RUIN MY LIFE

LUNA PIERCE

playlist

NOBODY GETS ME - SZA

TRIBULATION - MATT MAESON

RUIN MY LIFE - ZARA LARSSON

CAN I BE HIM - JAMES ARTHUR

1950 - KING PRINCESS

EMPTY SPACE - JAMES ARTHUR

ONE DAY - TATE MCRAE

YOU SHOULD SEE ME IN A CROWN - BILLIE EILISH

BRUISES - LEWIS CAPALDI

THIS CITY - SAM FISCHER

SORRY - HALSEY

YOU'RE LOSING ME (FROM THE VAULT) - TAYLOR
SWIFT

I DID SOMETHING BAD - TAYLOR SWIFT

DON'T BLAME ME - TAYLOR SWIFT

THE DEATH OF PEACE OF MIND - BAD OMENS

DEAR READER:

The contents of this book contain graphic material meant for mature audiences. Some situations and scenes are triggering, and I urge you to read through this list of triggers and make sure this book is suitable for you.

Mention of parental sickness, mention of parental death, non-consensual touching, murder, human trafficking, sexual assault, assault, systematic failure of the court system, parental manipulation, lying, mention of cancer, rape, infidelity (none of the main characters), murder for hire, illegal activities, forced pregnancy ideology, intimidation, death threats, mental health, stalking, passive suicidal ideation, parental abuse, child abuse (not at the hands of any of the protagonists), medical trauma, mention of animal harm, mention of woman and child abuse (not at the hands of any of the protagonists).

For a more comprehensive list of WHERE the triggers are located (spoilers), please visit https://www.lunapierce.com/trig gerwarnings

Book Cover Design by Opulent Swag & Design
Editing by Tori at Cruel Ink Editing & Design
Proofing by Tiffany Hernandez
First Edition 2023
ISBN 978-1-957238-11-1 *(paperback)*
ASIN B0BNJHYMYV *(ebook)*

*"They say I did something bad,
but why's it feel so good?"
— Taylor Swift*

To all the girlies who wanted to stab a man in the face with a stiletto heel for putting their hands where they don't belong...this one's for you.

1

CORA

I swallow the lump in my throat as Miller crosses his arms over his chest.

"Are we doing this or what?" he asks, his voice singing me a seductive lullaby.

He leans against the wall, the veins in his forearms bulging. It's everything I can do not to stare at him, at his hands, at the way his charcoal-colored shirt hugs his chest.

I'm not used to him this way.

Miller is stoic, quiet, reserved. He's a man of few words, but when he speaks, he commands authority. An authority that makes heat swell between my legs.

I shouldn't think these thoughts. I shouldn't acknowledge them.

But when he's standing in front of me like this, how can I do anything other than exactly that?

Someone clears their throat and draws my attention.

Alec.

Where did he come from?

"I'm game if you are." Alec's dark eyes meet mine.

I blink once, then twice. This can't be real.

"What do you mean?" I ask, finally ready to know what's happening here.

"Us, babe." Alec motions in a circle, implying what I can only assume is a dream come true. He steps forward and stalks toward me, his gait causing my chest to rise and fall a bit faster. He stops just as he reaches me.

Of course I want them, I have from the very first moment they entered my life.

But they are off-limits, and it's been made abundantly clear that it's forbidden.

Still, that doesn't stop me from licking my bottom lip and wondering what's going to happen next. I've been longing for the touch of a man; why should I starve myself of that because of a technicality I'm not even quite sure of? Especially two men, who are eagerly waiting for me to give them some kind of approval.

June and her guys quickly dismissed Miller as a potential suitor the second I brought it up, being evasive every step of the way. They said he wasn't interested in women, but how can that be true if he's standing here looking at me like he is?

There's undeniable chemistry between us, not just now, but all the other times we've interacted, too. Who am I to continue to deny that spark from igniting us both?

And Alec…June's driver. We flirt and banter, and I've always been attracted to his dark features and non-toxic masculinity. Alec feels safe, like he'd hold me if I cried or be there however I needed him. I don't know how I know that, it's just something I feel in my core. Still, though, there's a darkness to him, a sexy, illicit nature I haven't quite uncovered yet.

Maybe if I play my cards right, I'll find out.

I lean back on the bed, suddenly unaware of where I am, but quickly realizing I don't care, not when the reality of the situation sinks in. The burnt red comforter is soft under my elbows, and I scoot farther, eyeing both of the men in this decadent space with me.

"I want this," I find myself saying out loud in a whisper.

Miller and Alec exchange a glance, and from that very moment, it's like the energy in the room is charged with something fiery—one wrong move could set all of us ablaze.

But damn am I ready to feel the eruption consume me.

Miller grazes his fingertips around my left ankle while Alec cups the right in his hand.

My entire body throbs with desire, and my breath catches.

Miller smirks and yanks one of my legs away from the other, spreading me open and reminding me that I'm wearing a skirt with no panties.

My face flushes but somehow the heat that floods my core is an even greater intensity.

Alec climbs onto the bed beside me and distracts me momentarily. His brown eyes don't take themselves off of mine. "You're so fucking beautiful, Cora." He leans down, his hand finding my waist and sliding up under my shirt. Alec lowers himself so his face is only a wisp away from mine.

Meanwhile, Miller positions his body between my legs, both of his hands gripping my thighs and angling themselves closer and closer...

I moan as his warm breath finds my sex at the same time Alec presses his lips to mine.

Alec smiles against my kiss and latches onto the base of my neck, holding me in place to kiss me deeper. Our tongues frantically mingle, and I struggle to process the sensations coursing through me.

Miller wastes no more time and shoves a finger inside of me. "You're so wet for us, baby girl." He pulls it out and slides it over my eager clit, giving it the smallest attention before thrusting it back into me.

I moan again, this time breaking the connection between me and Alec and panting a bit.

"You like how he finger fucks you?" Alec repositions himself and reaches down to drag my skirt up, exposing me even more than I already was. He spits into his hand and immediately finds my clit, rubbing circles and applying pressure.

I drop my elbows and lie down on my back, arching toward their torment and dragging my fingers through my hair.

Alec glides his free hand up and under my shirt, pinching my already peaked nipple and sending another jolt of pleasure through me.

"God damn," I mutter.

Miller stops his movement abruptly and stares up at me. "If you're going to be moaning anyone's name, baby, it won't be God's. He can't save you from what we have in store for you."

"I-I'm, s-sorry." I clench around his finger and desperately ache for him to continue.

"Good girl," Miller says as he slowly begins to move again. But a second later, he fills me more, at least three of his fingers thrusting into me, deeper and deeper, harder and harder.

"Don't go easy on her," Alec tells him, rubbing my clit faster.

I stare between the two of them, wondering how the fuck I got this lucky to have their hands on my body at all, let alone at the same time. Is this what June's sex life is like, only with two more guys added to the mix? It's no wonder she's drunk in love and, for the first time in her twenty-something years, content with being in a relationship.

I can't say I blame her—having four guys completely enamored by you has to be a life-changing experience.

Not to mention, the four guys being rich as fuck and sexy as sin.

My release builds, and I chase it, grateful for the euphoria just on the horizon.

But instead of granting me my freedom, Miller frees himself

and brings his hand to his mouth, sucking my lust off his fingers.

Alec stops, too, his own hand trailing to his lips. "You taste so fucking sweet."

My chest heaves, and I bite at my cheek. "I was so close," I pant.

"I know." Miller sits up and unbuttons his pants. "I need to feel you come around my cock, not my fingers."

Throbbing all over, I grow even more impatient but remain in wait.

"Climb on his cock, babe," Alec tells me as he reaches out his hand to help me up.

I comply and rise onto my ass, tugging my legs behind me and doing what I can not to stare at Miller's rock-hard shaft as he frees it from his pants.

With Miller's eyes latched onto mine, he opens his mouth, spitting onto the tip of his cock and gliding his hand up and down it slowly. "Come here."

Inching forward, I surprise myself by going along with the request and let Alec guide me onto Miller, my hands resting on Miller's strong shoulders.

"That's it," Miller mutters, his breath mingling with mine. "I want you. Do you want me?"

I nod.

"Tell me," he says through clenched teeth.

"I want you. I want you so fucking badly."

Miller's eyes sparkle, and he grins. "Now shut up and take this cock like a good girl."

My heart thuds at the same time my pussy throbs, and I don't hesitate any longer. No, I must act before this opportunity is gone. I've wanted this for far too long, and there's no telling if I'll get this chance again.

Glancing over at Alec, he tips his head in approval and helps me onto Miller.

God damn this is hot.

I lower myself onto Miller, his tip penetrating me gently before he wraps his arm around my waist and lifts me from the bed. His cock buries deep within me as he carries me over and sits on the couch, keeping me on top of him. He leans back and releases me, his hot stare darting back and forth on mine.

"Fuck," I moan, his girth spreading me open.

"That's nothing, baby." A new, more sadistic grin settles on his face, and that's when I feel a familiar set of hands on my hips, holding onto me from behind.

"Hold still for a second," Alec tells me, but it's not just me that stops moving.

Miller and I pause, the anticipation making my heart race and my legs quiver.

"Don't be scared," Alec reassures me as his thumbs spread my thighs and skim over my pussy from behind. He slides the tip of his cock around my already full entrance, and just when I'm sure he's only moistening himself to enter my ass, he pushes onto Miller's cock and shoves into the same hole with him.

I gasp, the feeling foreign and unfamiliar but so fucking exciting.

Cautiously, Alec moves deeper until I'm in complete disbelief it's possible my body is handling what it is without breaking in two.

"You're taking us so fucking good." Miller cups my face in his hand and rocks his hips upward. He trails his hand down my chin and rests it around my throat, pressing slightly on the sides, applying just the right amount of pressure to restrict my airway.

My eyes roll back with pleasure, and I find myself moving against them, hungry for their cocks to ravage my pussy in a way I never imagined I would ever desire.

I'm on the brink of my climax as I bask in the fullness of

them, their hands on my body, their presence fully fucking consuming me.

"Yeah, baby, come for us. Come on our cocks while we fill you." Miller presses harder on my neck. "I want you to pulsate around us."

Alec thrusts into me harder with his hands digging into my hips. "Do what he says, babe. Let us feel you come undone."

But my impending orgasm becomes unreachable, my mind growing foggy as it struggles to focus on the men exploiting my body. Something else pulls my attention. Chatter in the distance.

No, focus, Cora. I arch my back to give them a better angle to fuck me.

"Don't leave us," Miller says.

"Stay here," Alec adds.

The commotion grows too loud, too distracting, my thoughts trying to decipher and make out the conversation. One voice familiar, one stern—too stern, too dangerous, and not in a good way.

My eyes dart open and my breath catches to gasp in air. Hands reaching out to the sides, I settle onto the comforter in my own room, my hands finding the book I was reading when I fell asleep. Some dark reverse harem novel I saw recommended in a reading group.

I sit up and rest my palm on my sweat-lined chest.

"Fuck," I mutter. "That was fucking crazy." My center throbs at the reminder of both Miller and Alec inside of me at the same time.

The noise that distracted me is still present as a conversation down the hall grows more and more heated by the second. I shouldn't, but I creep out of bed and tiptoe toward the noise to take my thoughts away from this very real reality and wish there were a way to rid myself of the embarrassment of such an intense dream. Of course, it was a dream—because that's my life, always wanting something I can't have. Not just Miller or Alec, but a man who stays, a man who worships me, a man who wants to please me.

No, those are reserved for the main characters, and I'm not the main character of this story, just a side character who probably gets killed off in the end.

2

CORA

I tiptoe out of my bedroom, making sure to open the door slowly to avoid the creak it usually causes. My oversized tee clings to my still-damp body, the remnants of the dream still lingering on my skin and causing the subtle ache between my legs.

I chew at my lip in a weak attempt to distract myself from the vivid dream and remind myself that it was simply that—a dream. Nothing more. And it never will be, because Miller isn't even interested in me, and Alec is off-limits. *Forbidden.*

Sighing softly, I navigate the spots on the floor that could potentially give me away and move closer to the chatter in my parents' house.

My dad's voice is the first that I make out. "I don't understand, I thought I had more time." His tone is clipped with each word, almost like he's afraid of whoever he's talking to.

A deep inhale, followed by the clicking of a tongue. "And that's where you're mistaken. You've been given plenty of time, and all you do is ask for more. More time. More money. More favors. That ends today."

"B-but," Dad says frantically.

"There are no more *buts*. Either you pay me right now, or I call it all off."

"You can't, please. Please don't do this. She'll...she'll die."

My fingers dig into the wall deeper as I hold my breath. *Who will die? And why is my dad borrowing money from who I can only assume is a loan shark?*

"You know I only agreed to do this favor because we share a mutual friend. But that isn't good for business. I give zero fucks whether she lives or dies. This was only ever about repaying a debt, and now, you're in deeper than what I bargained for." The mystery man clears his throat. "I'm done negotiating terms. I'm done having my men come back to me with some sob story about your wife. I. Don't. Care."

Wife? Is he referring to my mom? Why would she be dying, and what does that have to do with what's happening here?

"I'm begging you." A shuffling fills the space after my dad's plea with the ruthless man.

But is he all that ruthless if a deal is a deal?

Loan sharks are meant to be merciless. Otherwise, their entire business model would fall. How can I blame him for simply doing his job?

But loan sharks are also predatory—often setting rates and terms that are impossible to meet just because they can. People who seek them out are desperate and would agree to anything to get whatever it is they're after. And in this case, my poor dad was the sad sack that agreed to sell his soul to the devil.

Only, I don't understand why? I knew my parents were having financial trouble, but I never imagined it was anything worse than a few late notices and a couple extra shifts at work. They've always been able to bounce back throughout the years; what makes this time different?

And why do they keep talking about my mom dying?

Is this all a ploy from my dad to get the money in the first place? Some tragic story to hook this man into loaning him money?

Although, the sinking pit in my stomach tells me otherwise...that maybe there's some truth to what's being said.

I recall the few instances I've seen my mother lately. She's been busier at work. Later shifts, earlier shifts. Less time at home. I've caught a glimpse of her in passing, but other than that, she hasn't really been around much. She's been tired, a bit groggy, but I could easily chalk that up to her work schedule.

Unless...

My grip on the wall falters and I barely catch myself in time before I fall face-first into the hard surface. "Shit," I whisper.

Thunderous footsteps pound on the floor toward me, and for the slightest moment, I consider turning around and running, but there's no escaping the fact that whoever is out there knows I'm eavesdropping.

"And what do we have here," the man rasps as he rounds the corner and settles his sights on me.

I back away, my body naturally recoiling from him.

My dad follows him, grabbing onto his shoulder and attempting to pull him. "She doesn't know anything about this."

The guy shakes him off. "Don't touch me." He glares down at my dad and then settles his disgusting stare on me. Licking his lips, he drags his gaze up and down my body, sending a shiver across my spine.

The hairs on my arms stick up like a warning sign, but there's nothing I can do to evade his domineering presence.

I should have stayed in my room and minded my own business.

The man rubs his beard. "How old are you?"

"Twenty-three," I find myself saying even though I'd rather never speak to this man.

Come on, Cora, keep it together.

"Interesting." He steps closer, and suddenly, this already quaint home feels even smaller.

"Ricardo, please," Dad blurts out. "I'll do whatever you want, just leave her out of this." He reaches for the man again, but this time, Ricardo shoves him away, knocking him onto his ass.

I stifle a gasp and inch farther away, my eyes going wide at how easily he threw him down.

My dad isn't the biggest guy, but he has a foot on me and no doubt a hundred more pounds. If he was tossed aside with such a lack of effort, what would happen to me if I tried to get away?

"I'm not going to hurt you." Ricardo closes the distance between us, and once he's directly in front of me, he tilts my chin up toward him, a menacing look on his face. "At least not yet."

I ball my fists to the side and consider my options, quickly realizing I don't have any.

My phone is plugged in on my nightstand so there's no calling for help, and if I open my mouth to scream, Ricardo will surely snatch me up before I get a chance to cry out. There are no guns in the house, and even if there were, I wouldn't know how to use one. The only other weapon that comes to mind are the kitchen knives tucked away where they belong next to the toaster.

The only chance I have of making it out of this is going along with whatever it is he has in mind.

My nostrils flare, and my jaw tenses as I remain rooted in place. If I comply, maybe this will be over soon enough.

Ricardo keeps his mud-brown sights on me and says, "I accept this as payment."

Harshly, I swallow. "What?"

"You."

It's then that I smell the cigar and whiskey lingering on his breath, poorly masking a foul odor that could only be remedied by twelve gallons of mouthwash. Everything about him is repulsive. His breath. His crusty beard. The long, grey hairs wisping out of his nose. The dirt caked under his fingernails. The bulge of his belly as it pushes into me. The way he towers over me with no regard for my autonomy. Nothing is redeeming about him, and the more I'm forced to be this near him, the more my stomach turns.

I hate him, and I've only just met the man.

Ricardo skims his finger along my chin and up my cheek. "Solid bone structure." He twirls it through my hair. "It's been a while since I've had a blonde." His gaze travels south and he lowers his voice. "And I'd be thrilled to find out if the drapes match the curtains."

Without even meaning to, I shift back but not before he latches onto my arm and keeps me rooted there for his examination.

"You will stand here and obey me."

"I'm begging you," Dad says again from his spot on the floor. "I'll do anything. Please don't hurt my little girl."

In a flash, Ricardo has released me and withdraws a gun from somewhere on his body. He moves quickly, pressing the barrel to my dad's forehead. "Is this what you want? You want to fucking die?"

Dad's glistening eyes pinch shut, and I freeze, not knowing what it is I'm supposed to do. I hate how cowardice consumes me. I've been in situations where creepy men have made their advances on me. Most of the time I've been able to evade them, and a few times I haven't been as lucky, but now, this, this is something entirely different, and I do not know how to handle what's happening.

My fingers dig into my palms, and I desperately wish that this was another dream I could wake up from. I'd give anything for a gasping breath to bring me back to reality, safe and sound in my bed, but with each labored thud of my heart, I come to the realization that there is no waking up from this nightmare.

"What about you?" Ricardo turns his attention toward me and pushes the gun a bit harder into my dad's temple. "This could all be over right here and right now. You want your pops to die? You want your mom to die?" He chuckles, and I grow even more terrified. "I won't be the one to kill her, no. I'll let the cancer take her at its own pace."

I blink. *Cancer?* My head shakes, and I'm not sure if it's my doing or not.

"Oh," Ricardo quips. "You didn't know?" He laughs and repositions the gun in his grasp. "This just gets more interesting by the minute."

Tears trickle down my dad's cheek and confirm the truth that he's been hiding from me—that they've both been hiding from me.

My mom has cancer. My mom is dying.

And for whatever reason, this strange man knows more about it than I do.

"What'll it be, sweetheart?" Ricardo coughs the phlegm out of his throat. "You, or them?"

How can he ask me such a question and make it seem so fucking simple?

But shouldn't it be?

I give myself to him, in whatever manner he's referring to, and he spares my mother and father's lives.

I do the only thing I've ever been truly good at, the thing that's gotten me through some of the worst situations of my life. I flip the little lever in my head and disassociate from the decision I'm about to declare out loud.

"Okay," I spit out and step toward him, my hand shaking as I reach out to touch his arm in an attempt to get him to lower the weapon aimed at my dad. "I'll do it. Just don't kill them, please."

A wicked grin spreads across Ricardo's ugly face, only, it doesn't meet his eyes, and somehow, that makes it that much

14

more sadistic. "Atta girl." He holsters the gun and extends his hand toward my dad.

His nice guy act isn't fooling either of us, though.

Quivering, my dad rises to his feet and avoids my gaze. Defeat washes over him, but doesn't he see that I just saved his life? I fixed the problem. Who cares that I lost mine in the process?

I expect Ricardo to toss me over his shoulder like some kind of prize won at the fair and steal me away from life as I know it, but instead, he tilts his head toward me. "When I come for you, be ready." He pauses and then adds, "If you try to evade me, I will find out. And if you do, I will gut every single person you care about, starting with this pathetic excuse of a man you call your dad. Do not try to go to the police. I own them. There is nowhere you can hide. I own you now, too. Do you understand?"

I want to cry, but it's like my tears are too afraid of what's happening to come out. My lips part and I whisper, "I understand," even though there's nothing about this that makes sense.

Not the cruel man standing in front of me. Not the cancer he claims my mother has. Not the deal I just made with the devil.

One thing is certain—there's no way all of us are going to make it out of this alive.

So when he leaves and the door latches shut with a thud behind him, and the house grows eerily quiet except for the thumping of my heart which seems to be beating in my own ears, I recognize that this man is going to ruin my life.

"Cora." My dad finally breaks the silence.

I meet his gaze, and suddenly it's like I don't know him at all. A few minutes ago he was my father, a man I looked up to, a man I respected, a man I *thought* told the truth. But now the only thing I see is a liar, a pushover, someone who cannot protect me or my mother.

"How long?" I ask. "How long has mom been sick?"

His chest rises and he sighs. "Does it matter?"

"I think I deserve to know what I just gave up my life for." I do everything I can to keep my voice steady.

"We didn't catch it in time."

"What do you mean?" I question even though I already know what it entails.

"By the time we found it, it was too late. The cancer had spread." New tears well in his eyes but they do nothing to rid me of the anger building within me.

How could they keep this from me? How could they withhold the truth when it impacted me, too?

"Isn't there anything that can be done?" My fingers continue to dig into my palm, a sensation that keeps me grounded.

"Don't you think we've tried it all?" Dad exhales. "A buddy told me about this experimental treatment. Your mom has responded well to it. But it's expensive, and to qualify, you have to jump through a lot of hoops." He runs his hand through his disheveled hair. "The only thing I could do was get Ricardo involved. He had pull. Influence." Dad shakes his head. "When your mother finds out...she'll never continue."

I stomp toward him. "You will *not* tell her. Do you hear me?" Now, it's me that's in my father's face. "I don't care what kind of lie you have to spin. I don't know what she already knows about this whole arrangement. But this. What just happened here. You speak a word of it, and I will never talk to you again. What's done is done. The only thing that's important now is keeping her alive." My tenacity surprises even me because I was practically trembling five minutes ago. "That's all this was ever about, right? Keeping her alive?"

Dad bobs his head up and down. "Yeah, I..."

Holding my palm out to silence him, I say, "I don't want to talk about it anymore. There's nothing that can change what's already done."

He lied to me. He kept this secret. And now, I have to pay for his poor decisions.

I don't blame him for wanting to save her, but why couldn't he have realized that this was bigger than him? That nothing good ever comes from making a deal with the devil.

And with that, the reality of the entire situation sinks in.

My dad is a liar. My mom is dying of cancer. And I just sold myself to save them both.

I turn, walk away from him, and go back down the hall, shutting myself into my bedroom and locking the door. It does nothing to make me feel safe, and yet I do it anyway. Then, I flick off the light and crawl under my covers. Maybe if I wrap them around me tight enough it will stop my world from caving in.

But it doesn't, and there's no escaping the fate in store for me, so instead of finding a shred of comfort, I allow the emotions to break free and sob into my pillow as I silently wonder what I could have done differently to not end up here.

Alone. Afraid. Biding my time.

3
ALEC

I do the same thing I've done all week.

I show up at the mansion and wait for instructions.

Today is Thursday, which means June is more than likely working a shift at Bram's Diner. Something I don't quite understand, considering she's in a relationship with four of the most influential men on this side of town.

Dominic, the oldest of the bunch, is head of the criminal underground. He's also the most terrifying of the four. Don't get me wrong, the way June mouths off to him would make you think he's not that scary, but he's only soft for her, and the second you cross him, you might as well kiss your sweet ass goodbye.

Magnus is my favorite. He's the one who treats me most like a human being. Granted, I'm well aware that I'm here to do a job, but he still shows me respect. It isn't that the others don't, but Magnus acts more like my equal than the others, and that alone makes me glad when he's the one escorting June to and from. He makes it a point to ask about my day, make conversation about whatever the latest game was, and has even gone so far as to bring me something from the diner when I've been posted up in my car waiting for June's shift to be over.

But on this fine morning, it isn't Dominic or Magnus or even Coen with June, it's Simon. The lovesick puppy dog that follows so close to her heel that I wouldn't be surprised if he ran into her if she stopped walking.

It's kind of adorable, but has to be annoying.

Being that obsessed with someone has got to get old.

I sigh, knowing damn well the obsession is mutual, and if given the chance, I would love someone that hard, too.

Maybe I'm just bitter because I've never come close to something like that in my entire life. Let alone experience it as much as June does.

All four of her men are infatuated by her. Would do anything for her. Would risk their lives and kill anyone who dared to even look wrong in her direction. And that alone is why I keep my eyeballs to myself and do as I'm told, driving her wherever they command me and not for a second disobeying a single order.

It isn't all bad. Honestly, the pay is pretty damn good, and it's the only job that is flexible enough with the hours to work around my college schedule.

It's practically allowed me to pay for all my tuition upfront, too, along with saving a hefty chunk of cash—money that I'd otherwise be struggling to get if I worked a traditional job.

Sure, it comes with its risks, but isn't that what life is all about...taking risks?

"I've got it from here," Simon tells me with a hint of 'fuck off' lingering in his tone.

I tip my head in acknowledgment as I hold the door to Bram's Diner open for June and Simon to enter.

June offers me a soft smile which is a lot for her, since her default is resting bitch face twenty-four seven.

She's beautiful in a scary kind of way. That's why the

dynamic she has with those four ruthless men works so well, because she is one and the same. Her darkness matches theirs. June might be a petite woman in a soft and feminine package, but she is fierce, a bit psychotic, and just as fucking crazy as they are. Some might consider June a firecracker, but to me, she's more like a ticking time bomb with the potential to ruin any man who dares to look her direction.

"I'll be in the car, sir." I release the handle on the door and wait until Simon and June have greeted the wait staff before relaxing my shoulders and turning on my heel to make my way back to the blacked-out sedan I'm chauffeuring them around in today.

Not only is it blacked out, but it's bulletproof, too.

Only the best for June and her men.

Supposedly it wasn't always like that. But the second June came into their lives, Dominic had all their vehicles outfitted with every safety measure he could afford.

And that man can afford whatever the hell his sadistic heart desires.

Walking the few steps to the car, I slide a piece of gum out of the pack in my suit jacket and pop it into my mouth. The wrapper crumbles between my fingertips but I settle on shoving it into my pocket since there isn't a nearby trash can in sight.

I hop in the driver's seat and push the button to turn the car on, a moment later, pulling out and circling the block to find a parking spot that isn't directly in front of Bram's. It's not that I don't prefer being so close, but there are plenty of other people who frequent Bram's, and I don't need to be the dick blocking potential business.

Plus, June's shifts usually last a minimum of a few hours, so there's no real reason for me to hog such a prime parking spot.

Once I've found a new location across the street with a solid vantage point to the diner, I put the car in park and relax into the seat. My backpack seems to grow a pair of eyes that glare at me from its position on the floor in the passenger seat, but I make no attempt to reach for it. Not yet at least. Sure, there are some school assignments I need to catch up on, but for now, they can wait.

Instead, I slide my phone out and swipe the screen up to bring it to life.

Countless apps draw my attention and I thumb through them, not a single one pulling my attention. But because killing time is the plan here, I click on Instagram.

The first photo in my feed is an old Buick that was restored. I swipe through the before and after photos and then scroll to the next post to distract me from the clock slowly ticking away.

It's a video of some idiot eating shit on a skateboard.

I barely give it a glance and hit the search button, clicking the username that was already at the top of the list.

Her profile lags loading, and I grow impatient with the shitty reception on this side of town.

Finally, it pops up, her vibrant energy leaping out at me through the screen.

She's up to nine-thousand-eighty-three followers, and I'm sure I'm no better than all the other dudes drooling over her. It doesn't stop me though—it never has, and it never will.

I click the latest post, the photo taking up more of my screen and making my heart do this weird tremor-type thing. I should probably get that checked out, but I'd rather keep staring at her bright eyes and mesmerizing smile.

She's so God damn beautiful it's almost painful. There's a part of me that thinks she's completely aware of it, too, and that's why she posts photos like this, but then there's this other part that wonders if she'll ever see herself the way I do.

"Fuck," I mutter and run my free hand across my jaw. Closing my eyes and shaking my head, I click the button on the side of my phone and black the screen, because if I keep looking at her, it's only going to make the next few hours miserable with the very real possibility that I won't be capable of not thinking of her.

Although, I was having that problem before I even saw the damn picture.

I tilt my head back and pinch my eyes shut, allowing a heavy sigh to leave me.

"Come on, Alec, pull it together man, she's just a girl." But I know better than that. She's not just a girl. She's *the* girl. And I'd be lying if I said I haven't already pictured the next fifty years of our lives together at least a dozen times.

The first time was quite literally the first time I saw her. She was walking across campus, and my body and heart did a full stop. It was like I slammed face-first into a brick wall. I heard her laugh, saw her smile, and I was a fucking goner.

My friend had snapped his fingers in front of me but there was no coming back, no, not from that—not from *her*.

It wasn't until much later that our paths would ever actually cross, and when they did, I actually considered whether it was fate doing me the biggest solid of my life. This glowing beauty wasn't just some girl I'd only ever see in passing at my university —she was the best friend of one of my client's girlfriends. And what that really meant was she was completely off-limits.

It's not just my job on the line, but my life, too. These guys would kill me if I even considered pursuing her, so my only consolation is admiring her from afar and basking in the few moments we do get to share.

Maybe one day I'll get my happily ever after; it just won't be with her.

And that alone kills me a little bit inside.

At first, I thought it was simply infatuation, because who wouldn't fall for such a gorgeous woman. But the more I've been around her, talked to her, seen her exist, the more I realize how very wrong I was. She's not simply looks, granted she's fucking winning in that department, but she's intelligent, well-spoken, funny, kind, and ambitious. She has no shortage of admirable qualities. Her being June's best friend, the only fatal flaw. Sure, it allows me to catch a moment with her here and there, but it's the one thing that will never allow us to move forward.

Granted, it's bold of me to assume she would want that anyway.

She's friendly with me, some may even consider it flirty, but that's her personality. It's contagious. She's sunshine and the rest of us are fortunate to be in her radiating presence.

Every single time I'm around her it's like life is breathed into my body.

I'm aware of how fucking stupid that sounds, but I can't help it. Maybe it's because I can't have her that I want her so badly.

That's human nature, right?

Opening my eyes, I fumble with the screen on the dash until I find something to turn on.

Top hits, it says.

A soft and sad melody plays through the speakers, and I recognize it immediately. A Taylor Swift song that no doubt documents one of her many failed relationships. I turn the dial, the volume coming across a bit louder. I never understood why people give her so much shit for dating. I can't imagine how hard it is to live under such scrutiny, let alone try to find the person you want to spend the rest of your life with while living your life under a microscope. Things are hard enough as a non-famous person.

Gentle rain trickles down onto the windshield of the car, and the wipers automatically turn on to wipe it away. Across the way, a familiar blonde bombshell stops near the entrance of Bram's Diner. I hold my breath and watch her reach toward the door and hesitate.

She keeps her attention focused on the inside of the diner before a long moment passes, and she loosens her grip, letting go altogether. She takes a cautious step back and out of the way, letting another patron pass her and enter Bram's.

Without even thinking about it, I shut the ignition of the car off and shove my phone in my pocket as I slip out and into the street. I jog across the street with zero cares about the traffic that slows to avoid hitting me.

"Cora," I call out once I'm on the sidewalk near her.

God, even her name is beautiful.

Cora turns toward me, her brows pinched together momentarily before she activates her chipper persona. "Alec, hey, what are you doing here?" She crosses her arms over her chest like she's either cold or shielding herself in some way.

I slip out of my jacket and toss it over her shoulders, not allowing her to protest. "Here." I guide her under the awning as the rain picks up its pace. It's only temporary, the rain always is, but that doesn't mean it won't soak us while it's here.

"Thanks," she says.

"June's working." I throw my thumb toward the diner. "You going in to see her?"

Cora chews at the inside of her lip, and it's everything I can do not to reach out and graze her cheek to stop her from hurting herself. She shrugs. "I was going to, yeah, but she's working, so I figured I better not bother her."

I lean against the brick building and study her every move—the rise and fall of her chest, the way she clings to my jacket, the anxious energy that's usually a steady flowing positivity. "What's wrong?"

"What?" She narrows her gaze for a split second. "Nothing's wrong. Why do you think something's wrong?"

She's lying, that much is completely obvious. But it's not exactly my place to push the issue. She doesn't owe me the truth.

"Okay." I hold up my hands. "Nothing's wrong." I pause and then add, "But you know you could tell me if there was, right?"

Cora glances at the ground like she's contemplating something, and I wish like hell I could read her mind and figure out what it is. Surely by now, she can recognize my feelings, that I would do anything for her. But I shouldn't assume, not when I hold myself back from acting on it because if I did, June's guys would castrate me. Maybe my feelings aren't as obvious as they seem, which is a good thing since I'd like to keep my dick intact.

"Yeah." She forces a smile. "How's work going?"

Her attempt at changing the subject isn't lost on me, but I decide to entertain her. "Oh, you know. The usual. Get bossed around by one of June's grumpy men, try not to get stabbed or shot."

Cora chuckles. It isn't much, but it's something, and I take that as a win. "Yeah, sounds like a good time."

I lift my shoulder. "It isn't all bad." Especially when my workdays bring me the opportunity to see her, but I won't tell her that, not when it wouldn't do either of us any good.

Cora steps a hair closer and leans into the wall.

"You sure you don't want to talk about what's bothering you?" I ask her, my gaze trained on hers despite the strong pull to glance at her pretty pink lips. The shade looks a bit pinker than usual, and I want to ask her if it's new. I don't because that would be crazy. What guy notices those types of things?

"It's just been a long week, and I could really use a hug," she admits.

Like my body was fucking made for this very moment, I do the thing I absolutely should not—I stand and extend my arms. "Come on, bring it in."

Her blue eyes flicker through her lashes up at me. "You serious?" A bit of a smile flashes across her face, exposing those perfect teeth of hers. If she gets any prettier I'm going to die of a fucking heart attack.

"Deadly," I confirm and cup my fingers to motion her toward me.

Cora narrows her gaze and sighs, kicking off the wall and moving into my embrace. She's a bit stiff at first, but the second her arms go around my waist and mine around her shoulders, she relaxes and lays her head on my chest, the perfect height for me to rest my chin on the top of her head.

Cora exhales again, and I do everything I can to somehow relieve her of whatever torment she's experiencing.

"Thanks for this," she mumbles into me.

I smirk, knowing damn well this is just as much for me as it is for her. "I once read that people need eight hugs a day for survival."

She reels back and looks up at me. "No fucking way."

I bob my head. "Yep."

"No wonder I feel like shit, I'm hug deprived."

I tug her back into me. "There, there, little one."

She chuckles and goes along with it. "This is nice though."

"Anything for you," I whisper and wonder if she knows how serious I am with those three innocent words.

"You give really great hugs." Cora wraps her arms around me a bit tighter, and I breathe in her vanilla and lavender scented shampoo.

"Maybe that will be my next gig. Professional hugger." I rub a small circle on her back.

"I'd go broke." She chuckles and pulls away all too soon, holding me at arm's length. "You're a great friend, Alec, thank you."

And there it is. The *f*-word no guy wants to hear. *Friend.*

I force a smile through the agony of the nothing that is between us. "Hey, what are friends for?" It pains me even more to say it myself. If a friend is all she needs, or wants, that's what I'll give her, because there isn't anything I can't imagine I wouldn't do for her.

Call me foolish but I'm hung the fuck up on her, and there's no sign of me coming down from this love high anytime soon.

"How's work going for you?" I ask her in a sad attempt to keep her here a little longer and learn more about what's going on in that pretty head of hers.

"Honestly, it sucks." Cora's chest rises as she draws in a breath and releases it. "Don't get me wrong, it's great. The opportunity alone is fucking incredible. My boss, though? He's a fucking creep."

I catch my hand before it completely balls into a fist, and my whole body goes tense. "Did he do something to you? Do I need to—?"

She cuts me off, her cool hand pressed against my chest. "Simmer down, boy."

Her skin touching me has the exact opposite effect, though.

"He didn't do anything wrong, not yet. It's just his presence, ya know? He's a dick about everything, and there's always this undertone of disgusting male bravado that gives me the ick."

"The ick?"

"Yeah, Alec, the ick." This brings a smile onto her face, this time more genuine than the last. She shakes her head. "Those boys are keeping you under a rock or what?"

"Nah," I tell her, but if I'm being completely honest, between driving them around and school, I really don't get out much. I have a little bit of a social life, just not as much as most people my age. "But seriously, if you need me to do something about this boss of yours, I will."

The thought of anyone making Cora's skin crawl makes me want to rip theirs from every inch of their body.

Is it wrong to be this protective of someone who isn't even mine?

"It's fine, really. But thanks, I appreciate it." She reaches out and puts that tiny hand of hers on my biceps, patting gently. "Plus," her tone shifts. "I'm the lead on this new project. You know the giant high-rise going up downtown?" She doesn't wait for my nod before continuing. "It's a make or break for my career as an interior designer."

"Wait?" I say. "That's the job you got? That's fucking incredible. We've gone over the building design in one of my architecture classes. I hear that place is for like A-list celebs and shit."

Her cheeks redden slightly. "Yep. That's why I'm dealing with Mister Creepo, because if I can make a splash and start getting celebrity clients..." Cora's eyes lose focus like she's lost in a daydream of the future.

And boy would I do anything to make sure she gets exactly what she wants.

"Speaking of classes," Cora says. "How's that going? You almost done yet?"

"Yeah." I nod. "Only a few more months and one hell of a capstone project..."

"Are you worried?"

I scoff. "Nah, it'll be cake." Now I'm the one who is lying.

"I'm sure you'll pass with flying colors. How's your GPA?"

"Still going strong..."

Her eyes twinkle a bit as she looks up at me, a sense of admiration in her stare. "Just hang on a bit longer and that 4.0 will be all yours."

Sometimes I question if she even notices me, but then she remembers things like my weird obsession with graduating with a 4.0, and I realize that maybe she pays more attention than I think she does.

"I hope so."

"I don't doubt you'll pull it off. Neither should you." Cora adjusts my jacket over her shoulders, and I take a mental picture to keep forever, along with the feeling of her believing in me.

A throat clears as footsteps approach me from behind. "What's going on out here?"

My heart drops but I maintain my composure, turning to find Simon fucking Beckett standing a foot away from me.

Cora steps around me, putting herself between me and Simon. "Alec saw me get caught in the rain and was being a gentleman." She slides my jacket off and holds it out toward me, her gaze still on Simon. "You could learn a thing or two, pretty boy." Cora pats his chest, and I hold back a laugh at how she treats him. Doesn't she realize how powerful he really is?

There's the very real reality that she doesn't though, because June and the guys do what they can to keep her in the dark about what really goes on in their lives. Cora probably assumes they're influential men of some capacity, but not that they basically control this entire town, including all the illegal, and quite a bit of the legal activities.

Hell, even I don't know the full scope of what they're capable of. And part of me doesn't want to know. The less I'm pulled into that world, the better, because I don't plan to stay in it very long, and there's no telling what they would do to me if I found out too much.

For now, I'll take their cash and drive them around, not questioning the weapons tucked in their waistbands or blood speckling their cheeks when I pick them up at all hours of the day and night.

Maybe when I leave this world I can convince Cora to come with me, to get her away from the danger and potential threat that being friends with them poses. I would never ask her to walk away from them, but if she knew the truth about the situation, maybe she'd do it on her own free will. Maybe then I could tell her how I really feel about her. Maybe then I could protect her.

But until then, I'll do what I can from afar and savor these fleeting moments I do get with her.

"I'll see you later, Alec," Cora says on her way past Simon. "Thanks for saving me." She winks and it's everything I can do to remain upright. How in the fuck is it possible she has this much control over me?

Simon waits until Cora is inside Bram's Diner before he speaks. He clears his throat again, this time a bit exaggerated. He latches onto my shoulder, digging his fingers in and focusing his mildly terrifying stare right at me. "I don't care if you get your dick wet. You can fuck whoever you want." He shifts his focus between my eyes. "But if you even think about touching Cora, you know I'll have to kill you, right?"

I wait for a smile or a laugh to tell me that he's joking yet it never comes. No, Simon isn't joking. There's not a hint of sarcasm in his tone. He's dead ass serious.

And if he only knew the thoughts that ran through my head, I'd already be a dead man.

4
CORA

*I*t's been twelve minutes since Alec hugged me, and I can still feel his arms wrapped around my body. I cling to the comfort and safety and use it to pretend that everything is okay.

Everything is *not* okay.

"Hey, Cor, sorry." June slides into the booth across from me. "Busy shift today. What's going on?"

I plop my chin onto my hand and rest my elbow on the table. "Just wanted to come see you, is all." What I really wanted was to come here and tell her that my life is falling apart, and I don't really know what to do, but those aren't the words that come out of my mouth, and no matter how much I'm internally screaming for someone to help me, I keep my problems tucked deep inside to deal with on my own.

It's fucked up, I'm aware.

"Uh-huh, sure." June tucks her jet-black hair behind her ear and glances toward the kitchen as the chef shoves a plate through the opening. "Hang on, babe. I'll be right back." She darts out of the booth in a flash, making her way around patrons to snatch the plate and drop it off in front of its rightful owner. "Refill?" June asks the old man she passes, already on her journey to snatch the coffee pot to bring it back to him like she read his mind.

She really is a damn good waitress, even if she is a bitch most of the time.

That's what we know and love about her, though.

June cares in her own unique way, not in a warm and fuzzy manner. And that's okay. It's her.

I'm the bubbly friend, and she's the prickly pear. We have a very nice balance of darkness and light, only, mine seems to be dimming lately, and it's hard to counteract how fucked in the head I am.

It's temporary...nothing lasts forever. This shit storm I'm in will pass and everything will be okay.

Only, everything won't be okay, because I sold myself to some disgusting man who plans to use me however he pleases.

It's been two days since our run-in, and I haven't heard from him. He told me to *be ready*. But what does that mean? This entire situation has me looking over my shoulder every two seconds and questioning every single person who looks in my direction. The clock is ticking, and the worst thing of all is not knowing when my time will be up.

I should have asked him what he meant. I should have pressed for details. I should have negotiated. I should have done something other than give my life in exchange for my mom and dad's. What was I supposed to do? Let him blow my dad's brains out onto our living room floor and pick up the mess while wondering when my mom would be next? Things are already worse than I thought, but actually losing my parents would be worse than losing myself. I just have to come to terms with the fact that the life I had planned out for myself won't happen the way I expected.

When does life ever go as planned, anyway?

Ricardo didn't imply that he would kill me, so at least I don't have to die. But what if what he has planned for me is worse than death? Even the thought of him touching me with his disgusting hands sends a chill over my body and makes my palms sweaty.

I could have told Alec what was going on and maybe he could have helped me. The memory of Ricardo telling me he would kill everyone I cared about if I tried to escape him came rushing back in and stopped me, especially since Alec is high on the list of people I care about.

He's always seemed to care about me, in a manner that leads me to believe he sees me, not just the version of me that I portray to everyone else, but the real me. The insecure, scared me, the one that puts on a front because they're terrified that if they don't maybe people won't like them.

I'm not sure how to be anything other than that if I tried. I've spent so long pretending I'm not sure who I really am anymore. My need to people please outweighs whatever natural instinct I have for self-preservation. Hence me making a deal with the devil.

The bell on the door to the diner chimes as it opens, a tall figure appears through the entry.

I hold my breath until I make out the features of the handsome tattooed man and sigh as Magnus, one of June's boyfriends strolls in like he owns the place and goes straight to the counter where June stands on the other side, waiting for an order from the kitchen.

"Hey, princess," he murmurs.

June turns on her heel with a big grin across her face. "Maggie." She stands on her tiptoes to plant a kiss on his lips before going back to work.

It's nice to see her happy, especially after everything she's been through to get here. Her happiness makes my sorrows seem less, like I'm living vicariously through her or something.

If only. Then maybe I could have her criminal boyfriends fix the massive hole I've dug myself into.

Although, her guys never would have let it happen in the first place.

I don't know what kind of sketchy shit they deal with, June has never been open with me about what kind of jobs they *really* have. I'd be an idiot not to assume it has something to do with illegal activities though. There's no way they're that rich from anything legal. Sure, they might have some shit on the up and up, but they quite literally act like they've just come from committing murder every time I see one of them.

Not to mention, June has been super secretive, more so than she usually is, and has had really bizarre shit happen to her and given me super vague explanations for it. I'm all for privacy, I get that, but I'm supposed to be her best friend. She and her guys went through this rough patch when they were keeping things from her and she was hurt by it, so I don't know why she's okay doing the same to me.

I'm quite the hypocrite though, since I'm quite literally doing the same exact thing...

Only, my secret is staying tucked away because Ricardo literally told me he would kill people if I spoke a word about it. If that's not justification for keeping my mouth shut, I don't know what is.

"Sorry," June says and slides back across from me. "I should be good for a few minutes." She fumbles with the salt and pepper shaker at our table. "I need to refill these," she mutters under her breath, clearly distracted.

I don't blame her, she's at work, and that's what she's supposed to be doing—working; not talking to me.

"What's up?" I ask her. "How are things? When can we catch up?"

It's been a minute since June and I have gotten any quality time, and now feels like a pretty good time to make it happen since I have no idea when Ricardo plans to come for me or what that even entails.

Will I be allowed to see my friends ever again? Will he ship me away to some castle in never-never land and lock me in a tower or something?

I hate the ideas that run wild just because I don't have the facts. That alone might be the thing eating me alive the most— the not knowing. If I knew, then maybe I could come to terms with whatever fate is in store for me. Perhaps part of the punishment is not knowing. Maybe Ricardo enjoys a bit of psychological warfare before he claims his victim.

A shiver rushes over me.

"You cold?" June asks. "I'm sweating." She raises her armpit to her nose to take a whiff. "I've been running around here like crazy today."

"No, I'm good."

She reaches across the table and latches onto my hands, tugging me a bit toward her. "Speaking of catching up. Hear me out."

I raise an eyebrow at her. "Oh, God, what's this brilliant idea you have?"

"Hey, don't knock it until I've told you." June grins which only tells me how invested she really is. "So..." She leans in closer and lowers her voice. "Saturday, do you have plans?"

My mind goes wild with the possibility that I could have disappeared by then...there's no real way of knowing what the next few days have in store when I know nothing about what I've signed myself up for.

"I don't think so," I say anyway. "Why? What do you have planned?"

"I've been wanting to take Simon to a baseball game ever since he told me how special those used to be to him as a kid, and I ended up doing some research and this team he likes, the Dodgers or whatever, they're playing Saturday. I got us tickets."

Her eyes light up like a kid's on Christmas morning, and it's so strange and magical to see her this excited when she's usually less than thrilled about life in general. I guess love will do that to a person. It'll turn the darkest skies bright.

"Okay..." I can't help but wonder what the fuck her getting tickets has to do with me.

"Four tickets, silly. Me and Simon, you and a date. What do you think?"

I accidentally let out a laugh. "What date?"

She tilts her head and narrows her gaze. "Give me your phone right now."

"What? No. Why?"

June places her hand up between us, palm facing the ceiling. "Give. Now."

I exhale dramatically, yank the thing out of my back pocket, and place it in her hand. "Why do I not have a good feeling about this?"

"Thank you very much for your cooperation." June pokes in my passcode and swipes a few times, holding the phone toward her chest so I can't exactly see what she's doing.

"You're killing me, just tell me what you're doing. You're not calling anyone, are you? Oh God, J..."

"Hush," she says. "I'm getting you a date." June pokes a few more things then turns the screen around for me to see.

Facing me is a photo of a guy I matched with on a dating app a few weeks ago that I had been messaging back and forth with on and off. We'd never met up, even though he'd asked once if I wanted to grab a coffee with him. I had told him I was busy, because I was, but then he never bothered to ask again, and I didn't push the issue.

My phone vibrates and a notification scrolls across the top but I can't read it before she takes a look for herself.

"Perfect. He said he'd love to go to the game with you, and he'll text you to coordinate the details. I already gave him your number." She thumbs my screen and then swipes away, clicking the button on the side to shut it off and hands it to me. "You're welcome."

I roll my eyes and chuckle. "You're seriously the worst."

"And you love me anyway."

My heart pounds but I don't quite know if it's from the idea that I have a *date* or that I don't have a clue what the future holds for me.

Either way, June has a point...I need to put myself out there. And if I only have a limited amount of time before this creepy man comes for me, why shouldn't I be enjoying it instead of worrying twenty-four seven?

June may have just changed my entire outlook on this situation entirely without me having to say a single word to her about what was going on. Instead of dreading what's to come, I have something to look forward to. In the meantime, if Ricardo comes for me, maybe I can ask him for a few extra days so I can live a little prior to selling my soul to him. Although, if I could change the deal, I'd rather give him my soul than my body.

"Yeah, yeah," I finally say. "I do love you, you crazy bitch."

June smiles and I find myself smiling, too. We're not the most likely of friends but damn am I glad I have her. There's no telling what life would be like without her. Dull, boring, and probably a bit too mundane. June makes things fun and exciting and her guys add a layer of danger that's exhilarating...if only they'd let me in on their giant secret.

"So, are you in?" June asks me.

"Do I have a choice?"

"Nope."

"Fair enough."

My phone vibrates again and a notification from my date for the game pops across the top of my screen.

Maybe Kyle: Hey Cora, it's Kyle. Thanks for the invite to the game. Sounds like a good time.

"Is it him?" June raises her brows and leans back into the booth, stealing a quick glance toward the kitchen.

"Yeah."

"Well, what did he say? Are you going to text him back or do I need to do it?"

"You're out of control, seriously," I joke. "I'll message him when I get home."

June glares at me and it's enough to make me swipe open my screen and thumb a quick response.

Me: Hey, Kyle. Glad you're able to come. It'll be fun.

It's not the most exciting response, but I'm not that interested in the guy and if I'm being completely honest, I could think of a man or two that I'd rather go with instead. Both are completely off-limits, though.

"There, happy," I tell her. If looks could kill, I might already be dead.

"I am, thank you very much." She takes a peek over her shoulder where Simon stands across the room, his gaze flickering to her every point-two seconds—his level of obsession is endearing with a dash of creepy. "It's kind of a surprise though, so don't say anything yet."

"I won't," I confirm. It's not like Simon and I chat that often outside of when I see June anyway. He's friendly with me, and I mostly just give him a lot of shit, but we aren't friends like me and June. More like siblings who annoy each other. I love him, especially for her, and I'm glad he makes her happy. She deserves that.

"Cool." June reaches across and squeezes my hand. "Hey, you good?"

"Yeah," I lie. "I just wanted to see you is all. It's been a while."

"You can come over tonight if you want to. Magnus is cooking dinner so I'm sure it'll be something delicious and enough to feed a small army."

Any other night I would probably take her up on her invitation, but with all the things reeling around in my head, I'm not sure it's the best idea...I might cave and tell her what's going on, and the last thing I want to do is bring any more danger to her life than is already there.

"I'm supposed to have dinner with my dad," I lie again. The truth is that I've been avoiding my dad ever since what went down the other day. I'm repulsed by him. It's not that I don't understand why he did what he did, but it resulted in what it did, and it's going to take some time before I can forgive him for what he's done. What's worse is I haven't seen my mom lately, at all, and it worries me that Ricardo is making damn sure I don't back out of our little agreement. I could ask my dad where she's been, but I'm not ready to face him, not yet.

"Oh, that'll be nice." June pauses and then adds. "Hey, do you want Alec to drive you home real quick? He's probably bored sitting across the street waiting for my shift to end."

I shake my head. "No, it's okay, I could use the fresh air."

June's lip pulls into a frown. "It's really no big deal. He's on the clock anyway, wouldn't hurt to give him something to do."

"Maybe he's doing his homework." I slide out of the booth before she can push the matter any further. "Plus, I'm really good with walking."

"Ew, cardio." June rises to her feet too and nudges my shoulder. "Call me tomorrow and we'll talk details for this weekend, deal?"

"Yeah," I tell her. "I'll get ahold of you when I'm off work. I have that new unit I'm supposed to consult on tomorrow."

"Oh shit, that's exciting. I'm sure you'll blow them away with your design expertise."

"Order up," the line cook calls from the kitchen opening.

"Can't wait to hear all about it," June says before all but bolting away from the table to pick up the order and deliver it to the teenager sitting at the counter.

Making my way to the entrance of the diner, Magnus meets me near the door.

"Hey," he says in his typical suave tone. "You need a ride home?"

"I'm good." I flash him my signature smile and allow him to open the door for me. "But I will take a rain check on dinner."

"Sure thing," he says with a wink. "See ya later, Cora-bora."

I chuckle. "Is that the best you could come up with?"

Magnus clutches his chest with his tattooed hand. "It's not my fault you hate every single nickname I come up with."

"Psh. Hate is such a strong word." I slip out of the diner and onto the sidewalk, calling over my shoulder. "Catch ya on the flip side, Magpie."

Magnus hangs out the door. "You'll be happy to know I googled what that meant and according to the internet, Magpie are highly intelligent creatures, so I'm going to take that as a compliment."

I raise my hand and wave at him without turning around. "Whatever you say, Magpie."

One of the things I love about June having four boyfriends is that I have a different relationship with each one of them. It's like I have four brothers, and I either pick on them, or they pick on me. Magnus is probably my favorite since he's the most easy-going, but that doesn't mean I like any of the others less. They all have their redeeming qualities, and because they keep June happy, they're winners in my book. Don't get me wrong, their relationship has had ups and downs, and that's coming from an outsider, but whatever dynamic it is that they're working with, it fits them well.

I never thought I was anything other than the monogamous type, but I'd be lying if I said what they have going on isn't appealing. I love the idea of loyalty and commitment, only having it with a group of people instead of just one person seems fun and appealing. And more than likely totally out of reach for me.

I can barely find one person who is interested in me, let alone multiple—and then to get them to agree to share me...now that screams impossible.

But if June can get four of the most brutal men in this town on board with sharing and not killing each other, who's to say I couldn't figure it out too?

Maybe if I weren't destined to some disgusting loan shark I could explore the possibilities of making it happen.

The second I step onto the next block and out of range from Bram's Diner, my shoulders slump and the act I was putting on dissipates. The smile, the one that hurts my cheeks, fades, and the doom and gloom cloud that was once hanging over my head returns. I feel the comfort of Alec's arms around me and June's presence fading with each step I take away from them.

I swallow harshly and put my own arms around my body, rubbing my biceps and walking aimlessly in the direction of my parent's house. A place I don't want to be. A place that no longer feels like home. A place that isn't safe.

Nowhere is safe. Not home. Not Bram's. Not my own mind.

I'm trapped in my thoughts so much that I don't even notice the man who viciously latches onto my arm and drags me off the main street and into the alleyway. I trip over my feet and fall onto my hands, scuffing the skin in the process.

"For fuck's sake," the guy spits out and grabs me again, yanking me up and farther into the dark alley.

Tears well in my eyes as they adjust to the dimness. I guess this is it. The clock has finally run out.

So much for going to that fucking baseball game.

"Well, well, well," Ricardo says from his spot leaning against the brick wall of the building we're beside.

A chill creeps over me, and I'm not sure if it's from him or the coolness of this dark and dreary space.

"Let her go," Ricardo tells the brute who's manhandling me like he has the slightest sense of consideration for how I'm treated. It's all a part of his act, though. He doesn't care about me.

The man complies yet remains within a step of me as if he's waiting for me to run away from him at any moment.

I rub at the spot he had touched and wince a little. It's going to turn into a bruise tomorrow. Does that matter though? Now that my time is up.

"I'm pleased to see you haven't tried to evade me, yet." Ricardo rubs at his beard, and even in the darkness I can feel his stare trail my frame.

"You told me you'd kill everyone I loved," I blurt out.

Ricardo laughs and I do everything I can not to let it startle me. "I did, didn't I?"

I do something bold, something I'm not even sure I'm aware of until my feet move on their own and step toward him. "Can I have a word alone?" I glance behind me at the man who ripped me off the street.

"Hmm." I can't quite tell if Ricardo is entertaining my request or simply entertaining himself.

After what feels like a small eternity, he dips his head toward the man. "Check her first."

In a flash, the man is on me, his hands patting and trailing my frame. I understand that he's checking me for weapons, but his sudden and non-consensual touch still causes me to hold my breath and beg for it to be over.

"She's clear, boss," he says before walking back in the direction he pulled me and stepping into the light of the main street.

"What is it you'd like to speak to me about, pet?"

I cringe and wish I could claw his eyeballs out of his head and make him eat them.

"Can we discuss terms?" My voice remains steady even though I'm trembling inside.

"Ah, yeah, terms, how silly of me." Ricardo comes closer and tilts my chin up toward him. "We were in a bit of a rush the other day, weren't we?"

I clench my jaw and stand firmly in place. "It was rather unfair, if you ask me. To force me into a deal I don't even have all the information about."

When the fuck did I get so bold?

"Fairness is not something a man like me considers." Ricardo sighs. "But I'm not totally unreasonable, so if a negotiation is what you had in mind, I'll hear you out."

My heart skips a fucking beat.

"I do love a challenge," he adds, the stench of his breath turning my stomach even more than he already has just by being here.

"First of all," I start. "When you say you're taking me in exchange for my parents, what does that even mean?"

Ricardo skims my cheek with his finger. "I need a bride." He trains his eyes downward, onto my body. "You give me an heir, and I'll call our deal even." He raises his finger in front of my face to stop me from speaking. "But. I need a son. Someone to carry on the legacy. I already have a good-for-nothing daughter, I don't need another one."

Bile rises in the back of my throat, and I swallow it down. I should have known I wasn't going to like whatever it was he had to say; why did I expect it to go any differently? But the finality of it, to hear him say it out loud, what he plans on doing to me, it's enough to make me want to die right here and now. Only, if I did, he'd kill both of my parents—and that's the whole reason I'm doing this anyway.

"So, one son and we're even?" I ask him.

I never considered whether I would have children. I thought I had time to make that decision. I wanted to find myself first. To explore the possibilities of life and find love, and figure that out with the person I chose to spend the rest of my life with.

Now, having a child is no longer an option, but a necessity. One that I don't get to experience with the person I love, yet the person I hate most in this world. I'm supposed to bear an offspring for this repulsive man and then what, just hand him over? As a woman, as a mother, how am I going to be capable of not hating the one person I'm supposed to love more than anyone else—my own child?

Will I even be able to see it as my child if it's forced on me by this monster standing in front of me?

"Unless you'd like to give me more." He grins and shows off his yellowed teeth, a slight overlapping on the bottom.

"Can I have some time to get my affairs in order?" I ask him and hold my breath in anticipation for him to shoot me down.

He seems to consider my request. "One week."

I think about what can be done in a week. I can definitely make it to the game with June this weekend, but is that really the last of what my life will entail before I give myself to him.

"Six months," I counteroffer.

Ricardo laughs abruptly and I flinch. "*One* week."

Boldly, I place my palm on his chest gently. "Please."

He glances down at my hand on him and meets my gaze, his expression unreadable.

"I'm getting ready to start my period, anyway," I lie for what feels like the millionth time tonight. I still have another couple of weeks until my period starts, but I won't tell this creep that.

"A month, that's it," he seethes through his teeth. "Final offer. Ask again and I'll bend you over and put a fucking baby in you right now."

Don't get me wrong, I love a dominant man, but consent is consent, and I want nothing to fucking do with this repulsive old man other than to make him pay for everything he has and will do to me.

"Deal," I say knowing damn well this is better than what I had in store for me when I was dragged into this alley.

A month. Thirty-ish days to get my life in order. To say my goodbyes. To live life to the fullest before it's snuffed out.

Ricardo narrows his gaze. "You go home and flush your birth control down the toilet, pet, because once I start with you, I won't stop until you give me what I want. Do you understand me?"

I nod and try not to imagine his labored, hot breath as he finishes inside of me.

"Don't think you have the whole month off though. Every week between now and then, I will find you." He grazes my chin again. "I must keep tabs on my investments. I will have a driver pick you up and bring you to me. Your body is yours until then, but that doesn't mean I'm not allowed to admire it. I'll need to get your wardrobe picked out, so be prepared to model for me, pet. I need to make sure you're a suitable host."

With every single word, I grow numb to my future.

Not only do I have to allow him to fuck me, but I have to parade around like some fucking doll and play dress up as he pleases. What gives him the right to treat women this way? He can't find a wife the old-fashioned way so he forces one into the position? From where I'm standing, it makes sense that it's his only option, though.

"Okay," I say because what else is there? He's given me no choice in the matter and, if I want to make it out of this alive...if I want my parents to live, I must go along with his demands.

5

MILLER

"What do you mean the shipment was lost? How is that even possible?" My fist tightens into a ball, and I consider how much more of this bullshit I can take before I murder this crew.

The phone goes silent, and I pull it away to glance at the screen, confirming that it's still connected.

Sasha, the flight attendant, brings me another glass with two fingers of whiskey and walks away without another word.

"Thanks," I tell her anyway, holding the phone away from my mouth so the dipshit on the other line doesn't think I'm talking to him.

No, he is owed zero thanks. Honestly, he should be grateful I've kept him alive this long.

"Sir, I apologize for the hiccup, but it was seized by the police. We're lucky it didn't come back on us." His voice cracks a bit with each spoken word.

I rub at my temple and then reach for the drink. He has a point, but it still doesn't change the fact that this is the third shipment in the last ninety days that's been seized. Someone must be tipping the police off. The police that we're supposed to own.

I knew moving into new territory would be tricky, I just didn't expect to have this many losses in this short of time.

It's bad for business, and it makes me look like I'm incapable of running things.

"Figure out who the rat is, Harry, or you can kiss your daughter's tuition goodbye." I hang up the phone without letting him say a word, not that anything out of his mouth would have mattered.

I hate using ultimatums, but it seems to be the only thing to motivate that kind of man. Would I actually take away her tuition? Probably not. But I would put a bullet through his fucking skull.

It's all about balance.

Sighing, I flick through the messages on my phone and deem none of them that important enough to grab my immediate attention.

"How much longer until we land?" I ask Sasha, who makes busy work of the bar at the front of the jet.

She turns toward me and tilts her wrist to glance at her watch. "We should be on the ground in about forty-five minutes, sir."

Sasha is easily twice my age, old enough to be my fucking grandma, and yet she's calling me *sir*. I understand it's a respect thing, but it doesn't make it any less weird. I've told her countless times to just call me Miller, but she insists, and who am I to argue with this old, sweet lady?

She's been in our organization for over forty years, and if I had to guess, she's been subjected to arrogant assholes who command every person around them to bow down and kiss their ass.

Don't get me wrong, I expect my subordinates to do exactly that, but sometimes leading with kindness is the appropriate measure. At least, until the person attempts to walk all over me, then I rightfully put them in their place.

Six feet under if necessary.

"I've arranged for Alec to pick you up and get you to your penthouse at The Manor, sir. It's my understanding that Dominic will be meeting you to go over business. You meet with your interior designer tomorrow at The Wellerton. Is there anything else you need from me in the meantime?"

I shake my head and point to the seat across from me. "No. But you can sit the rest of the flight."

Sasha offers a soft smile. "That's not necessary, sir."

"Sit," I say with a bit more weight behind it.

"If you insist, sir." She comes over and settles her weight into the seat, her shoulders relaxing slightly. "Thank you."

"Do you want anything?" I lower my glass onto the table and stand. "What's your poison, Sasha?"

"Oh, sir, that's too kind. You don't need to do that." She begins to rise to her feet but I put my hand up.

"Seriously, it's the least I can do. It's been a long flight. Kick your shoes off and recline your seat. What will you have to drink?" I place my hand on the edge of her headrest and wait for her to answer me.

She swallows and seems to consider my question like it might be a trap of some sort. "I guess I've always been fond of brandy, sir."

I offer her what I think is a smile, but when I glance in the mirror, it appears more like a scowl. It's no wonder she's skeptical of me. "Brandy it is." I rummage through the selection of fine booze on the company's private jet until I find the one I'm looking for. I pour a healthy dose into the glass and ask, "Do you prefer it neat or on the rocks?"

"Neat, please, sir."

I return to our sitting area and place the drink in front of her. "Enjoy, you earned it."

Settling into my seat again, I observe her as she fidgets with the glass.

"Just say it, Sasha, I can see it written all over your face." I lean back and bring my own glass to my lips, sipping slowly.

"I mean this as no offense, sir, but you're just not like the rest of them."

"Compliment or insult?"

Sasha recoils a bit. "I would never insult you, sir. Truly. I have been in this...*industry*...for quite some time. You have a great deal of responsibility, but you handle it very well, without letting it change who you are. You are kind."

An accidental laugh bubbles out. "Didn't you just hear me threaten Harry?"

"Harry is lazy." She shrugs. "He needs to be threatened." Sasha dares to look me straight in the eye. "You can be ruthless and *still* a good, fair man."

"Think so?"

"I know so." Sasha tips her glass toward me. "You're proof of it."

I cheers her and lift the window shade to watch the clouds as we pass them by.

We don't speak the rest of the way, not until the pilot informs us to prepare for landing.

It's pleasant, her company, and when it's gone, I re-familiarize myself with being alone. It's what I'm comfortable with, my normal. I've always been a loner, adapting to the crowds around me and getting by. I've found ways to survive and have relied on nothing but myself. I learned at an early age that I was the only person I could count on and that was what kept me alive until Luciano found me. I pledged my life, and loyalty to him, and when he died, that transferred over to his son, Johnny, who is now head of the organization I help run. I'm the one people turn to when he's otherwise occupied, hell, the one *he* turns to, his advisor, a consigliere if you want to get technical.

We don't claim to be mafia, but we'd be fools to not recognize how everyone else views us.

Together, we are a group of highly influential people who work under an organized and structured system to use criminal means to get ahead. Not all our dealings are illegal, but the majority of them are, and the legal ones are to provide a smoke screen to hide the illegal shit.

Crime is committed on every level. Extortion, bribery, rackets, gambling, loansharking, weapons trade, fraud, torture, laundering, protection, murder for hire...you name it, we do it.

The only thing completely off-limits is human trafficking and anything involving minors. We might be ruthless criminals, but we have a moral code and we stand by it. If someone within our company is caught trying to dip their toes in anything of the matter, they're executed immediately.

We've had other organizations reach out and want to collaborate with us, but we refuse to deal with them if they don't at least have some line they draw when enough is enough. How can you trust someone if they have zero boundaries?

You can't.

The speaker in the cabin crackles to life. "Welcome to California, sir. Temperature is a comfortable eighty-two degrees. If you'll give me a moment to taxi over to your ride, I'll have you on your way shortly."

I rise from my seat and stretch my arms before latching onto my bag and putting it on the seat. The second I turn on cellular data, countless notifications pop across my screen. They come in too quickly for me to read them, and I pinch my eyes shut for a split second to turn my mind back into work mode. Not that it's ever off long, anyway. Three voicemails ding, and I don't check to see who they're from. I'll have time for that during the car ride from the airport to my hotel.

"I hope you have a great few days in town, sir," Sasha tells me on my way past her.

"Thanks, Sasha. Are you sticking around?"

She smiles softly. "I go wherever the wind blows me."

I reach out my hand to shake hers, slipping a few crisp hundred-dollar bills into her palm and exiting the lavish plane before she can react. I don't need a thank you.

A blacked-out SUV waits just off the tarmac, and Alec, one of the drivers for Dominic's organization, waits next to it with his arms crossed over his chest and a black pair of sunglasses covering his eyes. As I approach, he opens the back door for me, but instead of getting inside, I toss my bag in and shut the door.

"I'm not sitting in the back," I tell him and nudge him out of the way to get into the front passenger side.

"Yes, sir." He salutes me stiffly with a hefty dose of sarcasm and moseys his way around the front to get into the driver's seat.

"The guys might demand you call them sir, but just stick with Miller, okay?"

"Yes, sir."

I deadpan and consider stabbing him.

"Sorry, I thought it was funny." Alec pushes the button to turn the SUV on and shifts into drive. "How was your flight?"

"Well, I'd say it was successful since we didn't fall from the sky."

"Fair enough."

I pull my phone out to call Dominic but it won't connect. I try three times before giving up. "Can I use your cell?"

"Yeah, sure."

I reach for it and he turns toward me.

"Put it in front of my face to unlock it."

"Right, yeah." I do what he says and the screen lights up, the last thing he must have been looking at is still visible on his screen.

Her.

"Are you guys friends?" I ask, realizing all too late how accusatory my tone was.

"Wh-what?" Alec does a double-take. "Oh, shit, Cora. Yeah. I forgot to swipe out of that, didn't I?"

"So you are? Friends?"

Alec pulls the SUV onto the main road and shrugs. "I mean, no. Kind of. Maybe. Why?" He looks my way. "Are you guys friends?" He repeats the same question I had asked him with a similar jealousy lingering.

I shake my head and take a closer glance at her photo, admiring the way her hair falls into soft curls onto her shoulders and leads the eye directly to her cleavage. My cock twitches, and I blink a few times to distract myself but it's no use—she's so fucking pretty it physically hurts.

The first time I saw her I was completely taken aback by her beauty, and then when I spoke to her, I knew I had to know her. God, it was the strongest pull I've ever felt, but every time since then, it's felt like she isn't interested, and I won't force her to want me if she doesn't. I just wish she'd give me the chance to prove myself to her. But if I'm being honest, it's better this way —I'd only let her down. People like me are meant to be alone.

"No, not really," I tell him because it's the truth. Cora and I aren't friends. Sure, we've spoken a few times, but that's it. I had an immediate crush on her, and she was oblivious to it—and to me.

"Oh," Alec says, and I can't quite figure out if he's relieved or disappointed in my answer.

"She seems great, but like, way out of my league, you know?" I find myself surprised at my admission.

Alec laughs and continues driving. "Yeah, I know exactly what you mean."

I don't bother containing myself and thumb through some more of the photos on her profile, a small sigh leaving me. It's not that I haven't seen these photos already, I've looked at them countless times, and somehow every time is like I'm seeing her in a new light. I shouldn't want her; I'm damn well aware of that, but it doesn't stop me. Maybe it's because I can't have her. It only makes me want her more.

Or maybe it's something else entirely.

Closing my eyes briefly, I locate the rational part of my brain and ignore the pounding of my heart.

You don't know her, Miller. She's a stranger. Not some magical unicorn woman who belongs on a pedestal. There are plenty of other women out there that you can be with. Stop fixating on this one.

Although, I'm also well aware that it's easier said than done, and if I know anything about myself, it's that once I set my mind to something, it's impossible to break free. It's what makes me good at what I do. I'm thorough. And the second something is in my sights, I stop at nothing to make it happen.

Cora is a person, not a quest, I remind my irrational nature.

Did I buy a unit in the very building she's tasked to be lead decorator on just so I could get some time with her? Yes, yes I did. Do I recognize how *not* normal that is? Also, yes. Is that going to stop me? No.

"Something's been up with her lately." Alec breaks through my thoughts.

I turn toward him and study him with everything I have to try to figure it out quicker than he'll open his mouth and confess.

"What? What do you mean? Is she okay?" The desperation in my tone isn't lost on me. I must sound like a fucking obsessive psycho.

"I mean, I think." Alec drives us through an intersection and puts on his turn signal, focusing on the task of getting me to my hotel. "She mentioned her boss was being a dick, but when I pushed her about it, she told me not to be worried."

"And are you? Worried, that is."

My hand tightens into a fist, and I do everything I can to simmer the rage building within me. I hate how short-fused I am. I hate how little I can control when my anger sets in.

"A little bit, yeah." Alec glances over at me. "I think there's something else going on, too."

"Like what?" I press.

He shrugs. "I don't know. She just seems...*off*. Does that make sense?"

I swipe away at the photos on his screen and thumb until I find his phone, punching in the numbers to fix this problem.

It rings twice before a feminine voice answers. "Hello. Wellerton's office. How may I direct your call?"

"I'd like to speak to Charles Wellerton."

I ignore Alec's furrowed glance in my direction.

"I'm sorry, sir. Mr. Wellerton isn't taking calls at the moment. Can I take a message for him?"

"No. But you can get your ass up and go get him on the line. It's Miller Rossi."

"Oh," she says abruptly. "I'm so sorry, yes, let me connect you now, sir."

The hold music begins to play briefly before the line crackles.

"Miller, buddy. What can I do for you? Is this about your unit? Are you dissatisfied with the location? I can relocate you if you'd prefer a different view," Charles says.

"That building," I begin. "I want it."

Rustling comes through the line like he's repositioning in his seat. "What do you mean, the building? What are you talking about?"

"The entire building. The Wellerton. I want it. So you're going to sell it to me."

"I don't understand. What could you possibly want with The Wellerton?"

"That doesn't concern you."

"I—I'm sorry, Miller. That isn't possible. I can't just sell you the building. There are investors. There are hoops that you'd need to jump through. It's a lofty investment. I can't let that go. This is business, you must understand that."

Not for a second do I get discouraged at a single word he's saying, because from the moment the idea popped into my head, I knew I had the upper hand. I never would have considered it if I didn't. One way or another, that building is going to be mine—I'll either buy it from him or kill every person who stands between me and the deed to it. I don't favor one option over the other.

"Listen, Charles." I switch the phone from my left ear to my right. "We've known each other a long time." My tone remains steady, calm, calculated. "And because of this, your indiscretions have become something I'm quite familiar with. Now, I'm sure you don't want to dredge up the past, but I can assure you, that building is going to be mine one way or the other. I'll give you two options. You can sell it to me for a fair market value, or I can take it by force. Up to you."

"You...you can't do that," Charles sputters through the phone.

"I can, and I will. What will it be? Do you want the media to find out what happened to your last mistress? Maybe I could call Darla, your adoring wife, and fill her in on your indiscretions. Perhaps little Suzannah needs a visit at that fancy private school you send her to."

"Please, don't." His voice is barely a whisper. "I can't lose them."

And because I'm an evil and twisted man, I know this was the right button to push to get him to fold. He might be a cheating fuck-bag but he's always cared about his wife and daughter...even if it's shown in the worst way possible.

"One hundred million," I say with that same even tone.

"But it's worth—"

Alec pulls up behind a Rolls Royce in the valet of the hotel I'm staying at and creeps forward, waiting for a spot for him to pull into.

"I know what it's worth," I confirm. "You're lucky I'm offering you any money at all. Take it or leave it, Charles. What will it be? One hundred million dollars or the hard way?" I tap my free hand on my thigh and grow impatient with the theatrics of this entire conversation.

Finally, after what takes too fucking long, Charles exhales. "Fine, but it will take a few days to draft up the paperwork."

"Very well. I'll have my attorney contact yours. I'll be by tomorrow to get the employee manifest." I hang up without another word and hand Alec back his phone. So much for calling Dominic on the car ride over.

Alec accepts his cell reluctantly. "Did you just...*buy* The Wellerton?"

"Yeah, I guess so," I admit, not just to him, but to myself, too.

At the first hint of Cora having an issue, my initial reaction is to drop a hundred million dollars on a building solely to fire one employee. Is it irrational? Yep. Is it effective? For sure. And I'd do it again if it meant making her life the slightest bit easier.

"Dude. That's...that's a lot of money."

I shrug. "You realize I'm a billionaire, right? I can buy whatever I want."

Fun fact about me, though, I'm actually a tightwad with my money, that's why I have so much of it. I purchase the things I need, and occasionally splurge on the things I want, but for the most part, I live a very modest life. It's not unlike me to invest in real estate, but to do so on such a whim is unlike me, yet I won't tell him that.

"Holy shit," Alec mutters. "I knew you were loaded but...fuck man, that's a lot of zeros." He puts the SUV into park and slips out the door.

I exit, too, not waiting for him to open mine—I'm perfectly capable of opening my own doors.

Alec does manage to get my bag before I can, and he hands it out to me once I'm firmly planted onto the sidewalk in front of the building.

"Damn, that's a nice ass car." He eyes the jet-black Rolls Royce behind me.

It's then that I realize who the car belongs to. One of our long-time rivals—a man I greatly fucking despise. Someone who has tried to work with us numerous times, only to be shot down. Rumor has it that his syndicate is going under, and he's desperate to make moves to bring it back to life. There's even word that he's auctioning his daughter to the highest bidder in an attempt to infuse his business with the influx of cash.

What sick bastard would do that to their daughter...

He's reached out to both Johnny *and* Dominic, knowing damn well that they're spoken for—going so far as to crack jokes that they could use a woman like her...a *girl*...who's been untouched.

I have half the mind to put him out of his misery for everyone's sake, but a man like him still has protection and the means to ruin someone's life, even in the wake of his death. He's been around long enough to have strong connections and even stronger allies, regardless of how decrepit his reign has fallen. Men like him, the ones that have been around the longest, have a strange sense of loyalty to each other that can't be broken. He's a fucking cockroach. He's untouchable.

"It's not that nice," I tell Alec as I reposition my bag over my shoulder.

"Shit...is that who I think it is?" Alec watches the overweight old man stumble through the revolving door and toward his car.

"Yep." I watch in disgust and consider strolling over there and slitting his throat in front of everyone just because I fucking can. This world would be a much better place without him in it.

But the two rather large security guards trailing him stop me from making a scene. Not to mention, we're on sacred ground. There is to be no violence on The Manor's property. That's why it's crawling with criminals of every kind. There aren't many places deemed safe for the likes of us, and this is one of the few. It's often a safe haven for discussing business deals and doing negotiations because violence of any kind is forbidden. That's why I'm staying here until my permanent residence is complete at The Wellerton. I hadn't meant to plant roots on the west coast, but with as much business I do here now that Johnny and Dominic have aligned, it only makes sense to have a permanent place to stay.

I don't necessarily enjoy crashing amongst these types of people, anyway. I understand I'm no different than them, and I've been in it both deeper and longer than others, but it doesn't change that they aren't good company to keep. *I'm* not good company to keep.

We're a bunch of snakes and there's no telling when one of us will snap and turn on the other.

One thing you can absolutely trust—is that you can trust none of us.

Especially the no-good man walking directly toward me.

"Miller," he rasps, his voice cracking a bit. He hacks and pounds at his chest before extending his hand.

I don't take it, and it's a blatant sign of disrespect I do not care about violating. What's he going to do, shoot me?

"Mr. Gardella," I respond, because there's no way I can completely ignore him.

He coughs again. "I've always told you, you can call me Ricardo, kid."

"What can I do for you, Mr. Gardella?" I stand there, firmly rooted in place, my mind processing whether Alec and I could take both of Ricardo Gardella's bodyguards. It's possible, but probably unlikely, considering they're both nearing seven feet tall and easily twice our weight. Crazier things have happened, though.

Ricardo is a bold man, but I'm not sure he'd sick them on me simply for not calling him by his first name to his face, not here at The Manor, at least.

"I...I'd love to sit down with you sometime. Discuss a potential business venture."

"My apologies, Mr. Gardella. You must be under the impression that I'd work with a man like you." I step a hair closer, and his bodyguards both stiffen their stance. "I thought I've made myself clear in the past."

Ricardo's cheek turns up on one side and he laughs. "You're funny, boy." He slaps my shoulder, and I want nothing more than to end his life right here, right now, but I can't, and that alone kills me a little inside. "You're missing out. Business is booming. I just closed on this foreign deal that's set to make seven figures in its first two weeks. The time to strike is now, son."

He went from using my name, to calling me kid, and now son. Can this guy get any more fucking arrogant?

"And..." This time it's him that leans in toward me. "I hear you're still single. I could change that. You know I have a ravishing daughter..."

"I'm going to stop you there, Mr. Gardella." I close the distance until I can barely stomach the stench of his breath. "I would gladly purchase your daughter from you to get you to shut the fuck up, but I refuse to give you a penny of my money. Now, if you'll excuse me." I don't bother coming up with a reason for my leave; it's pretty damn clear I want nothing to do with this man—how he doesn't realize that I'll never know.

But that isn't my problem. And neither is his failing business.

He can claim he's doing well all he wants. The rest of us aren't stupid enough to fall for his lies, though.

I walk toward the entrance of the lavish hotel, not turning around to acknowledge any of them. Ricardo hasn't trained his attack dogs on me yet so if he were going to make an example out of my disrespect, the time for doing so has passed.

I'm sure I'll suffer the consequences at some point, but for now, I'm not going to concern myself with such matters. I have more pressing things to attend to anyway. Like the meeting I have with Dominic tonight and the one-hundred-million-dollar purchase I made just to fire one single man.

6

CORA

I stop myself from raking my hand through my hair. It's too perfect to fuck with, and I'm about to meet with a client, so I must look my best. Appearance is everything. I mean, that's quite literally what I do for a living—make things look good.

The desire to call the building's architect and berate him for the placement of the light fixtures in the living room is strong, but I know now that it can't be changed. Every fucking unit in this entire building will have stupidly placed lights, and there's not a damn thing I can do about it.

I went over the details at least a dozen times, and somehow the incompetent idiot still managed to fuck it up.

Sucking in a breath, I exhale and walk the rest of the unit, making notes on my tablet and killing time before my client arrives.

Each unit will have its own unique flare, including my client's visions and my ideas on how to bring them to life. This entire project is enough to make or break my career, and I'll be damned if I allow some shitty light fixtures to ruin it for me.

"Why does it matter, Cora? You don't even belong to yourself anymore," I whisper to no one but myself and make my way toward the entrance of the four-thousand-square-foot unit.

It's the biggest one available, and it's reserved for our high-end clients. I have no idea who's going to walk through that door this morning. It could be Beyonce or Taylor Swift for all I know.

On second thought, they probably have someone who does this kind of thing for them so it's possible I'll be meeting with some random assistant who handles shit like this.

But instead of either of those women walking in the front door, it's my asshole boss.

"Cora, baby." He comes right over and wraps his arms around me, pulling me into him without any consent given. "How's my girl?" Joshua plants a disgusting kiss on my temple and holds me at arm's length. "Let me look at you." His gaze trails my body, hovering way too long on my tits and waist.

I shake him off and find the closest mirror to fix myself in. So much for not fucking my hair up.

Joshua claps his hands together, and I flinch. "So," he says. "Today's client is a self-made billionaire at twenty-something."

I pat my hair down and wipe off the saliva he left on my forehead, making a mental note to douse myself in a gallon of hand sanitizer the second he's gone. Oh what I would give to drown him in a bucket of hand sanitizer...

The thought of murdering him has crossed my mind way too many times. More times than is probably normal for an employee/boss relationship. He's terrible, but there isn't anything I can do about it other than suck it up and deal with his demeaning remarks and wandering hands. He's never crossed the line enough that warrants HR to do anything other than tell me I'm being dramatic or exaggerating.

And since Joshua is friends with the owner of this building, it would be me getting fired way before he would be repri-manded for sexual harassment.

"I can handle them," I say with confidence once I've finally salvaged my appearance.

"I'm sure you can." Joshua licks his lips and raises his eyebrows. "You know..." Slowly, he strides toward me, and I step into the kitchen to attempt to navigate out of his path.

But the second my back is turned to him, he quickens his pace and is on me before I can realize what's happening.

I gasp as he spins me around and pushes me up against the counter, pinning me down with his hands on both sides of me.

"Wh-what are you doing?" I push my forearms into his chest, but he doesn't budge.

Instead, he presses into me. "I see the way you look at me. You're playing coy, aren't you, Cora?" He grinds his groin into me, alerting me to his already growing hardness. "We have time, baby. Let me show you what you've been missing." He leans closer, his mouth just next to my ear. "I won't tell anyone if you don't."

My stomach turns, and bile rises in the back of my throat. If I thought things were already worse in my life, boy was I mistaken. If it's not one guy trying to take my body for his enjoyment, it's fucking another. When will men get it through their heads that women do not belong to them?

"You've got it wrong," I tell Joshua and try to get him off me again. "I'm...I'm seeing someone." It's a lie, but usually, the only one that men seem to respect enough to quit. It's like their bro-code kicks in, and instead of accepting a woman just isn't interested, they accept that another man has claimed them.

Joshua laughs. "Oh baby, I'm married but that isn't stopping this from happening."

Sheer panic courses through me. There's at least another fifteen minutes before the client arrives, and I'm stuck here, at the mercy of whatever Joshua intends to do with me. I'm not strong enough to overpower him, and he's made it clear that I have no say in the matter.

Joshua lowers his arm to grip my hip, gliding his hand down to take a firm grasp of my ass. He snakes his fingers to the waistband of my dress pants and yanks hard, ripping the seams and causing me to stumble. "Yeah, I bet you fucking like it rough, don't you?"

Tears well in my eyes and drip down onto the tablet still in my possession. And with his grimy fucking hands now exploring my body, I use the lack of being completely caged in and pressed against him to free my own arm and crack him over the side of the head with the tablet.

"Fucking bitch," he blurts out and stumbles back.

Joshua touches his forehead and then glances at his crimson-soaked hand.

I rush past him, desperate to make it to the door and get the fuck away from him. My client will have to wait, because my top priority is putting as much distance as possible between me and this sad excuse of a man.

But despite his bulky size, he moves quicker than I can anticipate and latches onto my hand, spinning me around and toward him. "Where the fuck do you think you're going?" He drags me in closer. "We aren't done here." Joshua grazes his nose through my hair. "We're done when I say we are."

Trembling, I struggle to process how I'm going to get out of this. I could simply give in, let him have his way with me, and maybe I'll make it out of this alive. Or I could fight, and there's no telling how far he'll take this. If he kills me, what will happen to the deal with Ricardo? Will he care if someone else beats him to having their way with me? Will he rid my parents of their debt because of some technicality? The answer is more than likely no. It's safe to say neither one of these men is reasonable and I'm going to have to succumb to both of them.

When have I ever given in so fucking easily, though? I have fought for everything I have in life, why should this man get to take that away from me?

"Fine," I tell him. "Fine. You're right." I meet his gaze and place my hands on his chest. "But please, don't be so aggressive. It's not attractive."

Joshua hesitates but within a moment I sense the shift in dynamic, he's fallen for my trap. He swallows harshly and allows the smallest bit of space between us. "Tell me how you want it, baby. I've been dying for this moment for so long."

My skin crawls but I do everything I can to maintain my composure. "Me, too," I lie and look past him, hungry to find anything to help me out of my mess. That's when I spot it—my saving fucking grace.

"How about over here?" I nod my head in the direction I want him to go and he eats up every bit of it.

"Yeah? You want me to bend you over that island, baby?"

"Mmhm," I mumble and walk as much as he's willing to let me away from him, his clammy palm resting on my lower back.

We make it over to the edge of the elaborate piece of hand-chosen granite countertop and he nudges me into it, the force no doubt going to bruise where it impacted.

"You go first," I tell him. "I'm shy."

A sly grin forms on his face, and despite being fucking terrified, I turn around and press my ass toward him and lower my torso onto the cold counter.

"Fuck, baby, you're making me so hard." He grips my thighs and presses his hardness into me, aggressively thrusting his hips and making me wonder if he's going to come before we even take our clothes off. Maybe this won't be as bad as I expected it to be.

But either way, I don't want to find out.

So instead of letting him go any further, I reach toward the stack of papers the builders left behind and latch onto the box cutter tucked just along the bottom. In one fluid motion, I thumb the side of it, revealing the blade and spinning myself around toward my assaulter.

"I'm going to need you to back the fuck away from me, Joshua." My entire demeanor has changed, and it's almost humorous how long it takes him to realize I wasn't actually submitting to him.

And in that flicker of a moment I thought I had the upper hand, Joshua surprises me yet again and latches onto my throat, squeezing tight and flaring his nostrils.

"You think I'm fucking afraid of you, bitch? I'll choke you until you pass out and fuck your lifeless—"

I don't let him finish. No. My eyes blurring and my windpipe being crushed, I use the last remaining strength in me to pull away slightly and slam the sharp end of the box cutter into his neck. Blood spurts out, and for the first time since I arrived, I don't care that my appearance is fucked up. If anything, witnessing this man bleed is the perfect accessory to my outfit.

Doing the only thing my rational brain can think of, I yank out the blade and shove it back in, this time in his chest. He stumbles back, his eyes going wide with what I can only imagine is confusion and shock and terror. I plunge it in one more time, two times, three times. I keep stabbing him until he collapses onto the floor, and I climb onto his body, straddling his torso in a way I'm sure he never fucking imagined, and don't stop until the life has left him and I'm sure he can never touch me ever again.

It isn't until my ragged breaths are interrupted by the sound of the keypad at the front entrance that I return to reality, the blood-soaked blade in my grasp and my dead boss below me.

My chest tightens, and fear unlike any other washes over me. I just killed a man. My boss. I brutally murdered him. I didn't die by Joshua's hand but there's no way Ricardo will be content if I go to prison.

The door opens, footsteps follow, and then the door latches shut.

The person inhales, exhales, and then clears their throat. "Cora, you in here? I'm a few minutes early."

"I'm..." I rise to my feet as best as possible because what other options do I have. There's no hiding or denying that I'm covered in my mutilated boss's blood. "I'm right here."

A moment later, a figure comes into my blurry line of sight, the welcoming smile fading as he takes me in.

He moves quick and it causes me to lose my balance and fall, my ass hitting the floor hard.

"Cora, Christ." Miller's hands are on me in an instant, gripping my elbows and helping me to my feet. His blue-ish gaze trails over me hurriedly. "Are you hurt?" He takes pause at my waist where my clothes are ripped. "Did he—?" But he cuts himself off. "Talk to me, Cora."

"I'm okay," I manage to get out and let my attention fall to the man bleeding out onto the freshly laid tile flooring. That's definitely going to stain the grout. I should start cleaning it now if there's any chance of not causing permanent damage. "I need to..." I point toward the mess. "I need to clean this up." I sniffle and go to wipe at my nose and spot the box cutter still tucked so tightly in my fist that my knuckles hurt. "I...I killed him."

"Cora." Miller steadies my shoulder and uses his other hand to pry the weapon from my clutches. "Everything is going to be fine." His voice is calm and soothing, and I want to wrap myself up in it and stay cocooned in its protection.

"Bu-but...my client will be here any minute. Some billionaire guy. Oh my god. He's going to walk in here to this. To this fucking bloodbath." My heart races, and I can't seem to catch my breath.

"Cora," Miller repeats my name for what feels like the fiftieth time. He sighs before saying, "I'm your client."

I blink a few times and try to process his words. "What?"

"Yes. I bought a unit in the building. I was the client you were supposed to be meeting this morning."

Things start slowly falling into place...

How else would he have had the code to get into the unit in the first place? Maybe he really is telling the truth. Or maybe I've had a psychotic episode because I'm in shock over killing my boss. Maybe Miller is a safe person my conscious conjured up to save me from this nightmare. Maybe I can plead insanity when they take me to prison.

"Well," I say, my voice strained as I war with myself. "I...I should show you around before the cops come."

"I don't care about the design, Cora. I never did."

"Oh."

"And the cops aren't coming. I won't let that happen." Miller sets the box cutter on the counter and focuses his attention on me. "Are you hurt? I can't tell if the blood is yours or his." He hovers his hands near me but doesn't touch my body, almost like he's afraid I'm a bomb that will explode if he does.

"I'm fine." I turn my shaking palms up and take in the crimson staining them. My forearms are covered, too, as are my pale pink shirt and slacks. Without meaning to, I skim my fingers over the base of my throat, flinching a bit when I get to my windpipe. I swallow harshly and adjust to the pain.

I'm not fine.

I'm not fine at all.

Between having killed my boss, sold myself to some criminal, and my mother actively dying, it makes the little things that were stressing me out prior seem like nothing.

"Do you want to tell me what happened?" Miller asks me, his tone cool and even as if he's completely unfazed by the dead man bleeding out a foot away.

I nod but no words follow. I want to tell him, I do, it's just hard for me to believe it myself.

Did I really kill a man?

"I tried to get away," is what comes out. "It's my fault that he—"

"Cora," Miller raises his voice but not in a threatening manner. "What happened here was *not* your fault. Do you understand me? Christ...I'm so sorry I wasn't here sooner. I'm so sorry this happened to you." He breathes in and shakes his head. "What can I do? What do you need from me?"

When did Miller become so concerned about my well-being? When did he become so sweet? When did he start acknowledging that I exist?

It's a shame he's gay, because the way he's looking at me, the way he's caring for me...it's exactly what I want in a partner. And whoever he's with should feel damn lucky they have someone like that.

The first time I saw him, I was immediately attracted to him. He was talking business with one of June's men, and our eyes met from across the club. I thought he saw me, like a *hey, there you are* kind of way that souls do when they reconnect in another life, but when I pressed June and Magnus to introduce us, they told me of his sexual preference. I wanted them to be wrong, I wanted it to be a joke, but Miller never acted upon that first lingering look across the club, and that was enough to confirm what they had told me.

I just hope whoever he matches with makes him happy, because he deserves that. And if the only kind of relationship he's able to offer me is friendship, I'm okay with that, too. I could use all the friends I can get, especially lately.

Finally, I say, "I could use a hug."

Miller doesn't hesitate, yet pulls me in, wrapping me into his broad chest and holding me close. He rubs small circles on my back and I close my eyes and breathe him in—his scent is a mixture of cedar and something sweet, perhaps vanilla. He rests his chin on the top of my head, and at least a full minute passes of us standing there, holding onto each other, not saying a word.

Miller breaks the silence. "I need to call this in."

I sigh. "Okay." And come to terms with the fact that I'm going to go away for a very long time. I'd like to think self-defense would save me but, in a world where men rule everything, I wouldn't be surprised if the system fails me the same way it's failed so many other women.

"Everything is going to be okay; I promise," Miller tells me before pulling his phone out of his pocket. He thumbs the screen and dials a contact saved as *Silver*. He steps away, but not far, and waits for the line to connect. "I need a cleanup," he says through the phone. "Yeah, I'll send you a pin. And hey, that thing I called you about earlier. Cancel the order. It's been handled." The person on the other end says something I can't make out, and then the call ends.

"I don't understand what's going on," I admit. "Who was that?"

Miller's jaw tenses, and for a second, I think he's not going to answer my question. "That was a contractor of mine. His name is Silver. He's going to take care of this." Miller tips his head toward the dead body. "All of this."

"You mean like dispose of the body? Isn't that illegal?" The second I ask I know I should have just kept my mouth shut. Of course, it's illegal, dumbass.

"I don't want to lie to you, Cora." Miller runs his hand through his hair.

"You grew your hair out."

His dark brows pinch together for a moment, and he grins. "Yeah. Do you like it?"

"It looks good." I study him as a thick brown piece falls onto his forehead.

If I'm not mistaken, his cheeks blush slightly.

"Thanks." Miller slides his phone back into his pocket. "Cora, I don't want to scare you but..." He points with his thumb to the dead body. "This stuff, I'm used to it. I'm no stranger to violence. I hate that you went through this, I really do, but I'm not going to let you get in trouble for it. Not when there are other options available."

I wait for him to continue and when he doesn't, I open up my mouth. "Isn't it wrong though?"

Miller draws in a breath and slowly exhales. "Right and wrong, that's always the question, isn't it? Who gets to decide? What he tried to do to you was wrong, wasn't it? Doesn't that justify your actions? Just because something is illegal, doesn't make it wrong."

"Yeah..." I swivel the tip of my shoe into the floor and consider his words.

Joshua was going to rape me, and there's no telling what else. If I hadn't done what I did, who's to say what would have happened to me.

But to kill him...and to get rid of the body...

"Miller?" I don't take my eyes off the blood-splattered floor.

"Yes?" His voice is so calm that it's a bit eerie. How can he remain composed in a situation like this?

"What do you do for a living?" I ask the question I know I shouldn't. It's the one all my close friends avoid. They give me their version of the truth, but it's never the whole truth, and it leads me to wonder why they don't trust me enough to confide in me.

Miller sighs. "It's complicated."

I glance up at him, taking in his steady gaze. I expect butterflies or a whirlwind of emotions to flutter through my body but instead, I feel just as calm as his voice. *Safe*. With him. Suddenly, the fact that I just killed a man isn't as terrifying as it once was. I'm no different from him, from them, I'm a monster.

Starring into his eyes, though, a monster is the last thing I see.

No, Miller is kind, patient, and a bit dominant. He has this stoic nature to him and I wouldn't be surprised if he didn't have a darkness hidden deep within. There's no way he can stay chill all the time.

"It's not that I don't want to tell you." He continues, "It's just...a lot." Miller shrugs off his jacket. "Are you cold?" He drapes it over my shoulders without allowing me to answer.

"What about the blood?"

"I don't care."

It's then that my attention is drawn to his biceps, his fore-arms, the veins running along them and into his hands. My mind wanders back to the *very* vivid dream I had of him and Alec and if I'm not mistaken, my cheeks flush red. Why am I thinking about sex when a dead man is lying on the tile floor?

I wrap his leather jacket around me and try not to make it too obvious when I suck in a breath to catch a better whiff of him.

Miller's phone rings, and at first, he ignores it.

"Do you need to get that?" I ask him when it rings again. "What if it's the cleaner guy you called?"

He pulls his phone out and his jaw tenses. "It's Dominic. Do you mind?"

I shake my head. "No, not at all."

Miller steps away, not so much that I can't see him anymore, but enough that he's out of earshot. It's strange that with each foot he places between us, that comfortable layer of security dissipates. Maybe it's the dead body or the memory of my struggle with Joshua coming to the forefront, but it took Miller walking into the other room for me to realize I don't want to be alone, not right now.

I remain in the kitchen but move farther away from Joshua and try to block my line of sight to him with the island. If I can't see him, maybe his ghost can no longer haunt me.

But the second he's out of sight, this irrational fear that he isn't actually dead comes rushing in. My breathing hitches as my chest rises and falls quicker and I grip Miller's jacket in an attempt to shield me from the dead man. Without my consent, tears fall down my cheeks, and I hate myself for being so weak, so fragile, so emotional.

Why do I even care when this isn't the worst thing that's going to happen to me in the coming months?

If anything, this should just prepare me for the nightmare my future holds with Ricardo.

A chill washes over me, and I close my eyes. Leaning against the counter on the far side of the kitchen, I desperately search my mind for something good, something happy, something to distract my racing thoughts.

Nothing comes. Not a picturesque beach. Not a fond memory of a loved one. Just the box cutter in my fist and the terrified look on Joshua's face as I stabbed him repeatedly.

Kill or be killed, Cora, I remind myself.

What if he's done this to other women before me? What if he planned on doing it to someone after? I must remember the good I've brought the world by getting rid of him. I bite at my lip and know damn well that's not how the real world works. I am not the judge, jury, and executioner, and no matter what Joshua planned on doing to me, it was wrong to kill him.

"Cora," Miller says on his way back into the kitchen. "I have to run, it's urgent." He approaches me, his expression turning concerned as his brows pinch together. "Are you okay?" He stops in front of me, his hands hovering near my face. "May I touch you?"

I nod and sniffle.

Miller palms both of my cheeks in his hands and wipes away my tears with his thumbs. "Everything is going to be fine; I promise. You have nothing to be afraid of." He pauses and then adds, "I've got you, okay?" Miller surprises me by tugging me toward him and pressing his lips gently to my forehead. He wraps me into a hug, again, and I wonder if it's possible to just go ahead and die right here, in his arms. At least then I'll be content with the world around me falling to shit. Nothing can hurt me with him around.

Only, that isn't sustainable, and Miller isn't mine to keep. He's just simply being a good friend, one that gets rid of the body when you kill someone.

Miller releases me slowly and returns his right hand to my face, grazing my skin with such care. "I have to go," he repeats. "But Silver will be here any minute. He'll knock twice. I need you to let him in, and he'll handle everything, okay?"

I swallow down the panic that rises at the idea of some stranger coming in here and bearing witness to what I've done. But if Miller is telling the truth, neither one of them is truly a stranger to death, and this is part of their semi-daily life.

I trust Miller—I don't know why, I just do—so I have to trust this Silver guy, too.

"Okay," I confirm because I don't really have any other choice in the matter other than to call the cops and let them handle the situation. As fucked up as it is, I'm not so sure I'd like that outcome.

I've never been the type to stray away from accepting the consequences of my actions but when they involve me going to jail and potentially inadvertently killing both of my parents, that isn't the choice I'm willing to take.

"Here." Miller takes my hand in his, his warmth soothing the raging fire of my nerves. "Come sit on the couch while you wait. He should be here soon."

"But what about the blood?" I glance down at my body and wonder if I'll ever be clean of the gore.

"It's just a couch, Cora. I'll have it replaced."

"I think it's expensive," I tell him.

Miller guides me over to it anyway, nudging me to sit down. "I could buy you as many of them as you wanted."

It isn't until I'm sitting here alone after I've reassured him that I'm fine and he can leave that I realize he said to me, not the building owner or company I work for—that he would buy *me* as many as I wanted.

I allow that very simple declaration to consume my thoughts and pass the time, my mind reeling when a solid double knock hits the door. I flinch but rise to my feet, plastering on what I can of a fake smile to greet whoever is behind the door.

Clutching Miller's jacket around my chest, I turn the handle and pull, allowing the person to step inside.

"Hey," I say, which the second it's out of my mouth, feels so fucking inappropriate considering the circumstances.

We take each other in at the same time, his seriously dark eyes meeting mine. Silver is easily twice my age and size, and suddenly, I feel so small in his dominating presence. The salt and pepper of his beard matches the shaggy but well-kept hair on his head.

He clears his throat and does one final look up and down my body. "Where's Miller?"

"He had to leave."

Silver doesn't question any more about Miller, yet asks, "Where's the body?"

"Right this way." I motion toward the kitchen and assume that he will follow me. I glance over my shoulder one time to confirm that he does, but his footsteps are so quiet, despite his stature, I couldn't be sure without looking.

I lead him to the bloodbath and cross my arms over my chest at the foot of my dead boss.

"Murder weapon?" He points to the box cutter sitting on the counter.

I make my way over, grabbing it and confirming, "Yeah."

"I'll take it." Silver, or at least, I think that's his name, holds out his hand.

I place the bloodied thing into his rather large palm and ignore the heat of his skin on mine.

"You did this?" He raises a bushy brow and tips his head toward Joshua.

"Yeah." I don't know if I'm supposed to be admitting guilt or not, but it's not like things can get any worse. I'm covered in the man's blood...there's no denying it was me that stabbed him to death.

"Huh." Silver takes in a breath. "Well, I'm going to get started. Do you have somewhere safe you can go to get cleaned up and dispose of your clothing?"

"Um..." I don't mean to, but those pesky fucking tears well in my eyes again. I don't want to cry. Not here, not now. Not in front of this stranger. This murder cleaner-upper.

"Shit, what did I say?" Silver tilts his head toward me. "This isn't your first kill, is it?"

I nod without saying anything else.

"Fuck." Silver runs his hand over his beard. "I-uh, I don't know what to say. I'm not really good at providing comfort, I'm just the fixer."

"It's fine. I don't need it." I sniffle and wipe my nose. "I guess I could go home, but I've been avoiding my dad..." I leave off the reasoning and don't go into any further detail. Silver doesn't need to know how fucked up my life is.

"I mean, I probably wouldn't go somewhere that people are going to be asking you questions about all the blood." Silver chews at the corner of his lip. "You don't have anywhere else to go?"

The thought crosses my mind that I could go to June's mansion, since they're literally in this line of business, too, even though she won't admit it to me. She would understand the severity of the situation. But then I would have to tell them the truth. That I killed my boss. And then they would ask questions and want to know what happened and if I'm not careful, I might spill too many details about what's going on with my dad and Ricardo and the deal I made. I'd love to get their input and see if they had a solution for me, but Ricardo made it very clear that there was no getting out of this, and I can't risk putting them, or anyone else in danger when I could just isolate the damage to myself and handle it on my own.

"No," I say.

"Fuck." Silver scratches his beard, a nervous tick of his that I've already picked up on. Or maybe not nervous, but contemplative. A sign that he's unsure how to deal with something.

I wouldn't know how to deal with me either.

"I have a place near here," he finally adds. "You can shower and get a change of clothes, and I can get rid of the clothes you're wearing now." His nostrils flare slightly before he continues, "I don't do this. Like ever."

I throw up my hands slightly but don't let Miller's jacket fall away. "I don't exactly do this every day, either." I shake my head. "It's not a big deal, I'll figure something else out. Don't feel obligated to help me any more than you already are."

Silver narrows his eyes at me. "I'm not *obligated*. I *want* to help."

It's not lost on me that his jaw tenses at the last part of his statement.

"Why? You don't know me. You don't owe me anything." I put my hand on my hip and find myself a bit surprised by the amount of attitude I'm giving him. I'm sure he could snap me in half if he wanted to and dispose of my body before anyone suspected anything.

"You really are frustrating, aren't you?" He glances briefly at the dead body. "Is that why you killed him?"

I glare at him but don't give more of an answer than a simple, "No." He probably wouldn't believe me anyway. What man ever trusts what the victim says?

Silver sighs. "We've gotten off on the wrong foot." He steps toward me and extends his hand. "I'm Silver, what's your name?"

I tilt my head to look up at him, the closer he gets, the more he towers over me. "Cora." I place my palm in his and give it a swift shake.

"Cora," he repeats and keeps his gaze locked on mine. "If you'll excuse me, I need to tend to this mess, but when I'm done, the offer is still on the table."

"And what will I owe you in return?" I ask the question weighing heavily on my mind. No one does anything out of the kindness of their hearts anymore. There's always a string attached, even if it doesn't tug tight until it's too late to turn back.

"Nothing." Silver's face remains still, not a hint of an emotion showing through. He's a bit difficult to read, and I'm not quite sure if I find that terrifying or sexy.

I shouldn't be attracted to this man, he's literally a criminal, a *fixer*, but those words Miller said to me earlier float through my head about right and wrong. I should probably see all this as blaring red flags, but if I'm being honest, red has always been my favorite color.

Okay, I lied, maybe it's been pink, but isn't that the same damn thing?

"Why don't you relax on the couch while I clean this up?" Silver stares so deeply into my eyes that I'm worried he can see straight into my fucking soul. "It won't take long."

"That's what she said," I mutter, my sarcasm flaring up at the worst possible time.

"What was that?"

"Nothing." I point to the body and change the subject. "Do you need some help?"

The smallest grin flashes across Silver's hardened face. "No. I've got this."

"Suit yourself." I leave the bloodbath behind and go back into the lavish living room I was supposed to be showing my billionaire client and talking through design options.

Billionaire client...Miller. Is that even true? How could Miller be a billionaire? Surely a zero or two or three was misplaced along the way. He's young. There's no way he's much older than me. I barely have two nickels to rub together and he's fully fucking loaded? There's no fucking way. That must be a mistake.

I settle onto the stiff couch and bring my knees up with me, hugging them to my chest and wrapping Miller's jacket around to cocoon me in. Resting my head against the back of the couch, I consider how any of this could be possible.

Miller is a billionaire.

Silver is a murder cover-up guy.

I'm said murderer.

When I found out my dad was in over his head in debt, enough that I had to trade my life to keep him and my dying mother alive, I thought things couldn't get any more bizarre, but here I am, covered in my boss's blood and considering going home with a complete stranger—who happens to be twice my age and fine as fuck. I should be afraid, I should be freaking out, I should be doing something other than allowing my lids to flutter shut and become one with this overpriced couch.

But if I had to pinpoint how I felt about all of this, it would be numb. Numb to the debt, the cancer, the death, the deal with the devil. Life was once vibrant and mine for the taking, but now it seems like life happens to me and there's nothing I can do to control the outcome. I'm just here for the ride, even if it becomes the most terrifying rollercoaster I've ever been on.

I like to think of myself as an optimistic person. I've always been the friend to look for the silver lining in a bad situation. I've been the one my friends come to for help or advice. But who do I turn to when I don't have the answers? I've tried to think of every possible solution for the shit storm I'm in, but not only am I unable to find a way out, I keep digging myself further into the hole.

Murder, really?

Sweet, bubbly, doesn't even smash bugs, Cora...a fucking murderer.

And the weirdest part of all is that I'm not that surprised. No, when I shoved that box cutter into Joshua and yanked it out, his face lined with shock and mine speckled with his blood, I felt...

I reposition on the couch and try to distract my train of thought.

What I did was wrong. End of story.

And the only way I'm going to be able to make it through any of this is to do what I always do and shove it into a little folder in my mind along with all the other terrible things I refuse to acknowledge. So what if it's a shitty coping mechanism, it's mine, and it's what works for me.

Here's to hoping the lid on that little box of horrors in my mind stays closed because if there's ever a day when I lose control of the things I've hidden away, there's no telling what kind of darkness will emerge.

7
SILVER

I finish tending to the job I was assigned to and return to the crime scene.

There, on the couch, curled into a small ball of a human, Cora sleeps. Her chest rises and falls slowly, and damn if it isn't like I'm watching a fucking angel slumber.

She's nothing like I'm used to. No, in this business I deal with brute men and their evil wenches and occasional mistresses.

Never, in all my years, have I come across someone so...innocent.

Sure, she stabbed a guy countless times until he bled out, but that aside, Cora is like a bright beaming light that I haven't seen in ages, if at all. And damn if I don't have this strange, innate desire to protect it before it gets snuffed out.

Maybe if someone had done the same for me, I wouldn't have turned into the man I am today.

"Cora," I whisper but barely loud enough for her to hear.

She doesn't stir so I scoop her into my arms and position her close to my chest.

Cora nuzzles right in and wiggles her head to get more

comfortable, her hair wafting the sweetest mixture of honey and lavender up at me.

My heart pounds and I'm well aware of how fucking stupid this is. All of it. I should have never spoken to her other than the formalities of getting the job done, but how could I ignore how helpless she was in such an unfamiliar situation. I didn't expect *her* when I walked through that door. I thought I would be greeted by Miller, the man who ordered the job. The man I've dealt with countless times in similar scenarios like this.

The many years in this profession never prepared me for *her*.

So when I saw just how vulnerable she was, my stupid mouth betrayed me and offered to take her home with me.

Fucking idiot.

But how was I supposed to just leave her there to fend for herself when she had no idea what she even needed to do?

Christ, it was like watching a deer stand in the street staring right into a set of headlights. If I hadn't stepped in, there's no telling what would happen to her.

I hold her tightly and ignore the warmth of her body seeping into mine as I make my way out of the condo and down the hall. Luckily, the building is still vacant, otherwise I may have to avoid some awkward glares due to the passed-out girl in my arms. I've already scoped the place out, and the only people coming to and from are the occasional contractors finishing things up here and there, and they use the service elevator and stairwells. Not to mention, the unit that Cora and Miller were in has its own private elevator, saving me even more time in having fewer camera feeds to scrub once I'm done with the job.

Cora is light in my grasp, her petite frame weighing nothing compared to the brute she took down. It's a wonder she made it out alive, and from the redness around her neck and face, I can't imagine it wasn't without a fight.

Out of nowhere, anger rises within me, and if that man

wasn't already dead, I'd consider ending his life just because I could. I don't know what happened, or why things escalated the way they did, but if I was a betting man, I'd venture to say he fucking deserved what came to him.

My anger is suppressed by a slight sense of feeling proud of Cora for taking him down. I'm sure it wasn't easy, especially at her size and having never killed someone before, but she persevered all the same, and that alone shows just how capable she really is.

I carry her into the private elevator, my gaze darting down to check her breaths every few seconds, and then into the parking garage where my vehicle is. Holding her with just one arm, I open the passenger door and slip her inside. She stirs slightly but doesn't wake up, not even when I secure the seatbelt across her chest and buckle her in. I don't know whether I should be satisfied or worried about her lack of concern, but I know one thing is certain—she's safe with me.

At least, she is for now.

The scope of my job is to fix the situation, and maybe I'm stretching the description by taking it upon myself to take her under my wing, but what kind of man would I have been if I left her to her own devices? What if she was the loose thread that made all of this come undone and put the organization at risk? Those are the things I tell myself in a weak attempt to justify how very fucked up I am for thinking I should take her with me.

And it's what I continue to ponder as I drive the few blocks to my apartment on this side of town.

I drive straight into my garage and close the door a moment before I cut the engine, hoping like hell the tinted windows of my car prevented anyone from seeing the sleeping beauty in my passenger seat. I'm sure I'm being paranoid, but one can never be too sure, especially when you deal with the kind of evil shit I do on a daily basis.

Sighing, I shake my head and exit the driver's side, careful to shut the door with less force than usual. I stroll around the front and open Cora's door. She still hasn't woken up. Has the shock of the situation finally set in? I can't remember my first kill, it was a long time ago, so it's not like I can recall how it felt or what I went through emotionally. Mine was inevitable, though. When you grow up in a life of crime, death becomes the norm.

I unbuckle her seatbelt and hold my breath to see if she's going to move, and when she doesn't, I scoop her into my arms again, where it feels like she belongs, and carry her into my place. Despite the strong desire to not let her go, I lay her on my couch and step back, too afraid my presence will disturb her. Her breathing evens out, and she does that thing with her head where she nestles it to get more comfortable. I drape the dark grey blanket hanging on the back of the couch over her and drag my hand through my beard, wondering what the fuck I'm going to do now that I have her here.

What was I thinking? This is foolish. Quite possibly the dumbest thing I've ever done. I don't know her. She doesn't know me. I was called out on a job by Miller, and somehow, I thought it would be a good idea to take it upon myself to babysit the town's newest killer.

But damn if she isn't an adorable little murderer.

My phone buzzes in my pocket, and I step away, pull it out, and slide my finger across the screen to answer the call.

"Yeah," I say, a bit quieter than I normally would have.

"Silver," Miller greets me on the other end.

"Job is complete," I tell him part of the truth.

"And the girl?"

I exhale and watch her from across my apartment. I could lie to him and make up some story about how I sent her on her way, or I could risk being castrated by admitting I took her with me...

I consider both options carefully and choose the one that

will no doubt surprise both of us.

"She's here." I pause and add, "With me."

Miller audibly exhales. "Okay. That's good. That's good, right?" His tone shifts to something like nervousness. "Is everything okay? Let me talk to her."

"She's asleep," I tell him, suddenly realizing I have no idea what the connection between the two of them is.

Is she Miller's girl? Have I sort of kidnapped a very powerful man's woman?

"Yeah, of course she is," Miller says. "She's probably in shock."

"I didn't know what else to do with her," I admit. "She didn't exactly come across like our kind."

"No," Miller confirms. "She isn't. Not really."

He doesn't elaborate, and that only makes my mind wander even more.

Who is she to him? And why did he cover up for her?

"Whatever she needs, give it to her. I'll compensate you fairly." Miller clears his throat. "Whatever she needs, okay?"

"Yeah. Of course." I didn't need his order but now that I have it, at least there's some validation behind why I insisted on taking her. I want to question him and figure out what their relationship is, but Miller and I don't have that kind of relationship, so asking him would be too out of line. Instead, I'll just chalk it up to her being important to him, enough that he hired me to dispose of the body she killed, and to task me to take care of her.

"Let me know if anything changes. I'll be out of town for the next forty-eight hours. Can you keep an eye on her?"

"Yes."

"Okay. I'll wire you some funds now."

"That isn't necess—"

But Miller has already hung up, and within a few seconds, a notification pops across the top of my screen that twenty-thousand dollars has been deposited into my account.

If he had waited an extra second, he would have heard me tell him it wasn't necessary, that I would have watched over her for free, but then how would I have explained to him that his girl has got me under her spell?

It's better this way. Less risky. He gave me a job, and now that's what this is. A job. I will remain professional and do what is expected of me. Keep her safe and give her what she needs.

Dragging my hand through my beard, I sigh and shake my head. "Idiot," I mutter.

I use her slumber as an opportunity to slip out of the room and take a shower, washing away the remnants of her crime that lingers on my body and attempting to put space between us so my mind can think a bit more clearly.

Only, the distance causes this fucking pit in my chest that creates even more worry.

When have I ever worried about another human being? These *feelings*, these *emotions*, they're completely foreign, and I want nothing to do with them.

I slap my face, the water adding a nice cracking sound to it. "Get it together, Silver."

Any other day I'd stay under the shower longer, but I find myself turning the faucet off way sooner than usual and drying off in a hurry. Slipping into grey sweatpants and a white tee, I finish by towel drying my hair and accepting the mess that it is. This is the part of my day when I'd grab the paper and have a cup of coffee while I flip through the boring headlines to see what the media decided to tell us. I'd poke fun at the stories I'm well aware are fabricated and try to read between the lines of what is fact or fiction.

I'd cook dinner and eat it alone before settling into my chair and reading whatever my latest read is. Currently, it's some science fiction book I picked up off a stand near the checkout at the corner store. It isn't captivating or groundbreaking, but it does pass the time, and at this point in my life, that's all I can ask for. That's what I'm used to. Waiting around until I'm called into work and then fixing whatever problem arises with efficiency and discretion. My phone rings at any given hour, and I'm okay with that. It's nice knowing that my services are needed, and that people can rely on me to solve their problems. It's what I'm good at.

My work is my company. The dead bodies, loose ends, busted kneecaps, and helping people escape.

There isn't any problem I've been presented that I haven't been able to fix. I pride myself on being a man of my word and following through with any job I've been given. It's not for the faint of heart, and there are days when I question whether I can pull something off, but that has never stopped me from trying.

What it has stopped me from is living any semblance of a *normal* life. Not that I'd choose that, given the opportunity presents itself. I don't know anything outside of this life. At some point, I became so intertwined with it that I no longer see where the crime or my identity begins or ends. And I gave up trying a long time ago.

This is who I am. I am a bad man. And I am damn good at it.

I sit on the chair opposite Cora and watch her for what feels like an eternity and a second all at the same time. I notice her shoulders grow tense, her breathing change, and then even back out. I study her eyelids as her eyes dart underneath them, and I wonder what it is she's dreaming of.

She sucks in a sharp breath and sits upright, both scaring herself and causing my hand to ball into a fist, ready to fight whatever might be harming her.

Cora clutches her chest, and I want to rush over there, but I can only imagine that would startle her more. Instead, I allow her gaze to explore until her sights land on me.

"Where am I?" She rubs her eyes.

"My apartment," I tell her.

She glances down at her body and slides her legs off the

couch, placing her feet on the floor. "Sorry."

"What?"

"My shoes. They were on your couch."

"I don't care about my couch."

"Oh." She looks down at the blanket I wrapped her up in and tightens it around her body.

"Are you cold?" I ask.

"No."

"Do you require anything?"

Cora narrows her beautiful eyes at me. "That is the weirdest question anyone has ever asked me." She breathes in and leans back, relaxing enough to make me think she's not completely freaked out about being in my apartment.

"Are you thirsty? Hungry? Do you want to get out of those clothes?"

Her cheek turns up into a grin. "Are you trying to get me out of my clothes?"

I shake my head. "No. Of course not. I'm..."

She cuts me off. "I'm giving you shit, Silver. Chill out."

Right. Yeah.

"How did I get here?" Her smile fades, and I'd be upset to see it leave but it's etched in my memory.

"To my couch?"

She shrugs. "In general, yeah."

"I brought you."

Cora rubs at her neck. "I'm sorry. I must have been out of it."

"It's fine."

"You carried me?"

"Yes." *And I'd do it again*—but I don't say that part.

"That's embarrassing."

"There's nothing to be embarrassed about."

"Where are we?"

"Not too far from The Wellerton. Few blocks." It's a bit of a stretch but she doesn't need to know the specifics.

"It's cozy." She glances around from her spot on my couch, no doubt taking in the exposed brick and industrial vibe of my apartment. "I like it."

My chest tightens at her approval. "Thanks."

"I'm an interior designer," she adds. "That's why I was at The Wellerton. To meet with a client to discuss the design of their unit."

The pieces of the puzzle start to fit together.

"Miller was your client?"

She nods. "Yep."

"Oh."

"You sound surprised?" Cora raises a brow suspiciously at me.

"I thought maybe he was your..."

She laughs and cuts me off again. "No. Miller is not my *fill in the blank.* We're just friends, if you can even call it that."

But from the concern he showed on the phone, it's safe to say Miller doesn't think they're just friends. Or at least, he doesn't want to be only that. And how could I blame him? I've known this girl for a total of five minutes, and she has me questioning everything.

"Right. Friends." I loosen the fist my hand had made and tap my fingers along the armrest of the chair.

"You don't think so?"

"That's none of my business." I exhale. "I spoke to him while you were asleep."

"You did?" It's not lost on me that her eyes sparkle a bit more at the very mention of him.

"He wants me to look after you until he gets back."

"Where did he go?"

"I don't know. I didn't ask."

"When will he be back?"

"He said he'll be gone forty-eight hours," I tell her the limited information I have for no other reason than because I can. It's not like it will put her in danger or risk whatever Miller has going on. If anything, maybe it will convince Cora that she's safe here with me and follow along with his plan of me keeping an eye on her.

"That's oddly specific." Cora's shoulders slump, and it's obvious that it's caused by disappointment.

They're both clearly interested in each other, yet neither one of them seems to realize the other is.

How foolish of them to be so oblivious.

And how foolish of me for sticking my nose where it doesn't belong.

"You didn't answer me."

"About what?" Cora remains there, a beautiful addition to my apartment.

For a split second, I'm lost in the thought of her always belonging there, here, with me. But as soon as it comes on, I realize even quicker how irrational and stupid that thought was. She's a fucking stranger, and if I'm not mistaken, she's spoken for. And even if she wasn't, who's to say she's interested in me? I'm twice her age and much more corrupt a man than she deserves.

No, Cora deserves someone good and kind and gentle—not brutal and vindictive and malicious like me—like Miller. Neither one of us is deserving of her, and the sooner she sees that, the better.

"Silver." Cora tilts her head toward me.

I blink and look at her, my brain and my heart and my dick all tugging me in different directions over what they want. "Are you hungry or thirsty?" I rise from the chair. "I have water, coffee, tea. And if you want to take a shower, I can order takeout."

She brings herself to her feet too, and I'm reminded of just how small she really is. Sure, I could tell when I held her in my arms, but to stand here and tower over her...

The very caveman nature in me rises to the surface. That I could protect her. Provide for her. Satisfy her every desire.

"Okay. Yeah." Cora glances around the room again. "Where's the bathroom? Did you say you had something I could change into?"

"Mmhm." I point toward the door past the living room. "Through there. I set some things on the counter in the bathroom. Just toss your clothes out to me when you're done, and I'll dispose of them."

Cora shrugs off the blanket and grips the oversized jacket she's wearing. "This is Miller's, though."

"I'll take care of it."

"Okay," she says with a bit of reluctance. "Are you going to eat?"

I hadn't been hungry until she questioned it, but now that she did, I'm starving...in more than one way.

"If you'd like me to," I answer.

"Can we get pizza?"

"Sure."

"With pepperoni and pineapple."

"Anything else?"

Cora crosses her arms. "You're not going to fight me over the pineapple?"

"Why would I fight you on that?"

She shrugs. "Not everyone likes pineapple on their pizza."

"If I had an issue with it, I would pick it off or order one without it. If you want pineapple, you're getting pineapple."

"Can I have a Sprite, too?"

"Yes."

"I can Venmo you."

I roll my eyes. "You will do no such thing." Plus, Miller said she could have whatever she wanted. Even if I was prepared to get her anything she asked for, he quite literally sent me an excessive amount of money to take care of her for two days. I can't imagine this sweet, innocent girl asking for pineapple on her pizza costs more than twenty grand.

"I insist." Cora plants her hands on her hips as if it's going to somehow make her appear bigger or more dominant.

"Not going to happen, Angel."

Cora scoffs. "I'm not an Angel."

"Whatever you say, *Angel*."

"Wow." Cora breathes in and sighs dramatically. "You're not going to let that one go, are you?"

"Never." Not in a million years.

This time, it's her that rolls her eyes. "I'm going to take a shower. You don't have any creepy cameras hidden in here, do you?"

"Fresh out of creepy cameras. I can have some installed if you like?" It's the truth. I'd never put something in my apartment that could be hacked into and spied on. I deal with secrets like they're currency. I can't afford for anyone to threaten that.

"I'll pass." Cora makes her way toward the door I motioned to, the one that belongs to my bedroom with the attached bathroom. "Wait..." She turns to face me. "You mentioned coffee. What kind?" She presses the corner of Miller's jacket to her lips and it's everything I can do to focus on the simple question she asked me.

"What kind do you want?"

"What are my options?"

"Whatever you desire, I will provide."

Cora deadpans. "So, if I say I want a vanilla oat milk latte with an extra shot of espresso..."

"Then I'd ask if you wanted it hot or iced."

"You're not serious."

"Deadly."

"Okay, hot then. I'll have water, too. Spring, please." Cora, seemingly satisfied with her demands, continues into my room, leaving the door cracked behind her.

I waste no time pulling out my phone and ordering the pizza, an extra-large, and adding on breadsticks and two different types of desserts—an apple dessert pizza and brownies, along with her Sprite. It's from a place I frequent and know won't keep us waiting too long. Hopefully, she'll like it. And if she doesn't, I'll order her food from somewhere else until she's happy.

I bring my hand to my forehead and sigh. *What the fuck is wrong with me to care about something so stupid with someone I barely know?*

A few minutes after the door to my bathroom shuts, the water is turned on and the door opens again, only to shut a moment later.

I peek through, and once I'm sure she's not running around here naked, I enter the space and snatch the clothes she tossed out the door, leaving in a hurry to give her some privacy.

It's not that I wouldn't love to catch a glance of her in the nude, but consent is consent, and I might have some very grey morals but that is not one of them I budge on. Respecting women and their bodily autonomy has always been at the top of my list of lines I refuse to cross.

I'm walking through my apartment when I accidentally drop some of the garments she left out for me. Snatching her dress slacks off the ground, it's then that I notice something peculiar about them. I lay the rest of the things on my kitchen counter and examine the slacks, noting where the rip is and recalling a similar strand of fabric tucked into the victim's hand that I was tasked to get rid of.

Only, he was no victim at all. No, he was the fucking abuser, and if I'm not mistaken, the reason the fucker is dead is because he tried to force himself on Cora but he underestimated her ability to fight for herself. My fist tightens around the pants, and I grow furious at his actions. At the actions of so many men.

And all the women who never stood a chance against their attackers.

"Fucking pig," I blurt out to no one but myself.

If I hadn't already disposed of his body, I would put a bullet or two into his fucking skull for good measure.

But the time has passed for that, and all that can be done now is to make sure it never happens ever again.

I snatch everything except Miller's jacket off the counter, walk over to the door leading out onto my patio, and slip outside. I toss her things into the burn barrel and douse it with lighter fluid before tossing in a match. It ignites quickly, burns for a few minutes, and then dies down. I poke at it with my fire stick, and once I'm satisfied the evidence is gone enough to not be an issue, I grab the broom leaning in the corner and sweep up the fallen leaves from the tall shrubs lining my patio. They offer full protection from any prying eyes, but damn do they make a mess if you don't keep up with it. I toss the debris into the trash and return inside to finish my task. Grabbing a bag from my laundry room, I shove Miller's jacket inside and set it near the door so I don't forget to drop it off at the dry cleaners. If there's any trace of what happened today on it, they'll get rid of it and leave nothing behind.

The counters get a wipe down with a homemade but highly effective antiseptic and when I'm done, I wash my hands twice and scrub up to my elbows.

At the same time I'm finishing, the faucet to my shower turns off, giving me only a few minutes before Cora is back out here.

I stroll to the far side of my kitchen, opening the mini fridge at my coffee bar to pull out the thing of oat milk. I check the expiration date, grateful I had groceries delivered last week, and make quick work of her special-order latte. I pull the shots of espresso and pour them into an oversized mug with some vanilla syrup and steam the oat milk until it's perfect enough to add to the espresso. I hold the cup at an angle and do my best job of creating some foam art, but it turns into a weird blob.

"That smells good," Cora says as she enters the open space of my apartment.

I don't mean to, but my entire body tenses at her arrival. I complete the latte, anyway, and turn toward her with it in my hands, careful not to spill a drop.

"Holy shit." Cora comes the rest of the way. "You made that? For me?"

"You said you wanted an oat milk latte."

She towel dries her blonde hair, and it's then that I recognize the clothes she's wearing that I had laid out for her. A pair of my sweatpants and a tee shirt, the same thing I'm wearing, only they hang on her small frame instead of hugging it like they do on me.

"Yeah, but I didn't think you'd make one. I thought you'd order it or something." She cranes her neck to look around me. "Is that a DeLonghi?"

"Yes."

"Those things are so expensive..." She turns her attention to the mug in my hand. "Oh my God, is that a heart in the foam?"

I hold the thing out to her. "I tried. I'm not very good at it though."

"Are you kidding me? It's perfect." She brings it toward her and breathes in before taking a cautious sip, the foam lingering on her upper lip prior to her licking it away. "It's so good. Thank you. I love it."

My hand itches to reach and tuck the strand of hair that falls into her face but thankfully my train of thought is interrupted by the buzzer blaring in my apartment.

"Must be our food." I rush past her and press the button near my door. "Yeah?"

"Dinner's ready, sir," the person calls back.

There are few places I order takeout from, but every single

one of them has been vetted and knows certain phrases to use to get access to my building, and they change frequently in case anyone tries to pick up on them. One can never be too careful in my line of work.

I grant him entry and a few moments later, a solid knock sounds on my door. Reaching into my pocket, I pull out a hundred and slip it to the kid as he gives me our order.

"Thank you, sir," he tells me with a smile he can barely hide.

I had already paid our bill on the app I ordered from, but I always like to give the delivery kids a bit extra since there's no telling if their greedy bosses ever actually tip them out what's left on the mobile orders.

Returning to Cora, I find her pulling two plates out of the cabinet and making herself at home.

"I hope you don't mind," she says. "I got nosey."

"Not at all."

"Damn, what did you order?" She widens her gaze at the stack of stuff in my grasp and the bag dangling from my fingertips. "Let me help you."

"Well, you said you wanted pizza, so I got that...but I didn't know if you wanted dessert, so I got you two to choose from, and you can never go wrong with breadsticks." I slide the boxes on the counter and pull the bottles of Sprite out of the bag.

"Do you drink Sprite?" She points to the four bottles.

"No, but I figured I'd get you a few extra just in case."

"Just in case what? We get snowed in?" Cora laughs and fuck if the sound doesn't go straight to my cock and heart at the same time.

"Never know."

"You realize we live in California, right?"

"I'm sure crazier things have happened." I take three of the Sprites and walk to my fridge, placing them inside and pulling out a bottle of water. "And this." I hand it to her and she grins and shakes her head.

"I'm half tempted to ask for a horse and see if you miraculously pull one of those out, too."

"I know a guy."

"A horse guy?"

I nod. "Yeah. Do you actually want one?"

"No. I mean, yes, but *no*. Where would I put it? My bedroom at my parents' house?" The smile on her face quickly fades, and she fidgets with the bottle of water I just handed her.

"What's wrong?" I ask her.

"Nothing." She forces her cheeks upward but the expression doesn't meet her eyes. Clearly, she's faking it, but who am I to push her, especially considering the day she's had and the fact that I'm a complete stranger.

"Do you want to talk about what happened earlier?" I place my hands behind my back and weave them together.

"Nah, it's fine." Cora flips open the box of pizza and puts two slices on one plate and one on the other. "Here." She shoves the two slices toward me. "How many breadsticks do you want?" She pulls one out and bites off the tip before putting it on her plate. "Mmm, so good," she mumbles with a mouthful.

"You don't have to serve me," I tell her and take a stick from the box. "I'm supposed to be taking care of you."

"You literally disposed of a body for me today, pretty sure the least I can do is put a couple pieces of pizza on a plate for you." Cora covers her mouth. "Oh shit, I probably shouldn't have said that." She looks around suspiciously like someone might have overheard her.

"You can say whatever you want in here. Just watch it out there." I vaguely point away from us.

"Right." Cora slides onto a stool at my island and brings her plate and drinks toward her.

I grab a cup from the cabinet and fill it full of tap water for myself and take the seat on the other end, one chair between us.

"What, afraid I have cooties or something?" Cora glances

over at me.

"Just giving you and all of your drinks plenty of room."

She chuckles. "There's a method to my madness, I promise."

"Yeah? Do tell." I take a bite of pizza and wait for her to continue. I've never ordered pineapple on my pizza before, but I wasn't about to tell her that, especially after she thought I was going to cause an issue for her asking for it. It's surprisingly good, and I don't hate it as much as I thought I would.

"Well..." She points to the coffee. "This one is for caffeine." Then the Sprite. "This one is for taste." And then the water. "And this one is for..."

"Hydration," I add when she doesn't continue.

"Exactly. You get it."

"Do you pee every two minutes or what?"

"Three." She corrects me and nibbles off some of her pizza. Cora reaches for the stack of napkins, giving herself one and passing a few down to me.

"Thank you," I tell her, taking them. "What do you think?" I hold up my slice to her.

"Good, I approve." She finishes her piece but doesn't reach for another.

I hide a triumphant smirk and polish the two she plated for me off, along with my breadstick.

"Do you live here alone?" Cora breaks off a piece of her breadstick and eats it, turning toward me and managing to cross her legs on the small stool.

"Yes."

"No wife?" Cora averts her gaze to the breadstick she's picking at.

"No."

"Girlfriend?"

"No."

"Boyfriend?"

"I'm straight, if that's what you're asking." I wipe my hands on the napkin and swivel my chair toward her, too.

She shrugs. "You can never be too sure."

I clear my throat. "What about you?"

"I'm straight for the most part..."

I chuckle. "That wasn't what I was asking but good to know."

Cora takes a long swig of her Sprite. "Then what were you asking?"

"Do you have a husband or boyfriend wondering where you are right now?"

"No, I do not have either of those. I am very single." She exhales. "Very, very single."

"You mentioned your parents, do you need to let them know you won't be coming home tonight?"

Cora chews at her lip before answering. "No."

I leave space for her to elaborate on what feels like an open-ended answer.

"We aren't really talking right now," she adds. "My mom, she's...*sick*, and I haven't seen her lately. And my dad..." Her entire body seems to tense at the mention of him. "We got into a fight, and I really can't stand him."

"I'm sorry," I say because I'm not sure what else I can do to help her. I'm used to fixing people's problems, not help them process their emotions and shit like this. Give me a dead body and I'll get rid of it, but this...it's uncharted territory.

"It's fine," Cora mutters almost like a knee-jerk reaction.

Whatever is going on with her *isn't* fine, but why should she confide in me about it when we've only just met? It's strange how desperately I want to help her while understanding that I need to give her space. There's this big part of me that wants to grab her into my arms and hold her tight and never let her go, but *that* would be insane and would fully justify her stabbing me to death just like she did with that man at The Wellerton. Only the difference between me and him would be that I would be doing it to keep her safe, not put her in any further danger.

"Is it bad that I don't feel that bad about Joshua?" She glances up at me through her lashes, her voice barely a whisper.

It takes me a second too long to realize she's referring to the dead guy, but once I do, I shake my head and sigh. "I saw your pants. Before I torched them."

Cora tugs her top lip between her teeth and draws in a breath. "He was going to rape me."

I reach across the counter but don't touch her; I just leave my hand there and hope she knows I mean no harm. "You don't have to justify what you did to him. And you sure as hell don't have to feel bad about it. He deserves to rot in hell."

"When it first happened, I thought I would feel bad once my shock started to fade...but instead I feel bad about *not* feeling bad. Does that make sense?"

"Yeah." There are countless times when I fully understand that what I did was wrong, yet I have no remorse or guilt for having done it. I guess that's what separates me from others, and maybe it's why I'm so drawn to Cora, because in a way, I somehow knew we shared that similarity. A fucked up one. But as I watch her, the golden angel sitting in my presence, it's hard to imagine that she's fucked up at all. And maybe *that's* the real connection, that I see something in her that lives within me, only it's not this ugly terrible thing I once thought it was. In me, I thought it was a weakness, but in her, it radiates strength.

Cora reaches for her coffee this time. "I hated him way before today, you know?"

"Joshua?" I hate even saying his name.

"Yeah. He's a fucking prick. Well, he was, before I stabbed him to death." Her eyes widen briefly as she takes a drink of her coffee. "So crazy. I fucking stabbed a guy to death." She places the mug on the counter. "I ended a guy's life."

"You sure did." And damn did she do it well. She got him in enough vital places that there was no way he would survive. Whether she did that on purpose or accident, the fact remains, she fucked him up well. A familiar sense of pride washes over me.

"I wonder who's going take his place?" Cora glances over at me like I might have the answer, but I don't, not yet anyway. I'd be willing to figure it out for her, if that's what she wanted.

"I can look into it, if you'd like?"

"Nah." She shrugs. "Can't be worse than Joshua. Plus, now that I have you in my life, I can kill him if he sucks, right?" Cora grins and I know she's joking but I wish she knew I'd do it if that's what it took to keep her happy and safe.

Although, now that Miller bought the building, I can't imagine he'd employ anyone that would pose a threat to her once he's in possession and control.

It hasn't been made public knowledge yet, but after a little digging, I found out that Mr. Wellerton had sold the property to Miller. I can't imagine the chunk of change Miller paid to purchase it was small, but the way Miller threw me that money tonight without question, there's no telling how loaded he really is.

"I'm kidding," Cora adds when I don't follow her up.

"I'd hide your dead bodies whenever you needed me to." I wink at her and drink some of my water to distract me from staring at her. "You getting tired?"

"Nope." She swivels forward and extends to reach for the boxes of dessert, flipping both of them open. "Ah man, how am I supposed to choose between them?"

"Easy. Have one of each. Treat it like how you do your drinks."

"Hmm." Cora presses her index finger to her lips. "Yeah. Good idea." She does exactly that and then passes the boxes toward my side of the counter. "Which one are you going with?"

"Both." I wink at her again and for a split second, her cheeks flush before she turns away.

We sit there in silence, eating our dessert for a few minutes and I grow very comfortable with the two of us being near each other, existing in the same space, enjoying a meal together. It's been a long time since I've shared a meal with someone that wasn't work-related, let alone a person of the opposite sex. Sure, I've had my fair share of one-night stands, but to hang out in sweatpants and eat pizza...I don't know if I've ever done that.

"Would you like to add a fourth drink to your lineup?" I clear our plates away and tidy up the counter.

Cora sits there, cute as hell on her stool, and looks up at me. "What did you have in mind?"

I open the cabinet below the counter and kneel on the floor. "I have all your basic options. Bourbon, tequila, rum, gin, vodka..."

"What's your poison?" She rests her head in her hands.

"I'm usually a bourbon guy."

"Bourbon it is."

"I can make you whatever you'd like," I tell her, because not only did I go through a coffee phase where I bought a high-end machine and learned how to brew a damn good cup, but I went through a mixology phase, too. I got all the basics, stocked the appropriate tools and mixers, and became my own little bartender.

"I'm good with bourbon," she tells me again.

I snatch the bottle closest to me and place it on the counter before reaching for two short glasses. "Ice, no ice? Do you want a mixer?"

"How about ice."

I nod and go to my freezer, pulling out the circular ice tray and popping one into each glass.

Once I've poured the bourbon, I push one across to her and take the other.

"Thank you." Cora raises her glass. "What should we cheers to?"

"To staying alive."

She smiles and clinks my glass. "To staying alive."

We both sip our drinks, and I return the bottle of bourbon to its place in the cabinet.

"How come you don't have a television?" Cora asks me as she glances around my apartment.

I shrug. "Never really wanted one, I guess."

"So you're telling me you've never watched *Game of Thrones*, or I don't know, *Breaking Bad*?"

"Breaking what?" I drink some more of my bourbon.

"Wow. Really? You're not fucking with me?"

I shake my head. "I assure you, I am not fucking with you."

Cora hops off her chair and keeps her glass in her hand. "What do you do with your spare time then?" She walks slowly into my living room, glancing back at me for an answer.

"I read. I exercise. I learn. I don't know, what do *you* do in your spare time?"

She chuckles stiffly. "Other than having constant existential crises? I'd like to think I use my time wisely, but if I'm being honest, I doom scroll entirely too much and probably consume excessive amounts of television."

"You doom what?"

"Doom scroll. You know, like on Instagram or TikTok or whatever. You've never wasted four hours of your day accidentally scrolling the *for you* page?"

"The more questions I ask, the more I have." I follow her over but maintain a couple feet between us. "But no, I don't do that. I don't have those things. Are those social media apps or?"

Cora turns to me and narrows her gaze. "You're seriously telling me you don't have *any* social media?"

I rock my head back and forth. "Nope."

"Wow. I bet that's kind of wonderful." She returns her attention to my bookshelf. "Have you read all of these?" Cora floats her finger along the edges, flitting her gaze at me here and there.

"Most of them, yes. Some of them more than once. A few of them are new." I point to the three sort of haphazardly set on the shelf. "Do you read?"

Cora sighs. "Not enough."

"Feel free to borrow any of them if you'd like. There's quite a variety." I step a little closer. "Sci-fi, thriller, romance, mystery...I even have some non-fiction over here."

Cora snatches a book off the shelf and turns toward me. "You've read this?"

"Yes..."

"No way. I don't believe you." She flips through the pages and holds it between us. "What's it about?"

"Um, it's about a girl who's hiding out in a small town, and her three neighbors sort of take her under their wing and end up falling in love with her." I tilt my head. "Have *you* read it?"

She gently smacks me in the chest with the book before putting it back on the shelf. "Yes, I have. A few weeks ago, actually. I just never imagined you as the target audience for reverse harem novels."

"There's always the outliers, right? Plus, I thought you said you didn't read much." I swallow another swig of my bourbon, the heat of it warming me on the way down.

"Well, define *much*. You check my Goodreads and I'll have to kill you."

"Afraid I'll find your fairy smut stash?" I nudge her with my elbow and her eyes bulge.

Cora laughs. "You did *not* just say fairy smut."

"I did. And I'll do it again, don't tempt me."

Seemingly satisfied with my book selection, she continues on her journey of my apartment, stopping next at the record player. "How does this thing work?"

"Here." I push a few buttons and once the record starts to spin, I lower the tonearm until it makes contact.

My apartment fills with a soft piano melody, blurring out

the sound of my thudding heart. It's strange that I'm equal parts completely calm and yet so nervous around her. I'm a strong, feared man, why am I feeling like a thirteen-year-old boy looking for validation from a pretty girl?

"That's beautiful," Cora murmurs over the music. She closes her eyes and rocks her body slowly.

"Would you like to dance?" I ask her before I completely chicken out.

Cora's bright eyes open, and she grins. "I would love to."

"Let me have that." I take her drink from her and place it on the coffee table next to mine, extending my hand toward her, palm upward.

She places her small hand into mine, and I surprise her by spinning her toward me.

Cora giggles and lands firmly against my chest, right where she belongs.

With one of my hands resting above her hip and hers on my shoulder, we sway around my living room. Her grip on me tightens and for a small moment, the only thing is her and me and nothing else. Not the jobs, the crime, the money, the endless pursuit of the meaning behind it all...

"Where did you learn to dance?" Cora asks me, breaking my train of thought with her angelic voice.

"Believe it or not, I took ballroom dancing lessons."

"You're right, I don't believe it."

I break away from her slightly to spin her in a circle and then dip her back. She goes along with it, my hands guiding her body as it doesn't question, just accepts my lead. Holding her there, her delicate frame in my grasp, dangling horizontally to the floor, I wonder if anything could get more perfect than this moment.

She darts her gaze between mine and if I'm not mistaken, glances to my lips. "I changed my mind, I believe you."

Bringing her upright slowly, I say, "Good girl."

Cora smiles. "Did you learn that term in one of those reverse harem novels?"

"No." I hold her inches away from me and stare down at her. "Why? Do you have a praise kink?" I clench my jaw the second the question leaves my lips, knowing damn well how inappropriate it was to ask her such a thing. I don't know her, she doesn't know me, why would I think it would be okay to ask her about her fucking kinks?

But instead of making things weird, Cora winks. "Maybe."

We continue to dance—neither one of us bringing up the kink question again—for a few minutes. Cora lays her head against my chest with her small body pressed to mine. Spread across most of her lower back, my hand holds her to me and memorizes the very sensation of her.

Finally, Cora pulls back and looks up again, this time, something serious written across her face. "Can I ask you something?"

"Of course." I hold my breath.

"Do you think I'm pretty?"

"What?"

Cora releases me and steps back. "Sorry, I shouldn't have said anything. That was stupid of me."

"What?" I repeat, still somehow dazed by the turn of the conversation.

How could she question such a thing? Has she not seen a mirror? Has she no shortage of suitors that would gladly sweep her off her feet given the chance? Is she completely blind to what the rest of us see when we look at her?

Cora turns her back to me, reaches for her bourbon, and downs it in one gulp.

"Cora," I say as softly as I can.

"What?" She doesn't turn around.

"Ask me again."

8
CORA

"**W**hat?" I find myself saying the same thing he already did twice.

I should have never asked. I should have kept my mouth shut. I don't know what I was thinking. Why I let my insecurities get the best of me—why it matters to me what he thinks.

"I said." Silver's voice grows rugged. "Ask me again."

I face him but don't meet his gaze. "Do you think I'm pretty?" I hate the words more the second time around.

Silver brings his hand forward, slowly, cautiously, like I might explode if he touches me the wrong way, and rests it against my cheek. He tilts my head upward and forces my attention. "Yes."

I swallow the lump that forms in my throat but don't say anything. It's not as if he would have told me no. He might be a ruthless criminal but he's not a complete asshole. What I should have said was *attractive*, not pretty. Anyone can be pretty, but not everyone is attractive. And when it comes down to it, that's what I really want to know, if I'm attractive. To him. To anyone.

Except for Joshua, or Ricardo, or someone who doesn't respect me.

Someone who I'm attracted to. Someone who I want to want me.

"You're pretty," he confirms but then adds, "and beautiful, and gorgeous, and radiant and sexy and..."

My heart pounds at his declaration, and I wonder for a second if he can read my mind, although I'm desperately hoping that he can't, because I'd never want someone to know what goes on in my head.

"You don't mean that," I whisper.

"Why would I lie?" His dark gaze bores into me, and a strong part of me is terrified but a stronger part of me is electrified by his intensity.

"I don't know."

My cell phone buzzes in my pocket and threatens to steal my attention, but I don't allow it.

"Do you need to get that?" Silver maintains his closeness, his hand still resting on my cheek.

"No."

The music continues to play in the background, a perfect soundtrack to the evening.

"Angel..."

"Kiss me," I blurt out before I change my mind.

"What?" Silver doesn't back away. Instead, he rubs his thumb along my jaw.

"I said, kiss me." I stand up a bit taller, closing the distance between us, daring him to make good and prove to me that he isn't lying.

If my life is going to end soon, when I give myself over to Ricardo, I might as well live a little while I have the chance. And if Miller and Alec don't want to be a part of that, why should I pass up this tall, dark, and handsome opportunity standing in front of me?

I've been attempting to flirt with him all night but I haven't been sure whether or not he was actually interested or only going along with Miller's order to take care of me. I had been hoping that he was interested, I just wasn't sure if I was reading the vibe right or not. Miller is proof enough that I've been wrong before.

But when Silver leans in and presses his mouth to mine, I know damn well that for once, I got things correct.

His lips melt to mine and automatically, they part, our tongues dashing out and mingling. Silver wraps his strong arms around me and lifts me from the floor, my body light as a feather in his grasp and hungrier than ever.

I kiss him harder and envelop his frame with mine, my legs crossing behind his back and pinning me to him.

Silver slams us against the wall, one of his hands bracing himself and the other holding onto my waist. He grinds into me, his erection pressing through our sweatpants.

"Fuck," I pant and buck against him. "I want you."

"Are you sure?" Silver rests his forehead against mine.

"Yes." I reach down and grasp onto his cock through his bottoms, stroking the length. "Please."

He kisses me and hardens in my hand, and if I weren't so fucking impatient, I would enjoy this a bit more, but fuck, all I want is him to be inside me. I need to feel anything other than numb and broken. I yearn to be fucked in my pussy, not in my head.

Silver slides his fingers down my side and cups my breast, pinching my peaked nipple through the shirt of his that I'm wearing. He snakes his hand up and under, his touch lighting me on fire somehow more than I already was and sending heat shooting straight between my legs.

I moan into him and grip his shaft tighter.

He continues his exploration of my body, moving his hand under the waistband of my sweatpants and hesitating.

"Don't stop," I tell him. "Please don't stop."

At this, he carries on toward my center, his fingers inching closer and closer until...

"Angel, you're soaked." He glides his finger teasingly and then shoves it in, arching it upward.

I sigh and rock my hand up and down on his cock, gripping it harder. "Fuck," I whimper.

Silver positions his thumb along the edge of my clit and plunges another finger inside of me, spreading me open and then giving me one more. "I need to get you ready if you're going to fit me, Angel." He ravishes me with his hand, and it's everything I can do not to combust all around him. He finger fucks me like he's spent his whole life studying my body instead of learning how to dispose of dead ones. "You're doing so good."

I lean my head back and he takes the opportunity to graze his lips along my neck and kiss the sensitive flesh. He drags his teeth over it and then bites down gently while fucking my pussy harder. He applies pressure to his thumb, passing it over my clit and sending me crying out.

I climax hard and scream out, "Fuck!" as he doesn't let up his torment.

No, he keeps three fingers inside of my pulsating pussy and backs us away from the wall and into his kitchen, rocking my body against his fingers every step of the way.

He doesn't take them out until he's about to drop me onto the counter where we just shared a meal. Silver grips the sides of my sweatpants and stares directly into my eyes. "Are you still sure?"

"Mmhm." I nod expectantly for whatever he has in store for me.

I've been with older men before, but it's never been like this, like him. Silver is seductive and dominant, and fuck does he turn me on by just looking at me.

"I want to see you." Silver drags my pants over my ass, kneeling in front of me to remove them the rest of the way. "Is that okay, Angel?" He discards them onto the floor and waits for me to nod again before he places his hands on my knees and spreads them apart.

I want to close them, to shut the lights off, to grab a blanket and throw it over myself, not because I don't want this, but because I've never felt as vulnerable and quite literally as exposed as I do right now.

But when he says, "God damn, you're beautiful," I've also never felt as worshipped, either, and damn if that doesn't drive me absolutely fucking wild.

Silver sighs and runs his large palms over my thighs, inching them further apart on his journey to my core. He thumbs both sides of me and I lean back on my elbows and watch him do what he wants to me.

I even wonder if there isn't anything I wouldn't let him do.

Earlier today I couldn't stand the thought of a man touching me and now, I've never felt safer.

Am I a fucking idiot for baring myself to a complete stranger? More than likely. But is it worth it? Without a fucking doubt.

"Is this okay?" Silver glances up through his dark lashes, pausing his movement.

"Yes," I manage to spit out.

He shoves both thumbs into my pussy and spreads me open, swirling them around and back inside.

I whimper. "I want you to fuck me."

"Not yet, Angel. Not yet." Silver hooks my legs under his arms and pushes me further onto the counter as he leans down and licks at my center. "Not until I make you come on my tongue."

My eyes roll back and I reach down, swirling my hand in his hair and another up and into mine. "Silver," I moan.

He frees one hand to return it to my pussy, his fingers thrusting into me at the same time he sucks on my clit.

Every fucking nerve ending in my body ignites, and pleasure courses through me. I buck my hips and grip both handfuls of hair tighter.

Silver glides his tongue all over me and slows down his fingers, but thrusts them in harder, deeper.

I arch my back and practically beg with my body for release.

And because he's so attuned to my every desire, he gives it to me, darting his tongue across my clit and rocking his fingers just the right way to make me come once again.

I shiver and pulsate and I think there's no fucking way I can take any more.

But Silver stands taller, licking his lips and gripping my thighs to drag me closer to him. "Do you still want me to fuck you?"

"Yes," I breathe, unsure how it's possible to still want more.

He yanks down the waistband of his pants and grips his cock in his hand, stroking the already hard length and lining it up with my aching pussy. "Are you sure?"

"Yes, please."

"Say it."

"I want you to fuck me."

I barely get the last word out before he slams into me, his girth spreading me wider than his fingers ever could. I scream out and close my eyes, the pain, and pleasure mixing together into something truly fucking magical.

Silver places my legs on his shoulders and leans forward, fucking me deeper. "You're taking me so well, Angel."

"Mmm," I moan. "You feel so good." I bite at my lip, and he brings his hand forward and runs his fingers along my teeth and pops them into my mouth.

"Taste yourself, Angel. You're so sweet." He drags the same hand out of my mouth, up my body to grip the base of his shaft as he continues to fuck me. "You were fucking made for me."

Never in all my years have I been with a man that did dirty

talk.

Maybe a guy who tried to. Maybe said one thing here or there. But everything out of Silver's mouth is pure filth, and I fucking love it.

"Yeah, I was," I tell him as he pounds into me, my vision blurring with each thrust.

Silver rubs his thumb over my clit while still holding onto his shaft and burying himself inside of me, he stops his long motions but remains fully in there, his cock throbbing. He removes his hand and pushes the rest of the way in slowly, carefully, with great caution. But once he reaches my limit, he jabs his hips harder and tilts me up toward him to hit an even fucking better angle.

I cry out and clench around him, every nerve in my body exploding with pleasure.

His groin grinds against my clit, and he fucks me harder as I climax more explosively than I ever have. Part of me questions whether any of the times before in my life were orgasms or just mild pleasure, because this...this sends an earthquake through me that leaves me seeing fucking stars.

Silver pulls his cock out of me and finishes on my stomach not a second later, my weak frame quivering on the counter and still reeling with pleasure long after we're both done and left panting.

With my arm over my face, I catch my breath and wonder how I've ever lived life prior to this. Are other girls experiencing this level of orgasms on a daily basis and I've been starved of the pleasure? Or was this because I fully let myself go, knowing damn well I've sold myself to the devil?

Either way, I'll hold onto this memory until the day I die.

Silver cleans me off and brings me a glass of water, holding out his hands to help me sit up. "Are you okay?"

I nod and take the glass from the counter, downing a huge gulp. "Yeah. Are you?"

He drinks a full glass himself and tucks a strand of my hair behind my ear. "Do you want to shower?"

"I don't think I can walk." My legs shake as I try to get them to cooperate.

"No walking necessary." Silver scoops me into his arms with ease and carries me through his bedroom and into the bathroom, setting me on the counter again so he can turn the faucet on.

I rub my neck and wince, drawing Silver's attention immediately.

His eyes darken. "Did I hurt you?" He rushes over and with one finger, tilts my chin up to get a better look.

I shake my head. "No. It wasn't you."

Silver meets my gaze and like it finally clicks, he says, "I'm so sorry that happened to you."

"It's fine," I lie.

"No, it isn't, Cora. No one should have to go through what you did." He reaches past me and fumbles through his dopp kit. "I'll be right back." Silver slips out of the bathroom and returns not a minute later with my water and a couple pills. "It's over-the-counter pain medicine, I promise."

I take them from him without question and drink the rest of the water, fully realizing that I'm probably dehydrated despite having four drinks with dinner.

Silver looks at me, I mean, really fucking looks at me, and says, "If you hadn't already killed him, I would do it for you."

I'm not sure if I've ever heard anything more romantic in my entire life.

And I'm not sure what kind of person that makes me, but I don't really care, not anymore.

What's the point when all of this doesn't matter? Soon I'll belong to another man, and there won't be anything anyone can do about it. Not me. Not June or her men.

Not even Silver.

9
CORA

*L*ast night feels like a fever dream I never want to wake up from.

After Silver carried me to the bathroom and quite literally bathed me in the shower, he dried me off and applied lotion to every square inch of my body before tucking me into his insanely comfortable bed.

He held me and we talked, about nothing and everything, until at some point, we both fell asleep.

It was quite possibly the best rest I've ever had, and when I woke up, I was still snug in his arms.

The whole thing was perfect, from start to finish, and I can't believe any of it happened.

"Hey," Silver says through a yawn, his eyes heavy. "You sleep okay?" He turns toward me and tucks me into him, kissing the top of my head and rubbing my back.

"Yeah," I confirm. "Did you?"

He kisses me again and sighs. "Better than I ever have."

I wrap my arm around his torso and press my lips to his bare chest and wonder if I can stay here forever—safe and sound in his embrace.

But I know that isn't a potential reality, not for either of us.

"What time is it?" Silver releases me and rolls over, blindly grasping for what I can only imagine is his phone.

I lay my hand on his stomach and let his warmth soak into my fingertips. Maybe if I memorize every inch of him, it will somehow make leaving him easier.

"Shit." Silver blinks a few times and thumbs through whatever is on his screen. "Fuck." He sits up in a hurry, careful not to drop me too aggressively onto the pillow beneath me.

"Is everything okay?" I prop myself up onto my elbow.

"I fucked up." Silver swivels his legs off the edge of the bed but stops himself and leans back to kiss my forehead. "I have, uh, a work thing I need to do." He plops onto the ground and reaches for the closest pair of dark pants and puts them on in a rush. "I have to go, but it's still early, go back to sleep. Or don't, I mean, do whatever you want. There's food in the fridge, and I don't doubt you can figure the espresso machine out. Make yourself at home, snoop around, I don't care." He slides a shirt over his head and then darts into the bathroom for a minute.

When he comes out, he's somehow much more put together. His hair isn't quite as disheveled and his beard is tamer. He almost looks...happy. It warms my heart to watch him, and maybe in another universe, this could have been us, staying up late twisted in bedsheets and him going off and doing God knows what for work. Only, his work involves covering up dead bodies and getting away with various criminal acts, and the clock is ticking on when I will belong to another man.

"You're cute when you're in a hurry," I tell him.

He sighs and shakes his head. "You have no idea how badly I want to say fuck work and get back into that bed with you."

I pat the sheets and glance up at him.

"Angel, you're going to ruin me." Silver leans down and gives me one final kiss on the lips. "I'm serious. Whatever you want. My home is your home, okay?"

"Okay." I lie back on the pillow and tug the sheets up to my neck with a stupid grin on my face. "I'll be here."

"Right where you belong." Silver glances down at his phone and then at me. "I've really got to go this time."

"Get out of here, go," I say while shooing him, only everything in me is begging him to stay just a little bit longer. To hold me. To kiss me. To keep me safe. But that won't last. Nothing good ever does.

So, when he leaves, I lie there in silence for two whole minutes before I exhale and grab onto my own phone and see what I missed while I was in paradise.

A text from the guy who's supposed to go to the baseball game with me saying he's excited to *hang out*. One from June that's reminding me of said game. Two missed calls from an unknown number. And a voicemail.

I click it and wait for it to load, my pulse picking up without even hearing a single thing.

"Where are you, Pet?" Ricardo's disgusting voice leeches through my speaker. "I hope you haven't forgotten about our little agreement. Sure would be a shame if something happened to Ma or Pa." He clears his throat and hacks a bit. "I trust that you'll follow through with your end of the bargain. In the meantime, you'd do best with answering your fucking phone when I call."

The line disconnects, and nausea rolls through me at his demands. I rid myself of one creep and here's another, just waiting in the wings to do with me as he pleases.

Part of me wants to confide in Silver and see if he's able to help me out of this situation, but if Silver reacted the way he did about Joshua, there's no telling what he would do to Ricardo if he knew the truth. And because I care about Silver, I can't be foolish enough to involve him in something that could put his life in danger—more danger than his job already does.

He might be willing to slit Ricardo's throat, but what would happen to him after? What would happen to my parents? Those are risks I'm not willing to take. If I'm going to make it out of this, I'm going to have to figure it out myself, and so far, the only way out is through.

Even if it means having Ricardo's fucking baby.

A notification buzzes on my phone, and I'm grateful that's all it is and not a ringing of a call. It feels wrong to answer Ricardo while I'm still at Silver's place, like I'm somehow putting him in danger just by being here.

I glance at the screen and see an Instagram message pop up. I click on it immediately to bring up the chat screen.

Alec: Hey, guess who's driving you guys to the game?

Me: No way, really?

Dots appear immediately.

Alec: Yep! Simon has no idea. He's going to be pissed and I love it.

I chuckle and forget for a second where my last train of thought was.

Dots appear again, and it's strange how my heart patters in anticipation for whatever it is he's about to say.

Is it fucked up for me to be talking to Alec while still in Silver's bed? We just hooked up, but it's not like we're boyfriend and girlfriend or anything. Still, I dislike how it doesn't sit right in my gut.

I wait for the message and hop out of bed to head toward the bathroom to freshen up before I leave.

Alec: June told me your date will be meeting you there. Do you want us to pick him up on the way?

That's right. My date. I exhale and swipe over to the text screen with the random dude June matched me with. I do a quick scan of the texts and return to Alec.

Me: No, he said he's coming from work, so he'll head straight there.

Alec: Okay, cool...

Alec: Do you like him?

His question catches me by surprise as I'm brushing my teeth with the toothbrush Silver gave me last night. I spit into the sink and stare at those four words.

Me: I've never met him.

The dots appear again, but then disappear, only to show back up, and leave again. I watch them pop up and go away and wonder if Alec is typing and deleting, or just typing a giant message. Or maybe Instagram is being, weird and I'm massively overthinking this.

Finally, a message comes through.

Alec: Do you want me to get a background check? lol

I chuckle but realize he probably only added the *lol* to make him seem less serious than he really is. Knowing him, knowing *any* of the people close to me, I wouldn't be surprised if someone hasn't already checked him out thoroughly.

Me: I could give you his social security number if that helps, lol.

Alec: Perfect, thanks haha.

Me: I'm sure it'll be fine. It's a public place with lots of people around. And I don't know who's scarier, June or Simon...

Alec: Haha, June for sure. I wouldn't fuck with her.

Me: Me either.

Alec: How are things going with your boss?

I nearly drop my phone in the toilet when I read his question. My heart pounds harder, and I consider what the hell I'm going to respond...

It's not like I can tell him the truth. Especially over Instagram. Or the phone at all. But I don't want to blatantly lie to him.

How do I say that my boss came on to me, I stabbed him repeatedly until he died, and then Miller walked in and found me covered in Joshua's blood and called some random dude who came and got rid of the body.

Oh! And then I went home with said random dude, had the best evening, and then he fucked my brains out...and I'm still in his apartment and sort of have feelings for him?

Me: Better.

Alec: That's good. You had me worried.

Me: Nothing to worry about over here. I can handle myself ;)

Alec: I don't doubt that.

Alec: Hey, I gotta go. Duty calls. I'll see you Saturday.

Me: Have fun, see ya then.

I click the button on the side of my phone to shut the screen off and shove it into the large pocket of Silver's sweatpants I'm still wearing. If he thinks he's getting these back, he's sorely mistaken. The second he let me borrow them they became mine.

I gather the rest of my things, which don't amount to much, and head toward the door only to backtrack a moment later into Silver's closet to steal a sweatshirt, too. I'm sure he wouldn't want me to be cold on my journey home.

Taking one final glance around, I consider making myself a coffee, but decide I don't want to overstay my welcome, nor make a gigantic mess of his kitchen more than I already have. I slip out the front door and latch the thing behind me, the sense of security I once felt dissipating with each step I take away from his apartment.

The hallway is quiet, not a soul in sight, and it makes me wonder what his neighbors are like, and if they know what he does for a living.

My phone vibrates, and I tense as I scan the screen to see who it is. Some generic message from a game on my phone I haven't played in a while offering me free coins to come back soon. I swipe away and pull up the map to see how far away my house is from here. It's within walking distance, but once I step outside and look around, I dislike how exposed I feel. Usually, I'd be down for the extra steps and fresh air, but not when danger lurks in the shadows, waiting and watching.

Ricardo is a fucking creep, and there's no telling how many eyes he has on me, and from his voicemail, he's definitely keeping them busy in maintaining my whereabouts. The whole arrangement is fucking weird, and he has to take it even further by stalking me like a complete psycho.

I order a ride and walk to the next intersection to wait for it, hugging my arms across my chest and smiling politely to the people who pass me by. It's strangely comforting to be on a busy street, but I wouldn't put it past Ricardo to snatch me up in front of all of them without a care in the world. He seems like the type of man who gives zero fucks.

"Morning," a middle-aged man says as he walks by me, nodding his head.

"Morning," I reply and step closer to the curb to get out of people's way, glancing at the description of the vehicle I'm waiting for and keeping an eye out for it.

It appears two minutes later, a brown-ish Toyota Corolla with a matching license plate to the one stated on the app.

"Cora?" the older woman greets me.

"Yeah." I smile and wave as I slide into the back seat. "How are you today?"

She turns, watching me buckle up. "Doing well, how about yourself?"

"I'm well, too," I lie.

"That's great." She puts the car into gear, checking her mirrors before taking off.

The woman doesn't say anything else the rest of the drive, but glances in the rear-view mirror at me every so often. There's a sort of soft feminine energy about her that reminds me of my grandma. My heart aches at the memory of losing her.

I was just a kid, but the pain feels like it was just yesterday. One minute, we were putting a puzzle together in the dining room, and the next I was watching the paramedics load her onto a stretcher. At the time, I had no idea that would be my last moment with her alive, but still, it's etched into my mind and pushes its way to the front when I think of her.

Seven-year-old me had no idea what an aortic aneurysm was, but it sounded scary, and that's what took her away from me.

My grandma was my safe space, the one person I could count on and know would always be there. I didn't know how much I took that for granted until I was without it. I was never as close with my parents as I was with my grandma, and that was another thing I learned wasn't *normal* until I saw the inter-actions of my friends while growing up.

We didn't have bad relationships, and they weren't abusive, but I'd be lying if I said I didn't think I lacked something funda-mental that I couldn't quite put my finger on.

My driver pulls up in front of my house and puts the car in park. "Is this fine, dear?"

I blink in my surroundings and reply, "Yeah. Thank you," and leave the car.

Thankfully, my dad's car isn't in the driveway, but neither is my mom's, which only adds to the growing question of *where the fuck is she?* How can I be certain that she's even still alive if no one will tell me where she is or why she hasn't been home since I made this deal with Ricardo?

I tried to ask my dad, but he lacks the answers I seek and the rage that builds within me when I look at him overpowers any other desire to have him near. How could he let this happen? How could he be so foolish?

My time at home is short as I make quick work of rinsing off and changing my clothes to something a bit more presentable for work. I stand in the mirror for far too long, gawking and applying concealer to my neck to hide the bruises Joshua left behind. I don't need anyone else wondering what the fuck happened and potentially uncovering the truth about what really went down.

I'm not entirely sure what I'm supposed to say if questioned, but I do know one thing: I'm going to play dumb and act like I have no idea what happened.

10

CORA

*T*he office is filled with everyone who is normally here, minus Joshua, not that his schedule is ever regular anyway.

I go straight to my cubical, smiling politely at the few people I pass, and sigh as I settle into my chair.

"This is fine," I whisper. "Everything is fine."

Hitting the button on the side of my monitor, I wait for my computer to start up by grabbing the booklet of fabric swatches I was browsing the last time I was here.

Jamie, the girl who sits behind me, shoves her feet against the floor and scoots her chair over to mine. "Cora, hey, did you hear the news?"

My whole body tenses, and my face flushes at the same time my hands grow clammy. I sit there, frozen, unable to do or say anything.

Jamie glances around and then leans in close, lowering her voice. "The Wellerton is under new ownership."

"What?" I breathe a sigh of relief that she didn't bring up my dead boss but consider what this new information might mean.

Jamie presses her finger to her lips. "Yeah. It's not public yet, but I wasn't sure if you heard. You know, since you're lead on the job and all."

"How did you find out?" I ask her.

She winks and grins. "You know I find out everything."

"Then who bought it? Who's the new owner?"

"Now that...that I haven't figured out yet. Rumor is it's some rich bachelor, but the details have been hard to come by."

"I don't understand. Mr. Wellerton was so excited about this property...why would he sell it?"

Jamie shrugs, her dark hair moving as she does. She leans in again. "Maybe he was having financial trouble."

I scoff. "Unlikely. The dude is super loaded."

"Never know." She breathes in and exhales dramatically. "Anyway, just wanted to give you a heads up."

"Yeah, thanks," I tell her. "I appreciate it."

Jamie returns the same way she arrived, rolling herself from my cubicle to hers and turning her back to me.

With The Wellerton under new ownership, I'm not sure what that means for me. I was hired by Mr. Wellerton, but I don't know if that contract remains with whoever bought the place. They could easily restructure things, hire an in-house designer, pause or halt the project completely. There are count-less possibilities, along with the very big one of them finding out I killed someone in one of their units.

It's only a matter of time until the truth comes out, and I'm somehow in worse of a situation than I already am.

The rest of the workday doesn't lessen my worries about the situation at all. No, my mind spends two seconds thinking about the herringbone pattern I'm considering for a bathroom and then twice as much considering what the fuck is going to happen. This cycle repeats for hours and not only disallows me from making any progress at work, but distracts me from the fact that I haven't eaten or drank anything all day.

My stomach growling is the only thing that brings me back

to reality, the loud grumble catching me off-guard and reddening my cheeks. I place my hand on my belly and look around, hoping no one heard the intrusion, and reach for the bottle of water that's been sitting there since a couple days ago. My jaw aches as I take a long swig of the water. My body might be hungry, but it's hard to have much of an appetite when so many things are uncertain. I don't want to eat anything, but if I stand any chance of continuing work without my stomach betraying me, I need to consume *something.*

I stand from my desk, stretch my sore body, and walk a few feet to the break room. At least one perk of being tucked away in the back corner cubicles is being close to the break room. It's fewer people you have to walk by, and because of where I'm located, no one goes near my desk on their way to the room, either. The only downside is having to go past everyone on my way in and out of work, but usually I'm here earlier and stay later, so I can bypass that awkwardness. There are only so many fake smiles and forced pleasantries I can make on a daily basis.

The half-full coffee pot draws my attention first, and I pour myself a cup of the no-doubt-burnt java. I don't even bother tasting it before I dump in two little things of French vanilla creamer and give it a quick stir. Eyeing the box of donuts on the break table, I go over and check out the remaining selection. Only the regular glazed are left, and they're probably stale, but I take one anyway, bite off a chunk, and swallow it down with the coffee.

There, body, are you happy?

I eat the rest of the donut in record speed, but then remain in the quiet room and sip on my coffee. My thoughts wander, and I do nothing to reel them in. Instead, I let them run free, hoping that if I allow this, maybe I can shut them off and get back to work. I'll feel better if I can do *something* productive.

But my rampant mind is interrupted a short moment later by a commotion in the office.

"Excuse me, sir, you can't go back there," our receptionist says so loudly I can hear her all the way in here.

Has Ricardo shown up at my work in order to prove some point that he's in charge? That he calls the shots and if I don't follow along, he'll disrupt my life until I do?

I hold my breath and wonder if I stay still enough, maybe I will turn invisible, and no one will find me. But that never worked when I was a kid, so I don't know why it would now, either.

A large figure barrels into the break room, and his sights immediately lock onto me.

"Cora," Silver breathes, his shoulders relaxing a bit.

I kick off the wall I was leaning against. "Silver, hey, what are you doing here?"

He rushes over, his hands finding both of my shoulders and his gaze trailing over me. "I got home and was worried something happened. I thought you'd still be there."

He was worried about me?

"I'm sorry," I blurt out. "I had to work."

He lowers his voice. "After what happened yesterday?"

Another person comes through the entrance but remains near the door. Tommy from accounting. A typical, glasses-wearing, pencil-pushing, shirt always tucked in and his i's dotted and his t's crossed. "Is everything okay in here?"

"Yes," I say, genuinely meaning it. "Everything is fine, Tommy."

Tommy looks from me to Silver, then back to me. "Okay. Let me know if you need anything." He disappears in the direction he came, leaving me and Silver in here alone.

"I figured keeping up with appearances would be good," I tell Silver. "That I'd draw less attention to myself if I continued with things as normal."

Silver sighs and rakes his hand over his beard. "Yeah. Yeah. You're right. I just...I didn't know. I got worried."

My cheeks turn up into a smile. "You said that already."

"Fuck, I know." He shakes his head. "You're making me soft, Angel."

I tilt my face and doe-eye up at him. "You, a softie? C'mon, now."

"Plus," Silver continues. "Miller told me to keep an eye on you. I can't do that if you run away from me."

I slap his shoulder with my free hand and hold onto my mug with the other. "I did not *run* away. I took an Uber."

"I could have called a car."

Rolling my eyes, I say, "I'm fully capable of getting my own ride."

He rubs at his neck and for the first time, he almost looks...vulnerable. Silver shifts his focus to the empty doorway then back at me. "Do you need a place to stay?"

"What?"

"You mentioned things being weird at your parents. I'm offering you a place to stay, in the meantime, until you figure something else out. No strings attached."

"Silver, I'd never impose like that..."

"It's not imposing if I'm offering it." His face remains straight, and I can't tell if he's doing this because he wants to or because of the job Miller seemed to assign him.

In another lifetime I would take him up on his generosity and get as far away from my dad as possible, but maybe in that lifetime, my dad wouldn't have put me in a situation that makes me hate breathing the same air as him.

So many things would be different if that one single thing had been different.

But would that have led me to Silver? And because of that unknown, maybe I can't be entirely mad about how things turned out.

It's just a shame nothing can come from it because I'm already spoken for. Not my heart, but my body, and in a way, my soul. Because once Ricardo uses me to fulfill his sick fantasy, I'm not sure what shell of a human will remain.

Although, if I only have a few more weeks of freedom left, shouldn't I use every moment of it that I can? Shouldn't I enjoy the company of another man, one who respects and cares for me—even if it's partially because of a job that he was tasked with?

That alone doesn't really make sense either. Why would Miller be so concerned that he would ask Silver to look after me but not do it himself? And why does he care enough at all? Because he hired Silver, because he doesn't want to get caught? I guess that would make the most sense, because nothing else really explains why Miller would involve himself, or Silver, like that.

Finally, I say, "I'll think about it, okay?"

Silver's jaw tenses and he considers my words carefully before answering. "Okay." He shifts his focus to the cup of coffee in my hand. "That smells burnt."

I smile again. "It is."

"Gross."

"It's disgusting."

Silver winks. "You know where you can get a good cup of coffee."

"I'm seriously regretting not making one this morning."

"Why didn't you?"

I shrug. "Had to get to work."

"Can I at least give you my number?" Silver darts his gaze between mine and flickers his attention to my lips, the simple movement sending heat straight between my legs and my mind running to recall the events of last night.

"Yeah, of course." I pull my phone out of my back pocket, unlock it, and hand it to him.

He takes it and pushes a sequence of buttons before giving it back to me. "I texted myself. I hope that's okay."

"After what you did to my body, it's safe to say I'm okay with you having my number."

Silver reaches forward and grazes my cheek, cupping it gently despite him being such an aggressive and dominant man. "Hopefully you'll let me do it again."

I wish I could tell him the truth, that I would love nothing more than for him to explore my body however he sees fit, but that whatever we have is short-term, that it cannot last, not because I don't want it to, but because it can't.

11

CORA

I didn't sleep last night. Not for lack of trying. I was dead ass tired. I still am. I just couldn't.

I wasn't comfortable. My mind just wouldn't stop racing. And even though my dad was tucked away in his bedroom, I couldn't become okay with being in the same house as him. I don't want to hate him, but the situation makes it difficult.

So instead, I dozed on and off all night, tossing and turning and wishing I would have taken Silver up on his offer and at the very least, crashed at his place to get a decent night's sleep.

Not to mention all the other perks that would have come with it.

A lavish apartment with every amenity imaginable, minus a television, and a sexy man who seems so in tune with my needs that he knows what I want before I do.

But I didn't. I thought about it. Oh, did I consider it. But my self-control is greater than I thought it was and ensured that I stayed put at home, miserable and sort of alone.

Part of me was worried that Ricardo would call, and if I didn't answer it immediately, he would send out a search party.

I can't be certain he would really do that, but I don't put it past him, either. He's a loose cannon like that.

And if he did, I wouldn't want him to find me at Silver's. Because then he would ask questions I don't know how to answer and put Silver's life in danger. That would be selfish of me, and I've never really been the type to carelessly disregard how my actions impact others.

"How much concealer are you going to put on?" June asks me from her spot sitting on her bed.

"As much as it takes." I stand in front of the mirror in her bedroom and blend under my eyes. "I'm too young to have such dark circles."

She hops from the mattress and walks over, taking the stick from my hand. "Cora, you're fixating..." June replaces the concealer with my glass of bourbon. "Here, try this instead."

I roll my eyes at her even though she's totally right. I'm doing that thing where I focus on something I can control since everything else in my life feels so *out* of control.

"What's up with you lately?" June crosses her arms over her chest and stares at me. "And don't tell me nothing, because I know you...something is up."

Where do I even begin?

My mom has cancer.

My dad had such a debt with a loan shark trying to get her treatment that the guy showed up to the house, threatened my parent's life and I foolishly stepped in and offered my body in exchange for payment.

I went to work, and my boss got handsy so I stabbed him to death, and then Miller walked in, called some dude to clean up the body, and then he fucked me until I could barely walk.

My anxiety has been at an all-time high, even before this shit happened, and I can't seem to go twenty-four hours without having an existential crisis.

And, of course, we can throw in my latest, very persistent

insecurities that I'm unworthy of love and that I'll be forced to live a life of solitude with nothing but thirteen cats. Not that any of it matters anymore, since I have to quite literally have a baby for a completely *disgusting* human being that has little to no decency at all.

But I don't say those things. No.

"I think my period is coming," I tell her. "And I think there's a full moon this weekend...and an eclipse." I drink some of the bourbon and allow it to warm my insides and numb the chaos in my head. "You know how it is."

June narrows her gaze. "You can tell me things, you know?"

"Like you tell me?" I tilt my head at her. "Don't think I'm not aware of all the secrets you keep." I wave my arm around the room of this luxury mansion she shares with her four boyfriends. One of the many properties they have, in one of many states. I even overhead Dominic talking about property he owns in Spain and Portugal, leading me to assume that isn't the only place he owns homes.

"That's different," she says.

"Yeah, yeah, need to know basis..."

A while back she confessed that there were things she *couldn't* tell me. Not because she didn't want to, but because she actually couldn't. They weren't her secrets to share. By sharing, she'd be putting me and others in danger. I was forced to believe her—what other choice did I have?

But still, that doesn't make it any easier to stomach that June's keeping things from me...her supposed best friend.

Although, how can I be mad at her when I'm quite literally doing the same exact thing right now?

So for the most part, I keep my mouth shut about their incredibly suspicious lifestyle and go along with the vagueness she does offer me. Maybe one day we'll be past all the walls and shit that are between us, but I'm not confident we'll ever get there...our friendship apparently has limits and bounds.

"Are you excited?" I ask her in an attempt to change the subject. I plaster on my happiest attitude and do what I can to shift the direction of the conversation from anything involving me.

"I am." June glances in the mirror and tucks her dark hair behind her ears. "Is it weird that I'm nervous, too?"

I stand beside her, placing my hand on her back gently. "Not at all. But, he's going to love it."

A light knock patters against June's bedroom door, and when I turn, my heart does a little flip at seeing Alec standing there.

A small, okay maybe large, part of me wants to rush over and throw my arms around his neck and hug him, melt into his body and breathe in his *oh-so-Alec* smell. But I don't. I just smile and walk over to him casually.

"You girls ready to get going?" He keeps his eyes on me as I approach. "You look incredible."

"Thanks," I say, the smile on my face genuine this time. "So do you."

June waltzes over and shakes her head, walking between us. "Why don't you two fuck and get it over with already?"

My eyes widen and my gaze follows her out. "Um, excuse me, missy?"

June stops in the hallway and turns back toward me and Alec. "You guys clearly have chemistry, you get along well, and you're both hot and single, so just fuck and get it over with."

"I thought..." I find myself blanking at what to say.

She's always implied that nothing could ever happen between me and Alec because of him being her driver and all. This entire time I never pushed the possibility into place because I thought she wouldn't allow it. I've been going on shitty dates with loser men when this whole time I could have pursued the genuine connection I've had with Alec since the first time we spoke.

And now, the future we could have had is lost due to my deal with Ricardo.

Part of me wishes she would have kept her mouth shut, and I could have stayed ignorant to the lost potential of what could have been me and Alec.

"Don't let Simon find out though..." June shoots finger guns at us before spinning on her heel and continuing down the hallway.

"Don't let Simon find out about what?" Magnus chimes in from the entry of his own bedroom. He snatches June as she walks by and spins her into his arms, planting a kiss on her forehead and hugging her tightly. "I love secrets."

She softens into him, and I hate the jealousy in me that arises.

I'm happy for her, I really am, but when is it my turn to have a little love in my life? Love that will last. Love that won't be snuffed out by an ignorant agreement.

"Those two," June says and nods toward us.

"Oh, you guys are finally hooking up?" Magnus shakes his head. "Bout damn time."

I briskly glance up at Alec and avoid making direct eye contact, my cheeks no doubt blushing the same way his are.

"We aren't," I admit. "Alec and I are just friends."

Alec stands up straighter next to me. "Yeah, what she said. Friends."

Not to mention, *he's* never really made a move more than offering a comforting hug or paying attention to something I said. Those are things friends do. I shouldn't assume he's into me just because I'm into him. It would be nice if the crush was reciprocated, but as far as I know, it's not.

And that's okay. If friends are all we are, I'm okay with that, because he's a damn good one.

"Whatever you guys gotta tell each other to sleep at night..."

Magnus focuses his attention on June. "I hope you have a wonderful time tonight. Do you need money or anything?"

"Do *you* need money or anything?" June chirps back, her tone laced with heavy sarcasm.

"I could think of something I need." Magnus raises his eyebrows dramatically.

She grins and slaps his chest. "Didn't you get enough of that earlier?"

"Never." He kisses her forehead again, then her cheeks, and her nose.

"You two are going to make me barf," I say and take off from my spot planted next to Alec.

He follows behind a second later, as do June and Magnus, the two of them hand in hand when I glance back.

"You working tonight?" June leans in close to ask Magnus.

"Yep."

"Be safe, please." There's something she isn't saying, but the way she looks at him leads me to believe he understands completely.

"Always." He gives her one final peck on the lips. "Call me if you need me." Magnus points to Alec. "Keep my girls safe."

It's sweet of Magnus to include me like that when he could easily pretend I don't even exist. But he doesn't. No, Magnus is always very considerate of me when I'm around. Heck, the very first night June went home with Magnus, he brought us both here after a drunken night at the bar and got us pizza—even with pineapple. And when he was eye-fucking and flirting with June at the bar, he never cast me aside or made me feel excluded. It's almost like he knows there's enough room in June's heart and life for all of us, and he doesn't feel the need to fight his way to the front.

Golden retriever vibes for sure. But in a hot, *daddy* kind of way.

Tattooed golden retriever daddy, to be exact.

I chuckle at my own thought, and all of a sudden, it's like everyone is looking right at me. "Sorry," I say. "Thought of something funny that happened at work." Only, that's a blatant lie, and if I'm being honest, Silver marching into my office and storming into the break room to make sure I was okay was not funny at all, actually, it was embarrassing, but a bit hot.

Silver's protectiveness is definitely a turn-on, even if it is because Miller hired him.

Although, it's possible he doesn't take *all* his jobs so seriously. At least, that's what I tell myself to feel like he really does care.

June and I slip into the back of the blacked-out SUV and Alec takes his spot in the driver's seat. I climb into the third row and give June plenty of space for when we pick up Simon.

"You don't have to sit back there yet," she tells me.

I shrug. "No biggie." I grip the headrest in front of me and lean forward. "Stop being so nervous. Everything is going to be great. Seriously. This is so thoughtful of you." I pause and then add, "Can I tell you a secret?"

June turns toward me and lowers her voice. "Is it about Alec? Did you two really hook up?"

"I can hear you, you know," Alec calls out from the front of the SUV.

I close my eyes slowly and rock my head back and forth. "You're an idiot."

"What is it? The secret."

I take her in, like really take her in, noting the change a couple years can make. She used to be so reserved, withdrawn, and honestly, a bit difficult, but the June that sits in front of me is softer, in a more powerful kind of way. She opened her heart to her men, and yeah, they may have had hard times to get through in the beginning but damn if it didn't bring her to such a wonderful place today. She glows, and it's sort of magnetic and inspiring to witness how much she's evolved.

"It makes me happy to see you so happy," I confess. "You deserve it, really. And I'm so glad I get to bear witness to it."

June pouts her bottom lip. "Cor...that's so...sweet of you." She reaches out and grasps my shoulder. "I'm really glad we're friends."

She's never really been the type to confess her feelings so for her to say that, it means a lot. And it will be one of those things I cling to after these next few weeks pass, and I become the property of someone else.

"Me, too," I tell her. "Me, too." I give her shoulder a gentle squeeze and settle into my seat for the short ride to where we're picking Simon up.

Alec turns the volume up on the stereo just slightly so a soft melody fills the otherwise now empty vehicle. I catch his gaze in the rearview mirror but look away and out the window.

My phone buzzes, a text from Silver coming across the screen.

Silver: You doing okay?

I study those three words for far too long and finally thumb a response.

Me: Yeah, are you?

Silver: Always.

I start typing, the words *I miss you* staring back at me on the screen, but I delete it and shut my screen off to prevent me from saying anything too crazy. I hung out with the guy *one* time, that isn't enough to miss him. Or at the very least telling him. He'll think I'm a crazy clinger girl who caught feelings too quickly.

But isn't that what I am? I did catch feelings. And I do miss him.

I'm on the way to a first date with one guy, while being driven by another, and missing another. All the while I can't be with any of them because of my *circumstances*.

What the fuck is wrong with me?

Either way, I told myself I would try to enjoy what

remaining time I have left, so I need to get out of my head and do exactly that.

Alec pulls us to the front of a massive high-end hotel that I'm fairly certain is swarming with criminals. I've been here briefly with June, and it definitely gives off sketchy vibes but it's not like I could question her about it, since I'm on a need-to-know basis and all. If it weren't safe though, I don't think she would have brought me there. Maybe I was wrong, and I'm just being judgmental.

Simon, standing in a small group of men, glances our way, doing a double take. Alec hops out and rushes around the side to open the door in preparation for Simon's approach. I hate seeing him wait on them like this, but I guess it is sort of his job, and he's being paid to do so.

My breath catches as the man Simon is talking to comes into my line of focus.

Ricardo. The fucking cockroach is everywhere. Did he purposely infiltrate my friend group or was he already before I accidentally got involved with him? Regardless, it makes my stomach turn, and I do what I can to scoot closer to the window and get out of the line of sight. Here's to hoping the tint is dark enough that he can't see through.

Simon slaps Ricardo's shoulder like he's making an attempt to break free of him, and then he turns toward us. Only, Ricardo doesn't stay where he is, yet follows him over, his mouth still moving, his conversation apparently too important to end just yet.

Fuck, fuck, fuck.

"Christ, who is that guy?" June mutters under her breath and puts her arm out the door to wave at her oncoming boyfriend. "Hey," she says once he's a foot away. "We have reservations. We're going to be late."

It's a lie, but no one needs to know. And for all Simon does know, she could be telling the truth. I'm not sure what story she fed him to get him to play along.

"I won't keep you." Ricardo coughs into his shoulder and extends his hand. "I only wanted to meet the woman who stole the infamous Simon Beckett's heart."

June takes it reluctantly, and I do that thing where I try to become invisible, hoping and praying to any powerful entity that it will finally work. Hell, I'd accept sudden internal combustion if it meant getting me the fuck out of this awkward situation.

"June didn't steal it," Simon tells him. "I gave it to her willingly."

"Ah, and what do we have here?" Ricardo shoves his round face into the SUV and latches his sights on me.

My heart thuds and sweat pools between my tits. This can't be real. This isn't happening. This has to be some fucked up nightmare I'm going to wake up from any second. But when I close my fist so tight my fingernails dig into my palm, I'm not awoken. No, I remain right here, flabbergasted and confused about what the fuck I'm supposed to do.

Ricardo releases June and pushes his arm toward the back, toward me. "A friend of June's is a friend of mine. Ricardo, and you are?" The twinkle in his eye causes more panic to rise but somehow, I keep it the fuck together and lace my hand through his.

"Cora." I give him the fakest smile I've ever given anyone in my entire life and shake his clammy hand.

"What a beautiful name." He shifts his attention to June and then back at me. "Well, it sure was a pleasure to meet both of you." He doesn't take his eyes off me as he says, "We should all get together sometime. Dinner. On me."

Simon slips into the vehicle, forcing Ricardo out of the way. "Yeah, maybe." Simon shuts the door in his face and throws his arm over the back of the seat.

Alec makes his way to the driver's side and makes quick work of navigating us around the other expensive cars and onto the street.

It isn't until we're no longer in eye-sight range that I feel the pressure in my chest release, even if it's only slightly.

June offers me an apologetic glance. "Sorry about that," she says. "Guy is a total creep."

I smile and shrug. "No worries."

"I seriously hate him," Simon adds. "I wish I could put a bullet between his eyes."

"Simon." June scoffs.

"Oh," Simon blurts out and turns toward me. "Not like really, metaphorically, you know."

But I know damn well Simon was being completely serious. I've literally witnessed him kill someone else. How they think they can keep his illicit tendencies a secret is a bit mind-blowing, because it's not really a secret at all.

"Yeah," I say anyway.

Alec clears his throat. "I sort of met him the other day with Miller. He's not a fan of him either."

I never thought Alec was much of the gossip type, but it's a relief to hear Miller doesn't really like Ricardo. Still, that doesn't change the very apparent fact that no one seems to like him and yet he's still here, still alive, still tormenting people on a daily basis.

Simon brings June's hand to his lips and kisses it. "Yeah, he's a royal dick. Literally."

"What does that mean?" I ask even though it's not my place and they don't usually divulge this kind of information to me.

But before June can correct him that I'm on a need-to-know basis, he says, "He's been around for a while. The guy is untouchable. I don't understand it, really, since everyone hates him, but we're stuck with him. He's powerful in a weird and cryptic kind of way."

I swallow the lump that forms in my throat.

I may not know much about June and her men, but I was under the impression *they* called the shots on this side of town. But if what Simon is saying is true, Ricardo somehow supersedes that.

Which only confirms one thing: there's no way I can get out of this mess.

Even if I asked Simon or June or hell, any of the guys for help or advice, they'd give me the same answer—that nothing can be done, that Ricardo is, in fact, untouchable.

June dead stares at Simon and if I'm not mistaken, it's her way of telling him to shut the fuck up.

Sometimes I think he forgets that she doesn't confide their dark secrets in me, that I'm not one of them and he can't talk freely. But June reels him in pretty quickly and shuts him down before he spills too much. I hate that she's like that, but who am I to judge her when I don't fully understand the situation. Maybe she really does think she's protecting me by keeping me in the dark. Maybe she's afraid I'll judge her for whatever criminal things they do. If she knew about what I did to Joshua, maybe she'd think differently. But that same fear that she might have is the same reason I haven't told her what's going on either. I don't want to lose my best friend.

"Anyway," Simon blurts out. "Enough about creepy white dudes. Where are we headed?"

"It's a surprise," June tells him. "So, stop mapping out which roads we're going and trying to figure it out."

Simon pouts. "But love..."

"No buts." She presses her finger to his lips. "Just enjoy the ride. We'll be there soon enough."

He sighs and tugs her close, tucking her into the crook of his arm and wrapping his shoulder around her. "Have I told you lately how beautiful you are?" Simon kisses the top of her head. "God, I missed you."

June whispers something back that I can't quite make out, not that I want to anyway. It's not a lie that I really am happy for her, and them, but fuck it's nauseating at times how obsessed her men are with her.

I pull out my phone and swipe to my text screen, confirming I answered Kyle with the information about where to meet me. The old me would have been excited about this potential match but I find it hard to find joy in anything given the circumstances.

I've been struggling with my mind, even before what happened with my dad and Ricardo, so maybe that's adding to my lack of enthusiasm.

Kyle sent a thumbs-up after my text and I stare at it so long that it sort of morphs into a blur in my vision. I flick out of his text screen to skim Silver's, my thumbs itching to type something, anything, just to have him here with me. But instead, I close the messages and click on Instagram and read through my messages with Alec. Sure, he's sitting in the front seat, but it doesn't distract my mind the way I need right now. I kind of wish that I would have sat in the front, too, but that's never really been an option and I'm not sure what June or Simon would have thought. June is already suspicious of us hooking up and if I sat up there, that would no doubt potentially confirm that to not just her, but to Simon, too. And according to June, Simon isn't allowed to know we're into each other.

Simon sure is a great guy, but damn is he a cock block.

I scroll through until my app no longer wants to pull up older messages and shut the screen off and close my eyes. I lean my head back and wonder how long my mind will be safe before Ricardo creeps his way back in.

A millisecond.

But instead of letting the thought completely consume me, I recall the memory of Miller and how he reacted when he walked into the unit to find me covered in someone else's blood. He was so calm and collected and knew exactly what to do.

Miller held me and made me feel safe, and although he had to leave, he put me in the hands of someone who continued to maintain that safety. A small part of me misses him, too.

My phone buzzes, and I pause before flipping it over to see who it is. Maybe it's my date. Maybe it's Silver. But maybe it's Ricardo, and that alone is why I don't check immediately.

Only, the uncertainty eats at me too much to keep whatever it is in limbo for too long.

And boy am I surprised that I was wrong about every single possibility.

An unfamiliar number: Hey, it's Miller.

I read and re-read the text ten times as my heart races. Glancing up at the rest of the car, I consider if this is some sick and evil trick or if it really is him.

I guess there's only one way to find out.

Me: Hey, what's up?

Miller: I'm sorry I left like that the other day. Can we get together when I get back in town?

If this is a trap, boy am I falling straight for it.

Me: Yeah, for sure. And no problem, I understand.

Maybe he's back to business and wants to go over the designs we didn't get a chance to discuss when he walked in on me and a dead body. That must be why he wants to get together. What other reason could there be? Unless he wants to get our stories straight about what happened that day...or ask for payment for his help in covering things up.

Miller: I'll let you know when I'm back. Shouldn't be any later than Wednesday. This is taking longer than I thought.

I want to ask him what he's talking about, what he's doing, where he is, and why he wants to meet, but I don't do any of those things. Instead, I just let my mind wander and fill in the blanks.

Me: No rush. I'll be here when you're ready.

I regret the text as soon as I send it. It comes across as desperate and too available, but isn't that what I'm supposed to be—available? This is a job. I'm his interior designer. I'm supposed to be flexible and accommodating to his schedule. Especially since he's one of our high-profile clients...at least that's what I think since I haven't been told anything otherwise regarding the transition in ownership of The Wellerton. I keep waiting for an update from my superiors, but one hasn't come, so I do what I do best and overthink until the answers finally come to me.

Miller: Thanks, Cora. Talk soon x

I stare at my phone and wonder if I've conjured up the *x* at the end of his message. It burns into my memory and completely distracts me from the blaring horns and the traffic buzzing us by as Alec pulls us off the main road and near the curb.

"You're shitting me." Simon rises from his spot and looks from outside to June. "Is this what I think it is?"

June grins at him. "What do you think it is?"

"Are we going to the game?"

June nods and Simon wastes no time yanking her into his arms and smothering her with affection.

"This is the best surprise in the whole world. I can't believe it." Simon continues kissing her face. "You're the best, love, seriously."

June reaches into her bag and pulls out a Dodger's hat, plopping it onto Simon's head. "Only the best for the best."

Alec opens Simon's door and waits for him to exit. Simon does and reaches back for June's hand to help her out. I weasel my way through after them and dust off my black bottoms even though there's nothing on them. Habit, I suppose.

"I can't believe this." Simon looks at me. "Did you know about this?" He turns to Alec. "Did you?"

"Yep," I tell him. "Are you surprised?"

He shakes his head. "I had no idea. Seriously. Zero clue."

June smiles up at him. "You're so hard to surprise, too. You're like a sneaky detective who finds stuff out before I even have it planned. I've been working on this one for a while."

"I can't help it. I like to know things." Simon throws his arm around June. "But this...this is perfect. Thank you."

I scan the vicinity, not seeing the guy I'm supposed to be meeting here. Checking the clock, I see that there are a few more minutes until the time he said he'd be here.

"Why don't you two go ahead? I'll be right behind you," I tell Simon and June.

"What? No. We'll wait with you," June says.

"Seriously, it's just a few minutes. Go ahead. This is a special day for both of you. Get it started."

June narrows her gaze at me.

I shove her gently. "Go. Now." I flit my attention to Simon. "I'm going to beat you both up if you don't get going. Get some snacks and I'll be there by the time you get to your seats."

June reaches into her pocket to pull out her phone. "Fine. I'm texting you your tickets. If you aren't there soon, I'm sending out a search party."

I roll my eyes. "Why do I have a feeling that you're not joking?"

"Because I'm not." She points her finger at me. "I'm not kidding. Don't wait for that man more than five minutes. You hear me?"

"Yes, ma'am."

"Come on, love, you heard the lady." Simon nudges her toward the entrance of the place where hundreds of others are funneling in through the gates.

I've never been a huge fan of crowds, but lately, I prefer them. It's more witnesses that could prevent Ricardo from doing anything *too* crazy. At least, that's what I hope.

"You sure you're okay with this?" Alec shuts the door to the SUV and focuses on me.

"Yeah. No biggie." I check the time again. "He should be here any minute."

"I can wait with you."

Horns blare, vehicles floating in and out of temporary parking places in front of the venue.

"It's okay," I reassure him. "Plus, you might get a ticket or something if you stay there too long."

Alec eyes a security guard walking in our direction. "I don't care."

I place my hand on his shoulder and ignore the way it gateways into me wanting to hug him. "It's fine, really. I'll see you after the game."

"Message me if he doesn't show, okay? I'll have my phone on me." Alec stares at me with such intensity I think I might combust.

"Okay."

He exhales and hesitates before walking away, the security guard almost to us.

The blacked-out SUV drives off, and I'm left here among all these strangers, none of them the person who's supposed to be meeting me. I double-check the text thread and confirm I'm standing where I told him we'd be. The minute hand clicks over, confirming he's officially one minute late. But there's nothing wrong with that. We can't always be punctual, and with the traffic around the venue, how can I blame him for not being on time?

I send him a text just in case I've mixed things up.

Me: Hey, outside Golden State Gate C near the no parking sign. You close?

No dots appear.

Maybe he doesn't have his phone out in front of him. Maybe he's tipping his Uber driver. Maybe he's not coming.

I cross my arms over my chest, suddenly feeling so exposed to the outside world. What if Ricardo followed us here? I back closer to the outside of the gate in a weak attempt to provide somewhat of a sense of security.

Two more minutes pass. No text. No Kyle.

I scoff. Whose name is Kyle anyway? The only Kyles I've ever known have been Monster-chugging douchebags with a tendency to rough their women up. Why did I think this one would be any different? I shake my head to rid myself of the irrational thought.

"That's a generalization, Cora," I say to no one but myself and recall the time my old therapist had told me to challenge my intrusive thoughts.

Sometimes it takes me quite literally having to say it out loud for it to work.

The sun blares down on me and warms my skin while sending a little reminder that I should have brought a pair of sunglasses. Hopefully our seats aren't directly in its line of sight or I'll have to spend far too much money on a cheap pair of overpriced licensed shades. I pick a piece of white fuzz off my bright red crop top and position my hair behind my shoulders, then pull it back in front of them, only to shove one side back and keep the other forward. Unzipping the clutch in my hand, I retrieve a small compact, blot at my nose, and check my teeth.

Four minutes late turns into six, and I know the time is running out before June throws a fit and comes looking for me. I don't want her to feel bad since she's the one who insisted I bring this guy, so for her sake, I hope he shows up.

A tall figure approaches me, but they're blurred out from the shining sun. The person waves their arm, and I glance around to make sure I'm not the idiot about to wave at the wrong person. But when they come into my vision, I don't know whether I should be relieved or disappointed.

"He still not here yet I take it?" Alec approaches and leans

148

against the gate, kicking his foot up behind him and folding his arms over his chest.

"Nope." I examine my phone again to confirm my messages were delivered and to confirm the time. "No call, no show."

"I'll wait with you for a few more minutes." Alec reaches out and nudges my shoulder. "That's what friends are for, right?"

I tilt my head toward him. "Can you believe they think we're having sex?"

Alec blushes and a soft smile spreads across his face. "Would that be such a bad thing?"

My mouth drops open. "You're not serious."

Alec throws his hands up and laughs. "Sorry, didn't realize you despised the idea so much."

"Wait..." I fully turn toward him and put my hand on my hip. "What are you saying?"

"I'm saying." Alec shoves off the gate and steps toward me, his frame towering over me. "It should be me taking you on this date, not some random guy."

I blink up at him. "Wh-what?"

"You heard me."

"I didn't know you..."

"Cora," Alec purrs. "I've had a crush on you since the first time I saw you on campus. Months before we ever actually met. Do you realize how painful it is to be near you and not do this..." He hovers his hand near my cheek, slowly inching it closer until he finally does.

My entire body nearly melts at his touch and my eyes flutter closed briefly.

"Alec..."

"Tell me you don't feel the same and I'll never bring it up again." His dark eyes dart between mine like they're pleading with me to understand.

Little does he know, they absolutely do. I just had no idea until this moment that he felt this way.

"I do," I admit in a whisper. "I do feel the same."

My phone buzzes but I don't care who it is, the only thing I care about is right now, and for once in my life, I choose to be selfish and do something truly bold.

"Come to the game with me," I tell him. "Please."

Alec glides his thumb over my cheek. "What about your date?"

"He's late." I lean into his touch. "He lost his chance."

"Are you sure?"

I bring my hand up to press against his and savor the sensation as I weave my fingers around his and lock them together. "Let's go."

Alec grins and goes along with the embrace, even going so far as to take his other hand to cup underneath mine like he's afraid my hand might vanish from his. We take off together towards the entrance and I don't dare glance back to see if whatever his name is shows up. He's not who I wanted to be here with in the first place, so why would I ignore the glaringly better option presented to me?

Once our tickets are scanned and we're through the gates, I send June a quick text to let her know I'm on my way and to call the search party off.

Alec takes a breath in and says, "Simon is going to kill me."

ALEC

J'm not kidding. This may be the dumbest thing I've done in my entire life.

But with Cora's hand tucked between both of mine, I don't think there is anything in the world I would trade for this moment. Unless it was the chance to have many, many more. And when Simon, or Dominic, finds out, this short-lived slice of heaven will end as quick as it started.

"I'm sure it'll be fine, right?" Cora looks up at me and for the first time since we've met, there's something else there, like a spark of hope, maybe.

Cora is all bubbles and bright-eyed smiles on the outside, but I know she's hiding something. We all are. It's just a matter of how dark and deep it really is.

And damn do I want to find out.

So I can help her. Be there for her. Understand her.

"Doubtful, but I don't care." I slide one of my hands free to place it on the small of her back as I guide her through the crowd. I don't dare let go with the other, a sort of link that will keep me close to her.

God damn, I've waited for this moment for far too long and now I have to share it with Simon fucking Beckett.

Fingers crossed he doesn't actually shoot me in front of all those people in the stadium. I breathe a little easier knowing he had to go through security, but when has Simon ever upheld the law, let alone some pesky rules about no weapons. I wouldn't be surprised if June is packing, too. The both of them are a bit paranoid, but for damn good reason. They've gone through their fair share of close encounters, especially since June came into the guys' lives. I haven't been around the whole time, but some of the stories I've heard, I'm baffled that June was able to overcome some of the shit thrown at her in this criminal world.

I like to turn a blind eye to the ways of their world and play dumb, but it would take a complete fool not to see how fucked up and dangerous their lifestyle is.

"Can we grab a drink first?" Cora points ahead to a concession stand.

"Yeah, for sure." I guide her the rest of the way and we stop to get behind the rest of the people in line.

"Thanks for doing this," she says while turning toward me.

"Getting you a drink?"

Cora rolls her beautiful blue eyes. "Coming to the game with me, silly."

"Oh, are you kidding? There's no place I'd rather be." I hold out my arms and drag her in, my body starving from the lack of her close to me. I've thought about that hug from the other day a million and one times, and I've been dying to do it again, just to make the memory of it stronger.

"I missed this," she mumbles against my chest.

I breathe her in and kiss the top of her head softly. "Me too."

Cora breaks away, her gaze darkening. "Can we talk later?"

My heart pounds a little out of rhythm. "Yeah, of course. Whatever you want." I try not to let the worry of what the conversation will lead to get the best of me. I have her here now, and I don't want to taint that with my wandering mind.

Cora smiles but it doesn't meet those stunning eyes. "Thanks, Alec."

God, even hearing her say my name...drives me fucking crazy.

I've never been this insanely mad over a girl, and as great as it is, I can't help but consider how badly it's going to break my heart. I shouldn't get too far ahead of myself; I should appreciate what I have while I have it.

Cora isn't mine. She belongs to herself. And that's how I want it to stay. I want to be a part of her life, even if she feels like my whole entire world.

The couple in front of us grabs their drinks and walks away, giving us the opening to step up and place our order.

But instead of getting to the counter, a guy comes barreling over, almost knocking Cora down, and pushes in front of us.

I react without thinking, my hand latching onto his shoulder and shoving him away. "What the fuck, my guy." I reel back and throw my fist into his face, a couple of his teeth flying out of his mouth and scattering onto the floor.

People gasp and that's when I feel her cool hands on my body. One on my arm, the other on my back.

"Alec." Her voice is calm and immediately pulls my attention.

I release the guy and turn toward her, gripping her shoulders. "Are you okay?" I skim my gaze over her, looking for any sign that I should end this guy, right here, right now.

I don't care who bears witness.

"I'm fine." Cora cranes her neck and grasps my wrist. "Are you? Your hand..."

"What the fuck man, I just wanted a drink." The guy I punched holds his jaw and stumbles to his feet.

"I think you've had enough." I turn around as my hand balls into a fist.

But Cora grabs my arm again, her soft touch securing in me place.

"Break it up!" yells a security guard. He pushes his way past the crowd that gathered and stops to look between me and the guy bleeding from his face. "What happened here?" He glances at the horde around us and death stares at them. "Go somewhere else and get your snacks."

"This guy fucking decked me," the other guy blurts out immediately. "I think I lost a tooth." He runs his tongue along his teeth and his eyes widen. "I think I lost two." He starts toward me. "I'm going to fucking sue you, man."

The security guard slams his hand into the guy's chest to stop him and I know better than to act too irrationally in front of this guy, even if he is a rent-a-cop.

"And what do you have to say?" The guard faces me.

I shrug. "He had it coming."

The guard pinches his eyes shut and shakes his head slowly. "Really? That's the story you're sticking to."

Cora steps in front of me before I can stop her. "It was me. I hit him."

"What?" the guard asks.

"He's just embarrassed a girl knocked him on his ass. Here, look." She brings her hand forward and shows him her knuckles. "See. It was me, not him."

Her hand is red and inflamed, but from what, I have no idea. Unless I'm completely losing my mind, it was me who punched that guy. But shit, even she has me questioning who did it.

The guard narrows his gaze at her and then at me.

"Bitch is a fucking liar," the drunk guy slurs. "She didn't hit me. She fucking wishes." He grabs his groin and thrusts himself in her direction.

I move around Cora and raise my arm to swing again and the guard shoves both hands into my chest to stop me.

"Whoa, buddy." The guard plants his face in front of mine. "You want to calm down."

"You need to get this trash under control," I spit out as rage boils up and threatens to explode.

"Where do I know you from?" The guard gets distracted.

"I don't know, dude, but if you don't take care of this, I'm going to do it for you."

A lightbulb seems to appear over this oblivious guard's head. "I know. You hang with Dom's crew, right? I think I saw you with Beckett a few weeks ago."

I blink a couple times and try to place him in my memory, but I come up blank. Not that it matters. If he saw me with them, then he isn't wrong. There's no avoiding whatever fate has in store for me now that he's identified me as someone who hangs out with criminals.

"Yeah. That was me," I say, because I have nothing to hide and I'm sure as shit not letting Cora get in trouble for something I did.

The guard nods. "I thought so." He sighs and pulls his cuffs off his rinky-dink belt.

Fuck. The first chance I get to confess my feelings to Cora and take her on a date, I fuck it all up by decking a guy for disrespecting her.

"Yeah, fuck you and fuck whoever Beckett is," the drunk guy blabbers.

But instead of the guard cuffing me, he turns around and lifts his head briskly at the drunk. "Hands up, drunkie. Let's go see what management wants to do with you."

"What the fuck? This is an outrage...I'm a victim here." The drunk spits in my direction but it doesn't hit me, instead it speckles the concrete with his blood.

I flip him off, quickly turning it into a wave when the guard faces me.

"Sorry about this, son," the guard says. "Give my regards to the guys." He points to the badge on his shirt. "Jefferson. I work part-time at The Manor."

"Ohh." That's when it dawns on me where he must have seen me, and since that place is literally crawling with criminals, it's no surprise he's up to date on who's in charge around here. I guess my connection to them paid off instead of biting me in the ass.

He grips the drunk guy's hands after he cuffs them and takes off in the direction he came from, leaving me and Cora to stand here in a sort of empty concession area.

"Uh, did you guys want something to drink?" The young cashier stands there with her arms crossed over her chest, her jaw working the piece of gum in her mouth. She blows a bubble, and it cracks loudly.

"Vodka diet," Cora chimes in and turns to me. "What do you want?"

I consider the question and how I'm already going to be in a shitstorm of trouble with Simon. One, for punching some dude and using his name to get out of getting in trouble. And two, for literally being on a date with his girl's best friend. Do I really need to add drinking alcohol to the list of things he's going to be mad at me about?

"I'll have the same," I tell them, because what's the harm in having *one* drink. I mean, the game is probably going to last a couple hours—long enough for me to metabolize the booze and flush it down with a hotdog or something.

"And a lime if you have it," Cora adds.

"Lime for both of them?" The girl raises her eyebrow at me, still chomping on that hunk of gum in her mouth.

"Yeah, sure, fuck it." I reach into my pocket and pull out my money clip, stepping in front of Cora as she reaches into her small little purse thingy. I slide a hundred across the counter. "Keep the change."

"Thanks." The girl forces the biggest fake smile and goes to work making our drinks. She's sloppy but pours heavy, which is one thing I hate about getting mixed drinks. Unless the bartender is on top of their shit, there's no telling how much you're consuming. One minute you're pacing yourself and the next you're shit-faced because you drank a few triples instead of a single.

I take both of the drinks, handing one to Cora and grabbing her a straw.

"How did you know I wanted a straw?" she asks me.

I shrug and wink. "I know you."

"Oh, do you now?" She laughs and stirs her drink before taking a sip. "Tell me then, what's my favorite color?"

"Easy." I swirl my drink in an attempt to stir it knowing damn well all the booze has settled.

"Here." She plucks the straw out of her cup and shoves it in mine, mixing it around and taking it back out. "And if it's so easy, what is it?"

"Red, sometimes pink." I crane my neck to look for a nearby sign to tell me where we are. "What are our seats?"

"Uhh. Let me check." She pulls out her phone, the screen blaring with missed notifications. Cora swipes them away quickly and clicks on the tickets that June sent her, holding the phone out for me to see.

"Got it." I take another drink. "Do you need to check those?"

She shakes her head and puts her cell into her back pocket. "Nah. I'll deal with it later."

The way she says *deal* leads me to think it's more than just the date that was late messaging her, but I don't press. If she wants to tell me she will. The last thing I want to do is make her feel pressured.

Cora changes the subject, cupping her hand under my arm

and walking with me. "And the next question...hmm, when's my birthday?"

"That's easy, too. You're an April fools baby."

She releases me to smack my arm. "What? How did you know that?"

"I told you, these are easy questions. Give me something harder."

"What else do you know about me then? Did you get a Ph.D. in Cora?"

"I can't tell you all the secrets."

"Wait..." Cora slows down her train of thought. "When's your birthday? And what's *your* favorite color?"

"October 13th. And purple."

"Your favorite color is purple? I don't think I've ever met a man whose favorite color is purple."

"Well, there's a first for everything, I guess. Plus, it's a good color." I look over at her, taking in those bright eyes. "Although, baby blue is a close second."

She smirks and returns her hand up under my biceps and I die a little inside in the best way possible.

"Fun fact," I tell her. "I was born on a Friday."

"No way. You're a Friday the 13th baby?"

"Mmhm." I navigate us around a group of people and enter the corridor leading to where our seats are.

"What's your favorite food?" she asks me.

"Pizza..." I pause and then add, "With pineapple." I side-eye her in anticipation of her response.

"Shut up." She nudges me, and I can't quite tell if that's a good or a bad thing. "Are you just saying that because you found out that's what I like on my pizza?"

I chuckle. "I promise. I actually didn't know that. At least, I don't think I did."

It's entirely possible that I found out, and that's why I prefer it more lately, only I've liked pineapple on my pizza since I was a kid and for some fucking reason, it really offends people.

"Hmm." Cora seems to consider my response and decides it's sufficient. She sips her drink and points ahead in the direction of our seats. "Okay, moving on. What makes you angry?"

"Other than assholes who fuck with you." I brace myself for the wrath of Simon which is no doubt coming once we arrive.

Cora smiles politely at a woman as we walk around her. "Yeah, obviously, other than that."

"People who don't put their carts back at the grocery store." I'm sure she was expecting some more elaborate response.

She laughs. "That pisses me off, too."

I glance down at her, taking in her soft but stunning features. God damn she's fucking beautiful, in a blinding kind of way. Her teeth are bright white, and her smile could end a war and give me a heart attack at the same time. It's everything I can do not to trail my gaze down her chest and study the shape of her curves hugged tightly by her red shirt.

"What about you?" I ask. "What makes you angry...other than misplaced shopping carts?"

"Um..." Cora switches from walking down the right steps to the left to avoid a group gathered in the aisle ahead. "Honestly..." She glances back at me and takes another long drink, her cup already at the halfway mark.

I'm going to have to make sure she eats so she doesn't get too fucked up, too quick.

She continues, "The list is pretty long."

I chuckle and put my hand on her lower back again to guide her, only to remove it a second later when I can literally feel Simon's eyes burning a hole through my face. "You? Angry? Bubbly, sweet Cora?"

Cora scoffs. "You'd be surprised what's hidden under this makeup and blonde hair."

But doesn't she have any clue that I desperately want to find out? I want to uncover every layer she keeps tucked away from the world. I want her to feel safe enough to tell me, confide in me, and let me be the rock that she is to everyone else. Except, how can I say that without sounding like a complete psycho who's obsessed with her? We aren't even dating. Sure, I confessed my feelings for her, and they were sort of reciprocated, but this is new—too delicate. I don't want to scare her away with how much I care for her.

"I'd like to see it," I tell her, teasing that fine line of being too damn much.

Cora pauses in her step and turns around, placing her hand on my chest and breathing in deeply before saying, "There's a lot you don't know about me, Alec. A lot no one knows about me. I promise I am way more fucked up in the head than I appear on the outside. This"—she floats her finger in the vague direction of her body—"is a perfectly orchestrated act that I put on every morning when I wake up. If you saw the real me, you'd probably change your mind."

I open my mouth to speak, to protest, to make her understand that she's wrong, but Simon approaches, puts his arm over Cora's shoulder, and deadpans when he thinks she isn't looking at him.

"What happened to your date, Cor?" he asks her.

She tilts her head up toward him, and the look of disdain vanishes. "Stomach bug. He had to cancel. Alec subbed in." Cora slips out from under his grasp. "Hope that's okay with you because it's okay with me." She pats him on the back before walking away and meeting June halfway down the next row of seats.

Simon, with his perfect face and perfect hair and perfect girlfriend and perfect life, narrows his gaze. "A word."

It's not a question, definitely more of a demand.

I guess this is the price to pay for the short temporary bliss of finally telling Cora how I feel and acting on the impulses I've kept at bay for far too long.

He plants his hand on my shoulder, his fingers digging in. "I love you like a brother. You've been good to me, to June, to the guys. But Cora is June's best friend. What makes Cora happy, makes June happy, makes me happy. But what makes Cora sad, makes June sad, makes me furious. Get my drift, ponyboy?"

"Mmhm."

"You know I have no issue getting rid of a problem if it arises, right?" He stares back and forth between my eyes for a long second. "I'd hate to have to find someone to replace you."

There it is, the death threat that's cloaked in mystery.

"I understand," I tell him.

Simon squeezes me a bit tighter before releasing me. "Good. Good talk."

"But—" I blurt out as he's turning around, my foot no doubt being shoved in my mouth.

"Always a but." Simon pinches the bridge of his nose between his fingers. "Listen, before you tell me you love her, that you wouldn't hurt her, just know that I don't want to hear it. You filled in for her date, that's it. Cora is off-limits. I'll tell you the same thing I told Miller. *No.*"

He leaves without allowing me another word, the weight of that entire interaction pressing down and smashing me into the earth.

What did he mean he told Miller no? Had he already shown interest in her to him? And Simon shut him down? Miller is equally, if not more powerful than Simon, so if he's not allowed to pursue her, I sure as shit am not going to be able to. I have no authority here. I'm just a driver and almost an architect. Miller is the head of an entire East Coast criminal organization. But if Simon told him no, why did Miller buy an entire building, spending a hundred million dollars to fire a guy who was bothering Cora?

Maybe Miller isn't listening to Simon's threats...and maybe I shouldn't either.

What kind of man would I be if I backed down and missed out on what could be the greatest love of my life?

One thing is certain, something is going to get broken, and I don't know whether it's going to be all the bones in my body or my heart.

And I don't know which one would be worse.

13
CORA

*M*y head feels exactly the right level of buzzed to distract me from the shit show that is my life and allow me to have a little bit of fun. Maybe I'm high from Alec confessing that he's into me, or maybe I'm living in straight delusional land in my best attempt to stay sane right now.

Either way, I'm a hell of a lot less stressed than I was before I got here, and I'm going to ride this wave until it crashes to shore.

"Umm," June says while weaving her arm through mine. "Where's your date?"

I throw my thumb back at Alec. "Over there talking to lover boy."

She clears her throat and tugs me toward our seats. "You know that's not who I mean."

"Head cold." I catch my lie all too late. "No, sorry, stomach bug. I don't know. He's sick and couldn't make it." Although in reality, I saw his texts on my screen when I pulled up the tickets. He made it. He was just late, but by that point, I had already given his spot to Alec, and I'd much rather be here with him anyway. I don't need to share any of this information with June, though.

"Well, fuck." June stops in front of our seats and faces me. "I'm sorry. I picked a dud."

I shrug and fumble to find the straw in my drink to take a sip. "No biggie, babe. Let's watch..." I spin around to the stadium, my brain totally spacing on why we're even here. "Baseball."

June sighs and glances over to where Simon and Alec still stand. "I'm going to be really honest; I don't know shit about baseball."

I laugh. "Me either." I motion to the little area we're in. "This is cute. Was it *expensive*?" I take in the private but not too secluded area we're in, only the four seats with a barrier sort of around it so no one else can come or go but still open enough to not be totally excluded.

"Define expensive," June mutters. "Could I afford it a couple years ago, uh, no. But I also could barely afford the bare necessities to survive."

"What's it like?" I ask her, my lips hovering on the tip of the straw.

"What?"

"Being *rich* rich. You know. You could have anything you wanted. Like a houseboat or something."

June raises a brow at me. "A houseboat? Cor, how drunk are you?"

I hold my cup up to her. "I've had half a drink." But damn is it strong, the more I drink the less it tastes like alcohol and the more it tastes like a good time.

The guys approach, Simon first and Alec trailing behind, an unknown expression on his face—it could be fear or annoyance or maybe the realization that coming with me tonight wasn't worth the earful Simon no doubt just gave him.

"My love." Simon smiles and reaches for June, pressing his lips to hers. "I am so grateful for you, you know that?" He throws his arm over her shoulder and tugs her close, the two of them looking out onto the field.

That nauseating feeling washes back over me at their affection.

"Hey," I say to Alec, grabbing his arm and pulling him toward me. I weave my hand up under his biceps and stand there, his strong body giving mine the ability to remain upright.

I'm tired.

Tired of pretending I'm okay. Tired of pretending that my life hasn't gone to shit. Tired of the ticking fucking clock.

"You okay?" Alec asks me, his gaze darting to the nearly empty drink in my hand.

"Oh, I'm great. What about you?" I lower my voice as quietly as possible. "I see you're still alive."

The crowd cheers, the baseball players doing the baseball thing, and I'm unsure if it's good or bad for the team Simon is rooting for.

"Yeah." Alec laughs dryly. "For now."

I pat his arm. "It'll be fine."

Simon glances over his shoulder at us and the desire to punch him in his pretty face grows fierce.

"Do you want something to eat?" Alec reaches up to rub his hand along mine.

It's so strange that he's here, touching me like this. I've wanted it for so fucking long and now that I finally have it, I regret not pushing for it sooner. We've lost so much time, and there's only a little bit left.

"I'm good," I tell him, although, I can't be certain when the last time I ate was. Maybe that's why my head is swarming with the warmth of the vodka.

"How about a pretzel or a hotdog? You want some nachos? Maybe I can find a pizza place and bribe them to put pineapple on it for you." Alec rattles off options, and I get the strong idea that he isn't going to let this go.

"A pretzel does kind of sound good."

His eyes light up like I just gave a dog a bone. "I'll get you a pretzel. You want anything else?"

I hold my cup up. "Another one of these?"

Simon breaks from June. "Good idea, bud." He rubs his hands together for no real reason other than to annoy me. "Love, do you and Alec want to go grab some snacks? I'll stay here with Cora?"

June narrows her gaze. "You're up to no good, I just know it."

"Me?" Simon bats his eyelashes and retrieves his money clip from his pocket. "Here." He slides a few hundreds out of the stack and shoves them into June's reluctant hand.

"What do you want?" June grunts at him like they're an old married couple.

They're gross but adorable.

"Surprise me," he tells her and focuses on Alec. "Keep my girl safe?"

Alec shoots me a look before saying, "Ditto," to Simon.

My heart flutters, and my cheeks redden at his simple, yet bold statement.

Simon glares at him, and once June and Alec have left, I turn my attention to the game and pretend Simon doesn't exist.

"Do we want to talk about what's going on?" Simon approaches me, his shoulder only a few inches from mine as we stare out onto the field.

"I think..." I point forward. "That blue team has bases loaded." I squint. "Is that blue?"

Simon crosses his arms. "You know that's not what I meant."

I sigh dramatically. "What do you *mean* then, Simon?" I turn toward him. "Come on. Get it out. I know it's killing you." Waiting for him feels like an eternity, but damn if I don't want time to really slow down and make the next few weeks last for the rest of my life.

166

"This thing with you and Alec, it's just tonight, right?" Simon continues to watch the game.

"I don't know. Why?"

"Because that's all it can be."

"Why? You think Alec is too good for me or something?" It's hard not to hurt my own feelings at the very thought that's crossed my mind numerous times.

"What?" He shoots me a bewildered glance. "Have you lost your mind? It's the opposite, really."

I tuck my hair behind my ear and slurp the rest of my drink. "I'm going to need you to explain."

"You're June's best friend." Simon exhales. "And what hurts you hurts her."

"So this isn't about me at all; it's about her." I hate how defensive this spits out of my mouth.

"No." Simon rubs his chin and faces me. "Listen, I know you know more than June thinks you know."

I blink at him and don't respond because he's done nothing but finally spoken the truth.

"Am I right?" he asks me.

"Maybe." I shrug. "How am I supposed to know what I do and don't know if I don't know it."

"That was the most confusing thing I have ever heard in my entire life."

"And this is only adding to it, so just spit it out, Simon. You don't want me to be with Alec. Why? Because you're afraid it'll ruin your professional relationship with him if things go poorly?" I don't let him answer that, at least not yet. "I'm a grown-ass woman, Simon. I can choose who to be with. And if things don't work out, I'm mature enough not to let that screw things up for you. Heaven forbid you have to hire someone else to chauffeur you around."

Simon shakes his head. "This has nothing to do with that, Cora, you're putting words in my mouth."

"Then say what you want to say, what is it? Why does it piss you off so badly? You were okay with June picking some random stranger off a dating app but not Alec, who you trust quite literally with June's life every single day? Tell me how that makes sense."

Simon pauses like he's processing what I said, as if all the words strung together overloaded his fragile boy brain. "You're right."

"I am?" That sure as shit wasn't the response I thought I was going to get out of him.

"Yeah." Simon runs his hand through his hair, pulling it off his forehead and sweeping it back. "Can I be honest with you?" He darts his attention toward the entrance and returns it to me.

"That's all I've been asking for, lover boy."

"You're like a sister to me, okay? Not just because of June, but because I actually care about you. Yeah, it started because of your relationship with June, and there is a small part of me that doesn't want to see you hurt because of how it will make *her* feel, but it'll piss me off just the same, and I don't want another body on my hands, if you know what I mean?"

I chuckle. "You're telling me—let me get this straight—that you care about me, Simon Beckett?"

He nudges my shoulder with his fist. "Is that so hard to believe, you idiot? Christ, we bicker like brother and sister. Sorry for caring about you and your stupid feelings."

"You're the worst," I tell him. "Seriously. The number of times I think about punching you in the face on a daily basis is unreal. It's at least four."

Simon's green eyes widen, and his mouth opens dramatically. "How rude."

"Rude?" Are you serious? You're the overprotective *older* brother who won't let me date."

"Hey now, watch your tone with that *older* shit."

I glare at him. "Have you signed up for your senior citizen discount yet?"

"That's it, the next body I put in the ground is going to be yours."

He laughs and I laugh, and I know damn well that this is the type of conversation that June would smack him over. She hates when he alludes to violence and crime but I've come to realize it's just part of who he is—the life that they all live.

If only he'd make true on his promise, then I wouldn't have to go through with whatever Ricardo has planned for me. But then he'd kill my parents and I'd have to be haunted by them in the afterlife.

"Seriously though. I want what's best for you." Simon resolves to his oh-so-serious default expression.

"Yeah, yeah." I drink my drink even though there's nothing but a watered-down mess left behind.

"You know he got a job offer in New York, right?"

"What?" I do a poor job hiding the shock written in every feature on my face.

"Some big architect thing. Career changing."

"That's..." I digest the rampant thoughts that come to mind and struggle to find the right word to say. "Great."

"Yep. So. See why I'm concerned about you? I don't want you to fall for him and leave you high and dry. I'd have to track him down in the city and put a bullet in his head at Times Square or something. Sounds really messy. Then there's the possibility that he turns it down and stays here with you, which will probably only lead to a lifetime of resentment and guilt. Seems like a lose lose, and I don't want to see you get hurt. If this is a one-time only deal, go for it, live your best life, Cor, but if you actually have feelings for him, I'd strongly suggest you take a step back and look at what that means long-term."

Long-term. Something I don't have the luxury of considering. The truth is, I only have a few weeks. And even if I didn't,

Alec is leaving and moving on to bigger and better things. I guess in a way this is good news, because when I do give myself over to Ricardo, Alec will have something else to distract him from any potential loss he experiences from the death of us.

But if that's the case, why is this all such a punch in the gut?

I knew there was no getting out of the situation with Ricardo. I knew I'd have to give Alec up. I only just got him, and he's slipping through my fingertips like a child grasping onto sand at the beach. He was never mine to begin with, and somehow, I'm already mourning the lost potential of what we'll never be.

"Cora." Simon snaps his fingers and brings me back to reality. "Did you hear me?"

I nod. "Yeah. I heard you. And I get it. You're right. What we have is temporary. That's fine. I'm good with that. I don't have time for a relationship anyway. Busy with work and stuff. This new project is killer. I have my career. He has his. I'm happy for him, really." I force a smile, doing what I always do, playing pretend that everything is okay.

"You sure?" Simon claps his hands together and gets distracted by the game he's here to watch. "Yes," he cheers. "Sorry, Dodgers are on fire tonight."

I glance out on the field, watching the grown men on the field run around and throw a ball at each other. Baseball is a strangely elaborate game of tag I don't quite understand.

"Hey, that's why we're here." I elbow him. "You really were surprised, weren't you?"

"I was." Simon's eyes twinkle and it's sort of adorable to see his inner child come out since he's such a hardened man living in this dangerous world he's been consumed by. "I told her one time, before we even became what we are...and she listened." He meets my gaze. "Find someone who listens to you, Cora. Don't settle for anything less. I mean it. The little things matter a lot more than big grand gestures. Those are too flashy, almost fake, you know. Sure, they're great, and you deserve the big and the small, but the small ones, they add up over time to something more profound..."

Simon seems to get lost in his thoughts, and I allow the time to let his words sink in.

Someone who listens, someone who does the little things...someone who pays attention.

At that, Alec and June appear at the entrance of our small but lavish blocked-off area, both of them with boxes and drinks piled up and hanging from their limbs.

I rush over to Alec, taking the drink carrier he's about to drop. "Let me help you."

"Thanks," he says with a smile.

"What is all this?"

"Well," June starts. "I was hungry and couldn't decide, so we got a lot of everything." She walks over to the little ledge in the back wall that acts as our makeshift table. "We got pizza, pretzels, hotdogs, nachos, popcorn, umm what else?" She looks at Alec.

"Cotton candy, fries, cannoli..." He carries the rest of his stuff over. "And a couple burgers. I think that's it." He points to the drink carrier June is holding. "Oh, and milkshakes." He winks at me. "Chocolate with extra whip."

I crane my neck at June. "You told him?"

She pops a fry into her mouth. "Told him what?"

"My milkshake order."

"Actually, I thought you preferred vanilla, but he insisted I was wrong." June shrugs. "Guess Alec knows you better than I do."

Simon strolls over and grabs a bag of cotton candy, leaning in close to me and whispering, "Maybe I misjudged the situation." He kisses June on the cheek. "Thanks, love."

Alec smooths the hair off my shoulder, tucking it behind and rubbing my back. "Hey," he says softly. "I thought you should eat something before you drink anymore."

I melt into his embrace. "Are you calling me a lightweight?"

He pinches his lips together and says, "Maybe."

I lightly elbow him but it's hard to blame him when he's totally right. I should eat something to simmer the buzz from turning into full-blown drunkenness in the first hour of being here. "Fine."

Alec opens the top of the pizza box, revealing a whole entire pizza, half of it with pepperoni and pineapple.

The little things.

"You want a slice?" He reaches for it and eyes me.

"Sure."

He grins and pulls one out, plopping it on a napkin and handing it to me.

I take a bite, my jaw tense from keeping it clenched all day. I hadn't even realized it until I went to open my mouth wider than what is required to drink from the straw.

"This is good," I mumble.

June passes me my milkshake, and I down a huge gulp, brain freeze immediately settling.

"Fuck," I blurt out.

"Press your thumb to the roof of your mouth," Alec tells me.

"What?"

"Just do it and thank me later." He chews his pizza and watches me.

I squint through the headache and do as he says, awkwardly pushing my thumb where he told me to, and not a few moments later, the brain freeze subsides to a more tolerable ache. "How did that actually work?"

Alec reaches for a napkin. "I think what you meant to say was 'thank you'."

"Thank you," I say, drawing out the last syllable. "My hero."

He winks at me, and it sends my heart in a flutter. "Knight in shining armor ready to save the damsel."

If only he knew how badly I needed to be saved...

Simon cheers, reminding me that we came here to watch a game. June joins him, eating a burger at his side while he consumes far too much cotton candy in one sitting. She holds her burger out to him, and he bites off a chunk in between over-dosing on sugar.

"Thank you," I tell Alec again, but not for relieving my headache. "For all this."

It's nice to be spoiled for a change instead of always giving and never getting anything back in return. I offer myself uncon-ditionally, and I would never *expect* anything in exchange for my kindness, but damn is it nice to be on the other end.

"I hate that this counts as our first date." Alec wipes at the corners of his mouth. "That came out wrong. I'm grateful for it, really, I just imagined something grander, more special. Not a double date with Mr. and Mrs. Psycho over there."

I smile and look around, then at him. "I don't know. I'm having a great time. Best first date I've ever been on."

"You're lying to make me feel better, aren't you?"

"Not at all." I laugh. "I've been on some pretty terrible first dates though, so the bar wasn't *that* high." I sip some of the milk-shake, paying mind to not make the same mistake twice. "Wait, you have to tell me what this first date you envisioned was?"

"Well..." Alec grins. "Don't make fun of me."

I place my hand on my chest. "Never."

Alec sets what's left of his pizza on the little makeshift table and dusts his hands off. "Okay, so, picture this." He spreads his hands in the air like he's setting the scene for this story of his. "Dinner, by candlelight."

"Ohh," I mutter.

"On a rooftop."

"Ohh," I say, a bit more intrigued this time.

"But imagine it being lit with those string lights, you know the ones girls love?"

"Fairy lights?"

"Yeah." He points his finger at me. "Those. Strung all around the rooftop. We'd eat something fancy. I don't know. I'd hire some private chef and we'd sip fancy wine, and then mid-way through I'd ask you to dance to some fancy music and then I'd spin you around and the whole world would stop as we stare into each other's eyes and..." Alec seems to get lost in his train of thought.

"Wow," I tell him. "You really mapped it all out, didn't you?"

He shrugs. "I mean, only a couple details, nothing major."

I grin and shake my head. "Sounds absolutely magical." I glance up at the beautiful and kind man standing in front of me. "I'm going to hold you to it, though."

Alec smiles. "Yeah?"

"Mmhm."

The crowd erupts in a loud cheer, something big no doubt happening on the field. June and Simon high-five each other and hug, his arm lingering around her shoulder long after the chaos dies down.

"Oh, and I'd get you flowers, obviously. A big bouquet of..." He pauses and puts his finger to his chin. "I don't know what your favorite flower is."

"Hydrangea," I confess way too easily.

"That's going in the vault." He taps his forehead before reaching for the rest of his pizza.

I study him as he eats, watching the way his jaw moves as he chews, and his Adam's apple bobs when he swallows. I've known him for a while now, but there's still so much I've yet to learn about him. A whole lifetime of memories and stories and unknown baggage that we both have, daring to be unpacked. But if I open up to him, there's no telling how he'll react—or if he'll change his mind. Is that a risk I'm willing to take? Will I ever actually be happy with someone if I can't be myself?

And why does it matter, since all of this will be over in a few short weeks?

Still, I find my thoughts churning and my mouth opening to ask, "What were you like as a kid?"

"Um, well..." Alec leans against the counter and puts one leg in front of the other. "Awkward as fuck."

I laugh. "No, you weren't."

I can't picture Alec as anything other than tall, hot, and sweet. I figured he was popular and had tons of friends and every girl wanted him to pick her. I don't think he would have been a player, but I'd definitely assume he had a lot of options.

"I was," Alec continues. "I had braces and pimples and there was this one summer I grew like a foot. I was taller than everyone, even some of the male teachers. It was embarrassing. I got made fun of like every day of middle school."

"I'm sorry," I tell him. "That's fucked up."

He titters. "Yeah."

"But hey, at least you had one hell of a glow-up."

A smile breaks across his face and he raises his brows. "I did, didn't I?"

"Yep," I confirm. "You're super-hot now. But...I probably would have thought you were hot back then, too."

"No way," he says. "I bet you were a popular cheerleader or something."

This time it's my turn to laugh. "Hardly." I rummage through the massive selection of food and grab a nacho to shove into my mouth. "I was actually really shy in school, believe it or not."

"You're right, that is hard to believe. You're so...outgoing."

I eat another cheese-covered chip, covering my mouth as I chew and say, "I wasn't always like that."

"What changed?"

"Well..." I swallow the bite of food and attempt to rationalize my response. "Somehow, in my little teenage brain, I thought if I wanted people to like me, I had to be different. Because they sure as shit didn't like me when I was shy and reserved. It was the summer before senior year that I had this really rough patch. Bad boyfriend, bad breakup...some self-harming...it was a really dark time for me. I decided I didn't want that life anymore, so I just became a new version of myself, one that I thought people might like." I shrug. "And I mean, it worked. People started paying attention to me. I went from being invisible to someone who was invited to parties and stuff..."

I don't add the fact that it felt so artificial that I lost sense of who I was, and I don't think I've ever really been able to find my way back.

Alec places his hand on top of mine. "I would have been your friend before you felt like you had to change yourself."

I meet his gaze. "How can you be so sure when that isn't the version of me that attracted you in the first place?"

"It's your soul I'm attracted to, Cora."

My heart skips a beat, and a strong part of me wants to turn and run away while the other wants to kiss his lips. Yet, I'm too afraid to do either, so instead, I just stand here and pick apart everything he's said and wonder if it's all a lie. Because why would anything ever be real or genuine or good? There's always some shoe about to drop or rug about to be pulled out.

"Are there booze in those?" I point to the other carrier full of drinks.

Alec's gaze drops and I hate the energy shift I feel immediately. But it's better this way. I should keep a little bit of distance between us, if not physically, then at least emotionally. Even though I'd love nothing more than to reciprocate every little bit of what he's saying. I've been dreaming of someone coming along and saying the exact things he is, to do the sweet things that he does, to look at me in a way that makes me feel like I'm the only girl in the world. I would have killed for this a couple weeks ago, and now it kills me that it's here and totally out of reach.

"Yeah," he confirms and pulls one out to hand to me. "Here."

"Thanks." I take a very long swig, the entirety of it tasting like straight vodka as I will it to numb the ache building in my chest.

I don't want to hurt him. I don't want to hurt myself. But that's the only thing I see in our future, and there's no way around it.

14
CORA

I manage to toe a very thin line between what I want and what's right the rest of the evening.

But the more I drink, the harder it is for me to determine which is which.

Because every time Alec touches me, my body ignites with a fiery lust, and I consider how inappropriate it would be to jump his bones in front of my two best buds.

My phone buzzes, and I ignore it, the alcohol giving me a helpful crutch to blissfully not give a fuck about who might be contacting me. It could be Silver, but it could be Ricardo, and that's a man I'd like to avoid for the rest of my life.

Drunk me is just a bit bold and somehow very aware that I'm going to regret disobeying him tomorrow when I sober up.

"You good?" Alec steadies my shoulders.

"I'm great," I tell him and slap his chest playfully.

Or well, what I think is playful.

Everything sort of spins, and if it weren't for his hands keeping me sturdy, I might tumble over.

He guides me into a chair and hands me a bottle of water. "Here, drink this."

"I think I need to sit down," I mumble.

"Cor...you *are* sitting down." His brows pinch together, and I reach out and poke the spot between his eyes.

"I'm giving you wrinkles." I skim my hand over his cheek, the five o'clock shadow grazing my skin. "You're really pretty, you know that?"

Alec sighs. "And you're really fucked up."

I hiccup. "Oh, God."

"Are you going to get sick?"

"No." I hiccup again. "This is just really—" I hiccup. "Annoying."

"Here." He pushes the water into my hands, lifting them up.

I chug the water in an attempt to rid myself of the pesky hiccups and nearly choke on it as one fights its way through anyway.

June strolls over and plants her ass in the seat next to me, her body sort of doubling in my vision. "My little lightweight," she purrs. "You doing okay?"

"Mmhm." I nod a hair too aggressively, massively overselling the lie. I'm not okay. Not now, not before I got drunk, and not ever. "I'm tired." I rest my hand on Alec's shoulder. "Are you tired? Is it late? Why am I so tired?" I yawn and lean back into the seat.

Simon claps and cheers out, his back toward us, and then turns around and comes over. "Hey, buddy." He kneels next to Alec and puts his hand on my knee. "How about Alec takes you home, little lady?"

"But." I point out at the game. "It's not over."

Simon chuckles. "You haven't watched a single minute of the game, Cora."

"But like, I could. I was just waiting for it to get good."

"It's been good, and it's almost over. Alec can take you in the car, and we'll catch an Uber home." Simon shifts his focus to June. "That good, love?"

"Of course," she responds without hesitation.

"You haven't drank, right?" Simon asks Alec.

"Just one when we got here. Have you?"

"A few, yeah."

Alec breathes in, and I get lost in watching his chest rise and fall. "I could get her home and circle back to get you guys once the game is over."

"Nah, don't worry about it. We can be normal people for a change and take an Uber. It'll be fun."

"You sure?"

"Absolutely. But..." Simon stands. "A word, in private?"

Alec rubs my leg before rising to his feet and following Simon out of earshot range.

"I'm sorry I ruined your night," I say to June.

She turns toward me in her chair and pulls her leg up and over onto the other. "Tonight was great. You didn't ruin anything. I was happy to have you here."

If only she knew how badly I needed to hear that. That I didn't fuck things up. That I'm not ruining her life. Because I've already ruined mine and I can't stomach the thought of making hers bad.

Through blurred vision, Simon slaps Alec on the shoulder and the two of them part but return their places in front of me.

"Ready to go?" Alec holds out his hand.

I slip mine into his and allow him to help me up, my body strangely heavy and not as responsive as I'd prefer. The goal was to numb my anxieties, not get shit-faced, and here I am, way past the point of the level of intoxication I was going for.

"Are you mad at me?" I ask Simon.

He touches my chin with his thumb and index finger. "Never."

"Okay, good. Thanks."

"Get her home safely, please," June tells Alec and then looks at me. "Call me tomorrow?"

"Yeah, duh." I snatch my phone off the chair and shove it into my pocket, but then remember I came here with a clutch. "My bag..."

Alec holds it out in front of my face. "I got it."

"You're the best."

"And you're drunk." He wraps his arm around my body and tilts his head to the door. "Let's get you home and in bed."

"Mmm. Bed." I let him guide me, shooting a wave at Simon and June on the way out.

The noise from the stadium hits me once we're out of our little secluded area, my senses blaring in what seems like every direction. "God, why are the noises and lights so bright?" I squint my eyes and recoil into Alec a bit.

"Put these on." He takes his sunglasses off the top of his head and offers them to me.

"Have you had these all night?"

"Yep."

"Oh." I slide them onto my face and the relief is instant and a tiny sobering.

Alec navigates us through the crowd, and once we're outside, a sort of continued relief washes over me. He leads us silently the rest of the way until we eventually reach the car.

My phone vibrates again as I'm trying to get to the passenger door, and as I'm trying to look at it, I drop it onto the ground. "Shit," I mumble and bump my head on the car when I reach for it.

"I got it. Go ahead and get in." He helps me into the car and leans down to get my phone.

I rest my head on the seat, a sort of quiet falling between us. I glance over at Alec as he examines my lit-up screen.

"It's not broken, just a little dirty." He wipes it off on his shirt and gives it back to me, something strangely stern and deceptive in his voice.

I might be drunk but I'm still hyper-vigilant to any sudden or even subtle shift in other people's energies.

Alec shuts the door and as he's walking around to the front, I click the screen and spot the very aggressive texts that Ricardo has sent me.

Unknown: It was such a pleasure seeing you tonight, pet.

Unknown: You're not going to answer me, really?

Unknown: The more you try to hide from me, the worse this is going to be for you.

Unknown: You're mine whether you want to be or not.

Unknown: I will find you, and when I do...

Alec slams the door shut behind him.

I flinch and put my phone aside.

"I'm sorry," he says a second later. "I didn't mean to scare you." His voice is cool and even despite his fist wrapping around the steering wheel tightly.

"I...I don't want to go home. Not to my house." The idea of being this intoxicated and having Ricardo fuming at me grows a concern that can't be hidden by any amount of alcohol.

"Where do you want me to take you?" Alec pushes the button to start the SUV and waits for me to answer him.

I consider my options: home is off limits, so no to that. Silver's place crosses my mind, but I don't know how I would explain that to Alec or Silver. I guess I could crash at June's since there's no shortage of beds in that mansion.

"Can I stay with you tonight?" I blurt out the second the thought hits me.

"Yeah, of course." Alec pulls out of the parking spot and onto the main road, navigating around the slow traffic surrounding the stadium.

I tilt my legs toward the door and sort of fold into myself, my cheek resting against the seat as I stare out the window. I don't mean to, but I doze off, and when I wake, Alec is standing outside my door and scooping me into his arms.

"I can walk," I mumble.

"I've got you," he says without any indication he's going to set me onto solid ground.

Alec carries me the rest of the way through the garage and into his house, only stopping to set me on a cushy chair in the living room. "Let me help you." He takes each of my shoes off and sets them aside.

I sit up and scoot forward. "Hey."

"Hey." He grins back at me.

"Can we have sex?" I ask him, the question surprising even me as it slips out.

Alec closes his eyes briefly and looks down. "Cora, you're wasted."

"Yeah, but that doesn't mean I don't want to. Sober me wanted to earlier tonight." I inch closer to him. "Please?" I tilt his chin to force his gaze. "I want to."

He shakes his head slowly. "I'm sorry, Cora, but no. Not tonight. Not like this."

I sigh. "You're not attracted to me?"

Alec laughs abruptly. "Oh, babe, it has *nothing* to do with my level of attraction to you. You're fucking stunning. The most beautiful woman I've ever known. And you're going to remember exactly none of this, so I'm going to tell you something, okay?"

"Mmhm." I slump my shoulders and huff.

Alec carefully tucks my hair behind my ear and my eyes flutter at his touch. "I'm pretty sure I have loved you from the moment I saw you walk across campus, Cora. And every single second with you has only proven to me what I felt that very day. I kick myself for not having the courage to say something sooner but I'm here now, and I'm not going anywhere. Not unless you want me to go, not unless you tell me to. So, do I want to have sex with you? No. I want to make love to you, baby, because you deserve a gentle love, and that's not going to happen tonight. Not with you like this. I want you to want me in the morning when your head isn't being controlled by alcohol. I want to do this right. I want—no, I need—you to understand you deserve so much more than what life has dealt you so far. I'm going to prove that to you, okay?"

"Okay," I reply, only I blink and can't remember what I'm agreeing to. My body spins and I don't know if it's in my head or I'm actually moving or not. "Fuck."

Alec rises from his spot in front of me. "Come on, let's get you in bed." He grabs my hands and helps me up, everything going fuzzy and spinning all at the same time.

I arrive at a bedroom and break off from him, unbuttoning my bottoms and yanking them down.

Alec shields his eyes like I might be radioactive and turns his back to me. "Here, put these on." Without looking, he tosses me a pair of sweatpants, and I almost fall sliding my feet into them.

I collapse onto the bed and Alec pulls back the covers to tuck me in. He goes to walk away but I grab his hand.

"Will you stay? Please." I don't tell him that even though I'm drunk, I don't want to be alone.

"I'll get you some water and Tylenol and be right back."

"Okay." I close my eyes and wait for him to make good on his promise and return.

And although I'm not sure how long it is, he does. Alec slides into bed beside me but keeps his distance.

I roll over and scoot toward him, my head finding the crook of his arm and my leg crossing over his.

He doesn't protest and I'm grateful for it.

"This is nice," I mumble into him.

"Yeah, it is." He rubs my shoulder and holds me close, and I wonder if he knows how safe I feel here with him.

I want to tell him; I just can't seem to find the words.

"Hey, Cora?"

"Huh?"

"Is everything okay at work?"

"Yeah, I think so. Why?"

"I mean, your boss was giving you a hard time. Is he still?"

"Oh." I recall the memory of the box cutter blade slicing into him. "No, I killed him."

Alec chuckles. "That's good." He pauses and adds, "I thought maybe that's who texted you earlier. I didn't mean to look, but I was checking your screen, and you don't have message previews shut off on your lock screen."

"That's Ricardo. He's a dick."

Alec shuffles. "*Ricardo* Ricardo?"

"I only know one Ricardo. How many do you know?" I laugh at the idea of everyone's name being Ricardo. What a weird world that would be.

"Cora, what aren't you telling me?"

"Um, a lot, really," I mutter, unable to withhold information in my current state. Everything I've held back until this point feels like it's boiling over the edge of my tongue. "Ricardo bought me from my dad."

Alec sits up and catches me as I fall off him. "Cora, what are you talking about?"

I reach for him and attempt to get him to sit down. "Oh, stuff and things. It's not a big deal. It's under control. I've got it. Just have to have a baby. Then I'm good. You know? Easy."

"Cora, you're not making any sense." He smooths the hair out of my face. "Talk to me, tell me what's going on."

I struggle to keep my eyes open. "I did. I said it. I confessed. Wow. That feels great," I mumble with my face pressed into the bed. "I should have done that sooner." I breathe out exaggeratedly.

"What do you mean you have to have a baby?"

"You know. A baby. I don't know. It's not a big deal." I nearly drool on the bed but catch myself. "Don't worry about it."

"How can you expect me not to worry about it, Cora? After what I've already told you?"

"What?"

Alec tucks my hair behind my ear. "That I'm in love with you, Cora."

I open my eyes slightly and through the slits I make out his beautiful features. Even drunk he's sexy. "Can we have sex?"

"How about this?" Alec softens his resolve. "Ask me again when you're sober, and I'll consider it."

I grin and plop my face back down. "Deal."

"But you're going to have to tell me what's going on, too, when you're sober, okay?"

"Mmhm," I mumble, the weight of the situation easing at finally confessing to someone that I'm in trouble.

Maybe he can help me get out of this mess, or maybe I've doomed us both.

15

ALEC

I barely sleep a wink.

No. Instead, I watch Cora's chest rise and fall and wonder what secrets she keeps tucked inside.

I doze off here and there, but it's nothing to soothe the ache in my chest at the cryptic shit she was confessing before she passed out.

Part of me desperately wants to believe that she was mumbling nonsense in her drunken state, but a stronger part is convinced there is truth to what she said. I just don't know how any of it could be possible. How could she have gotten mixed up with Ricardo? She mentioned something about her dad...and a baby, but what did any of it mean? If she was in trouble, surely she would have gone to June for help, at the very least. Or there's me, or Miller. Clearly, he would help her. The dude spent a hundred million dollars to buy the company she sort of worked for because her boss was a dick, I can't imagine what he would do if he found out someone like Ricardo was making demands of her.

I slide out of bed and into my bathroom, brushing my teeth and splashing water on my face. Sighing, I take a look into the bedroom to make sure Cora hasn't disappeared. I don't want to leave her, but my duties are approaching and there's only so much time left before I have to head over to the mansion and drive Coen to a meeting.

He's not usually the type to have someone chauffeur him around but with the distance, he needs to use the drive time to catch up on work he can't do if he's behind the wheel. Understandable. And that's kind of the entire scope of my employment with them...to be their driver, no matter what the reason or location.

Quietly, I sneak into the kitchen and brew some coffee, my mind racing with endless possibilities of what Cora had said.

Not to mention the fact that I literally told her I loved her. I hope she forgets, not because I don't want her to know, but because I want to do it right and make it a memorable experience, not something I blurted out when she was drunk.

I froth some vanilla oat milk and pour it into both mugs and fill them to the brim with coffee. I return to the bedroom with a mug in each hand and pause as Cora stirs.

"Do I smell coffee?" She peers through one eye at me.

"Sorry, I didn't mean to wake you." I approach, hand her the cup, and settle along the edge of the bed. "How are you feeling?"

She draws in a breath and yawns. "Great, actually. Your bed is super comfortable." Cora presses down onto the mattress. "What is this, Temperpedic?"

"It is, actually." I take a sip of my coffee and contemplate my next words carefully.

"Damn." She smells the coffee and glances up at me. "Is this oat milk?"

I nod. "And vanilla."

Cora grins and shakes her head. "I don't know if I should be impressed or concerned with how much you know about me."

"Impressed, obviously." I wink at her. "But hey...can we talk about last night?"

"Oh God. What did I do? How embarrassing was it?"

"You mean other than the drool?" I attempt to lighten the mood even though my heart is pounding.

Cora wipes at her face. "Was it that bad?"

"You, uh...you mentioned something about Ricardo?" I eye her carefully.

"I did?" She takes a drink of her coffee without giving anything away. "That's the guy we met when picking Simon up, right?"

"Yeah," I confirm. "You never met him prior?"

She draws her bottom lip upward and rocks her head back and forth. "No. I don't think so. I mean, I think I'd remember him. He was kind of a creep."

"Cora, how much do you know about June and the guys and what they do for a living?"

Cora shrugs. "Enough to be aware that it's shady and illegal, but not enough to really build a case against them. Why?"

"Because if you think what they do is shady and illegal, then you have no idea the kind of shit Ricardo is into. He's not a good man by any means. He's dangerous. And if you're involved with him, I need to know."

"*Involved*? Are you insinuating that I'm into him or something? I'm not against dating an older man, but gross. Ricardo is repulsive. I mean from the short interaction I had with him, at least, you know?"

I narrow my gaze. "So, you're telling me nothing is going on between you two? And what you told me last night wasn't true?"

Cora drinks her coffee again. "I don't know what I said to you, Alec, but I can assure you, I'm not involved with him. Not now, not ever."

She's very convincing but I'm not entirely committed to believing her. The things she confessed were too bizarre to be a fabrication.

"Hey," Cora lowers her voice. "You don't have anything to

worry about, not with him." She raises an eyebrow at me. "I might not remember us talking about him, but there is something I remember..."

My chest heaves at my confession of love I thought she wouldn't have any recollection of when she woke up this morning.

"You said..." Cora scoots more comfortably onto her butt. "If I asked you sober...you'd consider my drunken proposition."

How can she remember that but not the rest of the night?

"You're not serious."

Cora smirks and I swear to Christ it's the most adorable thing I've seen in my entire life. "Deadly," she confirms.

"But...but aren't you hungover?"

"Nope." Cora drinks some of her coffee. "Unless you're having a change of heart, then I totally understand."

I glance at my watch and then at her, my cock already throbbing in response to her being so forward.

"Have somewhere you need to be?" she asks me.

"Fuck it," I blurt out. "I'm probably already going to get fired over last night, what's one more reason to add to the list?"

"I'll have a word with your boss." Cora scoots to the edge of the bed and places her cup of coffee on the nightstand.

I rise to my feet next to her as she reaches for the waistband of my pants and unbuttons them, her blue eyes flicking through her lashes up at me.

She continues on her mission, and I let her because this is all I've ever wanted. Me and her. In any way possible. I would have burned the world down just to hold her fucking hand, and here I am, being undressed by this literal goddess as she kills me with her sultry bedroom eyes.

Cora stands from the bed and nudges me toward it. She drags my pants over my ass and guides me onto the bed. I could easily overpower every single one of her moves, but damn is it hot as hell for her to take charge like this.

"You took care of me last night." Cora grips the base of my shaft, her hand so fucking tiny around it. "Now let me take care of you."

"Baby..." I smooth the hair out of her face. "You don't have to." But damn if I fucking want her to. I do my best to be a gentleman at all times, but I'd be lying if I said I hadn't thought about her perfect pink lips wrapped around my cock on occasion.

Cora leans forward, her mouth a breath away from my tip. "I want to." She swirls her tongue over the edge, the heat sending a spike of pleasure straight through me. "I've wanted to for a long time." Cora spreads her lips around the tip and tightens her grip on my base, and I stifle a moan.

"Fuck." I do everything I can not to bust in her mouth two seconds after she begins and force myself not to move my hips. God damn, I want to grab a fistful of her hair and shove my cock down her throat, but I refrain from allowing my intrusive thoughts to win.

No, I want to take my time. I want her to enjoy this, too. And never would I ever hurt her. Not in a million years.

But if she asked me to...that's another story.

Cora closes her eyes and swallows more of me down, her lips pressing against me as she strokes my length with each up and down motion. She hums slightly and the sensation makes me harden even more. She keeps her pace slow and steady, but deeper and deeper until I hit the back of her throat.

She glances up at me, and it's nearly my undoing.

"Fuck, baby." I cup her cheek and weave my fingers through her hair.

Cora releases me enough to place her other hand on top of mine and say, "You can pull it. I don't care."

"You don't care or it's what you want?"

She continues to stroke my cock and licks her lips. "It's what I want."

I throb in her hand and drag my fingers along her scalp to latch onto a fistful of her blonde hair.

Cora returns her attention to me and slides the length of my shaft along her tongue and hits the back of her throat. She pushes her hand on top of mine, pushing herself forcefully down onto my cock.

"God damn," I moan and buck my hips ever so slightly. "You're sucking me like such a good girl."

She smiles against me, and the change in sensation nearly sends me over the edge again.

"I want to taste you," I tell her and drag her face away from me before I come in her mouth too soon.

Cora glides her tongue over her lips and rises to her feet, my hands gripping her bottoms and yanking them over her ass.

I lean forward, breathing in her sex and wondering if it's possible to climax just from fucking smelling her delectable scent. Gliding my nose over her slit, I trace my tongue down and dip it along her entrance.

She whimpers and holds onto my shoulders.

I bring a hand up and tease a finger in the same spot, noticing just how she tenses with want seconds prior to me shoving it inside her. I rock it in and out and grip her hip with my other hand. "Sit on my face, baby." Scooting farther onto the bed, I guide her with me, helping her to climb on, her knees straddling both sides of me.

Cora hesitates as she hovers over me, her pussy inches from my mouth.

I lap at her and tug her closer.

"I don't want to smother you," she says.

"I'll let you know if I need air." I kiss and suck on her clit. "I'm serious. Bury me in your pussy, baby. Then I'd die a happy man." I drag her onto me and force her weight down, her scent the most heavenly experience I've ever had.

Cora relaxes and moves her hips with my help, my hands on

her hips and making their way up her torso, up under her shirt. She puts her palms on top of my hands and brings them to her perky tits, squeezing gently.

I pinch her nipple and she moans.

Submerging myself in her pussy, I glide my tongue over every inch of her that I can reach and dip into her when she fucks my face. Her motion increases and I tighten my hold on her nipple and release the other hand to latch onto her hip and keep her moving. I focus on her clit, sucking it with more pressure and rocking my tongue across it. My dick throbs with desire and if I weren't so focused on making her come first, I'd push her down onto me and fuck her through both of our orgasms.

But regardless of what I want, I wasn't lying about being a gentleman, and ladies *always* come first.

"Fuck," Cora moans. "I'm going to..."

But she doesn't finish, at least not her statement. Instead, she cries out and shatters onto my face, her body trembling on top of me and coating my mouth with her lust.

Cora pants and breaks away from me. "Did I crush you?"

I lick her slit and grin up at her. "Not even close."

She sighs and inches away more to reach back and grip my still-hard shaft. It twitches in her hand.

Cora climbs off me, only to climb back on, facing the other direction. She leans forward, giving me the perfect fucking vision of her ass in my face as she strokes my cock along the tip of her mouth.

I spread her ass and thumb my way along her soaked entrance, teasing it and gently penetrating her.

She arches her back and pushes into me, her body silently begging me to enter her. Cora circles her tongue on the tip of my cock, my precum mixing with her spit. She glides me in further and further and I shove both of my thumbs into her pussy. She tightens around me, and I almost come right there...my self-control somehow much stronger than I thought.

I rock my hips and gently fuck her pretty little mouth, each thrust putting me closer and closer to oblivion. I focus on her, my tongue slipping between my thumbs and out to dance around her asshole.

Cora moans and drives herself onto me as she sucks me harder and faster, her grip stiffening around my cock. She pauses and pulls me out of her mouth, but maintains her hand up and down. "I want you to finish in my mouth," she says through jagged breaths. "But I want to feel you inside of me."

I remove one thumb and slide it over her entrance, making sure to hit every nerve ending I can from this vantage point. "Whatever you want, baby."

She exhales and straightens her back, inching south on my body until her pussy is lined up with my shaft. Cora slides up my cock, her pussy on one side and her hand on the other, the sensation something from another world.

Holding onto her hips, I wonder what I did to deserve this. Maybe somewhere along the lines I've died and gone to Heaven...because that's the only explanation for this paradise on earth.

"Do you have a condom?" Cora glances over her shoulder.

"Nightstand." I point next to the bed.

Cora leans over me, her body splayed out even more than it already was as she reaches into the drawer and retrieves a condom. She bites off the corner and secures the rubber on my cock without a second thought, immediately getting back in place and positioning herself on the tip of my shaft.

I watch in complete awe as she sits down, my cock disappearing inside of her warm pussy.

"You're so fucking tight, baby." I keep my hands on her hips and let her maintain control for now. I so badly want to grip her harder and thrust into her, but I don't want to hurt her.

"Does that feel good?" Cora looks back at me as she bounces up and down at a quicker pace, each time going a bit more down.

"You have no idea." I can't keep my eyes off her pussy with every up and down motion, her plump ass right in my fucking face. "Is it okay for you?" I ask her.

She spreads her legs wider and rides me harder. "So fucking good."

I reach under her to grip my cock and tease her a bit more, my fingers finding her aching clit within seconds.

Cora moans again, and I lick the thumb on my other hand and press it against her tight asshole.

She whimpers and fucks me deeper, keeping me buried inside her and driving her weight down. "Fuck me, Alec. Please."

I buck my hips, thrusting up in her as I push into her ass and clit, my orgasm so fucking close. I lose control, sitting up in an instant and holding onto her as I toss her onto the bed and fuck her from behind, my hand wrapped around her torso and working her clit.

Cora grips the sheets and rears into me, her pussy pulsating near the edge.

"Come for me, baby." I thrust into her. "Come for me." I pinch her clit and rail her from behind, her body reacting within seconds to my command.

Cora screams and drives herself backward as her pussy contracts and spasms, and I follow her over the edge, a cry leaving my own lips while I'm pumping my orgasm into her. I slow my pace, making sure to ride this high all the way out and bask in her body trembling against me.

She twitches and sighs and finally, stops moving, her hands still gripping the sheets tightly. "That was..."

I kiss her shoulder and loosen my pressure on her throbbing clit, still barely circling it. "Incredible."

"Yeah," she breathes. "But if you're going to keep doing that..."

Her pussy clasps around my cock, and I take the opportunity to put two fingers on both sides of her clit and continue working it. Cora whimpers and gradually pushes back onto my still-hard cock, and I wonder how it's possible for me to be so fucking erect after such an intense orgasm. Usually, I need a little downtime between sessions, but right now, my desire is at an all-time high.

I ignore any preconceived notions and thrust into her, savoring the chance to allow her warm, tight pussy to consume me.

If I could curl up inside of it and live there forever, I would. But that's not possible, so instead, I fuck her senseless.

Cora pushes into me, and I buck against her, sitting up to get a hold of her hips.

I keep one hand circling her clit and spit onto her ass before pressing my thumb along her puckered hole. I listen to her body as it reacts to me and decide to push in slightly and apply more pressure.

Cora moans and shoves into me harder and my cock hardens in response.

Not holding back, I fuck her with more force and slide my fingers over her clit to send us both over the edge once again.

I slam her hungry pussy and don't let up until we're finished with each other.

"Holy shit," I blurt out. "That's never happened before." Slowly, I pull out of her and steady her hips as I guide her body onto the bed. "Did I hurt you?"

Cora lands on her side, her hair a mess and sweat gleaning on her forehead. "Not at all. That was fucking hot."

I press a gentle kiss on her lips and plop down onto my side, too, toward her. "Do you want to shower?"

She nods her head. "Yeah, but I don't think I can walk."

"I've got you, baby." I hold out my hand for her to latch on to, and once I have her up, I drag her shirt over her head and toss it onto the floor. I do the same with mine and admire her naked body for a second before inching her closer and scooping her into my arms.

My phone buzzes on the nightstand, and I know damn well I'm in trouble, but if I'm going to be fired...or killed...for being late, I might as well enjoy myself first.

16

CORA

*W*hy couldn't Alec have confessed his feelings for me a month ago...six months ago...hell, when we first met? Because maybe then I wouldn't have been so fucking stupid in signing myself up for being Ricardo's personal baby-making machine.

On paper, we get along well. Me and Alec, not me and Ricardo. We have ambition and drive and so much fun together. Our conversations are deep and meaningful and we still manage to bring out the inner child in each other. Don't get me started on the chemistry...it's off the charts.

Maybe it was meant to be this way? Had I known how Alec felt sooner, I could have sabotaged it. I could have pushed him away with my anxieties and darkness and we would have been doomed from the start. Either way, I would have ended up with my feelings hurt and alone. At least this way, I'm a bit more in control of the situation.

But the way he touches my body and seems to know me better than I know myself—it makes me question everything.

I thought my night with Silver was mind-blowing, and then

my world was rocked by Alec. Sweet, caring, so fucking sexy, Alec.

Never in my wildest dreams would I have imagined he would fuck like that. Sure, a girl could wish for it, but after getting absolutely railed by him, I'm not sure what reality I'm in anymore.

With my cheeks rosy and wearing nothing but some clothes I borrowed from Alec, I walk along the sidewalk outside of his place and make my way toward my parents' house.

I need to change and go over some work things and hopefully ignore the shit out of my dad.

Alec wanted to drive me, but I insisted. Partially because I needed some fresh air, but mostly because I was afraid once the sex left his thoughts that he would question me about what I said last night.

I may have been drunk, but I remember every word that left my mouth. Quite a bit of the night is blurry, except the very vivid memory of telling him I killed my boss and Ricardo bought me to make him a baby.

What the fuck was I thinking?

It's not that I *don't* want to confess to Alec and trust that he could help me, but how could I be so foolish? Alec isn't in the dark and dangerous aspects of that world the way that June and her men are. Telling Alec would only put him in danger, and I can't afford to be so reckless.

If I didn't care about him, I would. Not to mention the fact that he'd probably act on his impulses and confront Ricardo directly. Those are risks I can't take. Not with him.

June, on the other hand...the more I think about it, the more I consider it my best option. She's secretive with me, but maybe if I confide in her, that will change things and we won't have this gigantic wall between us. I love her like a sister. I trust her like family. She's the person I should have gone to from the start. I've been an idiot to wait this long when we could have been brainstorming ways for me to get the hell out of this nightmare. Especially now that Ricardo knows June and I are friends. She should be aware of the threat if he suspects I've told her. I have no doubt that he doesn't already surmise that I have.

A man and a woman who are holding hands walk past me on the sidewalk, and I smile politely at them on their way by. When no one is coming, I cross the street and hug my arms to my chest, breathing the city into my lungs. I like it over here, where it's not too crowded but you can still feel the energy of people in the near distance. A car buzzes by a bit too close, and I gasp before realizing everything is okay.

Only, everything is *not* okay.

Not now, and not when another vehicle comes screeching to a halt next to me. The door bursts open, and a large man jumps out. I don't have time to think, to move, to scream, to run. Instead, a cloth is put over my face and the next thing I know, my eyes grow heavy and everything turns black.

I wake up sometime later in someone's house, on someone's couch. I blink through the fog of my vision and take in my surroundings. Nothing is familiar. And yet somehow, I know exactly where I am.

Ricardo's.

Who else would have kidnapped me in broad daylight?

I rise to my feet, my heart pounding hard as I try to locate an exit. There's a window on the far side of the room and a door that's closed. Jumping out the window is always an option, but not knowing which level I'm on, I decide against it and advance toward the door, swallowing harshly.

My throat goes completely dry when I reach for the handle and it turns, Ricardo stepping through toward me.

"Pet," he murmurs with that familiar scent of foul breath and cigars lingering.

Cautiously, I walk backward to get away from him but he reaches forward fast and latches onto my arm, his fingers digging into my skin.

"You're hurting me," I tell him and try to pull away.

He tightens his grasp and glares down at me. "If you think *this* hurts then you're going to be in for a surprise once I get started with you."

My heart skips a beat, and despite my dry mouth, my whole body flushes with heat.

Ricardo releases me in a huff. "You're making it difficult to find you, pet." He brings his hand to his chin and taps it. "And to find out you're associated with Dominic's crew. Oh, how very interesting."

"I haven't told them anything," I blurt out.

Ricardo laughs. "As if that would do you any good. They can't save you." He shakes his head. "No one can." He clears his throat and walks across the room to pour himself a drink from a crystal decanter. "You underestimate me, pet. It's rather insulting."

I lean against the chair I woke up in and use it to keep me upright.

"Drink?" Ricardo holds his glass in the air toward me.

"No," I tell him.

He pours me one anyway and brings it over to me. "Drink it."

I clench my jaw and take the glass from him and down it in one swallow. The brown liquid burns on the way down and I can't quite tell what it is. Whiskey, maybe. Whatever it is, it's gross compared to the stuff my friends drink. But why would I ever assume Ricardo has decent taste in anything when he's such a piece of shit himself?

"You haven't been home lately," he says, as if I don't know that.

"I was on my way there when you *kidnapped* me."

Ricardo grins but it doesn't quite reach his eyes, a sort of falseness to it. "Kidnapped is such a strong word. I'm simply checking on my investments."

I cross my arms over my chest. "I'm not your property yet."

Ricardo snarls and latches onto my chin, forcing my attention. "You are sorely mistaken, girl. You were mine from the very moment I set my sights on you. You'd bode well to accept this."

My stomach turns from the alcohol and his proximity, and I consider how pissed he would be if I threw up on his overpriced suit.

"I don't know why you're resisting so much, pet." He leans in closer and runs his nose along my face, breathing me in. "This could be a rather mutually beneficial proposition for you."

I glare at him and wish there was a box cutter near so I could drive it into his fucking jugular and watch him bleed out on this fancy rug.

"Whatever you want, I can buy it. I can take you shopping, get you..." He peers at my oversized clothes. "Something that fits." He releases my chin to run his finger along the sleeve of Alec's shirt I'm wearing. "Something sexier."

"I'm quite fine with what I have."

Ricardo narrows his gaze and hesitates before slapping me across the face with the back of his hand. "You do *not* speak to me in that tone, do you hear me?"

I clutch my cheek and tears well in my eyes. "I hear you."

"You hear me, what?" He tilts his evil face at me.

"I hear you, *sir*."

"That's my pet." He tips my chin with his index finger and then returns to the other side of the room to refill his glass. "Every Sunday between now and when our agreement is fully in place, you will meet me here. I will have various items that you must try on and model for me." He turns toward me and sips his drink, watching me over the rim.

My breath catches and the reality of the situation only continues to sink in. He owns me. And I don't really see a way out. I have three weeks of being his personal model before I become his sex doll to use as he pleases that he plans on impregnating the second he can.

But the sooner I get it over with, the sooner I can return to my life. Only...even if he gets me pregnant the first month, there's no telling whether it will be a boy. I might get lucky the first time but I still have to keep the pregnancy viable and spend close to a year carrying his offspring.

How will I ever be the same after something so terrible?

"You start today," he continues and points toward the door. "There's a bathroom at the end of the hall on the right. I want you to go change for me now and meet me back in here. If you try to run, if you try to evade me, I will have my men stop you and hold you down while I fuck you unconscious. Do you understand?"

I nod. "I understand." If I thought there was any getting out of here today, he just completely took that away from me. It's only a few outfits, that isn't enough to risk him assaulting me today when I have a guaranteed few weeks of freedom.

He flicks his fingers to shoo me. "Go then, pet. Hurry back. I'll be waiting for you." Ricardo repositions his groin, and the nausea I felt earlier rises to the surface again.

I leave out the way he told me, stepping into the hallway where no one else is. I glance in both directions and consider bolting to the left, but that's exactly what he wants me to do. He wants me to run. He wants me to cause problems. Because if I do, then he gets exactly what he wants sooner than later. I was bold for negotiating with him once before, but the time for that has passed, and if I want to make it out of this alive, I have to play along.

Even if it kills me a little inside.

Tiptoeing down the hall, I approach the last door on the

right and reach for the handle, turning it slowly and slipping inside.

"Who the fuck are you?" a girl says as she's pulling her satin pants up. She buttons them, flushes the toilet, and approaches while I stand there looking like a deer in the fucking headlights.

Finally, words appear from my mouth. "Sorry, I..." I crane my thumb in the direction I came.

The girl, who is very much a woman, probably close to my age, with gorgeous red hair that falls in waves on her shoulders, says, "Oh, you're probably daddy's new pet, aren't you?"

She washes her hands at the sink and wipes them on the towel hanging nearby.

"I should have known." She motions to the stacks of clothes on the chair in the corner. "Daddy always likes to play with his pets."

"He's your...dad?" I fold my arm over my chest and study the person in front of me.

She's nothing like him. She's pretty and well put together and despite not being completely near her, she doesn't stink so bad it makes me want to vomit. She almost looks...normal. Aside from the designer clothing from head to toe and the very put-together appearance.

The woman exhales and puts her hand on her hip, reminding me a bit of myself, just much classier. "Unfortunately, yes."

"What happened to the other girls, his pets?" I ask her without fully realizing the question is out of my mouth until it is.

She turns her nails over and looks at them, not paying me much attention. "Honestly, I don't know what daddy does with them, but if I had to guess..." She meets my gaze, her green eyes staring into mine. "He probably drives them mad."

I swallow but there's nothing there, so I end up coughing.

She walks past me and pats my shoulder. "I'm sure you'll be fine."

She and I both know that's a lie.

"What's your name?" I ask her before she slips out the door.

She glances back at me. "Daddy doesn't like it when I befriend his pets. Not after what happened last time."

"What happened last time?" I whisper, a bit afraid of the answer.

She leans in close. "We tried to kill him."

My eyes widen. "You tried?"

She lifts up her shirt to show a thick, long scar on her torso that's healed but still a bit pink. "Daddy didn't take too kindly to it." She doesn't say another word as she disappears from the large bathroom and into the hall, leaving me here with the image of him hurting his own daughter.

If he would do that to her, there's no telling what he has in store for me. Every time I start to think I might be able to figure out a way to get out of this, I'm shot down with the realization that there is no escaping a man like Ricardo. The only way out is death, and even then, he would haunt me by killing my parents and probably anyone I cared for.

With shaking hands, I go over to the pile of clothes and hold the first piece of fabric up. It's red and sheer and leaves next to nothing to the imagination. I step out of the comfort of Alec's sweatpants and peel the T-shirt off, slipping into the piece of lingerie Ricardo has laid out for me. I wipe at the tear that rolls down my cheeks and turn to face the mirror, my eyes unsure of the person staring back at me.

Who am I and who have I become? And what's worse is the person I'm going to evolve into when Ricardo has finished torturing me.

If what he's making me do isn't bad enough, I quite literally killed a man and that alone weighs heavily in my mind.

Have I always been capable of such terrible things or did life push me over the edge and drown me in darkness?

I guess I'll never know because it's too late to figure it out and it won't matter either way.

My sights land on the heels stacked next to the pile of clothes. Ricardo put them there for a reason, and I'd be an idiot to think he won't be expecting me to wear them when I walk back into that room.

Once I have them both on, I take one final glance in the mirror and shake my arms. "You've got this, Cora. You can do this."

I force my mind to reach the depths, the place where I hide all my darkest secrets and worst memories. I shove this in there with it and know that soon enough it will be over. I will get through this. I've gotten through worse things, and I can only imagine things will get harder. I won't let this sick, twisted man break me.

My cheek aches where he slapped me but I put that into my little box of forbidden thoughts and walk confidently down the hallway and into the room I left Ricardo in. I stroll right up to him, ignoring the way his lazy gaze trails up and down my nearly nude body, and do a full circle around the room, only stopping when I get to the side closest to the door I entered.

He licks his lips. "I figured red would be your color. I wasn't wrong." He circles his finger. "Do a spin for me, pet."

I comply, rolling my eyes when my back is to him.

"Mmm." Ricardo sloppily drinks his foul-tasting liquor.

There's no telling how much he drank while he was waiting for me, and I suddenly realize how foolish of me it was to leave him unattended with his alcohol. He's already shown me what kind of person he is sober; I can't fathom the things he'd do while intoxicated.

Ricardo messes with his groin, tugging his suit pants down to reposition himself. "Making me hard for you, pet. Good job."

Bile rises in my throat, and I force a tight-lipped smile.

Ricardo raises his brow. "Come over here and drain me, and I'll give you an extra week of freedom."

I consider his offer and ponder whether a week is worth touching his disgusting cock. I'm going to have to eventually, but I never imagined that day would be today. And after how my morning started, am I really going to taint the damn good sex I had with Alec with the image of Ricardo's saggy balls? At least with the deal we have now, I don't have to be scarred by the thought of him every single time I'm with another man. These last few weeks are meant to be enjoyed, not another form of torture.

"I'm good with our original arrangement," I say, unsure if this was a trick all along.

"Very well." He flips his hand toward the door. "Next outfit."

I don't let out the breath I'm holding until I get outside the room, my heart pounding so wildly it's like my forehead is pulsating. I hold onto the wall to steady and pull myself together. It's only a few more outfits, it can't be worse than the next to nothing I'm already wearing.

But once I change out of the red and into a scrappy black thing, I'm proven wrong when I return to Ricardo.

There he is, sitting on the chair I woke up in, his pants unbuttoned and his flaccid cock in his hand. He strokes it lazily and scoots down onto his seat, his eyes not daring to look away from me.

"Come closer, pet," he murmurs. "Let me see you."

I walk over, my head held high, not letting him see me bothered. I do a spin when I reach his side and continue around the back of his chair to come to the other side. I get close but not within arm's length and stop, my hand finding my hip and the other laying slack against my slightly trembling frame.

"Such perky tits, pet. I can't wait until they're mine." His cock hardens in his hand, but it barely fills his entire palm.

At least when he has his way with me, he's working with potentially the smallest dick I've ever seen in my entire life. Even including the small penis humiliation videos my friends and I cackled about in high school.

"Next outfit," he demands. "But make it quick or I'll make you pay."

I leave the room, my bottom lip quivering once I'm in the hallway. Slipping out of the thin black ensemble, I throw on another red thing that takes me a second to figure out which thin straps go where. I'm not entirely sure I have it figured out, but it will have to do for now. These things should at least come with directions if there isn't going to be an obvious front or back, or hell, top or bottom.

I wipe another rogue tear and march my way down the hall, eager to get this entire thing over with. I complete the same pass around the room, spinning on one side and going to the other to do the same while Ricardo continues to jerk himself off.

"Come here, pet."

"But you said..."

"I know what I said." He grits his teeth. "I'm not going to touch you. And you're not going to touch me. I just want to...smell you."

I inch forward, closing the distance between us until I'm just inches from him and his gross cock.

He bends at the waist, his tiny dick still in his grasp as he lowers his face to my center and takes an exaggeratedly deep breath in. "Fuck, pet. Your cunt is sweet." Ricardo leans back, rests his head and closes his eyes as he picks up his pace, aggressively beating himself off. His lips part and instead of picturing him like this, I think about slitting his throat and watching him bleed out. Anything to rid myself of this nightmare living out in front of me.

Without looking, Ricardo reaches to the table next to him and fumbles until he plucks a tissue out of the holder. He returns his pace and furiously jacks off into the tissue, his face contorting with what I'm assuming is pleasure.

That's what I'm going to have to endure for the foreseeable future. His repulsive orgasm face.

"Pretty soon, pet, you're going to be on the receiving end of this cock." He cleans himself off and tosses the tissue onto the table.

I pinch my mouth shut as my nostrils flare. Is there anything he does that doesn't completely disgust me?

Taking a step back, I bump into the table and nearly knock myself down. I steady myself in these excessively high heels and grow curious about when this madness is going to end, at least today. I don't know how much more of this I can take without vomiting on the man or bludgeoning him with anything I can get my sweaty palms on.

Ricardo stands and tucks his shirt into his pants before buttoning them. He clears his throat. "This was fun."

A knock sounds on the door but it doesn't open.

"Come in," he calls out to the person on the other side.

His daughter pokes her head inside. "Daddy, you have a call, it's urgent."

Ricardo focuses on me, his stare sending a chill up my spine. "Every Sunday, you hear me? Be here at ten sharp or our deal is off."

I nod. "Of course."

He narrows his gaze.

"I mean, of course, sir."

Ricardo pats my head. "Good, pet."

My jaw clenches, and it's everything I can do not to break every tooth in my mouth at how tightly I'm squeezing it shut. I want to scream. I want to cry. I want to rip the fabric off my body since it's doing nothing to cover me and use it to strangle him.

"London can walk you out. I suppose you'll have no issue

getting one of those, what are they called...Uber's?" He leaves me to walk toward the door, fixing his shirt and suit jacket on the way. Ricardo pauses and looks his daughter up and down. "You think that's going to fetch you a husband?" He scoffs. "If you're going to spend my money, you might as well have a little taste."

"What's wrong with my outfit?" She glances down at herself but Ricardo wastes no time wrapping his hand around her throat and tilting her toward him.

"Other than everything?" His nostrils flare and even from where I stand, the stench of his breath lingers in my memory and no doubt assaults his poor daughter. "You disgust me." Ricardo shoves her on release and slams her into the doorframe. "Get out of my way." He leaves without another word, the silence deafening in his wake.

I walk over and reach for her. "Are you okay?"

She shakes me off. "I'm fine." London returns upright and dusts herself off. "Nothing I'm not already used to." She pats her red hair and no doubt does the very thing I do all the time, shoves the trauma away in a little folder in the recess of her mind.

It's not hard to notice she's so like me in this sense.

Honestly, I see a lot of myself in her, and it's a bit frightening to gaze into the mirror of her tortured eyes staring back at me.

"Are you?" She points to my face which is no doubt still beet red from where Ricardo hit me.

I nod. "I'm fine."

"You'll probably want to change before you leave." London opens the cracked door and motions for me to go ahead of her.

I steady a breath and make my way down the hall with her on my tail. My heels click against the floor and overpower the sound of my thudding heart. My torture might be done for the day, but the time spent here will haunt me long after I'm gone.

Once I'm at the bathroom door, I pause as London stops outside. "You can come in," I tell her. It's not like I didn't barge in while she was peeing and she isn't looking at me practically naked. We've only just met and somehow our relationship is strangely intimate already.

London doesn't bother questioning me, yet she strolls in behind me and latches the door. She goes to the oversized vanity and peers at herself in the mirror, primping her hair and smoothing out the bright red lipstick on her bottom lip.

I'm not entirely sure why I invited her inside. Maybe it was because I don't want to be alone, not in this house, not with her dad prowling about. It's not like she can protect me, but there's something calming about being near someone other than him. I can't imagine how she must feel when she's trapped in this mansion with him.

I fight the scrappy garment I'm wearing and huff when I can't quite figure out how to get it off.

London sighs and walks over. "May I?" She points to my back.

"Yeah." I go limp in front of her.

She tugs at one of the straps and pulls my arm through it. "There. That should help."

"Thanks," I tell her and finish getting out of the stupid contraption. I make quick work of throwing Alec's T-shirt over my head and savoring the comfort of his oversized clothing.

I'm slipping into my sneakers when she speaks.

"So, what are you in for?"

I blink at her. "What do you mean?"

London crosses her arms. "I can't imagine you're doing this for fun. I'm guessing it's money, but I can't fathom a price I'd settle with to do whatever it is he has in mind." She squints her eyes. "Leverage of some sort. He has something on you."

"My mom," I admit.

"He *has* your mom?"

"Sort of, yeah."

"Like he kidnapped her? Who is she? What does he want with her?"

I shake my head. "No, it's not like that. I don't think. She's sick." I tuck my hair behind my ears and try to make sense of the story for her. "My dad found some experimental treatment or something, I don't know exactly, but it wasn't cheap. He went to your dad and defaulted on payment."

"How does that involve you?" She taps her fingers on her crossed arms.

"I was there when he came for my dad. He threatened to kill him. Had a gun to his head. Said he'd let my mom die, too. I didn't have any other choice..."

London raises her head slowly like she's finally understanding. "You offered yourself in exchange for your parents' lives."

"Yep."

"What's that like?"

I furrow my brows. "What?"

"Having parents you'd sacrifice everything for?"

"I mean, look where it got me." I shrug. "I haven't seen my mom since this all started. I don't even know if she's still alive. And my dad...I can't stand being near him, not anymore. Not after he lied and kept this from me. Not after he let me give myself to such a..."

London laughs dryly. "You can say it. You're not going to hurt my feelings."

"I shouldn't be saying any of this. He probably has this place bugged. And what happened to us not being able to talk? I thought you said he'd flip his shit."

"First of all, Daddy is highly paranoid so there are no bugs in the house. He's too afraid someone could hack them. Secondly, I have no doubt that this is a test. After the shit I pulled with the last girl, he's probably convinced I won't do it again. He almost killed me. The only reason he didn't was because I'm an asset to him. The moment you no longer provide that man value, he has no issue in getting rid of you. It's not a lie that he doesn't want me to be friendly with his pets but when he told you my name and said I'd help you out of the house, he put the ball in our court. He gets off on people making mistakes, because then it justifies him punishing them. And that's all he really wants, is to punish people."

"He's a sick man," I say.

"Yeah, well, that's Daddy." London exhales and motions toward me. "Do you have everything?"

"Yeah." I shove my hand into my pocket to confirm my phone is there and realize somewhere along the way I lost my clutch. I had it when I left Alec's so either the man who kidnapped me took it or I lost it on the street when he nabbed me. Either way, that means I'm without my wallet.

And losing that means I lost my ID, my credit card, and the little bit of cash I took to the game yesterday.

"What's wrong?" London asks me.

"Nothing I..." I chew at the inside of my lip in an attempt to distract the tears from building in my eyes.

London comes closer, her floral perfume the best-smelling thing in this entire place. "Listen, we've practically already seen each other's vaginas and are being tortured by the same man. Just tell me what it is."

"I lost my clutch."

"Was it Prada or something?"

I chuckle and wipe at my nose. "No. It was some cheap thing from the mall."

"I don't see the problem."

"It had my ID and money in it. I'll have to call and cancel my credit card."

"Oh." London snaps her fingers and reaches between her boobs. "Here." She digs into a tiny little compartment and pulls out a single, crisp, one-hundred-dollar bill. "It's not much but it should help, right?"

I meet her gaze. "I can't take that."

She shoves the cash into my hand. "It's my emergency fund, you know, in case I ever fucking escape this place. I'll replenish it. No big deal."

"Thank you," I tell her, the words meaning more than she's probably aware. "Wait...why can't you leave now? You're an adult, aren't you?"

"Twenty-three to be exact." London adjusts her cleavage and fixes her shirt. "Part of the whole daddy not following through with killing me was so that he could use me as a business transaction."

"What?" My eyes go wide. "You're not serious."

London makes her way toward the door. "Yep. Selling me off to the highest bidder and my luck, the biggest creep, too."

"Is that what he meant about your outfit and finding a husband?" I follow her toward the exit.

"He's getting rather impatient." London stops at the door and presses her finger to her ruby lips.

I keep quiet as we walk side by side down the hall and into a grand entryway. I want to ask her more questions, to dig up more information about her and her shady father, but she asked me to hush and I have to respect that, especially after what she's done for me when she didn't have to.

At first sight, I thought London was a bitch, but it turns out she's in just as bad of a situation, if not worse than me. I don't know if I'd be as kind and generous as her if I had to spend my entire life with that bastard. I'm a couple weeks into meeting him, and I've already killed someone and questioned quite a few of my morals. I can't imagine what twenty-three years would do.

London opens the oversized front door. "Good luck," she tells me, and even though we just met, I'm convinced she means it.

"You, too," I reply as I step onto the front porch.

We exchange a final glance before she closes the door and severs the bit of comfort I found with her. In another life I could see us being friends, having fun together, gossiping about boys and brands.

But our fates have already been sealed in this lifetime, and we no longer belong to ourselves, not now, not ever.

17
MILLER

I pace the large boardroom in our West Coast office, picking up my phone and putting it back down countless times over.

"Get it together, man," I tell myself.

Why am I so nervous to make a phone call when my life is filled with crime and danger on a daily basis?

The thing buzzes in my hand, and I ignore the unknown number. That's a problem for another time.

A knock sounds on the door, a sweet older woman on the other side. There's no telling how long she's been watching me pace, the floor-to-ceiling walls of glass providing me with no shelter from prying eyes.

I motion for her to come in. "What is it, Marjorie?"

Her gaze stays toward the floor. "I'm sorry to interrupt, sir. I wanted to confirm your two o'clock with Mr. Adler."

"You didn't interrupt, but yes, I'm still on to meet with Dominic this afternoon."

"Very well. Thank you, sir."

"Marjorie?" I catch her before she leaves, her eyes darting up briefly but not meeting mine.

"Yes, sir?"

"You can call me Miller. No need for the formalities."

She smiles politely and nods. "Thank you, sir Miller."

The second she shuts the door behind her I yank out my phone and hit the button I've been avoiding the last half hour and press the device to my ear. It rings once, twice, three times.

Just when I'm convinced it's going to go to voicemail, it connects.

"Hello?" Her voice is a bit strained and cracks.

"Cora, hey, it's Miller."

"Oh." Cora's tone shifts and she sniffles. "Hey, what's up?"

"What's wrong?" I ask her. "Are you crying?"

"No, no," she blurts out. "It's my allergies. They're really bad this time of year."

Only, I checked the weather this morning and saw that pollen counts are at an all-time low and probably shouldn't be impacting anyone. Who am I to question or disagree with her though? Maybe she's not lying and she has some rare allergen that isn't listed on the weather app I was checking.

"Are you sure? I'm here if you ever need someone to talk to." I regret the words the second they're out of my mouth. It isn't that I don't want to be her soundbox, but she barely knows me, why would she trust me that easily?

"Thanks, but no, really, I'm okay." She sniffles again and my fist balls up at the idea of someone making her cry. "What can I help you with?"

"Oh, right. I called because I was hoping we could get together." I fidget the back of one of the boardroom chairs.

"Yeah, of course. We need to discuss the designs."

"Among other things," I add. Like the fact that she's become a borderline obsession of mine and despite doing everything I can, I can't get her out of my head. Every thought circles back to her. Would she like this? Would she prefer that? What would she think of this restaurant? Has she ever been to Venice? I find myself internet stalking her, and on occasion, in real life stalking her.

I know her drink order at the coffee shop near her work, the sections in a bookstore she gravitates toward, the type of salts she uses in her bath.

Okay, so I broke into her parents' house and went through her things...sue me.

I thought stalking her to find out more about her would help satiate my obsession with her but all it's done is fuel it even more.

"That, too," she says, distracting me from my rampant mind.

"How about tomorrow after you get off work?"

"Yeah, I mean, I don't have anything else going on. I was going to see if June wanted to get together, but I can do that Tuesday."

"We can do another day if you'd like."

"No. No. I'm good with tomorrow." A car horn blares on her end.

"Where are you? Do you need a ride?"

"I'm just outside the Haven District. I'm not too far from my house."

"Cora...that's still a far walk. I can send a car right now."

"Really, Miller. I'm fine. I've been trying to get my steps in any way."

When Cora isn't at the office, she spends her workdays walking million-dollar apartments and home goods stores to pick out the perfect pieces for her clients. She quite literally does nothing *but* walk. Another lie I can't quite question her about.

"If you change your mind, I'm a call away."

"Thank you. I appreciate it." She clears her throat. "Hey, you wouldn't happen to know anyone at the DMV, do you?"

"I do actually, why? What's up?"

"I can't seem to find my wallet and it had my ID in it. Being that it's Sunday and I have work all week..."

I cut her off. "Say no more. I'll have it taken care of immediately. Did you lose anything else?"

She sighs. "Just some cash...and my credit card."

"Call and have it shut off as soon as you can. I'll handle everything else and let you know when it's on the way."

"Thank you, Miller. I really appreciate it."

"Of course. Anything for you." I realize the second I say it how forward that must have come out. I ache for her to understand the lengths I'd go for her, but I don't want to come across as too much, too soon.

"What did you have in mind for tomorrow?"

"I was thinking of The Palazzo. I can send a car to get you from work?"

"Oh wow," she says. "I've heard that place is super exclusive."

"We can go somewhere else if you prefer."

Marjorie walks past the open windows of the boardroom with a stack of folders in her grasp. She's entirely too old to still be working, especially in a place like this. I'm going to have to do some digging and see why they haven't retired her yet.

"The Palazzo sounds wonderful." Cora's line cuts out a little and for a second it sounds like she's running. "Miller?"

"Yeah?"

A knock draws my attention to the door Marjorie entered not too long ago. This time it's a younger guy with a patchy beard.

"Could you stay on the phone with me another minute? This alley by the diner gives me the creeps."

I press my finger into the air to signal to the guy to wait.

"Of course. I'll stay on as long as you need me to."

"Thanks." More muffling comes through. "I take it you're back in town if you're wanting to get together tomorrow?"

"Yeah, I am. I'm sorry it took me a while to get back to you.

The trip took longer than expected. I hated having to leave you like that."

"Oh, it's totally okay. I've been busy since then anyway, you know?"

"And Silver took good care of you?" I hate that I wasn't there for her and another man was, but at least he's highly skilled and trained in that sort of thing. There's never been a job that he hasn't been capable of taking care of, so I felt fully confident in tasking him with keeping her safe.

"Yeah, he's great, actually. Really nice guy."

I laugh. "Wait, are you serious?"

Cora giggles, too. "I am totally serious. Did you know he doesn't have a single television in his entire apartment?"

"You went to his apartment?" I figured he would take her to one of the safe houses or to her own home, not his.

"I, uh, didn't have anywhere to clean up. I didn't want to involve June or the guys. I kind of panicked and he offered, and I figured if you trusted him enough I could, too. I hope I wasn't wrong."

"No, not at all. Silver's a reliable guy. One of our best. I'm just surprised." I don't add that I'm a tiny bit jealous, too.

"Well, he did a great job of keeping my mind off things. Sorry, I feel like I'm being cryptic. I don't know how much I can or can't say over the phone."

"We can talk more about this tomorrow, if you want."

"Yeah, that'll be good. I'll bring the portfolio and we can go over designs. But hey, I'm past the creepy alley, I can let you go. Thanks for keeping me company."

"Are you sure you don't want me to stay on any longer?"

"It's okay, my battery is dying anyway."

I shake my head. Lost her wallet. No ID. No cash or credit card. And a phone battery that's dying on her walk home. Can she stress me out anymore?

"Will you text me and let me know you made it home okay, at least? I worry about you."

"Little ol' me? I'll be fine. But yes, I can shoot you a text."

It's either she does that or I drive every block between the Haven District and her parents' house looking for her.

"Thanks, Cora."

I keep my finger in the air, the poor guy outside the boardroom waiting semi-impatiently.

"Talk to you later, Miller."

"Bye."

"Bye."

I don't hang up. Instead, I listen to the static between us and wonder where exactly she is and try to trace her steps in my head. I'm not completely familiar with this side of town but I'm knowledgeable enough to know she shouldn't be out there walking around by herself. Without a weapon. Without someone to protect her.

Hell, look at what happened at her work. A place where she's supposed to be guaranteed safety. Yet it was her very boss who pushed the limits and ended up with stab wounds all over his torso...every single one of them rightfully deserved. If she hadn't ended him, I would have tied him up and had one of Dominic's finest men guide me in delivering the maximum amount of torture. I've been known to fuck a person up here or there, but it's been for business, not for pleasure. And getting my hands on someone who even considered harming a hair on Cora's beautiful head would absolutely be for reasons completely foreign to my day to day.

"Miller?" Cora says through the receiver.

"I'm still here," I tell her, my voice low.

"Okay, I'm hanging up for real this time." She giggles slightly, and it's the most adorable thing my ears have ever been graced with.

"Okay."

"Bye."

"Bye," I repeat.

It takes her at least twenty seconds before she finally gives in and ends the call, a piece of me staying stuck in limbo with her there forever.

But the rest of me remains here, rooted in place, with meetings and business deals and fires that constantly need put out. I start with the one standing outside my door. I wave the guy in and he enters without hesitation.

"Sir, I apologize for the interruption, but Dominic wants to meet with you now. It's urgent."

I run my hand along my jaw and shift my mind back into work mode. I can't allow Cora to consume all my thoughts. Or at least not one hundred percent of them. "What's going on?" I move toward him and snap my fingers to get him to walk with me.

"It was another shipment, sir. He's calling an emergency meeting."

"With whom?" I glance at him briefly on my way through the hall.

"You and his chief of security, sir."

"Coen Hayes."

"Yes, sir."

I stop in my tracks and face him; he comes to a screeching halt next to me. "Can I trust you to do something for me?"

He nods eagerly. "Anything, sir."

"First of all, stop calling me sir, we're probably the same age. Second, I need you to contact our connection at the DMV and get a driver's license issued for Coraline Price. Twelve seventy-seven Ashwood Drive. Do you need to write this down?"

He shakes his head and taps it. "I have it up here."

"Very well." I pull the wallet out of my pocket and slide out the heavy black card and hand it to him. "I need you to add her as an authorized user. Ask Marjorie to help you, she should have all of my credentials. And..." I finger through the hundreds and split the stack in half, giving him the biggest chunk. "I want the license, this Amex, and the cash delivered to her house this evening. I want it personally handed to her; do you hear me?"

"I won't disappoint you." He takes everything from me and that's when I realize I have no idea who he is.

"What's your name?"

"Daniel. Daniel Young."

"Don't fuck this up, Daniel Young." I slap him on the shoulder and take off toward the elevator. "Shit," I mutter while glancing over my shoulder. "Where am I meeting them?"

"The Manor, sir." His eyes widen as soon as he catches his mistake. "Shit," he mumbles.

I chuckle. "It's alright, Daniel." I point at him on my way out. "Don't fuck it up. I'm counting on you."

A few minutes later, I'm climbing into the driver's side of the blacked-out sports car I had delivered this morning. If I'm going to be spending more time on the West Coast, I need a car that's actually mine instead of relying on one of Dom's drivers. Our career is a bit too dangerous to risk using one of those ride apps and I haven't been here enough to hire my own team. I use Dom's when I need to because I trust him but trust in this industry is paper thin when you can never be too sure who's willing to stab you in the back.

The car revs to life, and I shift it into gear, speeding across town in a hurry to get to The Manor.

My thoughts flicker between Cora and business the entire drive, Cora coming out on top every single time.

I check my phone and notice two missed calls from Dom and one from Simon, no texts from Cora. Exhaling, I plead with the universe to get her home safely. There's no telling what kind of trouble she could run into between where she was and where she needed to be. Maybe I should buy her a car, too, so she doesn't have to do so much walking. And if it's steps she's worried about, I'll escort her or buy her the nicest treadmill known in existence.

After what Johnny and Claire went through and how many times the guys almost lost June, I can't be too careful with Cora. The only problem is, she's not mine to protect, at least not yet. Maybe one day she will be. And tomorrow will be the first stepping stone in making that happen. She thinks I want to meet her about business, about the interior design in the unit she's in charge of decorating...when what I really want is to take her on a date, to court her, to see if she'd be willing to take a chance on me.

I've tried so hard to withstand and disregard my feelings for her. I heeded Simon's warning and heard Magnus out when he said he was just trying to protect Cora, but they have no idea how I feel. They got the girl. I didn't. How are they okay calling the shots about my love life when they involved an outsider and everything worked out fine for them?

And hell, there's four of them sharing *one* girl. I'd build a whole army if it meant I could have Cora in my life.

I press on the brakes in front of The Manor and pull behind that obnoxious Bentley parked out front and roll my eyes.

Ricardo Gardella. Literal scum of the earth, piece of shit.

I don't know a single fucking person that doesn't want him dead, and yet, here he is, alive and well, plaguing us all with his presence.

If putting a bullet between his eyes wouldn't end with me dying, too, I'd do it in a heartbeat. But he's got this weird kind of old-school-been-around-forever power that was passed on from his father and the next. It's a generational thing and despite him having next to no business sense and absolutely no tact, he holds a great deal of power. Enough to keep him aligned with just the right people and far out of everyone's reach.

I hop out of the seat and slam the door shut behind me, clicking the button on the key fob to lock it.

The valet walks toward me, but I don't stop. "Come get me if it needs to be moved." I slide a hundred into his hand on the way by and continue past everyone standing around the area smoking and chatting.

I'm not even through the revolving door when Ricardo spots me.

"Miller, son, it's great to see you." He hacks as he approaches and wipes his hand on his chest.

It would be great if the universe would do us a solid and take him out from natural causes instead of torturing us with his continued existence.

"Listen, Ric, I'm in rather a hurry." I point through the lobby in hopes that will be enough to get him off my tail.

"I won't keep ya, son. I just wanted to tell you, if you needed any help with your *problem* that I'd be more than happy to provide my assistance. For a price, obviously."

I exhale and turn toward him. "What problem?"

"I think you and I both know what the problem is. That's why you're here, isn't it?" He coughs again, and I wish I was farther away, so I didn't have to smell the stench of his breath. "You're meeting with Dominic and Hayes?"

I step a bit closer to him and square my shoulders. "You have no idea what you're talking about."

Ricardo throws both hands palm up toward me. "Okay. But don't say I didn't warn you. If you don't get this taken care of soon, it's not a good look for the east or west coast sectors. Maybe merging together wasn't the best idea after all."

"I'll keep it in mind. Now, if you'll excuse me." I don't bother letting him get another word in. I turn on my heel and march down the corridor to the private area Dom usually has us meet in when we're here.

This might be a criminal hotel with plenty of influential people, but with Dominic in charge of the West Coast sector and me running the East Coast, we're the most powerful people in this building. Sure, different people have different ranks or pull or influence, but if there was a war, Dom and I would come out on top, *especially* now that we've aligned.

I knock on the door twice, pause, and add another solid knock. It's silly, but it's effective.

The door opens a second later, Coen Hayes greeting me on the other side. His face is in its usual manner. Serious, stoic, and a bit like he has a stick up his ass. He's a strangely pretty man, like in a very beautiful kind of way, but damn is he the grumpiest and most bitter dude I have ever met. The only time I have ever seen him soft is with June, and according to the stories I've been told, even that took some time.

Apparently, June's the reason he turned into a major grump ass in the first place. They were childhood friends and were tragically separated. He was in love with her then, and the relationship ending fucked them both up badly. June turned into a stone-cold bitch and Coen, well, he turned into a murderous psychopath. Who knew fate would bring them back together ten years later when she was sleeping with his two closest confidants? Luckily it seems to have worked out, but I can't imagine how difficult it was to get to where they are today.

And even though he's gotten the love of his life back, he's still a royal dick. But damn is he good at his job.

"You're late," he groans.

"Traffic," I lie and step into the decently sized room.

"Thanks for meeting us." Dominic stands from his seat, his suit jacket folded neatly and laid over the chair next to him. His shirt cuffs are rolled up his forearms and his hair seems a bit disheveled. Still, he's properly put together, a hell of a lot more than Coen and I are, just not his typical over-the-top perfect Dominic.

It's sort of terrifying how orderly he is on a normal basis. Usually not a hair is out of place, nor is a wrinkle in sight on a single piece of his wardrobe.

226

Dominic has probably been in the life as long, if not longer than Ricardo, but the difference between the two is that Dominic earned every bit of his success and Ricardo had his handed to him. Dominic is a self-made man and did it through nothing short of sheer determination and a fuck ton of grit.

He might be an asshole to deal with on occasion, but I respect him entirely and truly admire his business ethic.

"Of course." I approach and shake his hand, his callouses rubbing against mine. "Talk to me. Tell me what's going on."

Dom points to a chair. "Have a seat. Can I get you a drink?"

"I can get it." I grab his empty glass on the way. "Refill?"

He nods stiffly and settles into his seat. "Thanks."

I make quick work at the liquor station on the far side of the room, pouring us both a hefty three fingers of Hawk's Mark, and return to where Dom and Coen are sitting. I slide his glass to him and take a sip of mine as I sit, too.

Dom shoots a look at Coen, and for a split second I wonder if they've somehow learned telepathy, because a second later, Coen opens his pretty-boy mouth.

"We lost another shipment today," Coen tells me.

"Which one?"

"The guns."

"The decoy or the actual shipment?" I hold my breath in anticipation of the answer I'm already sure is coming.

"We wouldn't have called a meeting over the decoy." Coen's jaw clenches and he adds, "We have a mole."

I lean forward, circle my glass, and swallow some of the golden liquid down. It's smooth and everything you would expect from a wickedly expensive bourbon. "I think we have another problem, too," I admit to them.

Coen is the first to speak up. "What kind of a problem?"

Dominic twirls his glass and waits for me to answer.

"Ricardo." I glance between them.

"What about him?" Dominic asks.

"He stopped me on the way in here. He knew about our meeting. He claims he knows about our *problem*. He offered to help."

Coen chuckles dryly. "At what cost?"

"Exactly," I reply. "But that's my point. He's aware of our business and offering to help in exchange for money. It wouldn't surprise me if he's the one creating the issues and turning around and lending a hand to benefit from them. How else would he know?"

Dominic sighs and rubs his greying beard. "I hate that guy."

"You and everyone else in this town," I confirm.

"He has everything to gain from it. Word is that his little empire is crumbling and he's desperate for an influx of cash. He's tried to sell me his daughter on numerous occasions." I take another drink of my bourbon and let it soothe my raging nerves. I still haven't heard from Cora and the clock is ticking on how long I'm going to give her before I storm out of here and go looking for her.

"He asked me, too," Dominic tells us. "Well, he more so was inquiring about leads on who would want her and how much to ask for, but he joked that he was willing to cut me a deal since I already had a woman."

My skin crawls at just how disgusting of a human he is. I can't believe his daughter hasn't smothered him with a pillow in his sleep just to get away from the fucker. But I'm no fool to understand a man like that has the means to crawl his way out of a grave and get revenge.

"What did you tell him?" I ask Dominic.

"All but that he was fucking crazy." Dominic swallows a heavy swig of his bourbon. "He's trying to get five hundred million out of her."

"If the money weren't going into his pocket, I'd do it just to get him to shut up and go away." Although I'm not stupid enough to realize funding him would only make him that much more annoying. "So, what are we going to do?"

Coen leans forward. "Without proof, no one is going to believe us, so it won't justify making a move on him. The first step is we need to find the mole and get him to talk. Maybe then we'll have the leverage we need, but until then, we have to continue with business as usual."

"You don't think we should halt deliveries?" I consider what that would mean for business, and even delaying a day would be detrimental, but so is hemorrhaging our funds because of lost shipments.

"We've had to deal with this before," Dominic says. "We got through it then, and we'll get through it now."

"Yeah, we can't afford to pause...the shipments going through will have to offset the loss," Coen adds and then looks directly at me. "How long will you be in town?"

I shrug one shoulder. "As long as I need to be."

"Good," he says. "We're going bare bones until this gets under control so we'll need all the help we can get."

"Should I bring in a team from the east?" Honestly, if I brought Claire in, she'd sniff out the mole in twelve seconds and get us back to business in no time.

"No. The less people involved, the better. Easier to track loose ends." Coen pulls his phone out of his pocket and pushes a few buttons on the screen.

I yank mine out too, my heart dropping at the lack of text from Cora.

Dominic clears his throat. "You bought The Wellerton."

I can't quite tell if he's asking a question or simply making a statement. Either way, I confirm, "Yeah," without looking up from my cell.

"Any particular reason?" Dominic asks.

"Diversifying my investment portfolio."

Dominic raises his head slowly and lowers it. "I see." He

doesn't buy my response, but I don't blame him, I wouldn't believe me.

I sigh and meet his inquisitive stare. "It was for personal reasons."

"Would those personal reasons have anything to do with a certain bubbly blonde?" Dom scratches his chin as he studies me with great scrutiny. There's no way I'm getting out of this one.

"Maybe." I set my phone face down, and as soon as I do, it buzzes. I turn it over immediately and relief washes completely over me.

Cora: Hey, I'm home. Sorry, I jumped right in the shower and forgot to text.

I thumb a quick response.

Me: Glad you made it. Let me know if you need anything else.

Cora types immediately, and it's strange to feel my heart patter the way that it is.

Cora: Thanks, I appreciate you x.

I stare at that little x so long that my vision burns.

"Everything okay over there?" Dominic inquires.

"Yeah." I put my phone down and focus on him. "What were we talking about?"

"You and Cora," he says bluntly.

"Oh."

I don't miss Coen's jaw clenching like he's a pit bull ready to attack and rip out my throat at a moment's notice. He doesn't say anything, but I can feel his disapproval radiating off him like a redhead at the beach.

Dominic downs the rest of his bourbon in one swift motion and sets his glass on the table a bit aggressively. He scoots his chair forward and looks right at me. "I get it, I really do. We went through it with June. The more we tried to stay away, the harder it was. But let me warn you, once you cross that line, there's no going back. So, make damn sure this is what you want. That she is what you want. It's not fair to her to put her at risk like that without certainty."

"I understand," I tell him, because I do. I've thought about this so much it made my fucking brain ache.

"How much do you even know about her?" Coen says, his tone as calloused as Dominic's hands.

I almost laugh but I catch myself. If only they knew how much I knew about her...maybe they wouldn't question me. But I can't tell them that without outing myself as a total psycho, and I'd rather keep that secret tucked away for no one to find out.

"It's not about that, Hayes, and you of all people should recognize that," Dominic snaps at Coen. "I barely spoke to June for weeks, and I knew deep in my bones that she was the one. Did I try to ignore it? Without a doubt but look what good that did. It put her in danger. It nearly got her killed, multiple times. It distracted us during one of the most pivotal moments of my career. I was a stubborn fool and I almost lost her." Dominic stares directly at Coen. "You did, too."

Coen rolls his eyes and ignores everything Dominic just said, focusing on me. "She went on a double date with June and Simon the other day."

My hand does that thing where it balls into a fist without me meaning for it to happen. I do my best not to let on how intensely bothered that immediately made me. How dare some stranger get to spend time with her in an intimate setting, especially with two people she cares deeply for. June and Simon are like her brother and sister.

"With Alec," Coen adds.

A weird sense of relief washes over me. Do I want Alec to be taking my girl on dates? No, absolutely not. But if she has to be spending her time with anyone, at least I know she's safe with him, cared for with him, and treated with kindness and respect.

I'd be an idiot if I didn't recognize Alec was madly in love with Cora, too. I see it plain as day because it's like I'm looking in the same love-struck mirror. I don't want her to love him back, but I wouldn't blame her, Alec is a great guy. He couldn't give her everything I could, but in his own way, maybe he could give her more, or things I couldn't.

Alec could give her a *normal* life. One free of crime and illicit activities that would only put her further in danger. Alec is in our world now but he's doing his best to get an education and a career that doesn't involve being a criminal. With him, Cora could go on and fulfill her dreams and not have to worry about looking over her shoulder every time she steps outside. She could love and trust and build a family with him, safe and out of harm's way.

I can never give her that.

And even though the thought of her choosing someone else breaks my heart, I have to be okay with the fact that maybe I'm not what's best for Cora.

18
CORA

$\mathcal{I}$ lie in bed with my hair wet and my blanket tucked tightly to my chest. I don't want to be here. Not in this room, this house, or this city. A strong part of me wishes I wasn't here at all. Anywhere. I don't wish to die, I just don't want to be alive, either. What a fucking contradiction.

And with those thoughts, guilt creeps its way like a shadow in a dark alley into my soul.

My life isn't terrible. Others have it worse. I shouldn't complain.

I slide my hand down to where my phone sits under the covers and pull it out to swipe open the screen. My eyes skim the texts from Miller and settle on the last exchange from Alec.

It was a long one, detailing how much fun he had at the game and how he can't wait to see me again. Plus, a little section about how when I rode his face it was the best experience of his life.

Alec is perfect. He's in touch with his emotions, he's able to communicate them clearly, and even though it took him what felt like forever to finally confess how he felt about me, he's been nothing but sweet and kind the entire time. Even when we were just *friends*, he never made me feel like I wasn't important or special.

And damn is he hot.

Fuck, when he took his shirt off and carried me to the shower, I thought I had died and gone to heaven. His muscles were apparent under his shirt, but the second it was off, each hard line was exposed and I couldn't help but drool a little bit. Especially when he picked me up with ease, pressing my naked body to his. I ran my fingers over his chiseled chest and circled the small dagger tattooed near his heart. I wanted to ask him what it meant, but my words were failing me at seeing him so...exposed.

He had just fucked me senseless and turned me into complete blubber.

Alec even spent his time with me in the shower, helping me wash my body and kissing me every chance he got. I felt cherished, adored, loved.

But as much as I've been waiting my entire life for someone like him to come along, I'm not stupid enough to think it will last. Not because of anything he'd do, but because of me.

If it isn't my *situation* that will ruin things, it will be the darkness I keep tucked away.

I cling to this idea that I want to be in a relationship and experience all the good and bad that comes with it, but deep down, it scares the ever-loving shit out of me. People change their minds. People put on an act. People lie and cheat and leave. And if I showed Alec the real me, the one I keep buried under the bright smiles and bubbly exterior, he would be no different than anyone else in my life.

Maybe that's why I sabotage every good thing that comes my way, because I don't think I'm worthy of it? But are the things ever really good or just some figment of my imagination that temporarily soothes the dull ache in my chest?

Maybe the people in my life never hurt me after all, and I'm the reason things go south.

Maybe *I'm* the red flag.

I thumb my screen and pull up the text thread with Silver.

The last thing he said to me was that he was hoping I was okay. I hadn't responded to his last three texts and as much as I wanted to, I couldn't bring myself to follow through. Silver is great, too, in his own way. He's a brute, and definitely the oldest man I've ever been with, but with that comes this sort of elegant, sophisticated nature I've never known before. He's dominant and commanding and somehow gentle and passionate. Not to mention hot as fuck.

Silver, in appearance, is *completely* different than Alec. Both are pretty tall, that's for sure, but Silver is broad and muscular in a way that isn't built from going to the gym like Alec. Silver's hair is a beautiful shade of salt and pepper, and his beard is the perfect length. It doesn't come off like he's trying too hard, but it's maintained enough to recognize he puts in effort to his appearance. His hands are strong and powerful and if I were anyone other than me, I'd probably be afraid of him strictly based on his looks.

When he stepped into the apartment I had just murdered a man in, I didn't know what to think. How could such a gorgeous man be capable of cleaning up dead bodies for a living? I knew that Miller wouldn't send someone that would hurt me or put me in more danger, but Silver wasn't what I expected. He was intimidating, hell, he still is, yet there's this subtle softness to him that peeks through that darkness every so often.

It's in the way he's so eager to enrich his mind instead of dulling it down with pointless television, how he attempted to make heart latte art and tried pineapple pizza because I said I liked it. It was in the comfort he showed me after absolutely destroying my pussy on his kitchen counter, and the concerned texts he's sent since then. Plus, him showing up to my office in a panic because I had slipped out of his place without telling him.

I'm safe with Silver. I guess he and Alec have that in common, too. Something that Miller shares with them, only Miller isn't interested in me the way that I am in him. I shouldn't want him, but that crush that appeared the second I saw him across that bar all those moons ago hasn't let up, and I don't know how to make it stop.

Miller is sexy in his own right, this sort of cryptic mysteriousness about him. He doesn't exactly fit in, aesthetically, into the criminal world. He's not overly muscular or arrogant in his nature. Miller is an enigma. He's well dressed, not in suits like a lot of the guys I see in that industry, but in fitted cashmere sweaters and pleated pants. He has great fashion sense, and now that I'm aware he's super wealthy, I wouldn't be surprised if he has someone who styles him.

Although his fashion sense could be explained by his...

The doorbell ringing takes me out of my thoughts, and I hug the blanket tighter to my chest, tugging it up to where it's almost covering my chin.

I listen intently, the shuffling of my father's footsteps going across the living room.

Our house is small, with thin walls. Nothing can be kept quiet here. A lesson I should have learned before I eavesdropped on my dad and Ricardo.

Muffled conversation appears, only for it to stop and my dad to walk away from the door. He doesn't close it, at least not from what I can make out.

Fuck.

He taps on my bedroom door. "Cora, you in there? There's a gentleman out here to see you."

A gentleman?

I sit up and consider who it might be. Other than Ricardo, Silver's the only one bold enough to show up unexpectedly, but do I really know Alec or Miller enough to put it past them? And if it isn't any of them, I don't know who else it could be. That alone sends a shiver down my spine.

With shaky hands, I throw off my blanket and slip off my bed. "I'm coming," I tell the man I've been avoiding and throw a cardigan over my shoulders.

My stomach tightens as I open the door and come face to face with my dad. I don't look him in the eye, nor do I even tilt my head toward him, instead, I keep it low and to the side for more reason than one. The bruises from Ricardo's slap are already forming on my pale skin.

I hug my cardigan to my chest and peek through the cracked front door at a man standing outside with a package in his grasp. He glances both ways and checks his watch.

"Can I help you?" I ask him once I've opened the door.

"Coraline Price?"

I cringe at the use of my legal name. "Yeah?"

"Here." He holds the envelope out to me. "It's from Miller."

"Oh." I take the package. "Thanks."

He nods. "Have a good evening."

"Uh, thanks. You, too." I stand there a bit awkwardly as he turns around and marches down the walkway and onto the sidewalk. I wait until he climbs onto a bicycle and peddles away before shutting the door.

"What do you have there?" My dad asks me, his proximity making me wish I never responded to his knock at all.

"I don't know," I tell him. It's not entirely a lie, but it's safe to say my driver's license is in here.

From the weight of the package though, that isn't the only thing.

"Well," he continues. "Are you hungry?"

I walk past him, not bothering to glance in his direction.

"I could throw a frozen pizza in."

I stop in my tracks but don't turn around. "Have you heard from her?"

My dad lets out a sigh telling me exactly what I need to know. "No."

"Is she even still alive?" Tears well in my eyes.

"I...I don't know, Cor. But I have to believe she is." His voice cracks, and as mad as I am at him, I can still recognize that he's suffering, too.

Still, that doesn't make me hate him any less.

I continue down the hall without saying anything else, darting into my bedroom and collapsing into the door behind me. My shoulders slump, and I take in the package in my grasp.

The metal prongs are cold and hard against my fingers when I pry it open. I sit on my bed and dump the contents out, my driver's license very much sprawled out on my comforter.

How it's possible Miller was able to get it so quickly I have no idea, but I'm grateful for it either way.

But that isn't all that was inside. Lying next to my ID is a stack of one hundred dollar bills and a black card. I pick it up, the weight surprising me, as does the texture. Is it metal? This thing is stout enough I could probably bludgeon someone to death with it. I skim my fingers along the bills, counting a minimum of seven of them.

What the hell was he thinking?

A small sticky note on the back side of the black card draws my attention and when I flip it over, it reads:

You've been made an authorized user, get yourself whatever you want x

Is that Miller's handwriting or someone else's?

I hold it to my chest and hope that it's his and savor the strange comfort his scrawled words give. Little did he know the best thing in this entire package would be the off-green Post-it note with his handwriting on it.

I reach across my bed and grab my phone, peeling the case

off and tucking the note inside for safekeeping. I give it one final glance and push the case back on and swipe the screen to life.

I send Miller a text.

Me: Hey, I got the package. Pretty sure you included more than just my ID in there...

Only thirty seconds go by before the dots of his text messages appear.

Miller: I'm glad it arrived. Use the card for whatever you want, there isn't a limit.

Cora: So you're saying I could buy a house if I wanted to?

Miller: Or a small island.

Miller: Maybe a big island, I've never priced them so I'm not sure.

I quite literally laugh out loud and my cheeks flush.

Me: Don't tempt me with a good time haha.

Miller: I can look into it if you'd like? Where were you thinking? Caribbean?

I chuckle again and shake my head.

Me: How about Fiji?

Miller: Near Fiji, or actually Fiji?

Me: I don't think Fiji is for sale.

Miller: Anything is for sale if you try hard enough.

Me: How about we start with a bottle of Fiji water?

Miller: I could probably get you the entire company if you want all the water for yourself.

Me: I think you've lost your mind.

Miller: I think you're right.

I scoot back onto my bed, resting against my pillows and pull my knees to my chest.

Me: What're you up to?

I shouldn't ask him such a personal question, but the line between our boundaries is a tad blurred considering he hired someone to cover up a murder I committed.

Miller: Boring work stuff. What about you?

Me: Why do I have a feeling nothing about what you do for a living is boring?

Miller: You'd be surprised.

Me: Try me.

Dots appear, then disappear, then appear again. I hate how anxious I am about the delay in his response. It almost feels...desperate, and I don't like it.

We're just friends, having a friendly conversation. Chill, Cora.

The same friend who somehow knew my legal name, where I lived, and now that I think about it...I never gave him my phone number. Maybe June did, or Simon. But that would mean he asked them for it, and I don't see that happening, either.

Wait, he must have gotten it from the team at The Wellerton. Duh. I'm designing his unit, that makes sense how he would have gotten it.

However, if my personal number is available to all the tenants, I'm going to have to have a talk with the company about personal boundaries.

Miller: There's been an issue...I can't really say much, but have you ever known someone was the problem, you just couldn't prove it was them?

I think about his question and ponder what the actual meaning behind it is. Who's causing him trouble? And why do I immediately want to solve the problem for him?

Me: What if you got them to reveal themselves?

Miller: And how could someone do that...asking for a friend, obviously.

Me: Obviously, lol

Me: Um, well, maybe tell them that you already know. Get them to admit it.

Me: Or, reverse psychology them and say they aren't capable of XYZ and see if they tell on themselves.

Miller: Not a bad idea...

Me: See, I'm good for something.

Miller: I'm sure you're good for more than giving me advice on my vague situation.

Me: I mean, I'm a damn good designer.

Miller: *sends an eye-roll emoji*

Me: Did you really just type that instead of actually sending an eye-roll emoji?

Miller: Seemed easier than scrolling to find it.

Me: You're telling me it's not your most used emoji?

Miller: Guess which one it is.

Me: Will you actually tell me if I get it right?

Miller: Scouts honor.

I click the emoji keyboard and look at mine and wonder what his might be. Maybe a generic smiling face. Or a thumbs up. He seems like a thumbs-up kind of guy. But I decide to take a risk and go for something bold.

Me: The knife emoji.

Miller: hahahaha

Miller: How did you know that?

I laugh out loud and cover my mouth to suppress the noise. Heaven forbid I draw any unwanted attention from that guy who happens to be my father.

Me: Was I really right?

Miller sends me a screenshot of our text screen with the knife emoji most definitely in the top spot.

I take a screenshot of mine and send it back.

Me: Great minds.

Miller: Wow, we're more alike than we seem.

Me: You should really check those two hundred and thirteen text messages lol.

Miller: If I ignore them long enough, they'll disappear, won't they?

Me: I don't think that's how it works...

Miller: A guy can dream.

Me: I think I'm going to pass out pretty soon, it's been a weird, long day. Thanks for talking...and thank you, for getting my ID for me, you have no idea how much that helped.

Miller: The pleasure was all mine. Let me know if you need anything else, otherwise, I'll see you after work tomorrow.

Me: Hey, real quick, I had a question...

Miller: Anything.

Me: Never mind, it's dumb. I'll see you tomorrow. Hope your work thing goes well and gets resolved soon.

Miller takes longer than normal to respond, those dots popping up and going away. I hate the uncertainty of not knowing what's going through his mind. And I hate that I even wonder at all. Why am I like this? Why do I care?

Miller: Get some rest. Text or call if you need me. I'm always here. x

I stare at the screen, that little x doing something sort of strange to my heart. I had added it to a text I sent him before, and now here he is, doing it back. It's probably meaningless, but it still makes me feel fuzzy all over anyway.

Holding my phone to my chest, I breathe in deeply and try to imagine what life would be like if I weren't destined for some gross, evil man who wants to use me for my uterus.

For the first time in my life, three guys seem genuinely interested in me. Silver and Alec for sure, Miller is questionably just my friend, but I can't deny that it feels like something else. Or maybe it's just what I want and I'm trying to force something that isn't possible. June told me I'm not his type. That he doesn't even like girls. Maybe she was wrong, or misinformed. Maybe I should just stop beating around the bush and ask him bluntly. But if June was right and I'm the one misjudging the situation, I'll ruin whatever relationship we have, and if a friendship with Miller is all that's on the table, I'm good with that.

Not that any of it matters. Because in a few short weeks, I'll have to give it up anyway.

My friendships and the potential relationships with Silver and Alec.

It's strange to mourn the future of something that might never be but the pain that aches through my chest is real nonetheless, and all it does is make me hate my father that much more.

His ignorant decision didn't just ruin my life, but it ruined whatever could have been, too.

19
SILVER

I've barely slept in days.

I have no appetite.

And it feels like I've lost part of my soul.

I don't know if I've ever felt like this, and I don't think I'd wish it on my worst enemy.

I *miss* her. Like deep in my bones, a visceral throbbing in my soul kind of miss.

I can't stop thinking about her.

Her lips. Her smile. Her perfect little nose. Those bright blue eyes. The way her face was speckled with blood when I found her. God, and the things we did in my kitchen...

I ache in places that I thought were dormant for the rest of my life.

And there's not a damn thing I can do about it.

I've texted her. I've reached out. I've sort of stalked her. And that will have to be enough.

If she wants to contact me, she will. I can't force the issue.

But do I want to drive to her work and throw her over my shoulder and disregard whether she protests or not as I bring her back to my place and lock her away so she can never leave me again? Yes, yes I do.

I hate the rational side of me that prevents that from happening.

I've never been clingy in my entire life. I've never lusted or chased after a woman like this. I've never wanted to literally carve my heart out of my chest and hand it to someone on a silver platter the way I want to with her.

I hardly know her. We spent one night together. And somehow that night set the course for my entire life, the light-bulb on my story finally flickering to life.

I rake my hand through my hair. "You're being an idiot, Silver. She's just a girl." I clench my jaw and grunt, knowing damn well that's not the truth. She's so much more, and anyone who comes within five feet of her would be able to recognize that.

Maybe this is what I get for refusing to keep my heart tucked away for all these years. The second I sensed a potential match, I turned into a blubbering mess and completely disregarded my very nature.

I am a lone wolf. I am a criminal. I am not a good man.

Why would I ever assume that I would be a good partner? Let alone what Cora deserves.

I should forget about her. That would be better for everyone involved.

"Are you going to throw him in there, or should I?" The guy at the morgue, Ronny, asks me.

"I've got it," I tell him and latch onto the bloodied man wrapped in plastic, hoisting him into the cremation oven.

"What's on your mind, Silver?" He pulls the white surgical mask down below his chin.

"Nothing, sorry, just a bit distracted."

Ronny widens his eyes. "It's unlike you is all."

"I know." And that's why I must make it stop. I have to forget about her.

I have to accept that what we had was great, and temporary. I'm too cold and heartless to have feelings anyway.

20
CORA

*W*ork drags.

I mean it truly feels like the longest day known to man.

It doesn't help that I check the clock every twelve seconds, the longer I stare at it, the slower it ticks by. I should be grateful that time has seemed to pause since soon enough I'm doomed to fulfill my obligation to Ricardo. Not to mention my truly disturbing Sunday duties of modeling for him while he jerks off.

I tremble at the thought and grow sick to my stomach.

Pulling out my phone, I glance around the office and pop open Instagram.

I type a name into the search bar and wonder if it will bring any results.

Her profile is the first one on the list and I click it immediately.

London Gardella. Three hundred eighteen thousand followers. And she follows precisely zero in return.

Her account is curated with perfectly posed selfies and model shots that would make any man's jaw drop.

I laugh at the idea of her father saying she can't fetch a husband, because any man in his right mind would be lucky to have her. But I guess for him it's a business transaction, so finding someone with enough money is more important than allowing her to choose a partner based on love.

I don't know why I'm surprised—the man is forcing me to have his child and according to London, tried to kill her because she turned on him. The scar on her side was brutal, and I can't imagine how terrible it must have been to be that brutally attacked by the very person who is supposed to protect you.

Skimming through her photos, I click on one here or there, zooming in on the designer clothes and fancy jewelry. It doesn't take me long to home in on the smile that doesn't quite meet the eyes and the fakeness of the persona she puts out. I guess I'm not the only one faking her way through life and putting up a front.

"Cora."

Tara, one of my co-workers, walks into my cubicle area and I nearly fall out of my seat.

I clutch my chest. "Sorry, you scared me."

She narrows her gaze. "Are you watching porn on the clock?"

"No." I click the screen dark and place it face down in my lap. "What's up?"

Tara holds out a stack of papers. "Would you mind going through these and double-checking my decisions? I feel pretty confident, but I'd love to get a second opinion."

"Yeah. Of course." I take them from her and do a quick glance at the clock.

"Obviously not today," she adds. "Sometime this week would be great. I don't have to turn the project in until Friday."

"Damn, you're ahead of the game." I thumb through the stack. "I'm sure you did great though, you always do. You should have a little more faith in yourself, Tara."

She blushes, her pale cheeks turning bright red, matching

her hair. It's a different shade than London's, a bit more orange than anything, but still pretty.

I always wanted to be a redhead but never thought I'd be able to pull it off. I considered trying it but the girl who does my hair told me she'd make me shave my head if she dyed it, and I changed my mind. I guess being bald could be a vibe, too.

"Thanks, Cora. You're always so supportive. I appreciate that." She leans in closer. "You're the nicest one here. In case you didn't know."

I chuckle. "You don't have to lie to get me to check your work, babe."

"And you don't have to lie and tell me it's good." Tara leans against the flimsy cubicle wall and crosses her arms. "Do you have a hot date or something? You're looking extra good today."

"Is it too much?" I hold out the sides of the muted green blazer that matches my skirt.

"Your boobs look amazing in that top." She points to my white spaghetti-strapped crop top. "And those shoes..."

I lift my leg to show off the pointed, black, stiletto heels. "I got this suit on sale at Zara. I haven't worn it yet. You sure I don't look stupid?"

Usually, confidence is something I wear with ease, at least on the outside, but today, this *meeting* with Miller, I'm more anxious than I've been in a while, and the time it took me to decide on what to wear this morning almost made me late for work.

I had to go with something I could wear both to the office and to the dinner, something that would be accepted at the restaurant we're going to, without being too over the top. I mean, after all, this is a work meeting, not a date.

"You look hot as fuck, Cora." Tara covers her mouth. "Just don't tell HR I said that, I don't want to get fired."

If only HR knew that my boss was a womanizer who ended

up dead, the cause of death the numerous stab wounds inflicted by yours truly...I'd be the one fired, not her.

It wouldn't put it past them to have known he was a piece of shit, though. Men always seem to get away with toeing the line of what's right and wrong, and as long as no one does anything to stop them, they'll continue to push it.

The minute hand on the clock by my desk ticks over, signaling that it's time to leave the office.

I stand and brush off my legs. "And as a matter of fact, I'm meeting a client," I tell Tara, not that it's any of her business. I have no reason to withhold that information and Tara is the one person in this office that I actually don't dislike. Everyone else seems to act nice to people's faces and then talk shit behind their backs. Tara has never done that, at least not that I'm aware of. We gossip, that's for sure, but it isn't anything that isn't already common knowledge or that we wouldn't say straight to someone.

Tara raises her brows. "Ohh," she purrs. "Is he good-looking?"

My phone buzzes and if it weren't for the fact that I'm meeting Miller soon, I would probably disregard it.

Still, I let out a sigh of relief when the message is from Miller and not Ricardo. I hate how he ruins even the smallest things like an alert on my cell. I'd mute his notifications if I could but he manages to contact me from unknown numbers, making it impossible to evade him.

"Find out for yourself," I say as I grab my bag from my desk. "He's outside waiting for me."

I send him a text to let him know I'm on my way out and Tara follows me like a puppy in hopes of catching a glimpse at the client who has me questioning if my outfit is acceptable or not.

Fighting my nerves, I plaster on my happy face and walk

through our office, my heels clicking against the floor once we're near the main area.

I step through the automatic entrance to the building and onto the sidewalk, shooting a look over my shoulder at Tara. "I'll see you tomorrow."

She trails me through but stops outside and offers me a wave, her sights scanning the parking spots in front of the building.

Perched against a black Porsche, looking like he just walked out of a GQ magazine, is Miller, his arms crossed over his chest.

He kicks off it the second he sees me and peels his sunglasses from his face. He's wearing a fitted black button-up with the sleeves rolled just below his elbows and black pants. Miller folds his glasses and tucks them into his slightly unbuttoned shirt and approaches me.

"Hey," he says with a grin he's trying to hide on his face. "You look...stunning. Green is your color."

"Thanks." I try to hide the blush that forces its way across my cheeks. I don't dare touch my face though—I spent entirely too long color correcting the hand imprint that Ricardo left behind this morning and I refuse to mess it up now. "You're not so bad yourself."

Miller places his hand on the small of my back and leads me to his car, reaching down and opening the door for me.

"I thought you were sending a car to pick me up?" I ask him as I slide in.

"I did...I just happen to be driving it." He closes my door and walks around to get into the driver's side.

I take a glance at the building, Tara standing there with enthusiastic thumbs up. I stuff my bag around my feet and attempt not to gawk too much at the super expensive car I'm sitting in.

Miller climbs in and pauses like his mind is processing something I can't quite figure out. He leans over and I completely freeze, all of me except my pounding heart. He reaches past me, grabbing onto my seat belt and pulling it across my body, his eyes killing me with their intensity.

"Thanks," I whisper with his face so fucking close to mine.

"You smell good," he says before latching my belt and breaking away.

"So do you," I respond like an idiot.

"Thanks." He turns the car on and the engine roars to life, rumbling my entire body but in a very sophisticated way.

"Is this your car?"

"It is." He glances over at me. "Do you like it?"

I nod. "Um, yeah, it's nice. Do you?"

Miller shrugs and pulls out onto the street, dodging cars and weaving through the traffic. "I'm not really a car guy. I told my team I needed a car, and this is what showed up."

"You're shitting me?"

He peeks at me briefly. "About what?"

"This is like a hundred-thousand-dollar car. Base price." I notice all the fancy embellishments and add, "And this is *not* a base model."

"I really don't know how much it cost. Is that a lot for a car?"

"I mean, I don't even own a car..."

"Do you want one?"

I tilt my head toward him. "If this is where you joke about buying me a car, we can skip that."

He throws his hands up in defeat. "Don't buy the woman a car, got it, noted."

"Oh and speaking of that." I reach into my bag and unzip the side compartment, pulling out Miller's property. "I cannot accept these."

Miller does a double take at what's in my hand and accelerates through an intersection. "Why?"

I shake my head. "You're my client, and my friend. This is too much."

"Can't you take it as a bonus or something? I mean, I'm paying you for a job, can't you consider it as compensation or something?"

I blink at him. "There's twelve hundred dollars here, Miller. And this..." I hold up the black American Express, which according to Google is reserved for the company's wealthiest clients who spend a fuck ton with them every single year. "I can't keep this."

"It's for emergencies." He pauses and then adds, "Or like, whatever you want."

"Do you give all of your interior designers access to your black Amex?"

Miller glances over and winks at me. "Just the pretty ones."

I swallow and clench my jaw in an attempt to force myself not to outwardly react. Did he say what I think he did or am I having a complete mental fucking breakdown?

"There are plenty of pretty people at my office. You should get a few more of these things made." I flip the card between my fingers, the weight of it so strange compared to normal flimsy credit cards.

Miller pulls the expensive car in front of the exclusive restaurant and puts it into park. "We can go somewhere else if you're not feeling this place."

"Like McDonald's?"

"Would you prefer that?"

"No."

"Okay. Good, because I don't think they have fast food on this side of town."

"That's a shame."

He trails his gaze to the card in my hand and the stack of cash resting on my lap. "You should put that away before you lose it."

I sigh and continue to hold it toward him. "I can't take this."

Miller breathes in and out. "Listen, if I take it back, here's what's going to happen."

I wait for him to continue.

"I'm going to have to sneak into your house while you're sleeping and put it back in your wallet. Then you'll be like *what the hell, where did this come from* and give it back again, and then I'd have to keep breaking into your place and putting it in there, and I mean, I don't sleep much as it is, so you wouldn't be fucking with my nighttime schedule but you'd probably end up feeling a way about it and it would be easier if you just held onto it. Don't you think?"

A valet worker opens my door before I get a chance to respond to him but it doesn't matter because I don't have words anyway.

He's persistent, and I can't quite figure out why.

So, I give in and shove the card and cash into the spot I had it tucked into my bag and latch onto the handle and hoist it out of the car.

Miller hops out and rushes around, shaking hands with the valet and whispering something into his ear.

"Yes, sir," the guy says.

Miller does that thing where he puts his palm on my back and I swear if it weren't for the fabric separating our skin, I'd probably pass out right here and now. I know he's off-limits and not interested, but it doesn't change the fact that I have a gigantic crush on him, and I have from the first moment I saw him.

"Do you remember that night, a very long time ago, when you went out with June at that club that Simon owns?" Miller guides me to the front of the restaurant and opens the door for me.

"I do," I confirm but don't admit that I was thinking about that moment as he was asking me about it.

"I was there on business. Meeting with Magnus, I think.

Those parts of the night are a bit blurry for me. But you..." He takes a break from his story to approach the hostess stand.

The girl perks up at the sight of him and practically jumps out from behind it. "This way, sir," she says without hesitation.

Our bodies get closer as we navigate the busy restaurant and mine comes alive at his proximity.

He doesn't like you, Cora. You're an idiot. This is a business meeting, not a date, dumbass. He's here to discuss design ideas, nothing more.

"I couldn't take my eyes off of you," he mutters to me from behind. "You were dancing and having fun, and I don't think I had ever seen anything more beautiful in my entire life."

My eyes dart to the side but I don't dare look at him. I move my feet forward and follow the hostess into a quieter and more private section.

She stops at a table and pulls out a chair. "Will this do, sir?"

Miller walks over to her and all but nudges her out of the way. "Yes. I've got this, thank you." He nods to the seat and pushes it in for me when I sit down.

What a fucking gentleman.

"Let me know if I can be of further assistance," the girl says before leaving the room.

Miller settles into the seat across from me, and I consider whether I'm going to be able to sit through a meal with him looking this fucking good.

"I probably shouldn't have said that." Miller puts his elbow on the table and thumbs his chin.

A sweet-faced waitress interrupts the tension. "Good evening, sir, it's a pleasure to have you back. I see you have a guest tonight. Would you like the chef to prepare something different than your usual?"

I hide yet another bout of shock at him being a regular at such a high-class place. I'm pretty sure we walked past George fucking Clooney on the way to our table.

"Perhaps, we need a minute to figure it out," he tells her.

"I'm good with whatever," I add to the conversation. If he eats here regularly, I can't imagine the food is bad, and at this point, I'm hungry enough to eat anything. Here's to hoping my appetite stays though...it's been a challenge having one lately with everything that's going on. The only decent meals I've had lately have been with Silver and Alec.

"Do you have any dietary restrictions or food allergies?" The waitress focuses on me, and it's then that I notice how bright green her eyes are.

"I don't," I tell her.

Miller meets my gaze. "Nothing with pine nuts."

I blink at him and wonder how the fuck he could have known that I have a pine nut allergy. It's mild and won't exactly kill me, but still, it's not common knowledge.

"Very well." She nods and glances between us. "In the meantime, can I get you started with drinks?"

I speak up first. "Martini. Vodka. Extra dirty."

"I'll do an old-fashioned," Miller tells her.

"We received a rare Whistlepig Boss Hog since your last visit if you'd like to try it, sir." She stands there with her hands behind her back, her posture strong and confident despite her fidgeting fingers. Is it Miller making her nervous or me? Surely if celebrities like George Clooney frequent this place, too, she should be used to being star-struck by now.

But I don't think it's that at all.

"Yeah, I'll try that, too. Neat, please."

She smiles and bows her head. "I'll be back with those drinks shortly."

The second she's out of earshot range, I lean across the table. "That girl has a massive crush on you."

Miller's brows wrinkle together. "She does?"

I laugh. "Um, yeah. It's obvious. Boys are so oblivious."

"Hm, I didn't even notice." Miller takes the napkin off the table and places it in his lap.

I repeat what he's doing and when I'm finished, he's staring right at me.

"Do I have something on my face?" I ask him.

He shakes his head slowly. "No." He lets out the softest breath.

With my elbows on the table and my hand resting in my hands, I think back to our conversation last night. "Did you get that super vague work thing figured out?"

Miller's hand twitches like he's restraining himself from making a fist. "No. It's more of an ongoing situation. Something that can't be remedied immediately."

"That's unfortunate."

"It is, yeah. It's costing the company a lot of money."

"Can I help?" I throw out the offer even though he'd never involve me in that line of business. Not even my best friend will discuss it with me, let alone someone I barely know.

"Are you a mind reader?"

I narrow my eyes and focus with great intent before saying, "Nope, sorry, just tried and didn't work."

His lips turn up into a smirk, and my heart flutters.

"Damn," he says.

"Speaking of..."

Miller pours some water from the carafe I hadn't even realized was sitting on our table into the glasses. He does mine first, and then his. "I'm also not a mind reader, if that's where you're going with this." He brings the glass to his mouth and takes a drink.

"How did you know I had a pine nut allergy?"

Miller doesn't seem to react, instead, he lowers the glass on the table and says, "I didn't. I have one."

"You do?"

"Mmhm."

"And the waitress, who happens to be very much into you, never asked you before?"

"Um, no, it never came up."

"Miller..."

"Okay fine I..." But he doesn't get a chance to continue because said waitress waltzes over with our drinks and a basket of fancy bread in all shapes and sizes.

"Your martini." She places the drink in front of me and then turns her attention to Miller. "Your old-fashioned. And the Whistlepig Boss Hog, sir."

"Thanks," he tells her, not paying her much consideration. He's polite, but it doesn't go any further than that.

"Can I get you anything else?"

I shake my head and he declines, sending her on her way a moment later.

"So," I say. "What's so special about that one?" I point to the golden liquid in the one glass.

"For starters..." Miller picks up the strangely shaped glass. "Whistlepig is hands down my favorite brand of Whiskey. And this one"—he holds it out in front of him like he's examining it— "is hard to find because there aren't that many bottles of it. The mash bill is one hundred percent rye. It's not even that expensive, but it's damn good." Miller extends his arm across the table. "Here. Try it."

"But...you're so excited, you can take the first sip."

"I insist."

Reluctantly, I take the glass from him and bring it to my face. "Are you sure?"

"Positive."

I sniff the whiskey, noting the warm spice and sort of maple scent and then take the smallest taste, not wanting to consume too much. It's savory, with a hint of sweet, and it goes down a hell of a lot smoother than I thought it would, leaving a lingering smokey flavor. "Damn," is all I say.

Miller smiles, and it warms my chest more than the whiskey does. "Good, isn't it?"

I nod and give him back his glass. "Damn good." Now I can't fathom my martini coming even close to matching that. Still, I drink some water and then try it, the saltiness of the olive juice is a complete contrast to the whiskey.

"Mmm," he mumbles after trying his drink as I try not to stare at him too much.

He's just so damn attractive, in a mysterious and tortured kind of way.

"How did you meet Dominic?" I ask, the question surprising him no doubt as much as it does me. The desire to learn more about him overpowered my desire to not cross the professional boundary I keep attempting to put in place.

"Well," Miller says. "It's sort of a very long story, that would require an excessive amount of back story, and I'd probably have to draw a little diagram of names and job titles and piece it together for you."

"I'm good with a long, winding story."

Miller tries his old-fashioned and points to my martini. "Is your drink good?"

"Very. Thank you. Is yours?"

Of course, it is, he comes here all the time, and he probably has the same damn thing. Why am I asking such stupid fucking questions? Can't I just shut up and pull out the notebook full of design stuff and have him make a few decisions so I can come to terms with the fact that this is very much a business meal, and nothing more.

"Yes, it is." He slides it across the table. "You can try it, if you'd like."

And because the idea of being anywhere near where his lips were, I accept his offer. "That is good," I tell him after swallowing. The whiskey in the drink is still very present, but it has a sort of subtle sweetness to it that makes it wickedly dangerous with how easily it goes down.

I return his drink and advance mine. "Are you a martini fan?"

"Can't say I am, but I don't think I've ever had one. Especially not a dirty one." He brings it to his nose and sniffs it the same way I had when I tried his.

I bite at the inside of my lip as his press to the rim of my glass, my eyes trained way too fucking intensely on a man who is simply tasting a martini.

"Not bad," he says. "Very...olivey."

I smile across at him. "That's what makes it dirty."

"Ohh."

"So, the long story, do I get it?"

God damn it, Cora, there you go prying.

"How can I sum this up..." He taps his chin. "Okay, so my old boss and Dom's old boss used to be rivals. That's another long story. They are no longer...in the picture..."

I nod slowly as the understanding hits me. "Got it."

"Dom took his boss's place. And Johnny, Claire's husband, took my boss's. Also, another long story."

"Why didn't you take his place?" I ask him, not quite sure how Johnny fits into all of this.

"He inherited it, rightfully so."

"I see...and you're like Johnny's right-hand man?"

"Yeah, something like that. And despite there always being a feud between the East and West, we decided to change that. That's how the connection started forming."

"So you guys have like an alliance or whatever?"

"You could say that, yeah."

I try to make sense of all of this with the limited information that I've been given. Clearly, they're all involved in a bunch of criminal shit, what exactly that entails, I haven't figured out.

"And your old boss, did you like him?"

That eager waitress comes over and places a bowl in front of both of us. "For your first course, a butternut squash soup." She keeps her attention mostly focused on Miller, and I sort of want to grab her ponytail and drag her into the back.

The poor girl hasn't done a thing wrong, and she honestly hasn't crossed a single line, and still, I feel weirdly territorial over a man who isn't even mine.

"Can I get you anything else?" she asks.

Miller looks at me first before saying, "No, I think we're good, thanks." He grabs the spoon and holds it over the bowl. "To answer your question though, yes. I liked him very much. He was like a father to me."

My heart aches at the tone of his voice, the shift in inflection at the past tense.

"What about your actual father?" I blow on a spoonful of soup and taste it, wondering how it's possible such a simple soup could be done this fucking well.

Miller's fingers twitch, and I worry that I've touched on a topic that he isn't willing to discuss with me. I mean, why would he, I'm practically a stranger.

"You don't have to tell me if you don't want to," I add in an attempt to diffuse the situation.

Miller pats at the corners of his lips with his napkin. "I haven't talked about him in years. I try not to even think about him."

"We can change the subject. I'm sorry for bringing it up."

His eyes meet mine with great intensity. "Don't apologize."

"Sorry," I whisper, the word slipping out.

"My dad and I didn't have a good relationship. My old boss, he gave me an opportunity to get away from my dad and I took it, never once looking back. In retrospect, he probably saved my life, even if what I do is dangerous from time to time."

The loss of such an important person makes that much more sense. I can't imagine losing someone who saved me...I can't really imagine someone saving me in general.

"I vowed my life to him," Miller adds. "I learned the business inside and out, there isn't anything I wouldn't have done for him. I sort of have a tendency to give my all to those I love and trust."

"I'm sure he was grateful to have you. Anyone would be."

"Maybe." He sips his old-fashioned and points to me. "What about you? What's your relationship with your parents like?"

My cheeks flush immediately and I avoid his beautiful blue eyes. "Um..."

"I guess we have that in common then."

"Yeah..." A flicker of a memory comes into my mind and it's like the floodgates have opened and I can't control what comes in. Unwanted tears fill my eyes and one spills over, speckling the white cloth on the table.

"Hey." Miller reaches across the table and places his hand on top of mine. "You don't have to say anything you don't want to."

I shake my head and try to focus on his skin on mine. *I'm safe here*, I tell myself. My past can't hurt me anymore. I wipe my cheek and force a smile as I reach for my martini and take a long drink. "I'm fine."

"You know you don't always have to be fine, right?" He circles his thumb on my hand.

"I disagree."

"Cora..." He sighs. "You don't have to do that with me."

"Do what?"

"Pretend."

I stare at him as he stares at me and it's like he's looking straight into my fucking soul.

He continues, "I see how hard you try to make sure everyone sees you as this perfect person. You're aware of everything. You take care of everyone. You put yourself last and prioritize their needs. You're allowed to be selfish every once in a while. You're allowed to ask for help. You're allowed to break down. And

you're absolutely allowed to talk about what's bothering you."
He exhales again. "Is this about your boss?"

I swallow and recall that day not too long ago when he forced himself on me, and I had no choice but to defend myself...his blood coating my face and clothes after I finished with him.

"Can I be honest about something?" I bend at the waist, leaning forward a bit.

"Your secrets are safe with me."

"I thought I'd feel worse about what I did...and I don't."

Miller smiles ever so softly. "There's nothing wrong with that."

"I think the legal system might disagree with that. Isn't remorse usually what lessens people's prison sentences?"

"You are not going to prison, Cora. I would never let that happen."

"How can you be so sure?"

"Do you trust me?"

"Yes," I say without hesitation.

"Then trust me when I say I won't let anything bad happen to you, not ever again."

Little does he know, there's nothing he can do to prevent that from happening—my fate is sealed, and it belongs to Ricardo Gardella.

"Why?" I ask him.

"What do you mean?"

"I'm nobody to you. Why does it matter if something bad happens to me or not?"

"Because I care about you." He gives my hand a pulsing squeeze. One, two, three. Like a morse code signaling that he's here for me, that he isn't going anywhere.

"Your soup is getting cold."

"I don't care about the soup, Cora, I care about you. Do you understand that?" His words are powerful and make me question literally everything.

How can someone look at me the way he is but not have feelings for me? Maybe he just feels sorry for me after what he walked into at the unit and felt obligated to keep an eye on me. Maybe the fluttering in my chest is mine and mine alone, and I'm like a kid sister to him or something.

Maybe I'm like our clueless waitress, fawning over a guy who isn't interested at all.

Be professional, Cora.

I slide my hand out from under his, the warmth of his touch lingering on my skin as I blurt out, "I brought the design portfolio so we could go over it." I reach into my bag and plop the thing onto the table, flipping through the pages and ignoring whatever it is that Miller might be doing. I can't face him, not yet. I need to pull myself together first and focus on why I'm really here.

Shoving the thing across the table, I point at the page. "I was thinking maybe something like this, but if you'd like, I can present a few other options."

"Cora," Miller says with a stern tone. "Cora," he repeats with a bit more intensity without raising his voice too much.

"Yeah?" I distract myself by downing the rest of my martini before looking at him.

"I did not ask you here because I was worried about the designs."

"Oh?" My stomach sinks at the endless thoughts that rack my brain. Is this because of what happened at the unit? Some sort of blackmail initiation? Why would he give me a stack of cash and his Black Amex if he had bad intentions though? None of this makes sense and the longer he takes to respond, the tighter my stomach curls into a knot.

"I wanted to see you."

"But what about the..." I glance down at the design portfolio.

"You can decorate the unit however you want to."

"But it's yours," I tell him, as if that will get him to have some input.

"And I trust that whatever you decide will look great." Miller's jaw tenses and his nostrils flare slightly. His lips part like he's holding back whatever he's about to say next. "Cora, do you find me attractive?"

My eyes widen. "What? I mean, yes, no, wait, I shouldn't have said that." I glance down at the barely touched bowl of soup. "This is good soup, don't you think?" I scoop some up and practically shove it into my mouth to shut me the hell up.

For the first time since we arrived, I desperately wish for that waitress to appear out of nowhere and bring me another martini or twelve.

Why would he ask me such a thing?

And why would I react like a blubbering fucking idiot who can't form words?

Miller tugs the corner of his lip into his mouth and drags his teeth along it before sighing. "Okay then."

"Sorry," I say, probably making things worse. "You're obviously a very attractive man, Miller. I didn't mean to imply you weren't. I was just surprised by the question." I swirl the soup around and wish there was a way to drown myself in it to escape how awkward I've made things.

"So you *do* think I'm attractive?" He raises an eyebrow.

"I just said so, didn't I?" I grin at him and point to the fancy bourbon sitting near him. "Can I have another drink of that?"

"Yeah, of course." Miller gives it to me without hesitation and then flits his attention around the quiet area until he spots his target. He raises two lazy fingers toward her and a moment later, my savior appears.

"Sir?" The waitress seems grateful, and I don't blame her.

"Another Boss Hog and..." He pauses and motions to my empty martini glass. "Another round of drinks."

265

"Thank you," I tell her as she nods and scurries away.

I busy myself with the soup and Miller does the same, grabbing one of the chunks of bread and breaking it apart and dropping it in his bowl.

The waitress comes back, leaving our drinks and taking our empty bowls. "Your second course will be out momentarily."

I meet Miller's blue gaze. "How many courses are there?"

He shrugs. "Hard to tell with Gus, just depends on what kind of mood he's in today."

"Gus?"

"The chef." He grabs his old-fashioned and holds it toward me. "Cheers."

I carefully take my martini and clink it softly against his. "Cheers."

"Okay, so, parents are off limits, what should we talk about next?"

I snatch a piece of bread even though I'm not really a fan, it's more to keep my hands busy while the alcohol settles into my veins and calms my nerves. "There's always politics and religion."

"Ah, yes, my favorite topics."

"Really?" I chuckle.

"No, I'd rather we talk about our parents." Miller grins and drinks more of his old-fashioned before sipping the other straight whiskey.

"You didn't have to give me this, by the way." I grab the oddly shaped glass and take a drink myself, savoring the decadent flavor. It won't be too long until the booze has caught up and my head will be swimming with the buzz of being a lightweight.

I like to think I can handle my liquor but with my eating habits lately, there's no telling how fucked up I'll get and when.

"Do you know the name of this particular glass?" Miller asks me.

"Uh, no, but I was just thinking about how weird it's shaped."

He smiles softly. "It's called a Glencairn glass. It's shaped like this to keep in the aroma but let off alcohol vapors. Or at least that's what Google told me one night at like four a.m. when I looked it up."

"Interesting."

For the next couple of courses, we talk about surface-level things. He tells me random facts, and as the alcohol sets in more for both of us, we smile more, laugh more, and the conversation flows with greater ease. It wasn't that it was difficult before, but the uncertainty of not knowing why we're having this meal together in the first place kept eating away at me.

Now, four drinks in, I'm just grateful to be here with him.

"But like, was that George Clooney in the other room?" I giggle and point in the direction we had come from when we entered the place.

"Probably," Miller says. "I saw Jay Z and Beyonce in here a couple of weeks ago."

"You're kidding."

"I shit you not."

The waitress comes over with our main course, and my mouth practically salivates at how damn good it smells.

"A twenty-eight-day aged filet mignon with roasted petite carrots and garlic-and-herb mashed potatoes." She clears our empty cups and refills our waters before leaving us with our food, the time of her lingering and stealing glances at Miller has lessened as the night progresses.

Or maybe I'm too intoxicated to pay that much attention to it anymore.

"This looks divine," I say and cut into the steak.

We finish the main course through more conversation and follow it up with the best chocolate cake I've had in my entire life. I moan with every bite and wish I could take an entire cake home since there's no way I'll ever be able to afford or even get a reservation at this place ever again.

Miller settles the bill and puts his elbows on the table. "Do you have anywhere you need to be?"

I pick up my phone and my heart thuds at the notifications on the screen. Two from Alec, none from Silver, and more than I can count from an unknown number. The magnificent dinner I just ate rolls over in my stomach and I breathe myself through the wave of nausea and try not to let it show externally.

"Is everything okay?" Miller does that thing with his hand where his fingers twitch.

"Yeah," I lie and put my phone in my lap. "Sorry, what were you saying?"

"I want to take you somewhere else, but if you have other plans, I understand."

I narrow my gaze and tilt my head. "What did you have in mind?"

"You have time?"

"For you? Absolutely." I rise from my seat and toss my phone into my bag and shove the inappropriate messages that Ricardo sent me about his cock and how much he enjoyed jerking off to me into the deepest corners of my mind.

I'm intoxicated and in great company and I refuse to let anything ruin that.

Miller slides the strap of my bag off my shoulder. "Let me carry that for you."

"You don't have to do that."

"I want to." He puts his hand on my lower back.

Without even thinking, I weave my arm around his torso and hold onto him.

My cheeks flush as we walk through the busy restaurant side by side out the same way we entered. I don't even bother looking around to check out who I might pass, the only thing on my mind is how much I enjoy being this close to him.

But once we're outside and the warm evening air hits my face, I'm reminded that this isn't right.

I drop my arm and glance up at him. "I'm sorry, that was inappropriate."

Miller doesn't say anything, instead, he continues toward his car.

Once we're there, I nervously fumble with my hands and turn around to face him. "Miller, I'm..."

But he doesn't let me finish. Miller drops my bag onto the concrete and steps forward, his strong arms caging me in on both sides.

I swallow and look up at him, his blue eyes burning into mine.

"What are you doing?" I whisper.

"What I've wanted to do for a very long time." His attention flickers from my eyes to my lips and back up. He takes a soft breath before leaning in, the entire world slowing down with his every movement.

Miller kisses me—soft and gentle and a bit unsure.

My arms remain at my sides, and I freeze, unsure of how I'm supposed to react. My brain, heart, and body are all screaming different things and practically short-circuit.

Miller releases my mouth but remains a few inches from me, his arms still caging me to his car. "*That* was inappropriate."

I blink up at him. "I don't understand, I thought you were..."

His ocean eyes narrow. "Thought I was what?"

"Gay," I whisper.

He brings his head even farther away, shock written all over his gorgeous face. "What? Why would you think that?"

My mouth drops open. "You're *not*?" I had my doubts, and they continued to add up every time I was around him, but I trusted June and the guys when they told me I wasn't Miller's type. I wanted them to be wrong, hell, I practically begged the universe for it, but I never thought it would actually happen.

"No, Cora." Miller removes his left hand from his car and brings it to my face, caressing my cheek. "Are you disappointed?"

"No," I say, the word coming out without thought. But that's when it hits me. This entire time I've been crushing on Miller, he's been available. And according to his lips just touching mine, he's been interested, too.

This whole fucking time.

Anger wells up inside of me, but it's overcome with the reality of the situation. That Miller likes me back.

"Miller?"

"Yes?"

"Kiss me again."

His eyes dart to mine and a small grin forms on his face before he trails his hand up along the base of my neck and presses his lips to mine.

I kiss him back and this time there's nothing soft or gentle about it. No, this one is full of passion and intensity and desire.

My hands wrap around his neck and his find my waist, tugging me toward him. His skin grazes mine, and fireworks practically shoot off in my body. Our tongues meet, and it's everything all at once and I can't get enough.

Finally, he breaks away, his forehead resting against mine as we catch our breath.

"You have no idea how long I've wanted to do that," he mutters.

"I think I have an idea."

Miller pecks my lips and then my nose, and fuck if it doesn't swell my heart and throw fire straight between my legs.

I want to get him alone, to take this even further but haven't I already done enough damage in sleeping with both Alec and Silver lately? Should I really add another to the mix? It's not like I'm in a committed relationship with any of them and how was I supposed to anticipate any of this happening?

Why is it that none of them came into my life until it was fully fucking falling apart? Even if I was able to choose between them, it's not like I could have a relationship. Not after what Ricardo has planned for me.

What's the harm in having some fun in the meantime? Even if that fun puts my heart on the line and will no doubt ruin me more than Ricardo will.

Maybe it was better when Miller and Alec were unattainable, and Silver was some one-night stand. But now that the possibility of a future with them is within reach, it makes it hurt that much more. Maybe if I knew what could have been, I never would have sold myself to the devil...but knowing me, there's a slim chance that I would have chosen my happiness over saving my parents' lives.

"I have a confession to make," Miller says, his fingers tucking my hair behind my ear.

"Uh oh."

"I bought a unit in your building just to get a chance to see you."

"You did not."

He nods. "I did. And it gets worse..."

My heart stutters and I ponder the meaning behind his words. What could possibly be *worse* than that? And how is that bad at all?

"Cora," someone calls out from nearby, drawing our attention.

I turn to the left, to the right, a familiar redhead approaching with her hand in the air. My arms slide down Miller's front and I release him because he's not mine to hold onto anyway.

"Hey," I say to London.

Miller joins me at my side and faces her. "London." He nods politely.

London points a finger between us. "You two?"

I shoot a glance at Miller and shake my head. "No. I mean, yes. No. It's...new."

Miller puts his hand on my back, and it strangely calms my nerves. "How do you two know each other?"

My chest tightens and the lie I need doesn't appear as quickly as I hope.

"College party," London says without faltering. "How did you guys meet?"

"Through mutual friends," Miller tells her.

I grow grateful for their ability to fill in the gaps because my brain can't handle the overload at the moment. Between the booze and the kiss and the daughter of my enemy standing in front of me, I can't quite think straight.

"Interesting," London purrs.

I want to ask them how they know each other but I have no doubt it will be some sugar-coated lie just like the ones already told. I'm well aware of who London is, and that Miller is involved in sketchy shit, but I'm still an outsider, and they aren't going to openly discuss that to me.

Still, the intrusive thought of whether Miller and London *know* each other nags at me more than I'd like to admit.

She's gorgeous and very much in that lifestyle. Being with someone like her would be more beneficial than a nobody like me.

And according to what I've heard, Ricardo is looking to sell his daughter to someone. Miller probably has the means to make that happen, aligning himself with a powerful man and getting a beautiful wife out of the deal. I don't have anything to offer Miller other than debt, excessive anxiety, and depression.

Why he would waste his time with me, I have no idea.

His money, too. I can't believe he bought a unit in the building I was decorating just to have a chance to see me. Now the reasoning behind the stack of cash and Black Amex makes more sense, but the fact that he chose me doesn't quite add up.

Miller glances down at me, his stare powerful and magnetic. "You okay?"

I force a smile. "Yeah, great."

"It was great to see both of you," London says. "Miller, do you mind if I have a word with Cora alone?"

He looks at me again before giving her an answer.

I nod approval and he releases me, latching onto the bag he had discarded when he kissed me.

"I'll put this in the car," he tells us.

London grins and weaves her arm through mine and tugs me a few feet away from Miller's Porsche. "I overheard Daddy talking about you being friends with Simon Beckett, is that true?"

"Maybe," I say. "Why?"

London glances over her shoulder at Miller. "You're hanging around some very powerful men, Cora, and Daddy is picking up on that. You need to be careful or he's going to make an example out of you."

"What do you mean?"

"I mean, you should tread lightly with who you're dating in public. If he catches wind of this, there's no telling what he'll do."

"Why are you telling me this?" I ask her, unsure what she has to gain from it.

London sighs and rubs my arm. "You seem like a nice girl, Cora. I'd hate to see you end up like Daddy's last pet."

Miller approaches and London immediately shifts her tone.

"We have to get together soon," she coos and hugs me quickly. "You did a good job with your makeup," London whispers into my ear. "Can't even tell." She releases me, holding my shoulders at length. "Text me and we'll catch up."

Lies piled on top of lies and I can't tell if any of it is the truth.

We don't have each other's numbers. We never met at a party.

And the first and only time I had seen her prior to today was when her father humiliated me and gave her shit for her outfit.

There's no doubt that he wouldn't do the same right now—her cleavage spilling out of her floral fitted top, her midriff exposed, and the pants she's wearing hugging every curve of her body. She looks like a high-class rich girl, but I'm sure Ricardo would have something negative to say.

"For sure," I tell her anyway to continue the charade.

London waves before leaving us behind, clutching her Gucci bag at her side and prancing along to the shopping center just past the restaurant we're parked in front of.

"What was that all about?" Miller asks me.

"What do you mean?"

"How do you two really know each other?"

My face grows hot and I dislike how easily Miller sees through the lies. "How do you guys know each other?" I attempt to change the focus of the conversation.

"Her dad is a prominent member of my *industry*."

"Oh," is all I can say. I already knew Ricardo was, but I wasn't sure if Miller would tell me the truth.

"And he's a fucking pig," he adds.

That much I'm aware of, too.

My breath hitches and my chest tightens. I press my hand to it, not realizing that I'm even doing so.

"Hey," Miller says softly. "I'm sorry, I didn't mean to..." He cups my cheeks in his hands and tilts my face up toward him. "Breathe, Cora. Look at me, just breathe."

I stare into his eyes, mine welling with unwanted tears.

"In through your nose, one two three four, out your mouth, one two three four five." He wipes a tear as it falls and continues to talk me down from the panic rising through me.

Finally, after an embarrassingly long minute, I blurt out, "I'm sorry."

"You have nothing to apologize for." He rubs his thumbs on my cheeks and in a perfect world, I'd stay here forever with his hands on me, his touch making me feel like there isn't a single thing wrong. "Does this happen often?"

I shrug and sigh. "Not really."

"How often?"

"Once a week, maybe," I admit. "But lately...more."

"Cora..." Miller drags me into his chest and forces me to reconsider my previous thought.

This is where I want to stay, in his arms.

"You're safe here, okay?" He smooths circles on my back. "I won't let anything happen to you."

I want to tell him not to make promises that he can't keep but it would ruin the moment, and I've already done enough of that.

"I'm okay," I lie and break away. "I'm fine, really."

Miller reluctantly lets me go and studies my face with great concern. His sights linger and my pulse picks up. "Is that a bruise?" He touches the spot in question, and I clench my jaw the same way I've done every single time he's touched it tonight in an attempt to stifle the pain. I had done everything in my power to cover it up and pretend like it didn't hurt when he touched me, but I'm only adding to the lies.

"Cora, what happened?"

"I hit my head," I tell him but don't include the part about it being against the back of Ricardo's hand.

"Did someone do this to you?" Miller's hand balls into a fist at his side. "Tell me. Who. Hurt. You?" he says through gritted teeth.

"No one, I..."

"Did Silver do this?"

"What? No. No, I haven't seen him since..."

"I'll kill him if he hurts you." Miller's eyes are wilder than I've ever seen, an intensity to them that equally excites and terrifies me. "Was it Alec?"

"No." I pause and place my hand on his cheek, this time I use my touch to calm him. "Miller, Silver and Alec would never hurt me, okay? You have nothing to worry about there."

"I can't stomach the idea of something happening to you." Miller softens his touch.

"I hit my head," I repeat again. "I'm clumsy. No one hurt me." I hate lying to him but I can't tell him the truth. One: because I have no idea how he'll react and two: I don't want to put him in danger.

"Did you go to the doctor? What if you have a concussion?"

"Miller," I say, my voice stern. "I'm fine. Now let's get out of here."

"I had something else I wanted to do before I took you home." He nods ahead to the direction London disappeared into.

"What?"

"Come on." He offers me his hand and my body reacts without my mind telling it to, my fingers sliding into his.

"Where are we going?"

Miller winks and tugs me toward the area full of designer stores. "Shopping."

I follow along but know there's no way I can afford a single thing in any of those stores.

"You lost your purse. I want to get you a new one. Oh, here's your phone."

I side-eye him and take my cell, sliding it into my back pocket. "It was like a fifteen-dollar bag, Miller."

"Then all the reason to get a new one." He pauses at the entrance of the open area.

Prada. Gucci. Chanel. Dior. Yves Saint Laurent. Tom Ford. You name it, if it's designer, this place has it.

"Isn't there a Target or something?" I ask him.

"Cora..." He tugs me into the area that I've only ever window-shopped in.

Most of these stores are appointment only and even if they did allow walk-ins, they'd be able to sniff out my broke ass within seconds and probably throw me out.

"What about this?" He points to Dior, my eyes trailing over the bags displayed in the front.

They're beautiful, but there's no way in hell I'm letting him get me one.

"Or this?" He motions to YSL. "Those look like your style."

But what actually makes me stop in my tracks is the Alexander McQueen store.

There, right in the window, are bags with what appears to be brass knuckles built into the handle.

"You like those?" Miller waits patiently next to me. "We can go in and check them out."

I shake my head even though every single one of them is absolutely perfect.

"Humor me," he says and releases my hand to put his on the small of my back.

I allow him mainly because I've never been inside this store before and if anyone is going to make it happen, it's him. Miller has this aura about him that makes it seem like everyone around him thinks he walks on water. It's sexy how much he's respected.

"Good evening, sir," a bubbly clerk greets him immediately, her eyes not once looking at me. "What can I help you with?"

"We're just looking, thank you," he tells her and guides me over to the selection of bags that drew my attention.

The little girl in me squeals with excitement but I keep it together. My fingers twitch to reach out and touch the bags, and even though I thought I was hiding my interest, Miller picks up on it.

"You like this one?" He grabs a shiny black bag with glit-

277

tering knuckles without a care in the world that it probably costs more than all the money I have saved.

That clerk comes over anyway and starts talking. "This is our Knuckle Collection, inspired by London street culture. It adds a tough aesthetic with a sophisticated class. Is there a color or bag type you prefer?" Finally, she directs her attention toward me. "Perhaps the Hobo Mini bag." She latches onto a shiny gold handbag and sets it on the glass counter near us. "It has a detachable chain if you prefer to wear it over your shoulder or crossbody."

Miller continues eyeing the selection and grabs the most beautiful clutch I have ever seen in my entire life.

"Ay, yes, this one is quite elegant." She holds her hand out to Miller. "May I?" The lady takes it from him and turns it sideways. "This crystal-embellished clutch is adorned with Swarovski encrusted rings and also has a detachable chain." She opens it up and pulls out the tag, setting it on the glass and showing me the inside. "Big enough for your phone, a small wallet, and a lip-gloss. Perfect for a night out. Actually, I have another one in the back you might prefer. Let me get it for you." She slips away without allowing us a chance to respond.

I pick up the tag and flip it over. "Um yeah, not happening. We should leave."

Miller snatches it from my hand and chuckles when he sees the price. "That's it?"

My eyes widen. "Are you crazy? That bag is over four grand!" I keep my voice low but try to make him understand the severity.

He leans against the counter and folds his arms. "I could get you every bag in here if you wanted, Cora."

I roll my eyes. "You're out of your mind."

Miller sighs. "It's just money. Let me treat you. Please?" He tilts his head and pouts a bit, and I swear to Christ I could melt into a puddle on the ground just at the sight of him.

"I can't."

"I'll do it, you know?"

"What?"

"Buy every single bag in this store if you don't tell me which one you want." A sly grin forms on his face.

"You wouldn't."

"You have no idea the things I'd do for you." Something mysterious lingers in his tone like he has an inside joke with himself that I don't know.

I don't press to find out, but I also don't put it past him to make true on his promise. He did help me cover up a murder, why would I assume he wouldn't buy an entire store just to get me a new purse?

We have a momentary stand-off, our gazes locked onto each other as we battle telepathically.

Finally, I say, "Fine," because I'm pretty confident I'm not going to win this war.

"You want this one, don't you?" He points to the black one on the counter.

"How can you tell?"

"Your eyes did this little thing. I'd call it a twinkle but that's cliché as fuck."

"You can call it a twinkle."

"Okay, it was a twinkle." He winks at me, and I die a little inside but in the best way possible. "What else do you want?"

I glare at him. "Nothing else."

"Come on," he says while nudging my shoulder. "This is barely a blip."

"To you," I poke him back. "One *very* expensive bag is plenty."

Miller shrugs and starts looking through the case of jewelry he's leaning on. "Guess I'll just have to pick things out myself then."

The clerk appears with three bags in her grasp. She sets

them on the counter and unveils them while giving her spiel about each one.

I listen politely, because what else am I supposed to do, tell her I can't afford any of them and that the guy I'm with apparently has more money than he knows what to do with?

"We'll take this one," Miller says while pointing at the black one I confessed I liked.

Liked is a massive understatement. It's fucking beautiful and perfect. It's edgier than my normal aesthetic but there's something dark and morbid about it that I can't deny fits that part of me that I keep hidden.

"And these earrings." He points to a gold pair in the case and doesn't bother looking to see my reaction. "And that bracelet."

I study the skull earrings with the dangling pearl as she brings them out, wondering how it's possible Miller continues to pick out items that I like. Maybe he knows me better than I think he does.

"There's a matching ring, too," the clerk adds. "And necklace, if you want the whole set."

"Yep," Miller blurts out, not holding back at how she just upsold him.

I do the math in my head, the total coming to over seven thousand dollars for the stuff he has picked out already. If he doesn't stop soon, I'm going to faint.

Miller snaps his fingers. "You need a wallet."

"This one would go nicely." The clerk reaches under the back of the case and pulls out a tray with wallets on them, settling on the simple black one with a gold Alexander McQueen logo. "It'll hold a few cards and cash but will fit well in the clutch."

"What about clothes?" Miller eyes the apparel section further into the store. "That red jacket is screaming your name."

It's as if he already saw my gaze flickering to it when I looked around the store. But I won't admit that, because then he'll insist on buying me it, too.

"It has matching trousers." The clerk smiles as if she's aware she could convince this man to buy me anything at this point. "Come. Try it on." She waves us over and takes off in that direction.

Miller puts his hand on my lower back and nudges me to follow her.

I sigh and comply, my eyes focused on the back of her head so he doesn't pick up on anything else I might be interested in. I can barely breathe without him noticing the shift in pattern. It's strangely comforting to know someone is paying that much consideration to what I desire.

Usually, I'm the one hyper-vigilant in keeping others happy —it's bizarre to be on the receiving end of that for a change.

The jacket is bright red, cropped, and oozing elegance.

"It has a concealed front fastener so you can wear the top by itself." The woman grabs it off the rack and snatches a matching skirt, too. "The trousers have this gorgeous bow on the side."

"What about this, too?" Miller runs his hand along the fabric of an electric navy dress.

"That chiffon dress is stunning." The clerk takes one of those, too, and walks toward the fitting room. "Feel free to grab anything else you like, too," she tells Miller.

I trail her to the private area. "I don't think I ever got your name."

"Sasha," she offers with a smile that seems mildly genuine.

"I'm Cora." I extend my hand once she's unloaded the clothes onto the hooks in the room.

"Your husband has a great eye."

"Oh, he's..." But I catch myself before I continue. "Yeah, he's got great fashion sense."

"I'll be right out here if you need anything." She slips out and leaves me with the few items.

I fumble with the tags and wonder how I'm going to make these look bad so he doesn't spend another eight thousand dollars. The dress alone is forty-five hundred. Here's to hoping he doesn't realize shoes would go well with these outfits, too. Good thing he doesn't know what size I wear...although it wouldn't be hard for him to figure it out.

A few minutes later, I step into the mirrored sitting area and Miller perks up in his seat.

"Damn." He blinks a few times and clutches his chest.

"Yeah?" I do a spin and even though this vaguely reminds me of how I spent my day yesterday, it's nothing like how Ricardo treated me.

"We'll take one of each," he tells Sasha as she approaches with a box in her grasp.

"Try these on," she says, pulling out a black heeled boot with blood-red heel and silver toe cap.

I flit my gaze at Miller and he grins. "Ah, come on."

The shoes fit perfectly and only make me continue to wonder how he knows everything he does about me. Shit that normal people don't know. Like my legal name and my food allergies. It's like he did an extensive background check to learn all the little and big details that aren't quite common knowledge.

I should probably think it's creepy but it's weirdly romantic.

"We'll take those, too." Miller leans into his chair and crosses one leg over the other.

I make my way back to the dressing room and hope the dress I haven't tried on yet is uglier than it appears. Because if I walk out there and it's remotely cute, he's going to insist on getting it and I don't feel comfortable leaving here with clothing that expensive. I don't own anything that costs as much as any of this, by itself or even added completely up. My entire life is worth less than the stuff he wants to buy me in this store.

And I have a feeling if I wanted to go anywhere else after this, he wouldn't protest in the slightest, and would probably encourage it.

But the second I slip into the dress and glance in the mirror, I know he and I are both a goner.

I tiptoe out of the dressing room and Miller's eyes light up like a kid on Christmas morning.

"Zip me up?" I ask him and he rushes over, practically shoving the clerk out of the way to do it himself.

His fingers brush my skin and send a chill over my entire body. Goddamn, I want him to touch me in more places but this is not the time or place for that.

I've wanted him for so long but thought he was out of reach, and now that the feeling is mutual, I can barely contain myself.

"Should I add the dress?" The clerk stands there and waits for a response.

"And shoes to match it," he tells her, not blinking an eye at how the bill keeps going up and up.

"I know a pump that would go quite well with this dress." She leaves the dressing room area and goes into an employee-only area, leaving us alone.

"You look fucking stunning," Miller says, his breath on my back. He grazes his knuckles against my flesh, and it pebbles with goosebumps.

I turn toward him and sigh. "You don't have to do all of this, you know? I thought you just wanted to get me a bag."

He cups my chin between his thumb and finger. "I'd get you the world if you wanted it, Cora."

"Why?"

"Because you deserve it."

"You don't know that. I could be a bad person."

"Being a bad person has nothing to do with whether you deserve it or not."

"You think I'm a bad person?"

Miller meets my gaze, his eyes darting to my lips briefly. "Don't put words in my mouth."

"That didn't answer my question."

"I don't think you're a bad person, Cora." He pauses and then adds, "But that doesn't matter, does it? You already think what you want about yourself. My opinion isn't going to change that."

"It might."

"So if I told you I thought you were the most special person I've ever met, that you're beautiful and kind and intelligent, and that no man is good enough for you, would you believe that?"

My heart stutters. "Probably not."

"See."

I avert my gaze. "Do you mean it, though?"

He gently forces my attention with his hand on my chin again. "I promise."

And because I'm an immature child, I bring my hand up and hold out my pinky. "Pinky promise?"

Miller's cheek turns up into a grin, and he wraps his little finger around mine. "I pinky promise." He leans forward, his face just a breath from mine. "And to make it more serious. I'll seal it with a kiss." Miller presses his lips to mine so softly I'm not convinced he touches them at all.

I kiss him back and wish I could rewind the clock and give us more time. I'd time travel to that night I saw him across the bar and march right up to him and say everything that was on my mind. That when I saw him, something sparked to life inside of me that never dimmed in all the time we've known each other. That every single moment I've been around him, my body has gravitated toward his and for no real reason at all, I've trusted him, and I've felt safe with him. So when he walked in to find me covered with my boss's blood, I was relieved that it was him and no one else.

But it's a lie that there's no reason for the safety and trust because if I think back to every interaction with him, he's always made it a point to offer gentle and secure dominance, walking on the outside of the sidewalk, stepping in front to block the view when I had to readjust my shirt, escorting me to the bathroom at the bar when I've been out with June, commandeering a drink that some random guy got me. I can recall countless occasions when he was there, watching and waiting to protect me, even if he was getting nothing in return from me.

He kept me safe when I was no one to him, I just hadn't really noticed until now.

Sasha clears her throat to interrupt us. She's holding an open box with a pair of simple black pumps tucked inside.

"Perfect," Miller tells her.

"I'll get everything boxed up," she says with a smile on her face.

I walk toward the dressing room but turn around and catch Miller before he returns to his seat. "Hey, can you come in here and unzip me?"

"Of course." He follows me in and the door latches shut behind him, giving us the first ounce of privacy since I found out he had feelings for me.

I turn around and move my hair out of the way for him.

Miller unclasps the hook and then slides the zipper down.

I face him and let the dress fall to the floor, leaving me there in nothing but my red lace panties.

He swallows harshly and meets my gaze, his eyes not daring to move another inch. Always the gentleman, this one.

"Kiss me," I tell him and step forward, pressing my nearly naked body to him.

Miller hesitates but not for long. He wraps his hand around the base of my neck and crashes his lips onto mine. Our tongues meet, our mouths parting and melting into each other's. My body comes alive with desire, and I find myself unable to resist the thoughts running through my head.

I reach between us and latch onto his cock through his pants, and he moans into me.

"Cora," he pants and breaks away. "You don't have to...."

But doesn't he realize this is exactly what I want? That I've always wanted him.

I keep my eyes on him and drop to my knees, my fingers unbuttoning his pants.

"I want this," I tell him as I free his cock. "I want you." I grip him harder and position the tip of his cock against my lips, swirling my tongue over his precum.

"Cora..." he breathes.

I take him into my mouth, slowly at first, my gaze still on his. Stroking him, I thrust him in and out and revel in how hard he becomes. Swallowing more and more, my eyes water, and heat swells between my legs—his pleasure only seems to heighten mine. My moan vibrates on his shaft, and I tighten my grip.

A knock sounds on the door but Miller grabs a fistful of my hair and keeps his cock buried in my mouth.

"We'll be right out," he says through labored breath and continues bucking his hips gently.

I stare up at him and dig my fingers into his thigh as he hardens in my mouth. My nipples pebble, and the desire to stand and bend over in front of him is strong, but we don't have time for that, not when Sasha is no doubt standing nearby wondering when she's going to get her commission. Working my hand, I pump him until he finishes down the back of my throat, and I pull him out, smiling against his cock and swallowing his climax.

"Jesus Christ, Cora," he pants. "That was...unexpected."

I rise to my feet and pull my white tank top over my head and slip into the skirt I was wearing.

Miller grabs onto my arm and drags me toward him, pressing his lips to mine. "I'm going to have to repay you for that later."

"I didn't do it to get even," I tell him. "I did it because I wanted to."

"Don't get me started on the things I want to do to you." Miller exhales and rubs his nose against mine.

He releases me to reposition his now soft cock and straightens his shirt in the mirror.

I finish getting dressed and slide my shoes back on as Miller picks up the *very* expensive dress I was kneeling on while I gave him a blow job.

We leave the dressing room with our faces flushed and find Sasha in the open area with her arms crossed and her posture stiff.

"I can check you out over here." She extends her arm to motion at the counter with numerous bags stacked on top. Sasha goes around the back and types into an iPad-looking device. "Your total is $22,341.19."

My mouth drops open, and I brace myself on the counter.

Miller doesn't bat an eye, instead, he reaches into his back pocket and pulls out a card that looks identical to the one he gave me yesterday. He signs a receipt and makes it seem so fucking easy to spend twenty-fucking-grand in like twelve seconds.

"It was a pleasure working with you today," Sasha says.

I smile politely even though the idea of spending that much money kind of makes me want to vomit. I reach for the bags but Miller takes the handles and insists on carrying all of them.

He holds out his elbow, and I slide my hand under it, partially because I need him to keep me upright.

Even with the booze still running through my veins, I'm well aware of the magnitude of that purchase.

Once we're through the double doors that are held open by Alexander McQueen employees, he pauses and asks, "Anywhere else you want to go?"

"You can't be serious."

"Especially after what you just did to me in that dressing

room...safe to say I'd buy you anything you wanted, Cora. Hell, I would have before that."

I pat his arm. "I think that's enough for one day, Miller."

My phone buzzes on the way back to his car and out of instinct, I check it and instantly regret doing so.

Only, this time it's not Ricardo.

It's June.

My so-called best friend.

The one who lied to me.

Who told me that Miller was gay so I wouldn't pursue him. Who keeps secrets and refuses to include me in her life even though she expects me to tell her every single detail of mine.

She's always been a withdrawn person, and I've accepted that there are things about her and the guys that I won't know, but to add that on top of her sabotaging my potential romantic happiness...it's hard to not be mad at her.

Finally, when I was coming around to the idea that I should ask her for help with my situation, I learn that she blatantly lied to me *and* got Simon and the rest of the guys on board, too. It makes it hard to trust any of them. And if I can't trust them, how can I confide in them about a situation that could put all our lives on the line?

I guess that's what I get for thinking that I could ask someone else for help—a reminder from the universe that I'm on my own, that I can't rely on anyone, that I have to do this myself.

21

ALEC

I haven't been able to sleep the past few nights, but that isn't really a surprise, I never sleep well. Lately, though, it's been worse, because my worry for Cora has only grown.

I can't get that conversation out of my head.

The things that she said, drunk or not, don't make sense.

I hate the way my mind runs wild, and I can't come to terms with her saying she was only drunkenly rambling. I'm well aware we say weird shit when we're intoxicated, but usually, there's some kind of truth to it, and if even a shred of what she said was true, how can I let that go?

It doesn't help that my bed still smells of her, and every time I toss and turn, I'm bathed in her scent and reminded of how fucking badly I miss her.

I'm trying not to come on too strong but it's hard when my every single thought revolves around her.

I glance at my phone and check the date and time to make sure I haven't made a mistake. Thursday at noon, Bram's Diner.

I'm a little early, but punctuality never hurt anyone.

I slip into the corner booth and wait for Miller to arrive, ordering us both a cup of coffee while I wait.

June sets two mugs on the table and fills both of them. "You're going to leave me a good tip, right?" She winks at me even though we both know she isn't going to let me pay.

I guess that's a perk of being her driver—free coffee and the occasional blueberry old-fashioned donut.

The door to the diner chimes, and when I look up, Miller walks in and glances around.

I wave him over, and he slides into the booth across from me. "What's up, man?"

It's now that I realize this is the worst place I could have asked him to meet me since June is literally buzzing about doing her job and no doubt spying on us every chance she gets.

I scoot farther into the corner of the booth. "Uh, do you think you could come over here?"

Miller narrows his eyes, and for a second, I wonder if he's going to shoot me for asking him something so fucking strange. "Dude, I don't know what you've heard, but I'm not gay. You're an attractive guy and all but I'm into chicks."

I shake my head and sigh. "That's not why I'm asking." I pat the seat. "Just trust me, please?"

Miller sighs and slips out of his side to join me on mine. He reaches for the mug of coffee and takes a cautious sip. "What is it, Alec?"

"It's about Cora," I say as low as possible without drawing anyone's unwanted attention.

Miller blinks stiffly and turns toward me. "Tell me everything."

I fidget with my own mug and pull it toward me. "So like, I might be totally overreacting."

"Let me be the judge of that." Miller taps his fingers on the table impatiently.

"Okay so, the other night, when we hung out..." I note the

way his fingers ball into a fist and wonder how much of this story I actually need to tell him.

"Go on," he says, his tone even despite his fist.

"She was a little drunk and—"

"If you're the reason her face is bruised, I will fucking slit your throat with that butter knife."

"Wait, what? Her face is bruised? When did *you* see her?" I try to keep my voice low but it's hard when we're talking about someone as important as Cora.

"Monday," he tells me. "You swear it wasn't you?"

I shake my head. "I saw her Sunday, and her face was fine. I would have noticed if it was bruised."

"That means it had to have happened sometime between when she left you Sunday and when I saw her Monday after work." Miller seems to get lost in his thoughts for a long moment. "Now that I think about it, she seemed upset when I talked to her Sunday, but she said it was allergies." Miller pauses and looks at me. "If this isn't about the bruise, then what is it?"

"Well, I've been worried about her."

"Why?"

"The other night, when she was fucked up...she said some stuff I can't make sense of."

"What did she say?"

"It was all kind of a blur..."

June approaches our table with a pot of coffee. "Hey Miller, I didn't know you were still in town."

"June, hey, yeah, I was gone for a few days but I'm back for the foreseeable future." Miller turns toward her.

"Oh, that's cool. Are you setting up a permanent residence?"

"Yeah, I got a place over at The Wellerton. Cora's decorating it, actually."

"I'm sure it'll turn out beautifully if she's in charge of it."

"I don't have any doubts," Miller tells her.

The forced awkward small talk is borderline painful.

"Speaking of Cora," June says. "Have you heard from her lately?"

"I've been in touch, yeah, why?"

June shrugs and her face seems to drop. "We were supposed to get together at the beginning of the week, but she's been blowing me off."

"She's probably busy with work. I can say something to her the next time I see her?" Miller's phone vibrates rather loudly, and he immediately reaches and slides it out of his pocket. He checks the screen quickly and disregards it.

"No, it's fine," June tells him. "You're probably right. This project she's working on is big. Anyway...did you two want to order anything?"

I shake my head and Miller adds, "No, I think we're good with coffee, thanks."

"For sure." She gives us her fake customer service smile. "Let me know if you need anything else."

"Thanks, June," I say as she's walking away.

It's strange to see the roles reversed—June's usually my boss and here she is, my waitress. I'll never understand why she works here when her boyfriends are loaded, but that's her life, not mine.

"You were saying," Miller continues where we left off.

"Yeah, so, the shit she was saying was off the wall. But hear me out, she mentioned..." I look out to make sure June isn't near before I say, "Ricardo."

Miller's fist tightens again, and he brings it onto his lap like he's trying to contain it as if it will detonate at any given second. "What do you mean she mentioned him?"

"I don't know dude; it didn't make sense. None of it did. I asked her the next day, and she said she was drunk and chalked it up to that."

"Why are you telling me this?" Miller asks me.

"Because man, you bought a whole fucking building just to

fire her boss. It's no secret you care about her. I was hoping maybe, I don't know, this is going to sound fucking crazy..." I hate that the idea even came into my head, but I can't think of anything else to ensure her safety.

"Just say it," Miller blurts out.

"Could you like, put a tracker on her or something? Monitor where she's going. Is that even a thing?"

Miller runs his hand through his hair. "Yeah, it's a thing. And..." He lets out an exaggerated sigh.

"Well don't leave me fucking hanging here."

Miller side-eyes me and lowers his voice. "I already put one on her."

"What? When?"

"The other day." Miller glances at June across the diner and turns toward me. "I took her shopping. She told me she lost her purse, so I took her to dinner and bought her a new one. I slipped a tracker in both of them."

"You bought her two purses?"

"Yeah, I mean, one's super small. You know the shit girls take to clubs and stuff, and the other one's a normal size." He shakes his head. "That's beside the point. I've been keeping an eye on her. She hasn't gone anywhere but home and work this week."

"Hold up, you said she lost her purse. She had it when she left me on Sunday. She must have lost it somewhere between when she left and when you saw her. And she was upset when you talked to her? It could have happened around then."

"Yeah, maybe," Miller says. "Either way, I have it covered. I see everywhere she goes." He scratches his chin. "We saw London on Monday night."

"Who's London?" I ask.

"Ricardo's daughter."

"Okay..."

"They knew each other." Miller reaches for his mug of coffee and takes a drink. "I thought it sounded suspicious but didn't have a reason to question it. What else did she say when she was drunk?"

"Something about a baby." I rack my brain and try to remember exactly what she said. "And that she killed her boss." I chuckle but the humor is gone when Miller doesn't seem to react the same way. I stare at him and when he doesn't respond, I smack his shoulder. "Dude. Talk to me."

Miller sighs.

"Is it true?" My heart pounds out of my chest because if even a fraction of what she confessed was actually true, there's a possibility that the rest is, too. And if that means what I think it does, she's in trouble with Ricardo, I just don't know how badly.

According to what I've learned of him, he's not the type of guy to fuck around with. He's ruthless, but not in the same way the guys I work for are. Ricardo has no moral compass. There isn't anything he wouldn't do, including selling his daughter to the highest bidder. If he'd do that to her, there's no telling what he would do to Cora.

"It's not *not* true." Miller glances around the diner again and focuses on me. "Listen, I don't want to tell you anything that you can't deny if the situation ever arose, but I can tell you that there is truth to what she said."

Cora killed her boss? How is that even possible? She's sweet, and innocent, and isn't capable of such a thing, right?

But when I think back to her telling me that if I saw what she kept hidden away, I wouldn't like her anymore. I wonder if this is what she meant—that she murdered a man.

Surely, she must have had a damn good reason.

He was bothering her, giving her a hard time. Maybe things escalated and she was forced to. Cora is a good person; she wouldn't just kill someone for the sake of killing them.

It had to of been justified, and if that's the case, I don't fault her for taking things into her own hands and doing what she had to do.

I only wish that she didn't have to carry the weight of that secret alone and felt like she could confide in me. At least she has Miller, and I guess that has to be good enough, for now.

"I know what plausible deniability is," I tell Miller. "I wouldn't say anything to anyone, even if I did know." Hell, I work for criminals every single day, there are plenty of secrets tucked away that I'd never confess.

Mainly because they aren't mine to tell, and partly because I don't want to end up dead in a ditch for betraying them.

CORA

I only agree to meet June after work today because I can't stomach the idea of being around my dad anymore. I've gone home every night this week and he's been there, lurking and trying to talk to me, providing me with zero answers to where my mom is and if she's okay.

I can't continue to listen to his evasive answers and exist in the same space as him. When he's in his room, doing whatever he does in there, it's easier, but every single night this week he's waited out in the living room for me to come home and basically corners me the second I walk in the door.

At least if I go out with June, I can arrive later than usual and potentially avoid him in the process.

My Uber drops me off at the outskirts of the Haven District, and I walk the rest of the way to one of the bars that Simon owns. I wouldn't be surprised if he has the entire Haven in his back pocket. Just when I think I have a grip on his investments, they surprise me by saying he's bought something else.

I'm not sure there's anything in this town that at least one of them doesn't have some kind of say in.

I still haven't figured out who bought The Wellerton, and

honestly, I wouldn't put it past Simon to have purchased that, too. Some kind of weird power play or maybe an overprotective brother vibe to give me job security. Once the initial concern of *am I going to get fired* wore off, it dawned on me that it very well could have been him who bought the building.

Who else has that kind of money around here?

The bars are buzzing despite it being early in the evening on a Friday. Usually, the rowdy crowd waits a bit later to come out but tonight, things seem to be getting wild already.

I sidestep a couple making out on the sidewalk and reach for the door to the bar. The thing swings open and slams into my shoulder.

"Shit, sorry," some college-aged kid blurts out and then continues to rush past me without any actual care that he could have caused any damage.

Pressing my hand to my shoulder, I make my way inside and take in the bustling crowd.

June waves me over from her spot at a high-top table near the billiards area.

"Hey," I say above the loud music and set my clutch on the table.

"Damn, Cora." June spots the expensive bag immediately, her taste having massively evolved since she got into a relationship with four very wealthy men. "Where did you get this?"

"Miller," I tell her, not holding back.

Her eyes widen and she bobs her head up and down. "Nice. I didn't know you two were..."

"Why?" I cut her off. "Because he's *gay*?"

"I mean, no, I just..."

I pour myself a beer from the pitcher she has on the table. "Cut the shit, June. I know it's a lie." I can barely believe how the words are blurting out of my mouth. I'm not typically this crass with her but it's been a long week, and I don't exactly have the time or energy to sugarcoat things anymore.

"Cora..." June says but I put my hand out to stop her.

"I don't want to talk about it."

"Is that why you've been avoiding me all week?" June pushes and I find myself getting more and more pissed off.

What doesn't she understand about me not wanting to talk about this?

I snatch my clutch and beer and say, "I want a shot. Do you want one? I'm going to go get one." I leave before she can say another word and head straight to the bar.

My sights skim the crowd and settle on Simon in the far corner, doing his creepy bodyguard thing he always does when June goes anywhere in public. If it's not him, it's one of the other guys, but usually, it's Simon.

He stares at me, a hint of concern lining his face, but I ignore him and continue on my way.

"Excuse me," I call out to the bartender who is clearly flirting with a patron instead of taking orders. "Hello?"

She rolls her eyes and mutters something to the dude in front of her and walks at the slowest fucking pace ever over to me. "Can I help you?"

"Two shots of tequila." I reach into my clutch only to realize I forgot to put cash in it from when I switched my bags over.

Miller had surprised me with another bag so I had been using that one all week to and from work. Tonight, I figured I'd go for something compact, opting for the bejeweled clutch I absolutely fell in love with.

"That'll be twelve dollars," she tells me as she pours the shots.

I thumb the black card tucked into the slim wallet he got me and slide it out. He told me I could use it, I'm sure he won't mind a twelve-dollar purchase.

The bartender throws her thumb toward a sign behind her. "Twenty dollar minimum for cards."

Shit.

"I'll take two more shots, make them doubles."

She takes my card and pauses to look at me. "Can I see some ID?"

I show her my driver's license, and once she's certain the names match, she plasters on a fake smile.

"Sorry about that," she says. "Bar rules. Is there anything else I can get for you?"

It's mildly entertaining how quickly her tone switched when she held that black American Express in her hand.

"A couple bottles of water."

"Of course." She looks out into the crowd. "Where are you sitting? I can have your drinks brought to your table."

"That won't be necessary." I down the original two shots she poured me and stack the shot glasses on top of each other. "I can carry everything."

She slides the bottles and doubles toward me. "Are you sure?"

"Yep." I secure the black card into my wallet and shove my clutch under my arm. Signing the receipt, I leave her a decent tip because, from my experience watching June work at bars, a little goes a long way. Sure, she started out being a bitch, but I'm well aware it's usually the guys you flirt with that end up leaving the biggest tips.

With one hand, I latch onto the bottles and the handle of my beer, and in the other, I grip the shots. Easy peasy.

Bypassing the bustling crowds, I make my way back to June and drop the drinks on the table.

"I don't like you being mad at me, Cor." June sits on the stool with her elbows on the table.

I sigh. "And I don't like being lied to." I shove the shot toward her. "But seriously, I don't want to talk about it. I just want to have fun. Can we do that?"

June seems to accept my request and asks me, "Do you want to dance?"

"Now you're speaking my language." I pick up my shot and hold it out to her. "To dancing away our troubles."

"I can cheers to that." June clinks her glass against mine, and we down them, the warmth coating my entire chest as it settles into my belly.

My head numbs and temporarily blocks out how mad I am at her. I just have to get through a couple more hours, then I can go home and curl up in my bed.

June latches onto the bottle of water I placed in front of her and downs a healthy swig of it. "That tequila is foul."

I laugh and do the same but am reminded of life when we were both broke and could barely afford to go out at all. I put our nights out on credit cards just because I needed them, because she needed them. Since getting my new job, I've been able to make a dent in that debt, but I barely make enough to survive, let alone pay much extra. Between my student loans, credit cards, and basic living expenses, there's no way I can move out of my parent's house anytime soon.

And if I stay there much longer, I'm going to fucking go insane.

I guess I don't have to worry about that in a couple of weeks when I become Ricardo's personal babymaker. I can't imagine he's going to allow me to live at home if he wants me at his disposal. Hopefully, I can keep my job and maintain the career that I've worked tirelessly at. If I happen to make it out of this alive, I need something I can fall back on when it's all said and done.

At some point, June signaled to Simon, because when I turn around to go to the dance floor, I run smack dab into his body.

"God, Simon, you're standing there like a fucking statue." I hold my nose and take a step back. "Did you spawn there or what?"

Simon pats my head. "You're just mad you're not as stealthy as me."

"Is that it?" I roll my eyes at him.

June strolls over and plants a kiss on his cheek. "Watch our drinks while we dance?"

His jaw clenches but he forces a smile. "Of course, love." Simon leans in close to her and whispers, "But if I see anyone touch you, I'm going to snap their neck." He kisses her back and settles into a chair at the table. "Have fun."

I down the rest of my beer before slamming it on the table and wiping my mouth. So very lady-like, but I don't give a fuck. I don't have anyone here I'm trying to impress.

"Come on," June says as she weaves her arm through mine.

We take off toward the dance floor, the music growing louder every step of the way. Some EDM tune pulses through my entire body and once we're deeper into the crowd, we both start moving to the beat.

The music and alcohol come to the forefront of my mind, and I give in to it and allow my worries to disappear. I sway back and forth and giggle as I latch onto June's hand and twirl her in a circle.

For a moment I forget everything and am taken back to a simpler time when my only concerns were college and keeping my trauma locked deeply away. Back then, my focus was being a good friend and keeping everyone around me happy. Not much has changed since then, except the added stress of giving myself over to a high-powered criminal and the continued deterioration of the relationship I have with my father.

I shake my head and rid myself of those thoughts. I'm supposed to be dancing, not thinking.

The rhythm of the music changes, and a new beat causes the entire area to start jumping up and down.

We join them and smile at each other, sweat glistening both of our bodies despite only being out here for five minutes.

Someone's hands find my waist and for a second, I go along with it and move with them. It isn't until their fingers dig a bit harder into my sides that I grow uncomfortable.

"Get your fucking hands off of her," June blurts out and shoves the guy off me. She slides her fingers under her waistband slightly and pauses like she's waiting for the guy to respond before making her decision.

Does she have a gun? A knife? A throwing fucking star?

I spin on my heel and push my palm into the guy's chest. "I'm not interested," I tell him.

He looks me up and down and licks his lips. "Didn't seem like you weren't interested when you backed your ass up into me." The guy, some twenty-something drunk kid with a sad excuse of a beard, grabs his junk and lifts his head as if he's performing some kind of disgusting mating ritual that must only work on drunk girls at the bar.

"Back the fuck up," I tell him above the music.

Everyone else around us continues to dance and doesn't seem bothered by the altercation. And I'm grateful for it, because when this dude refuses to take no for an answer, I slide my fingers into the clutch that Miller got me and slam my fist into the prick's face.

The gold-coated brass knuckles bloody his nose and if I'm not mistaken, knocks one of his teeth out. He covers himself, pulling away to spit blood into his hand.

"You fucking bitch, what the hell," he manages to get out.

I advance on him. "Call me a bitch *one* more time."

But he doesn't, instead, he scurries back into the crowd with his tail between his legs and disappears from my line of sight.

Another hand lands on my shoulder and I move quick and crane my arm back to throw another punch.

June raises her arms in front of her. "Just me."

Simon appears from fucking nowhere and scans the people around us. "Where did he go?"

I sigh and slide my hand out of the knuckles. "It's fine. I took care of it."

Simon grabs both of our elbows and all but drags us off the dance floor.

"If you're here, who's watching our drinks?" I shout so he can hear me.

Once we get to our table, my sights land on the answer to my question.

"Hey," Alec says in that perfectly charming voice of his.

I drop my clutch onto the table and rub my hand, wishing that more tequila shots would appear the same way Simon does the second June's in danger.

"Did I just see you sock a guy with this?" Alec picks up my bag and examines it. "Ew, his blood is on it."

"I'm going to get you some ice," June says and disappears before Simon can protest.

"And more tequila," I call out after her.

She throws her arm up in acknowledgment of my request and continues through the throng of bodies.

I pour beer into my mug, accidentally spilling some over the edge. I'm not that great at doing things left-handed and my right one is currently fucking throbbing.

"Haven't you had enough?" Simon asks me, his stupid green eyes watching me chug the beer.

"Haven't you?" I wipe at my mouth and burp.

"What does that even mean?" Simon's brows pinch together, and he climbs into the chair next to me. "What's up with you, Cor?"

"Don't *Cor* me," I practically spit at him.

Simon breathes in deeply and sighs. "What did I do now?"

"Other than exist?" Okay, I'm being harsh, but still, he pissed me off and the alcohol running through my veins is making me want to throat-punch him with the brass knuckle bag.

"You good?" Alec draws my attention, and it calms me more than I thought it would. But it's temporary, because the second I let it settle in, I'm reminded that it can't last.

"I'm fine," I tell him and shrug. "Why is everyone so worried about me?"

My chest tightens, and the symptoms I try to ignore often come rising to the surface. I push them down, desperate to make them go away. I can't let these people see me break. I won't let it happen.

Another song blares across the speakers, a mashup of Taylor Swift and Rihanna. It's weird, but it works.

"We should dance." I reach for Alec, but he doesn't move. Instead, his seriously dark eyes bore into me.

"Cora."

I hate the way my name sounds out of his mouth.

June pushes through to get to us, two shots in her grasp and a bag of ice in the other hand. "Here."

She plops the frozen thing on top of my hand, and I snatch one of the shots before Simon can persuade her not to give me one.

I shiver as the ice falls in the bag around my hand, my knuckles throbbing from the impact of the brass meeting that dude's face. It hurts, but it's a reminder that I'm in control, that I call the shots. Even if it won't last much longer than the next couple of weeks.

The tequila warms and numbs my body all at the same time. My thoughts grow fuzzy at the seams and the desire to scream and cry grows strong. My patience wears thin, and I bite at my lip to keep my mouth shut.

Only, it doesn't work as well as I hope.

"Why did you do it?" I ask June, my good hand on my hip.

"What?" She feigns ignorance even though she knows exactly what I'm talking about.

"Don't act stupid." I look to Simon, the deadliest man in this room. "You both lied to me."

"What's this about?" Simon glances at June for help.

"Cora, hey, want to get some fresh air?" Alec comes up behind me, but I shrug him off.

"Were you in on this, too?" I ask him, suddenly feeling way more defensive than I was a minute ago.

I don't like it, but that control I thought I had, is disappearing and my emotions are starting to get the best of me.

Alec throws up his arms and genuine uncertainty creeps across his beautiful features. "I have no idea what's going on. And you know I'd never lie to you." He inches closer. "You have to know that, don't you?"

I step away from all of them, the bag of ice still pressed to my sore hand. "Honestly, I don't know anymore." I focus on June. "I trusted you. I would have done anything for you. And you repay me by what, sabotaging my happiness?"

June tilts her head, her dark poker straight hair bunching up on one side. "Come on, Cora. That's not why I did it."

"Then why?" I blurt out and point to Simon. "You get him, and Coen, and Magnus, and Dom, and I get what? No one? Why do you deserve to be happy and in love?"

"I never said you didn't," June argues. "Of course, I want you happy. You're important to me."

I laugh sharply. "So important that you won't even tell me what's going on in your life? I have to piece it together myself?" Uncontrollable tears roll down my cheeks. "So important that you don't even see me suffering right in front of you. So important that..." I shake my head. "Never mind. I'm done. I can't do this anymore."

Simon reaches for me, and I yank my arm away too hard and fall back, hitting my head on a chair. He tries to help me up, but I smack him away.

"Don't fucking touch me," I snap at him.

Alec grabs my elbow and lifts me off the floor. "Cora, Christ, are you okay?"

His touch is cool and comforting and I know he's just trying to help, but I can't be here right now. Not with them, my so-called friends, the liars.

"I'm leaving." I stalk forward and grab my bag off the table. "Do not follow me." I enunciate each word harshly so they understand the severity.

"Cora!" June calls out as I turn my back to them.

"Let her go," Simon tells her.

"She can't go, she's..." But I don't make out the rest of what she says because I push into the crowd and shove my way through the bodies until I burst through the door and out onto the sidewalk.

The fresh air hits me like a ton of bricks, and I suck in a gasping lungful as the people standing outside gawk at me.

With my vision blurring and my chest tightening, I rush past them and stumble along the side of the building. Silent tears stream down, and I hate myself for cracking. This isn't what I do. I hold myself together at all times, never allowing anyone to see this side of me. The real me. The one that's falling the fuck apart.

"Cora," Alec calls out and rushes over, his strong hands reaching out to steady me. "Talk to me, babe, what's going on?"

I walk farther, desperate to get away from the noise of the Haven District bars, until I find a less noisy area. I slink down along the brick building and sit my ass on the hard sidewalk. "I can't do this anymore," I tell him.

"You don't have to, I'm here. I've got you." Alec kneels next to me and cups my hands in his.

I pull away. "You're..." I look up at him through my watery eyes.

He's so fucking pretty. Too pretty. Like he came out of a modeling magazine. He's perfect, and it pisses me off. Alec always knows the right thing to say, to do. Alec has his life together and will never understand the turmoil churning inside of me. He's meant for someone else. Someone who isn't pretending to be fine, someone who isn't falling apart.

"I don't love you," I hiss.

"Cora..." The hurt is written all over his face and still, he remains next to me.

"I don't. I never will." I choke back a sob. "And you don't love me."

"You remember," he says.

But does it matter that I do? Every single word he said that night was etched into my memory like it had just happened. That his confession lives within me and will be something I carry to the grave. I replay it in my mind, the sensation that rippled through me when he said it, something I relive over and over—one of the few good moments I'll hold onto forever.

"I'm not leaving you." Alec holds onto my hands.

"I don't want you here," I lie. "We were a mistake."

"You don't mean that."

I hate hurting him but this is the only way I can get him to understand this is never going to work. We will never work. Because we were doomed from the start.

"You should get back to work," I tell him and pull one of my hands free to wipe at my nose. "Don't want to upset your employers."

"I don't give a fuck about them, Cora. You're what matters to me." Alec's chest rises and he sighs. "I'm going to make a phone call." He stands up and pulls out his phone, turning his back to me momentarily.

I think about running but know that I'm too drunk and too uncoordinated to make it far. His legs are significantly longer than mine, and all that would do is make me look more foolish than I already do.

Deciding against fleeing, I slide my phone out of my back pocket and blink a few times until I can see the screen more clearly. I push a sequence of buttons and press the thing to my ear; the ringing way louder than I recall it ever being.

A thick, gravely voice comes across the line. "Cora?"

I sniffle. "Can you come get me?"

"Where are you?"

Alec turns around as I'm craning my neck to find a street sign or some landmark to give to Silver.

"Who is that?" Alec asks me and shoves his phone in his pocket. "Give me the phone, Cora." He snatches it out of my grasp and remains on his feet, way far out of my reach.

I lean my head against the building and close my eyes.

"Who is this?" Alec says into my phone. "Uh, Alec, yeah, that Alec." He pauses. "Haven District. I'll text you her location. Yeah, thanks. See you soon." A second later, he's back at my side and returns my phone.

"I can't breathe," I say with my eyes still pinched shut, tears rolling down my cheeks.

"Cora." Alec pulls my legs onto his lap and tugs me toward his chest. "Come here. You're safe, okay?"

I sob into him and wish I could make it stop. "I'm sorry," I blubber.

"Shh." He smooths my hair off my forehead and presses his lips to my skin. Alec rocks me and I lose track of time, the only thing I know is the steady beating of his heart and his arms wrapped around me.

I hate myself for being mean to him, for making a scene. I yelled at June and Simon, and I lied to Alec about my feelings for him. It's better this way, I remind myself, because here pretty soon, I'm going to go away and the relationships we had will be a thing of the past. If I don't cut these ties now, it will only make things harder in the future. I don't know why I thought I could enjoy these final few weeks.

"I'm going to lift you," Alec says moments before he rises to his feet with me still in his arms.

I blink through my swollen lids as he walks me away from the building and lowers me into a passenger seat.

"What happened?" Silver asks him, his voice gruff and demanding.

"Rough night." Alec exhales. "Promise me you'll keep her safe?"

"On my life." Silver clears his throat. "You're okay with me taking her?"

"You're the one she called." There's a sort of sadness in Alec's voice that rips my heart in two. "She chose you."

Someone shuts the door and I remain curled into myself even when Silver climbs into the driver's side. I can sense his dominating presence without even opening my eyes.

"You came," I whisper.

He lets out a breath. "You called."

23

CORA

I wake up in a bed that's more comfortable than mine in clothes that don't belong to me.

I rub my eyes and yawn, my breath foul and lingering of the excessive booze I drank last night.

"How did you sleep?" Silver's voice is calm and even and when I turn, I find him sitting in the chair in the corner, one of his legs crossed over the other.

"Okay, I think." I try to recall how I got here, but I come up short.

"There's coffee on the nightstand. And a water." Silver nods past me and rises to his feet. "When you're ready, come into the living room. We need to talk." He leaves the room without another word.

I feel like a child who's just been scalded and is about to get in even more trouble than they already are.

But because my bladder is screaming at me, I decide I better get moving sooner rather than later.

In his bathroom, I find three boxes of tampons lining the counter, the tops of them ripped open. My stomach cramps and reminds me that at some point last night, I started my period. I vaguely recall struggling to open the boxes, but how I got them to begin with is lost on me.

I make quick work of freshening up—changing my tampon and brushing my teeth being at the top of my priority list. On my way to the living room, I chug some of the water and take the coffee he had left out for me.

What I find when I step out of his bedroom is something I never would have imagined.

It's not just Silver in his living room, but Alec, too.

My lips part and I look between them, unsure of what's going on. "Um..."

"Sit," Silver says and pats the spot next to him.

I comply, only because I have no idea what other options I have.

"Does someone want to tell me what's going on?" I ask them and busy myself by taking a drink of the coffee.

Oat milk and vanilla, just how I like it.

Alec doesn't say a word. He remains there, stiff and unmoving, a pained look on his face. I hate it. As do I hate the trickling memory of the things I said to him last night. I was cruel, callous, and unforgivable.

"I'll go first," Silver starts and turns a bit toward me as he scratches his salt-and-pepper beard. "Cora, you don't know me very well." He clears his throat and I can tell he's trying so hard to soften his tone from his normal bravado. "And I understand if you don't want to confide in me. But your friends are worried about you. There have been things brought up that cannot be ignored, and I refuse to sit back and not get to the bottom of it."

Silver motions to Alec.

Alec rubs his hands together. "We need you to tell us the truth about Ricardo."

The coffee in my hands grows heavy and I lower it onto my lap so I don't drop it. I've already caused enough of a mess, I don't need to create a literal one, too.

Threats of killing those I love come flooding into my mind and I can't figure out the right thing to say when everything feels so incredibly wrong.

I shake my head. "I can't tell you."

My head throbs and tears dare to fall down my cheeks. How is it possible to cry any more than I already have?

"What do you need us to do in order for you to tell us?" Silver leans forward. "What can we do, Angel? I'm begging you."

I entertain his request and consider the options. What would make me willing to confess the secret that Ricardo all but swore me to keep?

I swallow harshly and look between these two drastically different men, both here for the same reason. "First, I need you to promise me you won't tell anyone else."

"Done," Silver says without hesitating.

Alec sighs. "What about Miller?"

"*Especially* Miller," I confirm.

"He's going to kill me." Alec runs his hand through his hair.

"That's the least of your concerns if I tell you the truth," I add.

"Fine, I won't tell him." Alec repositions in his seat.

"Next condition," Silver says.

"You cannot, by any means, do anything about it."

Silver scowls. "That's impossible."

"Then deals off."

Alec speaks up. "How do you expect us not to do anything if you're in trouble, Cora?"

I look right at him. "Because I said so, Alec. That's the only way I'll talk. Otherwise, this is my problem and mine alone. Do you understand?"

My heart pounds and for a moment I worry that they won't agree to my terms. It's strange to be this close to the truth yet so far away. I hadn't known I wanted to confide in someone else this badly until it was right on the edge of my tongue. It's wrong of me to ask them to stand down, but it's the only way I can guarantee their safety. Because otherwise, the second the secret is out of my mouth, there's no telling what Silver and Alec will do.

Alec is absolutely the more level-headed of the two, and the least criminal, but I wouldn't put it past him to drive over to Ricardo's house and do something that would result in Alec's imminent death. What kind of person would I be if I allowed that to happen?

"I can't agree to that," Silver tells me, his expression set in a straight and unwavering manner.

I stand from the spot on the couch and train my gaze on Alec. "Can you take me home?"

"Yeah, of course." Alec hops up and it's then that I see the blanket and pillow tossed aside.

Did he sleep on that loveseat all night?

"Sit down," Silver commands. "The both of you. You're not going anywhere. Not until you tell me what's going on."

Alec glances at me but I remain in place.

"Thank you for coming to get me last night," I tell Silver. "I'm sorry to have bothered you." I move toward the kitchen. "It won't happen again."

"Damn it, Cora," Silver says. "Fine, I won't do anything. Now sit back down and talk to us."

I smile but don't let him see that. Instead, I wipe the grin off my face and return to the spot next to him.

Alec settles into his seat, too, his hair a bit of a mess and sleep lines on his face.

"I need your word, too," I say to Alec.

He nods. "You have it."

I breathe in deeply. "I don't know where to start."

Silver lowers his voice again and says, "Start from the beginning."

And so I do, start at the beginning, as best as possible.

"My dad was in trouble, he owed him some money."

"How much?" Silver cuts in and asks.

I shrug. "I don't know. But it wasn't just that, Ricardo had done him a favor."

"What kind of favor?" he questions.

The answer isn't overly complicated, but I can't bring myself to say it out loud. Because if I do, it somehow makes it more real than it already is.

Alec leans forward, his elbows resting on his knees. "You can tell us, Cora, it's okay."

A single tear rolls down my cheek. "My mom is sick." I bite at my lip and continue, "My dad found an experimental treatment and went to Ricardo to get my mom in. I guess my dad couldn't pay him back, so he came to our house and threatened him. He was going to shoot him." I wipe at another tear. "That's when he saw me and said that he'd trade the debt for me."

Silver doesn't react. He just sits there sort of staring off into space. Is he in shock? Did I break him with the truth?

"What?" Alec blurts out. "What does that even mean? Can't we pay him off? Cover the debt your dad was in?"

Silver slowly shakes his head. "It's too late."

I wait for him to elaborate, my skin prickling at the seriousness of his tone.

"If the deal has been done, there is no dollar amount that will make him change his mind," Silver tells us.

"But like, Miller is loaded. He has more money than he knows what to do with. Surely there's a price he'd be willing to accept." Alec inches closer and frantically looks between me and Silver.

"You could flee town," Silver suggests.

"I can't," I tell him. "He'd kill my parents."

"There has to be something." Alec runs his hand through his hair again.

"How much longer do you have?" Silver asks me.

"A couple of weeks." I'd have to check an actual calendar, but I'm probably close to halfway done with the month I had negotiated.

"And killing him isn't an option?" Alec stands from the seat. "I know that's what you do for a living or whatever." He focuses on Silver for a second before turning to me. "And I know about your boss."

My eyes widen and my heart skips a beat. How could he possibly know what happened?

"I mean," Alec adds. "I don't *know* know, but I'm not stupid. He's dead, isn't he?"

Silver rises to his feet and positions himself between me and Alec. "Sit down, you're making this worse than it already is."

"Are you serious? You're sitting there doing nothing. Where are your brilliant ideas? What are we going to do?"

"Nothing," I say loud enough to hopefully make an impact. "You promised you wouldn't, remember?"

"Cora." Alec tilts his face and it pains me to see him this desperate. "You can't be serious."

"Please don't make me regret telling you."

"Who knows about this?" Silver asks.

"You two, Ricardo, and probably his daughter, London."

Silver lowers himself onto the couch and reaches toward me. "You haven't told anyone?"

"No." I sigh. "He told me he'd kill everyone I cared about if I did. That's why you can't do anything. You can't tell anyone. This has to be between us. Please."

Silver takes my hands into his. "I'm so sorry you had to deal with this on your own."

"It's fine," I lie but not entirely. I thought I'd feel better having told them what was going on, but I don't. Instead, there's this heavy weight of uncertainty about whether they will keep their word. What was once my life on the line is now theirs, too.

Alec exhales and draws my attention. His face is strained and he does nothing to hide how bothered he is. How can I blame him? I would probably feel the same way, especially knowing the things he does about this criminal world.

"Do you have any Tylenol?" I ask Silver. "Sorry, my head is fucking pounding."

"Yeah, of course." He leaves the couch without hesitation and disappears into his bedroom.

I take the moment of privacy to whisper to Alec, "I'm sorry."

He blinks and meets my gaze. "Cora..." Alec comes over and sits in the middle of the couch, closest to me. "You have nothing to apologize for."

"I was so mean to you last night."

"I understand why though." He places his hand on my knee. "I forgive you."

"You shouldn't," I tell him.

"Did you mean what you said?"

"No," I admit even though I should have lied and said I did. It would have made this easier for him in the long run if I pushed him to the point of no return. I want to confess that I meant the opposite of what I said. That he's a great guy and my feelings for him are only growing by the day, and that I wish we could go back and have all the time we lost by not speaking our truth sooner. But I can't. That would complicate an already fucked up situation and at the end of the day, this all ends the same: me belonging to Ricardo.

Silver returns a moment later and places two pills in the palm of my hand.

"Thanks," I say and hope like hell they dull the splitting pain in my head. I'm not sure if it's the hangover, the crying, my period, or my fucked-up life, but whatever it is makes it difficult to see straight.

Alec's phone rings and he pulls it out and audibly groans. "Fuck, I have to go." He faces me. "This conversation isn't over, okay?"

"Promise me you won't say or do anything."

Alec holds out his pinky. "I pinky promise."

I slip my little finger into his and give it a firm shake.

He gives his attention to Silver. "Promise you'll keep her safe in the meantime?"

Silver nods. "Yes, but I'm not doing that."

Alec presses a quick kiss on my cheek and tucks my hair behind my ear. "Don't give up, Cor, we'll figure this out." He leaves us behind, the tension of the situation not dying down at all with his absence.

Silver resolves onto the couch and faces me. He rests his arm over the back and props his head on his fist. "There has to be something we can do. Give me time to think and I'll figure it out, okay?"

I sip some of the coffee that's grown cold. He's asking for *time*, something I no longer have. But how do I convince him that this is a lost cause and there's nothing that can be done? I've thought about this from every angle I could and not a single solution presented itself that doesn't end in someone's death.

Ricardo has the upper hand, and the deck is stacked in his favor.

24
SILVER

"*D*o you love him?" The question leaves my mouth before I've had time to push it into the recesses of my mind.

"What? Who?" Cora furrows her brows and my thumb twitches to reach out and smooth out the wrinkle.

"Alec."

"Oh." She looks away and fidgets with her hand. "I mean..."

She doesn't have to continue for me to have my answer. If it were a no she would have said so immediately, and any other response is most definitely a yes. Even if she isn't aware of it, her heart has already made that decision. I see it written on his face plain as day. When he showed up and insisted on sleeping on the couch just to make sure she was okay and that he was nearby if she needed him, I knew with certainty that he was a goner.

There's a strong possibility that she loves Miller, too, especially when she made damn sure that we swear not to tell him. She did that to protect him, and what other reason would there be other than her heart belongs to him.

It's damn obvious those feelings are reciprocated, too. He

made that clear when he paid me to keep an eye on her. Not to mention the one hundred million dollars he spent to buy the building she's doing work at. It didn't take me long to figure out the connection, and once I saw how protective he was of her, the pieces of the puzzle only seemed to align that much more.

But what does that mean for me, for us? There are already two men who would do anything for her, where does that leave me? She might love them, but is her heart big enough for another? Why should I even consider myself a prospect when she's already spoken for?

On the other hand, though, I was the one she called last night. Not Miller, not Alec, who was quite literally with her...she sought me out in her time of need. That must count for something.

"It's okay, you don't have to explain," I tell her.

Finally, her blue eyes meet mine. "It's complicated."

I nod. "I know." My arms ache to have her in them, to tuck her to my chest and keep her safe, now, and always. I fucking hate feeling this way, so fucking vulnerable, so fucking alive for the first time in a long while.

"I don't want to go home," Cora says.

"You can stay here as long as you need to." I reach forward and place my hand on hers. "I mean it. I can sleep out here, give you the bedroom. Whatever you need."

She swallows and lets out a breath. "I can't impose."

"You're not imposing, Angel. I'm offering. And if you don't want to stay here, I can rent you something in the meantime."

"No, you're not going to do that." Cora takes a sip of her coffee and sets it aside. "Plus, what if he finds out I'm staying here?"

"Who? Ricardo?" Anger fills me at just the mention of his name. I want to rip every fingernail off and break every single bone in his body, slowly, one by one, until there's nothing left of him. I want to fucking gut him and shove his entrails down his throat. But I can't, at least not yet.

"Yeah." Cora brings her hand up to cover her mouth, and then lingers it around her throat, a tell-tale sign that she's holding back from saying something.

"What's the whole story?" I ask her.

"What do you mean?" She keeps her hand near her face.

"I can't help you if you don't talk to me."

"I didn't ask for your help."

I close my eyes, exhale, and remember that I'm talking to a woman here, not some insolent man. Normally, I'd torture whatever information I needed out of the person without a care in the world, but I can't do that to her, nor would I even have the desire to. With her, gentleness is key, and when the time is right, assertive dominance.

"I'm not going to fight with you," I tell her. "I know you didn't ask for my help. That's not you, it's not what you do. You go through life doing for everyone else and put yourself last. That's how you got into this situation, isn't it?"

Her eyes well with tears and her nose twitches like she's doing everything in her power to hold them back.

It fucking rips my heart in two to watch her battle with herself like this.

"I couldn't let him kill my dad," she whispers.

"I understand." I gently squeeze her hand.

"I hate him."

"I know."

"I don't mean Ricardo," she says while folding into herself.

"Your dad?" I ask the question despite already knowing. Of course, she hates him. How could she not after he allowed her to take the fall for him? A father is supposed to protect their child, not throw them under the bus when things get hard. He should have never involved her. He should have done anything other than seal her fate to one of the worst men in existence.

I would have gripped the barrel of the gun and shoved it into my mouth if it meant sparing her from this life. Never in a million years would I have put her in danger. Clearly, he has to see the magnitude of what he's done?

I want to ask about her mother, I want to learn more about her condition and what type of treatment she's receiving from Ricardo's black-market doctor. But there's a strong possibility that Cora has been left in the dark for a reason, and that reason might be that her mother is already dead.

Ricardo is a sick and cruel man, and I wouldn't put it past him to have lost his leverage and manipulated Cora into giving herself over for no reason.

I'm going to have to do research myself, without betraying her, and figure out the truth of what's really going on. I can't help her if I don't have all the information, and if she doesn't want to give it to me, I'll go out and find it.

At least I have an ally in Alec. He's not good for much, but he's loyal to Cora, and that alone is a huge asset. It would be great if I could involve Miller, because his pull is significant since he's a prominent member of the community and has endless resources at his disposal.

Maybe losing Cora's trust is worth keeping her alive. I'd rather her live to hate me than die because I was afraid of losing her. It's a sacrifice I'll have to be okay making in order to keep her safe.

"I can't believe he went behind my back," Cora starts. "Not only did he lie about my mom being sick, but he kept it from me, and made some stupid deal with Ricardo. He barely spoke up when Ricardo offered to take me instead."

"He was probably in shock."

Her blue eyes stare into mine. "Are you justifying what he did?"

I shake my head. "No. But it's not an uncommon reaction to

having a gun pointed at your head. People do unspeakable things when they're faced with death."

"I guess." Her shoulders relax.

"That doesn't make it right, though." I shouldn't have tried to rationalize it for her. That only made her retreat into her shell just as she was starting to open up about the situation. I need to tread lightly and understand that she and I are not the same person. We're very different and might not cope with things the same way.

I've been around death and violence and impossible scenarios my entire life—she's new to this, I have to remember that.

"What are the terms?" I attempt to get the conversation back on track.

"I have a couple more weeks."

"What does he want? Marriage?" Cora's parents clearly have no money, not enough that would interest him. She's not from a prominent criminal family, and aside from her connections to June and her men, she's not involved in the life. What could he possibly want other than...

My heart constricts, along with my stomach and fist. "He wants an heir, doesn't he?"

Cora blinks at me a few times and her lips part. "How did you—?"

"It's the only thing that makes sense." I attempt to hide my anger but there's no telling how well I'm doing. The simple fact that Cora hasn't gotten up and fled is a potentially good sign that I'm holding it together decently well. "And he gave you a month?"

"I negotiated for it."

"You negotiated with Ricardo Gardella?"

Cora nods and I don't mean to, but a fucking grin slips its way across my face.

"Why are you smiling?" she asks me.

"Because if you were able to do that, maybe this isn't a lost cause after all." I run my hand over my beard. "Ricardo is not the negotiation type, Angel."

"He made that pretty clear when he did this." She turns her head to the side and tucks her hair behind her ear. Her finger traces the outline of a faint bruise showing through.

"He hit you?" I nearly jump from my seat to move closer to her, taking her face in my hand and examining it. "You covered it with makeup, didn't you?"

Cora pulls away. "It's fine."

I sigh and wonder if she's ever going to realize she doesn't have to do that with me—the constant fake act she puts on that she thinks everyone buys.

"Why did you call me last night?" I ask her, but the answer is more for her than for me.

"I'm sorry. I shouldn't have."

"Angel." I attempt to get her to focus on me. "You called me for a reason."

She shrugs and avoids my glare. "I don't know, I was drunk."

"It was more than that and you and I both know it."

Cora scoots to the edge of the couch and tosses up her arms. "What do you want me to say?"

"The truth, for a change, Angel." I clear my throat. "You're scared."

She scoffs, glancing back before rolling her eyes. "Whatever."

"There's nothing wrong with being in over your head, Cora. I would be if I were in your shoes. I'd probably be doing the exact same thing. Internalizing and dealing with it on my own. I wouldn't want to involve anyone else, either. But the difference between us is that you actually have people willing to fight for you, with you." I pause and then add, "You aren't in this alone."

Cora drags her fingers through her hair and rests her head in her hands atop her elbows.

I inch toward her and place my hand on her back. "You

aren't alone," I repeat and hope the second time actually settles into her stubborn head.

Cora breathes in deeply and exhales, wiping a tear from her cheek. "I'm not used to this."

"Having help?" I rub circles on her shoulders.

She turns toward me. "Yeah."

I extend my arms and drag her legs up and over and pull her into my lap. She didn't ask for it but it's safe to say we both need this. "I've got you," I tell her as I wrap myself around her.

Cora stiffens but resolves into me, her head nestling under my chin. "Thank you," she whispers into me.

Those two words probably more difficult for her to say than one might think.

But I know the struggles she faces, and I understand her apprehension about accepting any assistance.

I've gone through life alone—always the fixer and the one people counted on. It's what I'm good at, what I'm used to. But year after year, I realized there was no one that I could count on. It was me against the world, and once you live that long enough, the isolation is daunting. Maybe that's what I saw in Cora, maybe that's why I was immediately drawn to her. I saw pieces of myself in her strength and willingness to persevere. I wanted to help her because, in a way, it was like I was helping myself—a past version of me, perhaps. She's young, impression-able still, and if I saved her from herself, maybe I could prevent her from turning out anything like me.

And maybe if I could help her, I wouldn't be a total lost cause. Saving her might be the very thing that saves me.

"What do you need me to do?" I say into her hair and press a soft kiss on top of her head.

"This is nice." She moves her hand from my chest, up my neck, and tilts my face down toward hers.

My dick betrays me by twitching right against her ass but instead of jumping off my lap, she grins and says, "Kiss me."

"Are you sure?"

"Positive." Cora tugs me closer.

I comply, kissing her with ease even though I want nothing more than to ravish her. I had been missing her terribly since our first sleepover, and despite having convinced myself that she was better off without me and that I was destined to live a life of loveless solitude, it never once mended my aching heart or stopped the incessant thoughts of her. Our sex was otherworldly, but even our conversation and banter were top notch, too. I hadn't had that much fun in all my life, and I had her to thank for it.

But with that, the longing I felt nearly unraveled me. My job suffered, my sleep and appetite were non-existent, and no matter what I did, I couldn't make it fucking stop.

So, when my phone rang and it was her on the other end, I knew there wasn't anything I wouldn't do for her.

And if dying at the hands of Ricardo Gardella is what it takes, I'll do it to keep her safe.

25
CORA

I don't want to feel anything other than Silver's mouth on mine, his hands on my body, and his hardness pressing up against me.

I breathe into him and kiss him deeper, my body reacting as I climb onto his lap fully and straddle him. His palms slide under the T-shirt of his that I'm wearing and mine dig into his hair. Grinding along him, I'm reminded that I'm very much on my fucking period.

"What's wrong?" he asks while resting his forehead on mine.

I swallow and consider my next words carefully, deciding the easiest thing is to just tell the truth. "I'm on my period."

Silver smirks. "I'm aware."

"You are?"

"You made it a point to have me stop and get you tampons last night."

My cheeks flush red. "You're joking."

"Where do you think all those boxes on the counter in the bathroom came from?"

I distance myself and cover my mouth. "Oh my God. That's so embarrassing."

Silver looks me straight in the eyes when he says, "What's embarrassing about a little blood?" He lifts me from the couch, my legs wrapping around his body and him securing me with just one hand. "Are you uncomfortable with doing things right now?"

"Define *things*." I hold onto him as he carries us toward the bedroom.

"There isn't anything I wouldn't do to you." He kisses me long and slow and heat swells between my legs, my libido heightened while on my period.

How fucking convenient.

Silver pauses his attention on my lips. "I'd go down on you right now if you'd let me."

My heart stutters, and I recall the one and only time I've ever had an intimate encounter while bleeding. I had no idea my period was so close, and I was hooking up with this guy I had been seeing for a few months. Mid-sex he looked down to find his dick covered in red, and he was so startled I thought he was injured or having a fucking heart attack. I was mortified and grateful I was in my bed and not his, but still, the fact that he ghosted me didn't really calm my insecurities about period sex moving forward.

Silver continues to carry me through his bedroom and into the bathroom. Gently, he sets me on the counter after swiping the boxes of tampons into the sink. He stares into my eyes, and my entire body comes alive.

"You're so fucking beautiful," he says.

I grip his face in my hands and tug him toward me, no longer wanting a single millimeter of space between us. I need to feel him on me, in me, all around me.

Silver's hands glide down my frame, stopping for a moment to take each of my boobs into his palms. He massages them, and I moan into his mouth as our tongues dance together, the intensity picking up with each passing second.

"I want you," I tell him between labored breaths.

He lowers his hands to the waistband of the sweatpants that I'm wearing and tugs them over my ass.

Embarrassed and exposed, I keep my legs together even though I want nothing more than to bear myself to him.

Silver breaks away from my mouth and brings himself to my center, kissing my side and my thigh. He grips my knees and shoves them apart, not flinching at all at the tampon string hanging out of me.

No, instead, he does something completely unexpected. He moves closer and grips the loose string between his lips and pulls the tampon out of my vagina.

My cheeks flush redder than the blood coating it, but Silver doesn't seem bothered one bit. He drops my tampon into the wastebasket and meets my gaze. He licks his thumb and pushes it to my clit, circling it with a firm pressure.

"Fuck," I whimper, my eyes rolling back and my head hitting the mirror behind me.

He teases my entrance with his thumb, and I buck forward, desperate for penetration. Silver slides two fingers into me, spreads them apart, and arches them upward.

I clench around him and feel the blood trickle out of me. "Oh God, I'm sorry," I blurt out.

"Do you think this bothers me?" Silver pulls his bloodied fingers out of me and wipes them across both of his cheeks. "I'll wear you with pride, Angel."

I sit there for a long moment, unsure of what to do with him, and how to react. Ultimately, my desire overpowers my embarrassment, so I reach for his hips and into his bottoms to grab onto his cock.

"Fuck me," I say while taking him into my hand, his hardness already telling me that he's ready to take me.

I stroke and pull him toward me in my attempt to get him closer.

He wraps his arm around my waist and tugs me to the edge of the counter, lining me up with his shaft. Silver glides his cock over my entrance and inches himself in a little bit at a time.

"Fuck, Angel, you feel so fucking good," he growls. "You're so warm and tight..." Silver shoves in fully and holds my hips up to keep me at a slanted angle.

It's fucking heaven, and it isn't long before I'm tensing around him, my pussy practically milking him as I climax around his shaft.

"That's it, come for me like a good girl." He thrusts through my orgasm and keeps pumping once it's finished. Silver keeps hold of me with one arm and slides the other under my shirt and up my body, pinching my nipple. He bucks his hips and lengthens each thrust until abruptly, he stops and pulls out.

"What's wrong?" I ask him.

"Nothing, Angel." He slides me off the counter and turns me around, backing my ass up to him and bending me over. "I want you to watch in the mirror. I need you to see how beautiful you are when you're taking me."

I lean down on the counter, my elbows resting on the cold and bloody surface.

Silver shoves into my pussy and holds onto my hips as he pumps inside of me. His gaze meets mine in the mirror. "You're taking me so fucking good, Angel." He slams into me and grips me tighter, his cock hardening in my pussy.

I brace myself on the counter and don't take my eyes off him in the mirror. Arching into him, my body practically begs for more.

He moans and digs his fingers into my ass. "You're mine, do you hear me? This pussy, it belongs to me. This body..." Silver skims his hand up my back and lowers it. "Mine," he growls. "This perfect asshole..." He glides his thumb over it, pushing softly. "Mine."

"Yes," I whimper and tighten around him, my pleasure heightened at each demanding declaration.

Silver fucks me harder, his body smacking against mine and mine backing into him to take even more than he's already giving me.

"That's it, Angel, come for me again." Silver slams into me and sends me spiraling around him, my entire being vibrating with pleasure from head to toe. He slows his pace but maintains the intensity of each thrust as he finishes inside of me with a groan.

I twitch around him and collapse fully onto the counter as I catch my breath. "Fuck," I whisper.

Silver pulses into me one final time before pulling out and taking a small step back. With one hand cupping my ass he says, "Goddamn, you are gorgeous."

I practically use all my remaining energy to bring myself vertical and face him. "We're both covered in blood."

Silver bridges the gap between us and presses the softest kiss on my lips. It's strange how externally dominating and intimidating he is, but then he's so fucking gentle with me. He's a contradiction and I love it. "I'd bathe in your blood if you let me."

I might not have much time left until I become Ricardo's, but at least in the short time with Silver I was able to feel utterly cherished and worshipped. My life might be ruined, and yet he gave me more in a short time than I've had in my whole life. The only downfall is that it can't last.

26
CORA

*S*undays are officially my least favorite day of the week. After a day full of wild period sex and plenty of relaxation, I woke up alone with a note from Silver.

> *I've been called out for work, but I promise you will not leave my mind, Angel.*
> *Stay as long as you'd like, maybe forever if you'll have me.*
> *Love, S*

I hold it to my chest and sigh, knowing damn well this will be over soon enough. I slip into the bathroom for a quick shower and freshen up, putting on the clothes I wore here Friday night that Silver had washed for me. I've been wearing nothing but his stuff since then, and as much as I want to steal all his oversized sweatpants and t-shirts, I can't go to Ricardo's wearing them without drawing too much attention to my personal life.

Ricardo already knows more than I'd like him to.

Once I've dressed and made myself somewhat presentable, I fumble through the desk in his living room for a piece of paper to write him a note. Last time I snuck out and it resulted in him tracking me down at work. The least I could do is inform him everything is okay and not to worry.

I rip off a piece of paper from a notebook and grab a pen.

Thank you for another wonderful evening. Text me later when you're home from work.
Your Angel x

J hesitate to write the last bit but figure it will put a smile on his hardened face if I submit to his pet name.

I'm shoving everything back in its place on his desk when a stack of paperwork catches my eye. I pull it out and skim over it faster than I have ever examined something in my life.

A contract for The Wellerton, the building I'm doing design work for.

I scan the words frantically, flipping each page, looking for the answer I've been wondering around since the sale of the building. I find it, but it leaves me without any closure since it's a business name instead of a person's name. I fan through the rest of the paperwork, my chest tightening at the very last page. The owner of the business who bought The Wellerton.

Miller Rossi.

I gasp and hold the stack of papers over my mouth. Is this even possible? What does it mean? Why would Miller buy the building? He said he purchased a unit within it, not the entire fucking thing. And if he did buy the whole building, why wouldn't he just tell me that? Why lie and keep it a secret?

I scan for a date, finding the day I killed my boss.

Like I found something I shouldn't have, I shove everything back onto Silver's desk and tidy it up as best as possible. If he didn't tell me, maybe he didn't want me to know either. But why? Why would either one of them keep this a secret? And why was Silver investigating it at all? Did he have something to do with it? Maybe he and Miller are weirdly conspiring together behind my back? Did Alec have knowledge of this, too? What do any of them have to gain from keeping this from me? Or from the purchase of the building in general?

I leave everything the way I found it, or at least, try my best to make it appear that way, and grab my clutch on the way to the door. Silver was kind enough to wash every bit of blood off of the knuckles of my bag as he told me how proud he was that I punched a guy for groping me. He offered to kill him, but I declined. It wasn't the first, and it wouldn't be the last time a drunk guy got a little too handsy at a bar. If I allowed him to murder every one of them, it wouldn't be long until a massive pile of bodies added up.

I thought he had been joking at first, but when he asked me to describe the guy who touched me, I realized he was oh-so-serious in his pursuit to end the guy's life.

"Any man who upsets you deserves to die, Angel," he had said.

My phone buzzes, a notification from June coming across the top of the screen. I swipe it away and put it with the countless others from her and Simon. I don't want to talk to either of them, and I'm not sure if I ever will. I was drunk last night and flipped out on them, but it doesn't change the very real fact that they lied to me, betrayed me, and attempted to derail my happiness. How dare they think they have that kind of say in my life. If they don't trust me enough to keep their secret, then I want nothing to do with them. I've proven myself to be a good friend over and over, I don't deserve some half-assed friendship in return.

Although, I'd be lying to myself if I said I wasn't pushing them away to make it easier when this shit with Ricardo comes to fruition. I can't have them trying to save me and put themselves in danger. I might be mad at them, but I don't want them dead.

I slip out of Silver's comfortable apartment and type Ricardo's address into my ride-share app and click on the first one that pops up. Three-minute wait, with an estimated time of arrival one minute before Ricardo's demanded meeting time.

Shit.

Hugging my arms to my chest, I tap my foot to the ground and wait for my ride. I press my fingers to my lips and recall Silver's on mine. He's so fucking sexy and dominant and has an understanding of my body unlike anything I've ever experienced with a man.

Even after he's fucked my brains out, he's gentle and affectionate, taking extra care in bringing me water and cleaning me up. He even got a hot water bottle out for my cramps last night when I barely held my hand to my uterus and groaned. How he can go from talking about killing someone one minute to holding me the next, I'll never quite grasp. I think if we hadn't been intimate, I'd be afraid of Silver. In a way, he reminds me of Dominic, one of June's partners. He's ruthless and constantly has this severe intensity about him that makes you question how many men he's killed and how many of them he did for enjoyment. They're both older with this sophisticated nature that's equal parts comforting and alarming. I see the way Dom softens for June, and only June, and it's exactly how Silver treats me.

Honestly, I'm surprised he let Alec into his place and didn't kill him just for showing up to check on me. But it's safe to say

Silver only did that because he knows it would hurt me if he hurt Alec, and for whatever reason, Silver prioritizes what matters to me.

A grey Acura pulls up in front of me, and a middle-aged man rolls down the passenger window. "Cora?"

"Yeah." I check the license plate and slip into the back seat.

The guy smiles politely in the rearview mirror but otherwise doesn't say another word. I'm grateful for the silence and lack of awkward small talk but it does nothing to ease my nerves as we get closer to Ricardo's house.

I offer him thanks as I exit the car a few minutes later and make sure to leave him a rating and tip before I forget.

My stomach turns with each step toward Ricardo's front door. I swallow down bile and knock on the hard surface with the elaborate golden lion knocker.

A moment later, a familiar, and non-threatening face greets me from the other side.

"Hey," London says and opens the door for me to step inside.

I join her in the mansion and flit my gaze around nervously. "Hey."

"Daddy isn't home yet," she tells me. "But you can follow me back." London takes off, not bothering to wait for my response, her red hair pulled halfway up with a loose braid knotted into the ponytail. It's so effortless and makes me wonder how long it took her to do.

Everything about her screams trust fund baby but not in a completely offensive way.

London leads me into the room where Ricardo had me model for him until he jerked off into a tissue.

A shiver rolls over me as we step inside. Does she know what her dad does in this room? How can she possibly live in the same house as him when he's as disgusting as he is?

My dad merely sold me to hers, and I can't stand to be around him.

I can't imagine having to exist around a man who quite literally tried to kill me and then only decided to keep me alive so he could sell me to the highest bidder.

I guess if that's all she's ever known though, she might be more used to how fucked up the relationship she has with her father is than I am.

"Do you want something to drink?" London stalks straight to the bar at the far side of the room and pulls out two glasses from the silver tray. She pours golden liquid into both and carries them over, handing one to me.

"It's ten in the morning," I tell her but take it anyway to numb whatever it is that Ricardo has planned for me today.

London shrugs. "It's five o'clock somewhere." She sips the drink and settles onto the couch.

And because I want to avoid the one he pleasured himself in, I lower myself next to her, holding the glass to me like it might protect me in some way. It's a stupid thought.

"I like the bag." She eyes the clutch tucked under my arm. "Can I see it?"

"Yeah, of course." I let it fall and set it in my lap. "Actually." I fumble with the clasp until it opens and pull out a hundred-dollar bill. "Thanks for this."

London shakes her head. "That's not necessary, really. Plus, I already replenished my emergency fund."

"Take it," I insist. "Never know if you might find yourself in need." The words slip out of my mouth like some strange foreshadowing of what's to come. I shake off the chilling thought and shove the money into her hand.

She sighs and takes it, tucking it into her bra. "Thanks." London checks out my bag next, examining it and turning it over. "It's beautiful." She gives the thing back to me and meets my gaze. "Miller buy it for you?"

I nod, unsure of how much I should say.

"He seems like a nice guy," she adds.

"Yeah." But then I'm reminded of the paperwork I found before I left Silver's apartment. Is he actually a nice guy or does he have some weird ulterior motive? Am I a pawn in some sinister plan I'm not even aware of?

"Are you two dating?" London brings her glass to her mouth, and for a moment it's like the two of us are just two girls gossiping about boys.

"No," I tell her. "I mean, not really. I don't know, it's complicated." I pause before saying, "Are you dating anyone?"

London chuckles as if I should already know the answer to that question. "Yeah right, Daddy would kill us both." A sort of sadness washes over her, and her expression darkens. "Literally."

"Why haven't you left?" I blurt out.

Her intense gaze meets mine. "You don't get it, do you? Once he stakes his claim, there's no escaping him. He'd hunt me to the ends of the earth. There is no getting away from him. Not ever. Not really."

London's words sink in and only solidify what I already knew as truth, and I wish desperately that there was a way to turn back time and change the fateful course I set myself on when I stumbled into that conversation between him and my dad.

Instead of mourning my future, I'd be mourning the loss of my parents, and without the knowledge of the situation, would that have been worse or better than life as it is now?

I guess I'll never know.

"Do you at least get a say in who he marries you to?" I ask her.

She fidgets with her glass of whiskey. "No. Not unless I find someone wealthy enough that he would approve." London exhales. "The likelihood of that is slim to none, though. Any decent man won't co-mingle with Daddy's shady business practices. The few prospects that have even considered it didn't have a strong offer. Although, he's getting rather desperate. I wouldn't put it past him to settle just to get rid of me and line his pockets sooner rather than later."

"I'm sorry," I tell her, the two words falling flatter than I'd hope. I can't imagine what she's going through; I can only compare it to my experience, and that alone is nothing I'd wish on another person.

"It's fine," she lies. "I've grown to accept it."

"What did you mean by shady business practice?"

London crosses her legs and licks her lip, sucking the bottom one between her teeth. "Well." She turns toward me. "How much do you know about the industry?"

"Um, assume I know nothing." Because let's face it, the only bits and pieces I've gathered have been wild guesses with no evidence to truly back them up.

"Wow, hm, let me see." London takes another drink of her whiskey. "You're friends with June, aren't you?"

I nod. "Yeah, why?"

"Her partners are head of the West Coast. Well, Dominic is. Coen is their security lead. Magnus is an advisor. Simon is well, Simon." She chuckles and continues. "He's a pretty face but is in charge of operations. They handle the ins and outs of all illegal activity on the West Coast. If someone has their hand in something dirty, they have ultimate control. It's like they have their thumb on the pulse of the entire coast. Obviously, there are sub-sectors and the occasional turf war, but they hold the most power. Daddy is part of the old-school formation. He still has significant authority and a great deal of influence, but it's different than theirs. And the shit Daddy deals with goes against the new way."

"Like what?"

"Imagine any type of crime that could be profitable, Dominic benefits from it. But he has his limits. Nothing involving women and children, no human trafficking, no prostitution, no harming animals." London laughs again. "They'll torture and kill a man any day of the week, but they draw a line for certain things. Daddy does not. He doesn't care if it's his flesh and blood, if he can make a penny off it, he'll do it. He has no moral compass."

"So, drugs, extortion, loan sharking, tax fraud, murder, corruption..."

"Yep. They do it all. Stock manipulation, gambling, protection, art smuggling, they even have their hand in many legitimate businesses around town. And obviously now with their alignment to the East Coast, it's only strengthened their foothold."

In a matter of minutes, London has told me more than June has during our entire friendship. And nothing has changed, not my feelings towards them, not my safety. There's no reason she couldn't have sat me down and had this very same conversation.

"June played a huge role in them securing their position," London adds, almost like she can read my mind.

"Really?" I down nearly half the liquid in my glass.

"Yeah, she almost died a couple times if I'm not mistaken."

"I knew she had gotten hurt, but I had no idea..."

London bobs her head up and down. "Pretty sure she was kidnapped, tortured, stabbed, shot, assaulted."

My heart aches for what June went through, and if I had to put myself in her shoes, I suppose I understand why she would want to keep that from me. Still, it doesn't make it hurt any less that she didn't think she could trust me with that information.

London barely knows me and is willing to tell me anything I ask her, why couldn't June do the same?

"She didn't tell you any of this?" London drinks the rest of her whiskey and wipes her mouth.

"No, not really."

The door to the room flies open and Ricardo walks in, my heart almost lurching out of my chest at his sudden arrival. The liquor in my stomach does nothing to calm my nerves as he barges into the room and grabs London by the arm and yanks her up. "Out, now!"

"Unhand me, Daddy," she cries out and yanks herself free of him.

But Ricardo doesn't care for her reaction and hits her across the face, knocking her onto the floor and sending a lamp falling off the side table.

I rush around him and reach for her as her eyes well with tears, her hands clutching the side of her head where it hit the corner of the table. She pulls them away, blood coating her fingertips.

"Don't you dare fucking touch her." Ricardo latches onto my hand and rips me backward, a popping sound rattling from my arm and pain shooting in its wake.

I fall back onto the couch and choke down a sob. I came here to model some clothes for him, not watch him assault me and his daughter.

London scrambles to her feet and wipes her cheek. "I'm sorry, Daddy, I..."

He points to the spot on the couch next to me. "Sit your ass down now and let me make something very clear to you." Ricardo coughs and hacks and spittle flies out of his mouth. He narrows his gaze at each of us. "You two are *not* friends. Do you hear me? You will not *ever* be friends. If I so much as think there is a friendship brewing between you, I will throw you in the cellar with a knife and make you fight to the death. I don't give a fuck who wins. Do you fucking hear me?"

London nods aggressively. "Yes, Daddy."

I chew at the inside of my lip and think about all the ways I'd love to end his life. I'd rip off my fucking arm and beat him to death with it if I thought it were possible.

Ricardo grabs my chin and squeezes it, his fingernails digging into my flesh. "Do you fucking hear me, or do you need me to make it more clear to you? I am in charge. I will bend you over this couch and fuck you right here if that's what it takes to make you understand."

"I understand," I say through the pressure he holds on my face.

"Good." He shoves me, and my hand moves from holding onto my injured arm to my chin. Both firing bouts of agony through me in different ways.

I don't mean to, but I cry, silently, and look over at London to find her doing the same thing.

Ricardo's phone rings and he answers it immediately. "What do you want?" The expression on his disgusting face darkens. "What do you mean he's outside? What does he want?" He hangs up and points between us. "You stay here and don't say a fucking word."

The second he disappears, I turn toward London. "Are you okay?"

She shakes her head but says. "I'm fine." London blinks and it's like she rises from whatever fog was covering her vision. "Are you?"

"Yeah," I lie and motion toward her head. "Let me see that."

London turns in my direction, the blood soaking and blending into her red hair.

"You should probably get that looked at. You might need stitches," I tell her. I'm no doctor but the gash looks deep enough to need something more than a measly Band-Aid.

"Your shoulder." London points at my arm laying limp at my side with my other arm holding onto it.

"It's fine, no big deal." I force a smile even though I'm pretty damn sure it's dislocated. Every time I attempt to move it, a sharp pain shoots through me.

"Where is she?" A distant voice yells and a door slams. "Where. The. Fuck. Is. She?"

My breath shudders and I inch toward London as if

together, we could conquer anything. When in reality, as long as we're in this house, neither one of us will be safe.

The door to our room bursts open and bounces off the hinges.

Miller scans the space until his sights double-take on me. He turns around and shoves Ricardo. "I fucking knew you had her here, you bastard."

Ricardo throws up his arms and feigns complete ignorance. "I had no idea. London and your girl must have been hanging out. I simply just returned home, right girls?"

I swallow and don't say anything because I don't know what the right thing to say is. Anything out of my mouth would be incriminating and there's no telling what Ricardo would use against me if I tried to cover for him.

London on the other hand goes right along with it. "Yeah, Daddy's right." She reaches for her empty glass. "Cora and I were having a drink and catching up."

Miller storms over. "At ten in the fucking morning?"

I go to shrug but end up wincing, my hand still holding onto my injured arm.

Miller yanks a gun out of his waistband and points it at Ricardo, backing him up until he's flat against the wall. "What did you do to her?"

My mouth drops open at seeing him like this. Miller is always calm and collected, never talking at a louder-than-normal volume. He's serious and solemn, and right now, he's a version of himself I have never witnessed before.

"I must warn you, Miller. You are in *my* house, with a gun pressed to *my* head. I don't care what connections you have, you're making a mistake, boy." Ricardo doesn't seem all that bothered like he has a trick hidden up his sleeve that will get him out of this situation without any danger coming to him. Or he's just that fucking crazy and doesn't give a fuck that a gun is trained on his forehead.

"I don't give a fuck whose house I'm in." Miller presses the end of the barrel into Ricardo's temple. "You don't fuck with Cora and get away with it." He glances over his shoulder. "Up, now."

It takes me a second to realize he's talking to me.

"Both of you," he continues. "Up. Walk to the door."

Ricardo dares to move but Miller shoves him into the wall again.

"Do not fucking test me, Gardella. I will plaster your fucking brains on the wall and deal with the consequences later. I don't fucking care who you think you are." Miller shoves the gun harder and takes the opportunity to check on us as we approach.

Once we're near the door, he positions himself between us and Ricardo and lowers his weapon.

"We're leaving."

"The hell you are. You can take your bitch, but you aren't taking my daughter. Not unless you want to pay for her." Ricardo spits on the floor near Miller's feet.

Miller takes his free arm and shoves us through the entry and aims the gun lazily at Ricardo's leg. He pulls the trigger, the sound loud and reverberating through me.

Ricardo falls to the ground and blurts out every obscenity he can muster. "I will fucking kill you, son. You don't know who you're messing with. You're going to regret this."

"The only thing I'm going to regret," Miller tells him. "Is not killing you right now." He turns around and pushes me and London in the direction of the front door. "Keep moving." He only looks back once, and I assume it's to make sure Ricardo isn't following us.

"Oh my God," London says, her voice breaking.

Once we're through the front door and out onto the side-walk, Miller points his gun-laden hand toward his Porsche. "Get in, both of you, now."

London reaches the car first, not hesitating as she opens the door and climbs through to the back. I slide into the passenger seat and Miller slams the door behind me.

"Are you okay?" I look back at London as she's cramped into the small space.

"I'm good."

I hold onto my arm and breathe through the panic that consumes me. Miller wasn't supposed to find out. No one was. This was all a secret, one that none of them could find out. Now, not only does he know something is going on, but he fucking shot Ricardo and threatened him.

What if Ricardo retaliates by killing my parents *and* everyone I love?

"What the fuck were you thinking?" I blurt out the second Miller is in the car.

With his hand still gripping the gun, he shoves the car into gear and takes off, his tires peeling out on the pavement.

His jaw clenches and he checks his mirrors as he speeds away. "I'm taking you to the hospital."

"No, you fucking aren't," I tell him and reach into my pocket to pull out my phone.

Miller glances over, his gaze wild and unlike him. "Why are you wearing your clothes from Friday?"

"Why does it matter?" I scoff. "And how do you even know what I was wearing Friday. Are you following me?"

How else could he have found out where I was? It's either that or one of the guys told him. They both swore to me that they wouldn't, but am I a fool for trusting them?

"No," Miller says unconvincingly.

"I'm not going to the hospital," I say again. "You think he doesn't have men everywhere? You pissed him off! You fucking shot him."

He looks over at me, this time doing a double take. "Put your seatbelt on."

"I can't." I keep my arm at my side.

"Cora."

"She's not lying," London speaks up from the back seat. "I think her shoulder is dislocated." She presses the spot on her head where she was bleeding and checks her fingers for fresh blood.

"Somebody had better start talking." Miller accelerates around a few cars and runs through an intersection at three times the speed limit.

"Take me to Silver's," is all I say. I thumb through on my phone until I find his number and hit the dial button. Surely, he'll know what to do, about my shoulder, about this entire situation.

The line goes to voicemail and a tinge of disappointment hits me.

"That's where you were last night." Miller's tone is more factual than accusatory.

"How do you know where I was last night?" I ask him and wince as he hits a bump in the road, a spike of pain shooting up my arm.

Miller doesn't answer me. He actually doesn't say anything. Not for the next few minutes it takes to get across town to Silver's place. I'm not even convinced that's where he's taking us until we pull onto a familiar street.

I glare at the side of his head, the perfectness of his chiseled jaw and baby-blue eyes pissing me off more than they should. He can't help it he's good-looking, but he can help that he's keeping things from me.

But the second I allow that anger to set in, my stupid fucking conscience reminds me that I'm doing the same damn thing. I've been harboring the biggest secret of them all, but it impacts no one but myself, so the justification seems prevalent.

"Come on," I tell them and slip out of the car toward Silver's apartment complex. I don't bother turning around because I'm completely certain they have no choice but to follow me.

I punch in the code at the door that Silver had given me and enter the gated area, walking straight to his front door and using the other code there.

Noise carries from inside his apartment and without thinking about it, I snatch the gun out of Miller's hand and aim it at the bedroom.

"What the fuck are you doing?" Miller loudly whispers.

"Shh." I step closer to the bedroom, all fucking James Bond-like, and realize I must look like a complete fool. I think I'm being sly, but with my slack arm at my side and the thumping of my heart, sly is the last of what I am. Still, I advance before Miller can get the gun from me.

"Cora," he says as I disappear into the bedroom. He's on my heels a second later, not giving me a chance to fully confront who's in the bathroom alone.

But just as I'm about to point the gun at whoever is in the bathroom, a gun trains on me from the other side of the door.

Silver being the one who's attached to it. He sighs and his shoulders relax for a slight second before he points the gun at Miller.

"Whoa, buddy." Miller throws his arms up. "It's me."

Silver nods to the gun still in my hand. "Who gave you a gun, Angel?"

"Oh shit, sorry." I lower the thing and give it back to Miller. "It's his. I thought there was an intruder."

Silver raises a brow and I fully take him in, the bathroom steamed up and the towel wrapped loosely around his waist. Water, still beaded on his chest, and his hair damp from the shower.

I don't mean to, but my mind immediately goes to the gutter.

He winks at me and says, "Think I could get dressed and then you two could tell me what's going on."

"Yeah, of course." I hold onto my arm and rush out of the room, ready to put a bit of distance between me and Miller.

I care about him, deeply, but I'm equally pissed off at him at the moment and my hormones are putting me at risk for doing something I might regret once I can think clearly.

London perks her head up from the kitchen and turns toward us. She was snooping, and I don't blame her, I probably would have been too if I were her.

"Find anything?" I ask her and settle onto a stool at the counter.

"This man is obsessively tidy," she tells me.

Miller comes over and crosses his arms over his chest as he leans against the counter. "What's going on, Cora?"

I look him right in the eyes. "I could ask you the same thing."

"What? What do you want to know? You'll talk if I do?"

I pinch my mouth shut in a firm line.

"That's what I thought."

We remain there, having a standoff, for at least an awkward moment or two until finally, Silver exits his bedroom with dark dress slacks and a black button-down shirt.

He rolls his sleeves to his elbows and glances up at us. "Oh, hello." Silver nods at London.

She strolls over and holds out her hand. "London Gardella."

Silver slides his palm around hers and the idea crosses my mind that I should have left her behind at Ricardo's house.

"Silver Franco."

He tilts his head. "You're bleeding."

"Meh." She shrugs and points to me. "Her shoulder's dislocated. Probably worry about that first."

Silver reacts immediately, his blasé demeanor shifting to intense concern. "What happened?"

I spin on the stool and face him, his gaze trailing my face and no doubt seeing the small cuts and bruises already forming around my chin.

"If we're going to talk," I say mostly to Miller, "You should call Alec."

"What does he have to do with anything?" he asks me.

"Just do what the lady says," Silver snaps at him. "Come over here on the couch and let me look at you."

I hop down and follow him over, my body releasing some of the tension from being around Ricardo now that Silver is near. There's just something about him that makes me feel safe, I can't help but gravitate toward.

"Lie down," he says.

I comply and hold onto my arm as I lower myself horizontally.

Silver kneels next to the couch and pokes and prods until he shakes his head. "Yeah. It's dislocated." He lets out a sigh before returning to his feet. "This is going to hurt, but I promise it'll be over soon, Angel."

I nod stiffly and can't imagine it could possibly get any worse than the radiating pain already piercing through me every single time I move.

"Try to relax, okay?" Silver puts his sock-covered foot near my armpit and slowly guides my arm away from my body.

I pinch my eyes shut and wait for it to be over.

"Breathe, Angel, breathe." He continues moving my arm until the thing snaps back into place.

I gasp and open my eyes to find him smiling at me.

"You did so well." He helps me to sit up and guides my arm across my stomach. "You should probably try to keep it immobilized and ice it. I think I have a sling."

"Damn Cora," London says as she comes into my line of sight. "You're a baddie."

I chuckle dryly and stand from the couch. "Not hardly."

Silver returns a moment later and fixes me up with a sling that's clearly too big for me. "I had shoulder surgery once," he tells me and meets my gaze. "You're going to need to take it easy, Angel."

"I'm fine, really." The pain has dulled to a subtle ache and isn't anything I can't handle now that I know my arm isn't more severely injured than I had worried it was. Whatever fate Ricardo has in store for me now that Miller fucking shot him is way worse than a measly dislocated shoulder.

"Alec will be here in a few minutes," Miller announces to the rest of us, his gun still casually resting in his hand.

"You plan on using that thing or did you maybe want to put it away?" I saunter into the kitchen and return to the stool I was sitting in before Silver doctored me up.

"I'll keep it out for the time being." Miller comes over and places his hand on the counter in front of me, his stature towering over me. He lowers his voice. "I need you to tell me what's going on, Cora."

"We'll talk when Alec gets here." I tilt my head toward Silver. "Can you take a look at her head? I think she needs stitches."

"Yeah." He waves London over. "Better lighting in my bathroom."

I hate the idea of them being alone but come to terms with the reality that Silver is not mine, and I have no claim over him. If he wants to fuck London on the bathroom counter the same way he did with me last night, that's his prerogative. How dare the thought even cross my mind to be jealous when I'm messing around with Miller and Alec. I'm being selfish, especially considering I can't keep any of them.

Whatever future I thought I had after Ricardo is surely over after what happened today.

A buzzer in Silver's apartment goes off and Miller slips away to push the call button near the door.

"Who is it?" he asks through the receiver.

"It's Alec. Let me in."

Miller grants him access, a moment later opening the door

for him with his gun tucked behind his back. He doesn't relax in the slightest until the door is shut behind them.

Alec's sights quickly land on me, his face contorting from a smile to a frown. "Cora, babe, what happened?" He rushes over and takes my face in his hands. "Who hurt you?"

"I'm fine," I lie.

"Ricardo Gardella," Miller answers him. "That's who fucking hurt her."

Alec glances from Miller to me. "Is that true?"

"Yeah, but it's okay. I have it under control." I wonder how many lies I can keep up with before every word out of my mouth becomes one.

"So did you tell him?" Alec keeps his voice low, but it isn't low enough.

"Tell me what?" Miller steps forward and all but slams the gun down on the counter.

"Dude, seriously? Put the gun away." Alec turns around and throws his arm in front of me. "There's a lady in your presence, have some tact."

Miller exhales dramatically and holsters his weapon. "There. Happy?"

"No, not really." Alec plants his hands on the edge of the counter. "Where's Silver?"

I nod in the direction he and London disappeared, only for them to come out a second later.

"Two ladies," Alec corrects himself.

"Alec, London. London, Alec." I introduce the two and hope the formalities won't increase the rampant jealousy overpowering the pain in my body.

"Hey, 'sup?" Alec shakes her hand briskly and nods to Silver.

London climbs onto the stool next to me and Silver steps into his kitchen area to lean on a counter, his arms crossing over his broad chest. He keeps his eyes trained on me and I can't help but wonder if he hates the distance between us as much as I do.

"Alright." London smacks the counter. "I'd like to start this meeting by saying, *what the fuck?*" She looks directly at Miller. "You realized you signed your death wish when you shot him, right?"

"Shot who?" Alec is the first to follow her up.

"Ricardo," I fill the rest of the group in. "Miller shot Ricardo after he stormed into his house and found me and London." I narrow my attention on Miller. "How did you know I was there?"

Alec shoots a stare between Miller and me, his head practically whipping back and forth.

"I put a tracker on you, okay? Shoot me." Miller throws up his hands. "What else was I supposed to do, clearly something was going on and you wouldn't tell anyone? I had to do something."

"Where is it?" I ask him. "The tracker."

Miller draws in a breath and exhales. "It's in both of the bags."

"You took me shopping," I say through gritted teeth. "Just to put a fucking tracker on me?"

"That's not the only reason," he blurts out. "I wanted to. I also just happened to see an opportunity that I couldn't pass up."

I shove the overpriced clutch across the counter. "Take it back. I don't want it anymore."

Out of the corner of my eye, I see London perk up, her eyebrows raising and her finger pressing to her lips. "I mean, if you don't want it, I'll take it."

"You're not helping." I glare at her and quickly turn my attention to Miller.

Alec clears his throat and then rubs his hand on it. "It's not entirely Miller's fault." He flinches like he's anticipating being hit.

"What did you do?" I ask him.

"I'm the one who brought it up." Alec takes a cautious step back and puts up his hands in defeat. "You got drunk and said that shit about Ricardo and killing your boss and shit. I panicked. I didn't know what to do. I knew he cared about you, and I shouldn't have invaded your privacy, but I was worried. I'm sorry."

I want to be mad at him, I really do, but damn is it hard when he's looking at me the way that he is. With remorse and actual concern. None of which Miller is exuding.

"And what's your excuse?" I turn my attention to Miller. "What else are you hiding from me?"

"Are you kidding me?" Miller barks back. "When are you going to tell us what's going on with Ricardo?"

London scratches her head and averts her gaze, matching the same expression that Alec is wearing. Silver keeps his arms crossed and glances around the room.

"You all fucking know?" Miller finally catches on. "And I'm left in the dark, why?"

"Probably because you're a loose cannon," London chimes in. "You shot him without even thinking twice. It's no wonder she didn't trust you enough to tell you."

Miller's face drops and for the first time all day, I actually feel sorry for keeping him in the dark. "Is that the truth?" His blue eyes don't dare leave mine. "You don't trust me?"

I shake my head. "It's not like that, Miller."

"What is it then?" He shifts his head toward Alec and Silver. "You trust them but don't trust me?"

"It wasn't supposed to be this way." I clutch my injured arm to my chest and wish I could disappear from thin air. I hate this, the weight of his disappointing stare. I never wanted to hurt him, any of them, but that's all I seem to do.

I don't know how to not let people down even though all I've ever wanted is to make them happy.

27

MILLER

"Can we talk in private?" I ask Cora.

"We can talk right here."

I steady a breath and try with all my might to calm my raging nerves. I've never been quite this...unhinged, and I don't know what to do with it. If I don't get some kind of clarity soon, I'm going to fucking explode.

"Cora," Alec says, his voice low. "Hear him out."

I flit my attention from him to her and back to him, wondering what I did to get him on my side. I'm not even entirely on my side.

"Fine," Cora huffs and looks to Silver. "Can we borrow your room for a minute?"

He nods stiffly.

Cora turns her attention to me briefly before hopping off the stool. "You have five minutes." She walks straight into his bedroom without looking over her shoulder.

Murmurs fill the space in the kitchen where the guys and London are no doubt gossiping about whatever the fuck is happening, their circle tight and excluding me.

I shut the door behind me and stand there like a statue, my entire body itching to step closer to hers, to fix what I've broken.

But now that I have her here, I don't think it's possible. What if I've already ruined things beyond repair?

"So?" Cora turns around and puts her hand on her hip as she juts it out. Goddamn, even when she's mad she's fucking adorable.

Somehow, I convince my legs to move, and step toward her. "I'm sorry," I say, fully meaning it. "I'm sorry you couldn't trust me. I'm sorry for tracking you. I'm sorry for keeping that from you."

Cora narrows her bright blue gaze. "You're still not telling me everything and you know it."

"What is it that I'm keeping from you, Cora?"

"You're the one with the secrets Miller." She runs her hand through her hair and tugs at it. "Why are you so frustrating? Why can't you just be honest with me?" Cora lets out an irritated sigh and walks away from me, pacing Silver's room until she stops near his dresser, her back resting against it.

I try to think about what she's referring to, but I can't be certain what it is. Is she referring to me breaking into her house and looking through her things? Surely there's no way she found out about that, unless she has cameras that I'm unaware of. I left no trace that I was there the few times that I had done it.

I approach her but keep my distance. "Is this about the building?"

"What about the building?"

For a second, I'm afraid that I've shoved my foot into my mouth and that this isn't what it's about at all, but when she shoves my chest and says, "Why didn't you just tell me?" I know exactly what she's referring to.

I breathe in deeply and exhale. "Because it's crazy."

"Miller..." Cora tilts her head to the side. "Why did you do it? Why did you buy The Wellerton?"

I look anywhere but her face as I say, "Because I heard you were having problems with your boss, and I wanted to make sure he got fired."

Cora chuckles and it draws my attention. "Oh, he got more than fired."

"Yeah." I rub at my neck. "I should have acted sooner and none of that would have happened. I'm sorry."

Cora reaches forward and presses her non-injured hand to my chest. "You bought an entire building just to fire my boss?"

My body comes to life with her touch. "Yeah."

"Do I even want to know how much it cost?"

"Probably not." I place my hand over top of hers. "It wasn't that much."

"How much?"

"A hundred."

She pinches her brows. "A hundred thousand?"

"Million."

Cora's eyes widen. "You spent a *hundred million* dollars to fire my boss?"

I shrug. "It's not a big deal."

"Miller, that's fucking insane. What the hell were you thinking? You could have just contacted Mr. Wellerton and asked him to let him go."

I shake my head. "I had to be sure."

"What am I going to do with you?" she asks, her shoulders slumping with the breath she lets out.

"I'm sorry," I tell her again.

"Will you stop saying that?"

I boldly take my other hand and cup her cheek, running my thumb along her delicate skin. "I keep failing you, and I'm sorry.

You have no idea how much you mean to me. I'd give all the money in the world to keep you safe. It pains me to know you don't trust me. I'd give anything for your trust. Anything, Cora, just name it."

Cora leans into my touch and closes her eyes briefly. "It had nothing to do with trust, Miller. I promise." She pauses and adds, "I do trust you. I always have."

Then, she does something completely unexpected, she stands on her tiptoes and gently kisses my lips.

I kiss her back, soft at first, but melt into her embrace, my hands roaming her body as my tongue dances with hers.

She continues to take me by surprise and runs her hand between us to grip my cock through my pants, stroking my length.

"Cora," I pant. "You're hurt."

"I don't care." She unbuttons my trousers and yanks them down. Cora kisses me deeply before breaking away and turning around, unzipping her own pants and dragging them over her ass. She backs up into me and looks at me in the mirror above Silver's dresser. "Hurry up, I don't want to keep them waiting."

And because I lack complete and utter self-control, I slide my cock along her entrance and shove it in her.

I bite down a moan and reach around her to find her clit with one hand and her breast with another. I massage both areas and fuck her from behind, my dick buried inside of her.

Cora braces herself on the dresser and forces herself onto me, her tight pussy slick. "You feel so good."

I apply pressure to her clit and rock it back and forth between my fingers as it throbs against me.

My cock swells as I feel her pussy contract.

"Goddamn baby girl," I mutter while grabbing a fistful of her hair and tugging her toward me.

She turns her face to the side and my lips find hers, our tongues frantic to reunite. "Harder," she moans.

I slam into her and groan into her mouth, my climax spilling over into her.

Cora whimpers and bucks her hips as her orgasm rattles her body.

We both slow down and kiss the rest of the way through the wave of pleasure.

She giggles and lowers herself onto the dresser to rest.

Slowly, I pull out of her aching hole. "Fuck, you're bleeding. Did I hurt you?"

"No, shit, I'm still on my period." She turns around abruptly. "I forgot. I'm sorry."

I breathe a sigh of relief and kiss her nose. "Don't ever apologize for being a woman."

Cora practically waddles to the bathroom, and I follow her in to wash my dick in the sink as she uses the bathroom.

She cracks the door to the toilet area. "Hey, toss me a tampon?"

I eye the boxes strewn about on the sink area and grab one at random. "Here." I pass it to her and avert my gaze to give her some privacy.

Cora exits the enclosed area and washes her hands as best she can with the sling confining one of her arms. "This thing is stupid." She slides the strap around her head and tosses it on the counter. "I'm not wearing it."

"Are you sure?" I step toward her. "You're not in pain?"

She shakes her head. "It's sore but it's not painful."

I can't quite tell if she's lying or not. Cora's damn good at pretending everything is fine when it isn't.

"Tell me if that changes, okay? You don't need to hurt for no reason." I tuck her blonde hair behind her ear. "And for the record, I didn't ask to speak to you alone to hook up."

Her gaze flickers between mine. "I know you didn't."

"I still need to know what's going on though," I say. I hate to push her, especially when she's just stopped being mad at me, but I have to figure out how to help her, and I can't if she keeps me in the dark.

"Come on." Cora weaves her good arm around my biceps and tugs me toward the bedroom. She leans in and whispers, "Think they know?"

"Probably. I think the dresser was bouncing against the wall." I follow her through the bedroom and back out into the open area, all eyes on us the second we're through the door.

Cora releases me and takes her spot on the stool she was sitting on earlier. "First things first," she starts. "I'm not wearing that brace." She focuses directly on Silver. "It's bulky and itches and I don't think I need it. Thank you, though."

I walk back to where I was leaning against the counter and wait for what she has to say, my cheeks no doubt flushed from the quickie we just had.

"Secondly, I guess now is the time when I get everyone on the same page. I'm going to tell this story one last time, so listen up because I'm not going to do it again." Cora's eyes settle on mine. "But before I do, you have to promise me that you won't do anything, and you won't tell anyone."

"Why are you looking at me?" I glance at the other guys.

"We've already promised," Alec announces. "Silver and I both have."

Cora stares right into my eyes like she might catch me on fire with just a glare if I don't agree.

"Fine." I throw up my hands even though I'm not entirely sure if I believe the promise I make to her. How am I supposed to sit back and do nothing when Ricardo is causing her harm? I barely have any information, and it's enough to make me want to strangle him to death; if I have the whole truth, who's to say the lengths I will go to make him pay?

"That's not very convincing," Cora says.

"I won't do anything unless I get your official consent, okay?"

"Very well." She sucks in a breath. "A couple weeks ago, Ricardo came to my house and threatened my dad. I overheard them and accidentally stumbled into the room. He was going on about my mom being sick and needing treatment. Treatment that apparently Ricardo was capable of providing."

London raises a finger to interject. "Sorry to interrupt already but Daddy does deal with experimental medical stuff. It's one of his rackets."

"What else do you know?" Cora turns toward her. "Do you know where it is or who does it or anything?"

London shakes her head. "Sorry, I don't. But I can try to find out." She pauses. "That is if he doesn't kill me first." Her intensely green eyes peer right into my fucking soul. "Thanks to you."

I keep my arms crossed over my chest, not saying a word in response. I understand she's furious, but what she doesn't get is that I would do anything for Cora, including put her life in danger. I won't be winning any points with anyone in this room if I say that out loud, though.

So instead, I keep my mouth shut and hope that Cora will finish this story that I'm the last to hear about.

"Go on," Silver chimes in, his face emotionless as he stands in the corner with his arms folded, too.

I've known him for a long time—longer than I have Dominic and his guys. Silver was around back when I worked for my previous boss, those two having been acquaintances for quite a while. Silver was always reliable and discreet; someone my boss could count on even during the fallout and the war that ensued. They kept in contact, and if I'm not mistaken, would have considered each other friends. That's a rarity in this industry. There's no shortage of backstabbing, and that doesn't equate to any of us having many, if any at all, friends. On the rare occurrence that you do find someone loyal and trustworthy, you stay with them to the death.

Cora clears her throat. "So, my dad was in debt to Ricardo, and he couldn't pay. Ricardo threatened to kill both of my parents but said he would take me in exchange."

My fingers dig into my forearm, and I consider all the ways I want to torture and kill him.

"I agreed, and then a few days later, he found me, and we discussed terms. I negotiated for a month to get my affairs in order. And part of that deal was that I would come to his home every Sunday to try on clothes for him. That's what you stumbled into today, Miller." Cora glances over to London. "London and I were chatting because Ricardo was running late, and he came in all pissed off and thought something was going on, that we were conspiring against him or some bullshit. I don't know."

Silver sighs dramatically. "Tell them everything, Angel."

I glare at him for the use of the pet name but quickly remember I just had sex with her in his bedroom. If anyone should be shooting vicious stares it should be him, not me.

"Part of the deal is that I owe him an heir. A son. He says the deal will be done if I can do that."

I blink a few times and process the information. Did she just say what I think she did? Did I hear that correctly? Was I so distracted with Silver and Angel and sex that I misheard the words she spoke?

"Excuse me?" I drop my arms to the side and step off the counter.

Cora slowly lowers her head and raises it to confirm my worst fears. "A baby. He wants me to give him a baby."

"Abso-fucking-lutely not," I all but shout, the rage coursing through me at an all-time high. Just when I'm convinced this can't possibly get any worse, it does.

"See," Cora says. "This is why I didn't want to tell you." She glances around the room. "I never wanted any of you to find out. This was supposed to be my burden to carry, my issue to deal with."

I grip the edge of the island she's sitting at and steady myself as best I can given the circumstances. "You are not dealing with this alone, Cora. Not anymore. We're going to figure this out. I don't care if I have to take your place, you are not going to have to go through with this."

"You don't understand," Cora utters. "He already has my parents. He said he'd kill anyone I cared about if I told anyone or tried to get out of it. What do you think he's going to do when he finds out you all know?" She shakes her head. "This is why you can't do anything. I can't lose anyone else." A single tear rolls down her cheek, and before I can reach to wipe it away, Alec beats me to it.

"I'm with Miller, Cor," he speaks low. "You're not going through this alone. Whatever it takes, we'll get through this."

I shoot a look at Silver, who leaves his spot in the corner to come over and show his solidarity.

"He has power, but he's a dumb man. We'll figure this out." Silver stands at my side and I grow grateful for the relationship he had with my former boss. That by itself gives me faith that his follow-through game is strong, and he'll be a great asset to have to solve this seemingly impossible situation.

"Let's go over the facts," I say, my problem-solving nature kicking in. "How much time is left?"

"Approximately two weeks," Cora tells us.

I tap my chin. "Okay. And you have how many Sundays left?"

Cora shrugs. "Either one or two. Not including today." Her gaze falls to the counter. "I don't know what's going to happen after today."

"Since you shot him," London points out once again.

"It was a flesh wound," I announce. "It's not a big deal. He's lucky I didn't aim for his dick."

Silver rasps his fingers against the counter. "It does pose an issue, though. There's no telling if he'll change his timeline or terms."

"I could always say it was a misunderstanding," Cora suggests. "He doesn't need to know anything else. I could tell him part of the truth, that Miller had put a tracker on me and saw I was at his house and got jealous."

"You're going to need to go into hiding," Silver says.

"No fucking way." I cross my arms. "Not happening."

Cora cocks her head to the side at me, those blue eyes blinking up at me. "Miller."

"Yeah, dude, Silver's right," Alec agrees. "From what I've heard, Ricardo is not someone to mess with. I mean, isn't that the reason he isn't dead already?" He glances between us.

"His position does make him rather difficult to exterminate," Silver answers him. "If I knew his strongest allies, if I could turn them against him, it would make it easier."

"You guys are failing to grasp the part where he said he'd kill me, my parents, and anyone I told." Cora gawks at all of us, settling on London. "Tell them what he did to you."

London's lips part and for the first time since she's been here, she looks vulnerable. "I don't know, it's not a big deal."

"Are you serious?" Cora points at London's side. "Don't tell them then, show them."

London sighs and lifts up the corner of her shirt to reveal a thick ass scar on her torso.

"Holy shit," Alec says without a filter. "Did he do that to you?"

She nods and covers herself up. "Yeah. The only reason he agreed to keep me alive is to sell me off."

I swallow down the reality that Ricardo has offered his virginal daughter to me on numerous occasions. I had no idea the situation was as dire as it is, otherwise, I would have taken him up on the offer just to free her of his madness. Even if I could come to terms with the idea of handing him over a small fortune, there's no way he'd be willing to accept my money to pardon his daughter now that I barged into his house and shot him in the leg.

"I'm sorry," I tell her. "I didn't know."

London keeps her chin level and her shoulders set into a straight line, her exterior solid like if she maintains her composure maybe she won't fall apart.

She reminds me a great deal of Cora, in how she pretends things are fine when they really aren't. It makes sense that they would immediately be drawn to one another.

"In light of what happened to me," London continues. "I can vouch that Daddy is not someone to cross. He loves a good challenge, and the only thing you've done is give him a reason to pursue whatever methods he deems fit to make you pay. If I were you, I'd leave town."

"I'm not leaving town." There's nothing that could make me leave Cora in her time of need, not now, not ever.

"I can tell him I'm not interested," Cora proposes. "I can be rather convincing. I'll say that you pursued me, and I wasn't into you and beg him to forgive the situation."

"I wouldn't beg," London tells her. "Begging insinuates that he has the upper hand. You have to be strong, but not too strong. Know what I mean?"

Cora nods like she knows exactly.

Silver speaks up. "I'll continue to do some digging and see what I can uncover. But in the meantime, we have two weeks to figure this out. Not a day more. Cora, I suggest you stay here where I can protect you."

I glare at him. "And you think I can't?"

Silver pinches the bridge of his nose between his fingers. "He's going to come after you, Miller. Do you want her to be with you when that happens?"

"No," I practically whisper.

"She can stay with me, too." Alec stands tall at the counter, ready to be of assistance in whatever way he can. "We can alternate, take turns you know, so he has a harder time finding her."

"You're not safe at home." I focus on Cora and try to get her to understand without telling her that it was very easy to break into her parents' home.

"Can I at least get some things?" Cora motions to her body. "I'm wearing Friday's outfit."

"I'll get them. Make me a list."

Cora scowls at me but it makes no difference. I refuse to allow her to go home where she's most vulnerable. I don't care if he wants me dead, he's going to have to come do it himself and if he's that bold, I fucking dare him. I'm not afraid of some decrepit old man.

"You'll spend tonight here," Silver declares. "We'll figure out the rest of your schedule on a whim so he can't figure it out." He centers on London. "And the less you know, the better."

"I shouldn't be hearing any of this." London licks her lips and raises her brows. "You guys are all going to die."

"Thanks for the support." Alec chuckles and checks his phone, which only reminds me of the one that's been buzzing on and off in my pocket for the last three hours.

There's been another situation with shipments and if I don't get ahead of it soon, there's no telling how much damage it will do to the West Coast sector.

"Silver," I say as the idea sparks. "Can I talk to you for a second? In private."

Cora is the first to speak up. "Secrets don't make friends."

"These secrets aren't secrets, babe." It's more of a hunch that I could use his advice on but I don't tell her that because I don't want her to think I'm not capable of handling shit on my own.

Silver nods toward the living room, and I follow him over, noting how closed off his body language is.

"What is it?" he says with a hint of annoyance in his tone.

"First of all, thank you for taking care of her when I couldn't."

He raises a grey hair speckled eyebrow at me. "That's what you asked me over here for?"

"No." I flit my gaze back at the group who talk quietly amongst themselves. "Can I trust you with something else?"

Silver sighs. "When have I ever made you feel like you couldn't trust me?"

"Fair enough." I rub my neck and consider the weight of what I'm about to confess. This isn't just my business information I'm putting on the line, it's Dominic's, too. He's told me to keep it between me and his men, but what if it could somehow help us solve the situation with Ricardo for all of us.

"Get on with it," Silver adds impatiently.

"There's been some issues lately impacting the West Coast sector."

"What kind of issues?"

"Shipments have gone missing, some being turned over to police, you know, typical turf shit."

"What does this have to do with anything? Do you need me to figure out who's behind it?"

"I think I know who's behind it."

Silver stares back and forth between my eyes as the realization hits him. "Ricardo?"

I nod and keep my voice low. "Yeah. Seems we have a common enemy. I haven't been able to prove it yet, but he approached me the other day with information he shouldn't have had unless he's in on it."

"Okay."

"That's it? Okay?"

Silver scratches his beard. "This gives me more to go on. I'll see what I can do about proving it and figure out a way to discredit him. Once we get all the pieces in place, we kill him."

"I thought Cora told us not to do anything," I say even though there's no way in hell I'm going to be able to stick to my word.

Silver looks directly into my eyes when he says, "I'd rather die than let something happen to her."

He and I may be two very different men, but at least we can agree on one thing—we will sacrifice ourselves to save the girl we love.

2 8
CORA

S omehow, I convince the guys to let me go back to Ricardo's with London.

It's probably a stupid idea, but the sooner I get a handle on the situation, the better.

My phone had been blowing up non-stop since Miller stormed in and shot Ricardo, and if I didn't make amends soon, there was no telling how bad things would get—for me, and for London.

My injured arm stays at my side as I walk through the door and into his mansion, my stomach coiling with regret the second I'm inside. I breathe and remind myself that everything will be okay, that with the support of London and my guy friends, I will survive this.

How? I don't know, but I'll figure it out as I go.

I follow London silently down the hall and watch her poke her head into each room we pass. It isn't until I hear commotion that I'm not entirely convinced Ricardo is here at all.

"Well, well, well," he says and steps out of his weird jerk-off room. "What do we have here?" Ricardo hobbles a little but is otherwise upright and well. If only Miller had shot him in an artery that would have made him bleed out instead.

"Daddy, we can explain," London is the first to open her mouth, probably because she's dealt with him before. But what kind of person would I be if I allowed her to take the lead on something that wasn't even her fault?

"Sir," I speak. "I'd like to offer you my official apology for what happened and assure you that it will never happen again."

Ricardo lifts his arm to signal for us to enter the room. "Come, have a seat, let's discuss this." His mild tone brings more concern than it should. I expected him to be outraged, immediately abusive, something other than even-tempered.

We slip past him and I try not to gawk at the remnants of blood on the floor where Miller had shot him.

London lowers herself onto the couch and I take the spot opposite of her and brace myself for what's to come.

Ricardo sits on the seat he masturbated in last Sunday and leans back. "So, do tell how long you and Miller have been together."

"We aren't." I shake my head. "This has all been a great misunderstanding. Miller, well, he's obsessed with me. He had been following me and saw that I was here and got jealous that you and I were together. He's a psycho and overreacted."

Ricardo rubs his bearded chin. "And you expect me to believe that?"

"It's true, Daddy," London chimes in. "I saw them at the shopping center the other day. Cora looked very uncomfortable, and I didn't know until today how bad things were. I heard her tell him that there was nothing between them."

"And how did Miller take it?"

"Not well, Daddy, but I reminded him of how powerful you are and that he shouldn't dare cross you again."

"Give me your phone." Ricardo holds out his hand to me. "Now."

Frantically, I pull the thing out of my back pocket and fumble to input my password and slide it into his palm. I swallow harshly and wait for him to look at whatever he's after.

He squints his eyes and pokes the screen a few times, and then scrolls, my heart pounding every second that he's holding my phone.

What if he sees something that incriminates us? What if our lie falls flat because I forgot to delete something?

Only, an antagonizing minute later, he tosses the thing at me and sighs. "Very well."

I hide my smirk as I shove my phone back into my pocket, our plan working just as we wanted.

Thanks to the new unsend and edit feature, I was able to go through my texts with Miller on my phone and his and make it appear like he really had been sending me inappropriate texts and I had been telling him I was not interested. We fabricated the whole thing to corroborate our story and it worked like a fucking charm. I even made sure to delete the threads with Silver, Alec, and June, just in case Ricardo got curious and wanted to snoop through those, too. The only ones I left behind were work-related, distant family and friends, or automated texts that send those annoying verification codes.

Ricardo pats his knee and focuses on me. "Come here, pet."

My heart stutters at his request but I have no choice other than to comply. Slowly, I rise to my feet, walk over to him, and sit on his lap.

His hands are on me in an instant, one on my lower back and one digging into my thigh. "I want you to tell me you're going to obey me, pet, that you're going to be a good girl."

Teeth chattering, I find the strength to get it together and say, "I will obey you. I will be a good girl."

Ricardo slides his hand up my back and into my hair, gripping it tightly. "Good, pet, good." He yanks hard, and I lose control over my posture, him tugging me toward him. "I get what I want, do you understand me. You're lucky I don't fucking kill you right here for that little *show* he put on earlier. If you weren't such a *candidate* for an heir..." He clenches my hair harder and jerks me at his mercy.

I don't even see it coming when he releases his other hand, forms a fist, and slams it into my stomach. My entire body curls inward and he repeats the motion, this time clamoring me in the ribs.

Instinctually, I try to free myself, to cover my belly with my hands, to do anything I can, but he is stronger and there's no getting away.

London says something I can't make out through the ringing in my ears.

Ricardo stands abruptly and tosses me onto the ground with a great thud, his leg reeling back and driving forward into my gut. "Mine! Do you fucking hear me? Mine!"

He draws his leg back again and London screams at him to stop.

"Daddy, Daddy! Wait a minute." Her breath is ragged as she pleads with him.

Through my watery gaze, I see her holding her hands out and I try to warn her, to tell her not to interrupt him, but nothing but choked air comes out.

"What?" he screams at her.

"You have to listen to me, Daddy. If you want her to make you an heir, you have to stop."

I clutch my stomach and gasp through the pain flowing through my body.

"Okay," is all he says as he steps over my body. "You're right, London girl, you're right."

I reach to grab onto his ankle, but he slips right past me, and I know with certainty that there's nothing I can do to stop him.

His gentle tone leaves quicker than it arrived and he all but growls as he takes a fistful of her red hair and drags her down. "If she can't take the beating, then you will."

"No," I cry out. "Stop." My voice is nothing but a raspy whimper.

He kicks her square in the side and she recoils inward, her face pinched together. He repeats it again, and again, each time throwing her around on the carpet.

Ricardo takes a momentary break from her and turns toward me. "See what happens when you disobey me." He thrusts his foot into my side and a snapping sound shoots a spike of pain through my torso. "Fucking bitch."

Tears roll down each of my cheeks, and I cough, a metallic taste coating my mouth.

I'm frozen in place, my body trembling with fear and agony as I watch him return his attention to London.

"You. Will. Obey. Me." Each word is enunciated with another blow. "But only for so long, London girl, because I have found someone who will take you off my hands."

He kicks her repeatedly until she's left in a sobbing heap on the floor, her mascara-soaked face in my direction.

"*That* is what you both deserve." Ricardo spits onto the rug between us and leaves the room with a slam of the door.

How he's able to push through the pain of his gunshot wound is beyond me, but nothing he's ever done has made much sense. He's a monster.

Seconds pass that turn into minutes, and I grow unsure of what will happen when he returns. Did he go to get something to finish us off? Or is he done with us for now?

I dig my fingers into the carpet and drag myself toward London as she lies there unmoving.

"Oh God, London," I force out and smooth the matted hair off her cheek. "London, are you..."

My worst fear consumes me and a new bout of tears crash

down at the possibility that London didn't survive another one of his brutal attacks.

But as I intensely stare at her chest to monitor if it will rise or fall, London coughs and blood coats her lips. She blinks her red eyes open and frantically looks around until her eyes land on mine.

I force myself upright next to her and pull her head into my lap. "I'm going to get us out of here," I tell her without really knowing how. "I'm going to get us help."

Considering my options, I realize I have to call someone. If I call 911, they'll ask too many questions that I won't be able to answer. If I call Miller, he'd come in an instant and tell me how stupid I was for agreeing to come here. Silver would come, but he'd probably burn Ricardo's house down, leaving me only one option left.

Alec. My only hope is that he isn't busy doing some errand for June or her guys.

I can't have them find out about this, partially because I'm still infuriated at them for lying to me, but mainly because I cannot afford to get anyone else involved in this already terrible situation.

"Cora," London mutters.

I pat her head. "Shh. I've got you." I wince as I grab my phone out of my pocket, swipe open the cracked screen and push the call button.

It rings once, then twice, my stomach dropping with each obnoxious sound.

"Cora, hey, is everything okay?" Alec's voice comes through the other end loud and clear.

"Yeah," I whisper. "Can you come get us? I need you to keep this between us. Not tell the other guys." Every word I speak is more difficult than the last. Even breathing is a burden I no longer wish to have to endure.

"I'll be there in five minutes."

I hang up, shove the phone in my pocket and glance down at the battered and broken girl in my lap. "London, can you stand?"

Despite being beaten bloody, she nods with her lids heavy and swollen.

Slipping out from under her, I put my hands up under her armpits and help her into a seated position. I ignore the pain and force both of us to our feet, knowing that things will only get worse if we don't leave now. Ricardo did enough damage for one day, and that will have to be enough to tie him over until he can torment us again.

I sling London's arm over my shoulder and wrap mine around her waist, doing the best I can not to apply too much pressure to her wounded frame.

She cringes but remains next to me and does her part in keeping herself vertical.

"You're doing great," I tell her. "One step at a time, London. Come on. We can do this."

Together, we move inch by inch closer to the door, my heart pounding so intensely it thuds in my ears, making it hard to hear what's going on outside the room.

What will I do if Ricardo comes barreling back in and demands us to stay and inflicts more damage? How much more can London take before she succumbs to his abuse? Although, if memory serves me correctly, he mentioned that he found her a husband, so wouldn't that be a reason to keep her alive to get his payoff?

I cling to that and hope it will be what we need to get us through.

We reach the door, my injured arm reaching out to grasp the handle. My shoulder burns but I push past it and turn the knob and prepare for what might be waiting for us on the other side.

Holding my breath, I weasel us over the threshold and pause to glance both ways, my vision still a bit blurred.

The hallway is eerily quiet, like that moment in a horror film before there's an excessive jump scare. Cue the suspenseful music as I conclude that it's now or never.

London coughs quietly, almost as if she's aware of how dire things are and how if we aren't careful, we might not make it out of this. Blood speckles out of her mouth and onto the light-colored tile flooring. Her heels drag against the hard surface, and I stop us to kick them off both of her feet. It's no easy task, but I fight through the pain and make it happen.

With one final glance behind us, I push forward and guide us toward the front of Ricardo's mansion. I grow grateful that his weird torture room isn't that far in, because I'm not that confident I could carry her much farther than I already have.

Every step I brace myself for him to jump out from a darkened corner, but he never does. Is he even aware we're leaving at all? What is he going to do when he finds out we have? I guess that's a problem for future me because my main concern is getting London out of here and getting her medical treatment.

Summoning all the strength I have left, I grip the handle of the front door and crack it open, my sights grateful for the blacked-out SUV that pulls up in a screeching halt.

I practically fall through the doorway and manage to regain my composure to tug the door shut behind us. I do everything I can to hurry because if I don't, Alec will get out of his vehicle and expose himself to whatever exterior surveillance that Ricardo has.

London had said he doesn't keep cameras in his house, but if that phone call he received when Miller showed up signals anything, it's that there might be some outside.

But I can't voice that to Alec in time because he jumps right the fuck out of the driver's side and rushes across the lawn toward me.

"Fuck, Cora." He grabs the other side of London and takes the brunt of her weight from me.

"Help me get her in your car." I continue to carry what little of her I can, only releasing her once we arrive at the back passenger door to open it.

"Climb in," Alec tells me and I do it without question, allowing him to guide her into the seat with me a moment later. He takes a sobering glance at me before slamming the door shut and running around to return to the driver's seat.

London groans and lays on her side with her head in my lap. Her hair is crusted to her bloodied head, and I try to pull it away but it's no use.

"Everything is going to be okay," I tell her even though I have no clue if what I'm saying is a lie. Between her injuries, what Ricardo could do to her in the future, and the husband he claims he's found, there's no shortage of things that could prevent it from coming true.

Alec's gaze meets mine in the rear-view mirror as he slams the gear shifter into drive. "Are you okay?"

"I need you to take us to the hospital," I say with great urgency.

"No," London groans, but I don't care, she needs to be seen by a professional, not Silver or anyone else who's used to tending to less serious criminal wounds.

Keeping one hand on London, I move the other to my ribs and wince as I apply the slightest pressure.

"I take it things didn't go well?" Alec says to me from up front.

I swallow the coppery taste in my mouth. "It went fine. He totally bought the story."

Alec glances at me and turns his attention to the road, swerving around a car that pulls out in front of us.

"Really," I insist. "He bought it but that didn't mean that we still didn't have to pay for what Miller did."

The desire to say *I told you so* is strong and yet I keep it to myself—it wouldn't do any good, especially with Alec, who has done nothing wrong.

"I'm sorry," Alec says, his voice low.

"Focus on getting us to the hospital."

"Is she going to be okay?"

I look down at the bloodied girl in my lap, my heart aching at witnessing what she deals with on a normal basis from the one man who is supposed to always keep her safe—her father. "I don't know."

The rest of the drive is quiet, my eyes only taking a break from London briefly to check where we are every so often. I study her chest, the slow rise and fall, and the tension that coils in her at each bump in the road.

"Pull straight up to the emergency room." I point ahead at the sign to guide Alec on where to go.

He does exactly as I say and jumps out, rushing around the side to open the door. Without being told to, Alec scoops London's frail body into his arms and bolts through the gliding entrance.

This is the part in movies where hospital employees come running out to greet us and ask what happened and insist on putting the injured person on a gurney and escort her back immediately for help, but none of that happens. No, instead, we're greeted by the many eyes of the packed waiting room who no doubt wonder if their ailment will be put on hold to tend to the broken girl we just brought in.

I slam my hand on the receptionist's desk, and the woman blinks up at me, chewing her gum obnoxiously.

"I'll be right with you," she says with no sense of urgency.

I snatch the phone out of her hand and shove it onto the receiver. "You'll help us now or I'll make sure this is your last fucking day." Whether I mean at work or alive is left to interpretation.

The curly-headed middle-aged woman continues to smack on her gum. "Listen, lady, take a number." She points to the stand with tickets and then at the monitor on the wall. "Someone will come get you checked in shortly."

I lower myself onto the top of her desk and take a fistful of her shirt into my hand. "I think you'll help us now. See that girl right there?" I tilt my head toward London hanging in Alec's arms. "That's London Gardella, Ricardo Gardella's daughter." And for extra emphasis, I add, "Friend of Dominic Adler."

At the mention of the last name I dropped, her eyes bulge and she hops up from her desk, shooting her chair out of the way as it rolls toward her.

"Come around here." She cups her arm and waves it around the corner of her desk. "Right this way."

I tilt my head to signal to Alec to come on and follow her wherever she's taking us.

The woman bangs on a door and opens it a second later without allowing the person to respond. "Doctor Trevani. You have a patient here who needs to be seen immediately. London Gardella. Ricardo's daughter. Mr. Adler's friend."

The man snatches his stethoscope off the small table next to him and drops his drink, spilling it without a care. "This way." He doesn't question us until we're in a small patient room, the receptionist lingering behind him. "Set her down here. What happened?"

Alec lowers her onto a hospital bed gently and steps back.

"We were mugged," I blurt out, the only lie I could think of off the top of my head.

Trevani meets my gaze, his brown eyes boring into me with great intensity. "I don't need to know what happened, but I need to know *what happened to her*, do you understand?"

"She was kicked, repeatedly." I do everything I can to block out the image of Ricardo slamming his shoe into her over and over, her body growing more limp with each blow. I don't think there was a part of her that he didn't inflict at least some pain on. Mainly her torso, but he spared no remorse for her legs, her arms, or her head.

When he was finally done, she was contorted and bloody and barely moving.

"Get my care team in here," Trevani tells the receptionist and then looks at us. "Get back." He leans toward London, his hands working over her body, lifting her shirt and taking in what he can.

London's breaths grow choppy and ragged, and a blue hue starts to appear on her skin.

A group of men and women rush into the room.

"What's happening?" I ask anyone who will listen.

The doctor announces to the room, "Possible pneumothoraxis, get me a needle, stat!"

"A needle?" I frantically look to Alec but he doesn't have the answers he needs.

A second later, one of the guys comes over and pushes on my shoulder. "You're going to have to wait outside."

The people, collectively, start attaching monitors and various devices to London and cut her clothes off.

Alec takes my hand. "Come on, Cor, there's nothing we can do for her."

"But, but..." I shove past him toward the doctor. "Don't tell anyone anything," I say above the beeping of the machines and chatter amongst them.

"I won't," Trevani confirms with his brows pinched together. "Someone get her out of here."

The man who tried to get me out already positions himself between me and the doctor and forces his chest into me to nudge me out of the way, his hands up on both sides like he's ready to put them on me but is really trying not to.

"Cor, give them their space." Alec guides me out of the room, the door latching shut behind us and my back finding the closest hard surface to lean against.

Tears spring from my eyes. "What if she doesn't make it?"

"Ma'am," the receptionist says. "Do you need to be seen?"

I shake my head, water trickling from my face onto the hospital floor. "No, I'm fine."

"Yes," Alec interrupts. "Yes, she does."

"This way," she tells us.

I blindly follow them but pull my phone out of my pocket and try my best to spell the word the doctor just said. Thoro-something. I wipe my face and blink to see the screen more clearly. "What did he say? What was that word?"

Alec keeps his hand on my lower back but takes my phone from me to thumb the word into my search bar. "What happened to your screen?"

"Ricardo," I whisper so the receptionist lady doesn't hear me and read the words that take forever to load on my phone.

Pneumothoraxis, in layman's terms, London has a collapsed lung. All because of her terrible fucking father and his incessant need to hurt anything and anyone in his path.

I understand he was mad about what happened with Miller, but how was that London's fault? Really, how was it anyone's fault but his own?

"This room right here." The receptionist stands in a doorway and motions for us to enter.

"I don't want a male doctor," I blurt out before she leaves.

She smiles kindly, turns on her heel, and walks away.

"Cora, sweetheart." Alec sighs and pats the empty hospital bed.

The guilt of everything comes crashing over me—the fact that I told the guys, the unknown of whether London will make it, hell, even the people stuck in the waiting room while I barged my way straight to the top of the patient lists. I wanted her to be seen, not me. I don't care about the ache in my side or my shoulder. I wish everyone would see that I'm okay, I'm not the one that people should worry about.

"I'm fine," I tell him, hating how the two words come out so fucking aggressive. He hasn't done anything wrong, in fact, he's done everything right. Alec has been nothing but kind and patient with me since the moment I met him, and I've done nothing to deserve how he treats me. I lower my voice and comply with his request, settling onto the too-sterile bed. "I'm sorry," I say quietly.

"What are you apologizing for?" Alec stands in front of me, his cool hands on my cheeks, tucking my hair behind my ears. He leans down to kiss me and it's then that I realize how much taller he is.

"How tall are you?" I ask totally changing the subject.

A soft grin forms on his beautiful face as he shrugs. "I don't know. Six-one, six-two, maybe."

"You're like supermodel hot, you know that right?"

"Did you hit your head?" He cups my chin between his thumb and finger. "You're worrying me."

"No, my head is fine." At least physically, maybe not mentally...I just don't mention that last part. "You're just really pretty." I weave my hands under the hem of his shirt and poke my head under. "And you have a lot of abs. More than normal."

Alec swats away my hands playfully. "I have the normal amount of abs, thank you very much."

"No, I'm pretty sure there's a few extra." I chuckle and release his shirt. "But I'm apologizing because I've been an asshole to you, and you deserve much better. I was really mean to you, Alec, I'm sorry."

Alec draws in a breath and lowers himself onto the bed next to me, weaving his fingers through mine. He studies our entwined hands and meets my gaze. "You've been through a lot, Cora, probably more than you've even told me. I don't fault you for that. I don't blame you for pushing me away, or at least, trying to. I get it. I understand. I'm not mad at you for it. And I wish you'd stop punishing yourself for something I don't hold against you. This..." He holds onto my hand between his like he's afraid I might slip through his fingers like sand. "Us, that's all that matters to me." He looks at me, really stares into my eyes, his soul begging mine to comprehend how serious he is. "You're all that matters to me."

He swallows and it's as though that simple movement changed everything about his tone, his demeanor, because when he opens his mouth back up, it's unlike anything I've ever heard come out of his mouth. "I am not a violent man, Cora. I am cool-tempered, I do not yell, I do not start fights, I do not have a thirst for violence like a lot of men do. But watching you struggle like this, witnessing you go through something no other person should, well, it's sparked something to life in me that terrifies me, and I'd be lying if I said there weren't any lengths I wouldn't go through to keep you safe."

"Alec..."

"I want to kill him, Cor. Like really kill him. Make him suffer. Make him pay. Make him dream of the day he never laid a finger on you or even looked your direction. I get it now, how psycho the guys get over June...the things they've done." Alec shakes his head. "Unspeakable things. Things that will make them go straight to Hell...things a person cannot come back from. I would do that and worse, just to get you justice. To get revenge." He pauses for a second and adds, "If it's the last thing I do, I will kill him for you."

My heart pounds a little harder with each word he says, my brain unable to grasp whether he's real, whether the things he's saying are a part of my imagination, some vision I've conjured up because in reality, I died there on that crusty floor in Ricardo's torture room.

But when he squeezes my hand and averts his gaze like he's

embarrassed by his confession, I know that this is real. He is real. The love we have for each other is real.

Love. I love him.

And with that realization, my chest tightens even more. How can I love him and still feel the way I do for Silver and Miller?

29
CORA

The doctor checks me over. Both the doctor and Alec insist that I get a CT scan to rule out any internal damage, and I'm told exactly what I already suspected—my ribs are fractured.

Per the doctor's orders, I'm supposed to: take pain relievers, ice regularly the first few days to reduce swelling, and rest. The same goes for my shoulder, too. The doctor told me I was lucky, but nothing about my life feels very lucky.

There's been no update on London, and I don't know if that's a good or a bad thing.

"No news is good news, Cor," Alec attempts to reassure me but it does nothing to soothe the raging pit inside of me.

How could I let this happen? Why couldn't I have protected her?

"What time is it?" I ask him since my phone screen is too cracked to read it clearly.

He pulls out his cell and mutters, "Fuck."

"What's wrong?"

"I have like thirteen missed calls from Miller." Alec pushes the green button and presses the phone to his ear, Miller answering without it barely ringing.

"Where is she?" Miller says so loudly I can hear him from my spot next to Alec.

"We're at the hospital," Alec tells him.

"What room? Where are you? Tell me *right* now."

Alec slides off the bed and makes his way to the door, popping his head out to check for the room number. "Uh, two nineteen."

Miller appears out of fucking nowhere, shoving past Alec to barge into the room, his gaze frantic until it meets mine.

I rise from the bed and stand there as he approaches.

Miller plants his arms on my shoulders and studies me from head to toe. "You're hurt. What's wrong? Tell me, what did he do?"

I shake my head. "I'm fine." But the nagging tears fill my eyes anyway, no doubt bringing him the opposite of comfort.

Alec interjects. "She's got a couple broken ribs and minor bruising, but she'll be fine. The doctor went to see if she could get an update on London."

"Your tracker," Miller says, his eyes never leaving me. "It shows you're still at Ricardo's."

I blink as the realization dawns on me. "I must have left my purse there. I'm sorry."

Miller sighs and closes his eyes briefly. "I'm just glad you're okay." He pulls me into him and I bury myself in his chest. His embrace is gentle but exactly what I needed.

"How did you find us?" I ask him, suddenly unsure how he was at the hospital the second Alec told him where we were.

"When I didn't see you at the house, I checked Alec's location." Miller rubs soft circles on my back and kisses the top of my head.

"What the hell dude, you put a tracker on me?" Alec scoffs.

I pull away. "Are you stalking Alec, too?"

Miller shrugs. "I'm not sorry."

Alec rolls his eyes and crosses his arms. "Whatever."

"London?" Miller takes a step back to glance between us.

"I don't know. She has a punctured lung." I wipe my cheek and exhale. "Ricardo beat the shit out of her."

"I told you it was a bad idea," Miller says.

"Not going would have been worse. He would have found us. He probably would have killed us all." I try to search for some kind of silver lining but it's hard not knowing if London will make it. I don't want to admit that I might be the very reason she doesn't pull through. I have to believe that this was the best possible option, even if they were all shitty to begin with.

"Yeah, you're right," Miller admits and surprises me a bit.

The doctor, a soft-spoken older woman named Jenny, comes back into our room, her blue eyes latching onto Miller the second she steps through the door. She nods to him and draws in a long breath. "I'm afraid I don't have much of an update. You were correct that London did suffer from pneumothorax, a collapsed lung. Preliminary recordings show she has several broken bones, including some skull fractures. She's in surgery for the time being but I don't know when she'll be out." She swallows harshly and adds, "This probably shouldn't have to be said, but I'd like to remind you that this is confidential information that I'm not able to give out, so please keep this to yourselves for now."

Miller is the first to speak up. "Of course. We wouldn't jeopardize the ongoing relationship we have with the hospital staff here." He extends his hand. "Miller Rossi, I don't think we've met before."

"Jenny Durk, ER Doctor."

"Thank you for the unofficial update," Miller continues.

Jenny glances at us each curtly and settles on me. "Meds. Ice. Rest."

"Got it," I tell her and wish that she would have kept her

mouth shut. I don't need another reminder to the guys how fragile I am. They already worry about me enough as it is.

Jenny leaves me and the guys alone, the silence nearly deafening.

"I want to wait until she's out," I make my formal declaration while expecting them to protest.

Miller pivots toward me. "We have no idea how long that's going to take."

"He's right," Alec adds.

I consider darting out of the room and hiding somewhere for an update that London's made it out of surgery, but knowing Miller, he'd hunt me to the ends of the Earth if I tried to evade him—Alec more than likely helping him in his pursuit of keeping an eye on me.

"It's not safe here." Miller watches a person walk by the doorway suspiciously. "There's no telling if Ricardo is going to come after you again."

I pull out my phone, cutting the tip of my finger as I swipe the screen to life. "I have a text from him thanking me for the visit. He said he's looking forward to our last Sunday together next week."

Miller looks over my shoulder, his jaw tensing. "It could be a lie."

"I think what he did today deeply satisfied him, even with you pissing him off, I still think he's temporarily satiated." I wouldn't be surprised if Ricardo went somewhere more private to masturbate after beating me and his daughter up. He's a deeply twisted man and he seems to get off on hurting women.

"Sick fuck," Alec murmurs.

"I'm going to have someone trail him, that's the only way we'll know for sure. I don't feel comfortable with you out and about without being certain of where he is. I won't put you at risk like that. I shouldn't have allowed you to go today." Miller's fingers twitch like he's refraining from making a fist. He does that a lot, leading me to believe he's often on the brink of exploding with rage.

"Where's Silver?" I ask.

"Doing what we talked about." Miller focuses on Alec for a second. "I think I'm going to take her with me."

"Uh, hello, she's standing right here." I snap my fingers between them.

The two of them face each other with me on the outside in the middle.

They're both about the same height, making me practically crane my neck to glance up at them.

They share similar qualities but are somehow so different. Alec's skin tone is a bit more olive and darker than Miller's, and Alec's hair, scruff, and eyes are all brown. Miller's hair is lighter, and his eyes are bright blue. They're both strong, Alec's muscles showing a bit more than Miller's. They're equally capable of being models, or at least thirst traps on the internet. How I got them both interested in me, I'll never know.

"Are you listening?" Alec says and snaps me out of my trance.

"Uh, what?"

His lips turn up into a grin. "What were you thinking about?"

"Nothing, why, what's up? What's the plan?"

"You're going with him," Miller tells me. "For now. He's going to take you to The Wellerton, and you'll wait until I arrive. You'll stay with me tonight."

"I have to work tomorrow," I blurt out without much thought.

"Take a sick day," Miller suggests.

Only, I'm not so sure it's a suggestion as much as it is a demand.

"I mean..." I rub my neck and consider my options. "I guess I could tell them I'm working at The Wellerton tomorrow. And I very well could."

"Perfect, there you go," Miller says.

"But wait, I thought I wasn't supposed to go with you. Why are we changing things now? And what will we do about my stuff? I don't have things at your place. Do *you* even have things at your place? I don't think *anyone* has moved into their units yet, is that even allowed?"

Miller shoves his hand into his pocket, leaving his thumb out as he faces me. "You do realize I own the building, don't you? If I wanted to kick every single person out of it, I could. It's ours."

Something about the way he says that last word sends a rush of heat over my body.

Ours.

He didn't mean it the way my first instinct took it, but it's still nice to pretend.

"And as for your things, that will be taken care of, don't worry," he adds.

Alec stands there patiently like a well-obedient dog. It's sort of adorable how he's willing to roll with whatever, but also has a completely unhinged side that makes him want to brutally murder Ricardo. It's romantic, if you ask me.

"What about London?" I ask, the idea of not knowing if she's going to make it still eating at me.

"I will make a call and verify that we are the first to find out when she's out of surgery." Miller dodges each of my questions with an answer that pacifies all my worries.

He steps toward me, squeezing my chin between his fingers and tilting my face up toward him.

"Everything will be taken care of, trust me." Miller presses the softest kiss on my forehead and I do the thing I find hardest in life—I trust him to handle things.

"I'll take one of those," Alec says and tips his head down at Miller.

Miller rolls his eyes and shoves him lightly in the chest. "I am not giving you a forehead kiss."

"Ah, man, come on," Alec laughs playfully and reaches for my hand. "You ready queen?"

I raise an eyebrow at him. "Queen?"

He shrugs. "I always hear Magnus call June princess; you've got a more queen vibe to me."

"I like it," Miller confirms and pats my head. "Our queen." He winks at me, and I nearly die. "I'll have to get you a crown."

"Do not get me a crown!"

"Nothing too flashy...a proper tiara." Miller takes off in the direction of the door, the noise of the hospital buzzing once we're through it.

The three of us walk side by side with me in the middle, Alec's hand wrapped around mine and Miller's resting on my lower back. It's...different...to be in public with them like this. There's a strange intimacy about how we're existing together. Neither of them is overly possessive of me, at least not with each other, and for a second, I allow myself to consider the possibility of what it would be like if we had a similar situation like June does with her men.

None of them are into each other, and they're all focused on her. I wonder if that's something Miller and Alec would be willing to do. As of right now, the way they're taking turns driving me around and babysitting me, it leads me to think that they might. But then there's Silver...the oh-so-serious old man who never in a million years would share me.

Although...he does read reverse harem novels and is very aware of June's relationship dynamic. Maybe being together isn't as farfetched as I once thought. Not having to choose between them would be ideal, because if someone put a gun to my head right now and asked me to, I don't think I could.

I like each one of them, all for different reasons.

Alec for his excessively thoughtful nature.

Miller for his psychotic tendencies.

And Silver for his assertive dominance laced with sweetness.

It's not traditional and doesn't really make sense, the three of them with someone like me, but it feels right, and I don't want to lose what we've just begun.

Only...the ticking clock on turning my uterus and body over to a man who beat the shit out of his daughter in front of me is a reminder that my happily ever after is far from reach.

30
SILVER

I overturn every single stone I can uncover.

I make phone call after phone call, digging up whatever dirt I can find on the man who thinks he has a claim on my angel.

"I don't know, Silver," an old pal of mine, Dravin says through the receiver. "You're barking up the wrong tree if you think I'm going to cross him. You should tread lightly, son. If he finds out you're on a witch hunt, he'll come after you himself."

Honestly, I wish he would, then I could end things and guarantee that he dies without ever laying another finger on Cora.

"You can't give me anything? Really? Everything I've done for you, that's how you do me?" I tell him, hating myself a bit at such a low blow.

All our transactions have been equal. I get paid to do a job. A favor is returned with a favor. We're even. Sure, I've helped him out of shitty situations, but I've never left empty-handed. To insinuate that there's an imbalance here is fucked up on my behalf, and still, it's the angle I play because I'm desperate.

"You're killing me, Silver." Dravin sighs dramatically and clears his throat. "Listen, you didn't hear shit from me, okay, but word is he's got some guy on the inside of Dom's organization giving him info. You hear about those shipments that keep going missing or getting picked up by the coppers? Yeah, it's Ricky, my man."

"Thanks, Dravin, I appreciate you. I won't forget it."

"Just leave my name out of it, alright, Sil? I trust you, but Ricky still has pull, and he'll have my head if he finds out I was talking shit."

"I have no intention of breaking your trust. You have my word. But hey, really quick, before I let you go, do you have a name?"

"You're killing me, Sil."

"Come on. I'll owe you one."

"You fucking better."

"When have I ever not been a man of my word?"

"Alright, alright. But you didn't hear it from me. It's some dude named Harry. Can't tell you a last name cause I don't know it so don't even ask."

"I can work with this, man, thank you."

"If this shit blows up, I'm not taking the fall." Dravin hangs up the line, leaving me with more than I had when I called him, and that alone is better than what I've figured out all day.

Ricardo has tons of dirt on him, but he's a criminal, so it's expected. What's hard to figure out is anything that can get his longest confidants to turn their back on him. People can point fingers and talk shit but until you have some rock-solid evidence, it's all hearsay, and that shit only starts pissing matches that fizzle out quicker than they start.

I dial another number, knowing exactly who I need to talk to.

He picks up on the third ring. "Find anything?"

"Can you talk?"

"Yeah, what's up?"

"I need you to tell me what all has gone missing."

Miller exhales dramatically. "I'd have to get you a full inventory, but everything from guns to art. Why?"

"Did it go to the cops or is it MIA?"

"Most of the guns were taken by the police, yeah. But some high-dollar art is completely missing. I'll have to call my guy and figure it out."

"Who's your guy?" I ask him.

"Why?"

"Because I got the name of a rat, someone working for Dom that's playing double agent."

"Tell me the name."

"Tell me who your guy is and I'll tell you if it's him."

Miller pauses like he's considering my question. We've worked together a long time and I've always liked the kid, but he reminds me a bit too much of myself, the bad parts of me. "His name's Harry."

"I'm going to need you to send me Harry's information."

"Is he our guy?"

"Yeah."

"Fuck," Miller blurts out and quickly pulls himself together. "I'll handle this."

"I'm going with you," I insist. "I'm not taking no for an answer. I'm trained in interrogation."

"Fine."

I could easily hang up, but another unknown lingers in my head. "How's our girl?"

"Broken ribs, pretty shaken up. Alec's taking her to The Wellerton now. That place is a fortress, she'll be safe there."

I want to scream, to cuss, to throw shit and punch things, but I remain even-tempered and allow the rage to simmer until it's time to unleash it. There's no sense in getting upset when there's nothing productive that can be done.

"And the other girl?"

"I don't know, man. It's not looking good. Cora's a mess

about it, and I hate that there isn't anything I can do about it. He beat her close to death."

"That could have been Cora."

"It won't be. We won't let that happen."

"We let her go over there today. It was fucking stupid."

I run my hand over my beard. "If he wants her to make him an heir, he isn't going to risk that. He's not stupid. He knows he got lucky with her. That's why he took it out on the daughter and not Cora. He's trying to intimidate her into submitting. It's part of his plan."

Miller doesn't say anything for a long moment and I wonder if he's hung up on me.

Finally, he says, "I can't talk about this right now."

"What are you doing?"

"Breaking into Ricardo's house to get Cora's purse back." He pauses and adds, "I'll talk to you later."

31
CORA

*A*lec and I wander through the unit that Miller advised us to go to in The Wellerton.

"This place is..." Alec takes it all in, his head practically whipping from one direction to the other. "Massive."

It's nearly identical to the one where I killed my boss, but it's mirrored and doesn't smell of fresh blood. Not that it would anymore—the blood would be old, and no doubt long gone since Silver was in charge of clean-up.

What a strange situation. I wonder if Miller or Silver knew back then that they would become what they are in my life now. Or Alec, for that matter. It's only been a couple days shy of a few weeks and things have blossomed into something...complicated.

I run my fingers along the back of the couch that's in all these display units and cross my arms over my chest as I walk further into the place. It's cold, but not just temperature-wise. The entire place lacks that lived-in vibe. There are no decorations aside from a few generic ones that the company I work for placed in here for sample purposes.

But when I walk into the kitchen, I notice a few things that don't quite belong.

A state-of-the-art espresso machine is the first thing that draws my attention. I open the fridge to find it fully stocked, a lot of my favorite foods adorning the shelves.

"That's weird," I whisper to no one but myself.

"What's weird?" Alec comes over behind me and peeks into the fridge. "Damn." He snatches a yogurt smoothie off the shelf. "I love these things." He twists the lid and side-eyes me. "What? I'm hungry."

I smile and shake my head as I continue to scan the contents. Mangoes. Blackberries. Raspberries. No strawberries, which is fine, because I don't care for them. Mushrooms, the cremini ones, not the basic white ones; also, my preference.

It's almost like this was stocked with everything I like in mind. There's no way that's a coincidence.

I latch onto the handle of the pantry and look inside there, too, and am not even surprised to find more things that I like. Things I wasn't even entirely sure if I liked, but appear to be something I would. Hint-of-Lime tortilla chips, pre-packaged granola bars, the kind with the red raisins, not the regular ones, almost as if the person knew that was the type I preferred. Boxed brownie mix, but the cake-like ones, because I don't love when they get hard and too crunchy.

"This is weird."

"You said that." Alec downs the rest of his yogurt and spins around in what I assume is in search of a trash can.

I point in the direction it should be and continue scanning the shelf. "All this food. It's stuff I like."

He returns to me a moment later with his hands empty. "What's so bad about that?"

"I mean...nothing, I guess." I grab a canister of honey-roasted cashews and turn toward him. "I have never had these before, but I'm pretty confident I'll love them."

Alec raises his eyebrow. "You do know he's super obsessed with you, right?"

I return the nuts to the shelf and shut the door. "What do you mean?"

"I mean, the guy spent a hundred million dollars to buy this building just because you didn't like your boss."

I shoot him a look that could probably kill. "*Didn't like* is a massive understatement. The guy was a fucking creep."

"Did you actually do it? Kill him, I mean." Alec follows me at my side, his hands behind his back, just going along with whatever I do.

I pause at the island and replay the scene in my head, my eyes darting across every bit of the kitchen he had cornered me in before I climbed on top of him and stabbed him repeatedly until eventually, he stopped moving. It was interesting, watching the blood flow slow from his wounds as his heart stopped beating.

"I did," I whisper, almost afraid to admit it to him. He already knows the truth, but saying it makes it something I can never take back.

Alec places his hand on my shoulder and tilts his head. "Hey, I don't judge you."

I glance up at him. "I'm a murderer."

"The only difference between you and me, Cor, is that I haven't done it yet." His dark gaze peers deeply into my eyes. "That makes us the same." He loosens a breath. "Actually, that makes me way worse, because it's premeditated. Pretty sure I'll go to jail for a long time. You were acting in self-defense."

"I wanted to kill him long before that."

"Yeah, then maybe we're more alike than you think." He presses his finger to my nose. "You're not going to convince me you're a bad guy, babe."

"I'm kind of tired," I tell him as I leave the kitchen and change the subject. It's not a lie, I'm exhausted, but I try not to think about what happened with my boss because it brings up other things that have happened in my life I would rather forget.

"Yeah, of course." Alec kicks off from the spot where he is standing and joins me in my pursuit of finding a place to crash.

"If I'm not mistaken..." I turn down the hall and walk a few steps before stopping at a door. "This should be one of the master suites."

"One of them?" Alec asks.

"Yeah, there are three suites and two other bedrooms—not including the office and study that could easily be considered bedrooms, too."

"Damn..." Alec reaches for the handle and pushes the door open. He leans against the frame and glances inside.

I walk in slowly, taking in every little thing. The plush throw blanket hanging on the edge of the bed, an exact replica of the one in my room at home. The nightstand has a few books that have been on my to-be-read pile for ages, but I haven't gotten around to reading them yet. And tucked between two pillows is a stuffed teddy bear that I've had since I was a kid...

Picking it up, I hold it to my chest and wonder how it's possible Miller could have gotten it here.

"Like I said, I think he's obsessed with you," Alec says from the doorway.

I glance back at him, the bear still in my grasp. "This is too much, right?"

He walks into the room and opens the double closet doors, revealing a massive walk-in closet with tons of clothes. "I mean, give him credit for being thorough."

I go to Alec's side and study the items that more than likely fit my body perfectly. "It's giving...stalker," I say.

Alec shrugs. "It's kind of romantic if you ask me."

I had the same thought but didn't want to say it out loud and risk him judging me. But Alec has never, and probably would never judge me, even if it is an irrational fear of mine.

"It is, isn't it?" I step in and run my finger over the clothes, all of which still with their tags attached.

How did he have time to do all of this? And how was he so sure I'd like what he picked out?

I slide a drawer open and find undergarments, and the next drawer filled with sweatpants. I kind of figured Miller would spring for silk pajamas but apparently he does know me better than that and opted for something more comfortable.

"How long are you staying?" I ask Alec as I pull out a spare change of clothes.

"I have to take Simon to do a thing in a little bit, so not much longer." His face saddens for a second. "But I'll be back. Promise."

I pause in the doorway between him and the frame and look up at him. "Thanks," I whisper.

Alec plants his hand above my head on the frame and inches closer, his other palm inching forward to lay along my cheek. "What for?"

I lean into his touch. "Taking care of me."

He runs his thumb along my skin, his dark eyes darting between mine. "I'd do anything for you." Alec lowers his head slowly and skims his nose against mine, his lips pressing a soft kiss on my lips.

My body comes alive with desire but ultimately is overpowered by exhaustion and a dull ache that consumes me.

I kiss him back and sigh, my heart happy and safe here with him. Oh, what I would give to turn back time and go back to when this could work. When we could all work.

"You should rest," Alec says just a breath away from me.

"Yeah." I position my forehead against his chest and bask in his earthy smell.

My phone buzzes in my pocket, and I groan at the interruption.

Alec chuckles and steps back to give me space I didn't want. "Are you going to shower first or get straight into bed?"

"I should probably shower; I have hospital germs on me." I glance down at the clothes from Friday that Silver had washed for me that got kicked by Ricardo. "I wonder if Miller has some matches or a lighter somewhere."

"What for?"

"To burn these clothes."

"I'll look for some while you shower." Alec takes the handful of clothes from me. "And in the meantime, I'll put these in the bathroom so you can check your phone." He leaves me in the doorway and opens two more doors before he finds the ensuite bathroom.

I pull the thing out of my pocket and struggle to get my broken screen to unlock. Once I do, I find a couple texts from June checking in on me and asking if we can talk. Nothing else from Ricardo, Silver, or Miller.

My chest tightens as my mind wanders to London and how she might be doing. I shove the thought and my phone away because neither is doing me any good right now. Worrying is only going to make me experience the pain twice if something does happen to her, and I've experienced enough torment for the day.

I have to be okay with not knowing until there is news from the hospital.

"I turned the water on for you," Alec says when I step into the bathroom, the mirror already steaming up.

"Thanks." I smile at him and kick off my shoes.

He goes to leave the room, but I catch his arm on the way out.

"You're not leaving, are you?"

"No. Just going to give you some privacy."

"Okay." I want to ask him to stay, to at least sit in here with me so I'm not alone, but I can't bring myself to admit I'm terrified of solitude right now. I've never shied away from personal time in the past, and yet here I am, afraid of the person I've become and hesitant to be stuck in a room with her.

"I can stay if you want?" Alec asks the question like he's unsure if that's what I'd prefer.

"No, it's okay," I lie and go back to stripping the rest of my clothes off.

"Let me go see if I can find a lighter and either way, I'll be right back."

He gives my hand a gentle squeeze before leaving, his eyes not trailing down to my nearly naked body.

I finish slipping out of my bra and panties and step into the piping-hot water. Closing my eyes, I tilt my head back and let it wash over me, and do what it can to rid me of what happened today. Only, as the water continues to flow, none of my worries disappear.

I wipe my face with my hand and blink through the droplets of water to find some shampoo. The bottle is nothing like the one I have at home, but it is the same scent, and if I'm not mistaken it's a brand I could never actually afford. As I massage it into my hair, I can already tell my hair is going to want to thank Miller later. He spared no expense on the conditioner, and once I get to the body wash, I'm already prepared for it to be the best I've ever used.

"Hey, what's your favorite movie?" Alec asks, and I rub at the fogged-up glass to peer through at him.

"Uh, I don't know, why? How long have you been in here?"

"A few minutes. I told you I'd come right back."

I shut the water off, not quite ready to get out, but ready to get into bed.

Alec greets me with a towel, wrapping it around my body the second I'm done. "I was going to put it on the TV for you."

"Oh..." I ignore the throbbing in my torso, secure the towel around my chest, and reach for another one to wrap my hair up in. "You don't have to do that."

Alec narrows his gaze at me. "Let me love you, damn it."

I stop my rummaging through the cabinets to turn toward him. "How about *Crazy, Stupid, Love?*"

"That's the one with the guy...what's his name?"

"Ryan Gosling," I tell him as I continue my search for body lotion.

Alec snaps his fingers. "Yeah, that's it. And that other guy, the funny one."

"Steve Carrell."

He snaps again. "Yes. And that girl, oh man, what's her name, don't tell me."

I smile and realize the lotion I was looking for was right in front of my face the whole time. I pump some of it into my palm and smooth it over my body, starting with my legs and working my way up.

"Emma Stone," Alec says triumphantly.

"Good job," I mutter and look through the rest of the contents of the drawer until I find a face lotion.

"I never knew something so simple could be so hot." Alec leans against the wall and shakes his head, his eyes a bit wide.

"What?"

"You. That lotion. I don't know. It's doing it for me."

I yawn and hate the way the pressure pushes on my aching ribs.

"Shit, Cor, you okay?" Alec rushes from his spot across the bathroom to my side in an instant.

"I'm good, really, it just caught me off guard." I pat his hand and force a look on my face that is supposed to resemble a smile but probably comes across more like I'm constipated.

"You don't have to lie to me, it's okay not to be okay." Alec tips my chin and steps away, grabbing onto something sitting on the counter and bringing it over to me. "I found this though, thought you might want to wear it." He holds the sides of the top to show me a beautiful, cushy, light blue robe.

Without hesitating, I slip my arms into both sleeves and fold it over my chest, tying it loosely and wiggling out of the towel covering my body. "This is the most comfortable thing I have ever worn in my entire life." I bring it to my nose and breathe it in. "It even smells good. Here, smell it." I extend some of the fabric toward Alec and he sniffs it obediently.

"Damn, it does smell good. What is that, lavender?"

"I think so." I snatch the towel I dropped around my ankles and hang it on a nearby hook to dry and follow Alec out of the bathroom and into the bedroom.

He's pulled back the covers on one side and gotten me a glass of water and a bottle of pain reliever. Alec even brought a chair that was originally perched in the corner of the room next to the bed.

"I can't stay much longer but I thought I'd sit with you while you fall asleep," he tells me, my heart swelling with every word he speaks.

Alec is so fucking thoughtful it begs the question, how the hell is he still single and what did I do to deserve this treatment from him?

"That would be nice," I tell him and climb into the spot he had made for me, the mattress already alerting me to the good night's sleep I'll probably be getting soon.

This definitely isn't the standard issue one brought in here for staging purposes...no this is one of those expensive mattresses that only rich people have.

I should brush my hair out and see if Miller got any leave-in conditioner, but my body is too thrilled to be horizontal, and the second my towel-covered head hits the pillow, my eyes close.

"This is the most comfortable bed I've ever been in," I mumble into the pillow.

"Yeah?" Alec settles in the chair next to me and I reach out toward him.

He takes my hand between his, and I lie there silently, listening to the faint in and out of his breaths.

It isn't long until I fall asleep, but it also isn't long until the nightmares start.

3 2
MILLER

*C*ora has been asleep for a very, very long time.
I study her chest as it rises and falls and watch for any sign of distress.

She's woken several times, but never enough to keep her awake long. No, she's startled by her own whimper or quiet scream, a gasping breath, and then frantically, she looks for me, grabs onto my hand, and falls back into a deep slumber.

Every single time it breaks my heart a little more, and I worry that my presence isn't enough to rid her of those demons haunting her.

I lie here with her far longer than I'm ever known to be in bed, but I can't fathom leaving her, not when the only thing that seems to calm her is my simply being here.

Alec left, and Silver came and went, both coming into the room to stare at our sleeping beauty and no doubt contemplate murder as they take her in.

It's bound to happen, soon enough—one of us finally reaching the depths which we can handle before ending this once and for all.

Cora stirs, her face pinching together like she's in pain.

"Shh," I whisper and tug her tighter to my chest.

She lets out a soft cry, and her eyes flutter open, her gaze darting until she settles on me. This time is unlike the last, almost like she's really awake instead of the in-between she's been stuck in all night and morning.

"Hey." She yawns, her hand coming up to cover her mouth. "What time is it?"

I remove my arm from around her to check my watch. "After two."

"In the morning?"

I tuck her ratty hair behind her ear. "No, two p.m."

She sits up abruptly and glances around like that's going to somehow change what time it is. "Holy shit, why did you let me sleep so long?"

I reach for her hand and fall short. "I think you needed it, Cor."

Cora hops out of bed and flinches, her palm quickly covering her side. "Fuck."

"You're working from The Wellerton today, remember?" I pat the spot she just left. "Get back into bed. But take your medicine first."

She follows my pointed finger to the nightstand where a water and pain reliever sit. Alec told me she fell asleep before she could take any last night, her tolerance for discomfort clearly no match to her level of exhaustion.

Cora swallows two of the pills and downs about half the glass of water before climbing back in with me.

I hold out the blanket for her and tuck her in, my head propped up on my hand as I rest on my side.

Cora turns toward me and brings the comforter to her chin. "Why do you have so many things I like in your apartment?"

My cheek twitches as I try to hide my smile. "What do you mean?"

"Well," she begins, her eyes darting away like she's recalling a memory. "I'm pretty sure everything in the fridge and pantry is something I've eaten and loved, or something I might enjoy. The closet is full of clothes that fit me, and the bathroom is stocked." Cora reaches behind her without looking and reveals a stuffed bear. "And this? Where did you get this?"

I pinch my lips together. I knew this day would come, the day when she would ask the questions I wouldn't want to give her answers to. And still, I'm no less prepared for them than I was the day I began my pursuit of her.

Cora brings the bear to her chest and nestles it. "I do love Mr. Snuggles, though."

"Is that his name?" I ask, clearly avoiding the previous request for information.

"Just admit it." She looks directly into my eyes.

"What?"

"That you've been stalking me."

"And what if I have?"

Cora breathes in deeply and exhales into the bear. "Tell me the truth, Miller, please."

The truth...where do I even begin?

"The truth is..." I reposition my elbow and adjust the way my head was resting on my hand. "Yes, I have been stalking you."

"For how long?"

"A year...maybe closer to two."

"Have you broken into my parents' house?"

"Yes."

"How many times?"

"A few."

"Define a few," she says, her expression unreadable.

"Six times."

"Have you followed me?"

"On occasion."

"Is there anything you don't already know about me?"

I recall everything I've learned and the surface-level things that are on display for anyone who is paying attention. I've deduced things based on other facts, but there are plenty of details I don't have, like the freckle on her collarbone that I must have overlooked until now.

"This." I poke the darkened spot. "I didn't know you had a freckle here."

"Do you have any freckles?"

"A few."

A grin creeps across her face. "Like six?"

"Maybe."

Cora surprises me by reaching out and running her hand along my cheek, her eyes trailing the places she caresses. "You know all this about me, and I know nothing about you." Her gaze meets mine. "Tell me something true."

I swallow the fear that had been rising at not knowing how she would react to my admission that I've been stalking her. It's not exactly a redeeming quality, and it's enough to get me put in jail, and yet she's still here, her body not having moved an inch away from mine.

She should. She should run and get as far from me as possible, because a man like me is dangerous and bound to ruin her life, but I'm too selfish to let her go and part of me is sick enough in the head to think she likes it.

"Something true..." I want to open myself up and allow her to see whatever it is she wants, but that's never been easy for me. I've gone through life with very few friends and people I could trust. I've longed for the type of relationship I've witnessed others having, I just never thought it was possible for me. I'm not even entirely sure how to give her what it is she's asking for. So instead, I settle for, "You're gorgeous."

Cora rolls her eyes. "That doesn't count."

"What do you want to know?" There, maybe if she gives me something specific I can answer her instead of having to come up with the data on my own.

"How many people have you killed?"

Her question doesn't surprise me as much as the answer does...because as hard as I think about it, I'm not entirely sure.

"A few," I reply.

"Why do I have a feeling you do not mean six?"

I chew at the inside of my lip. "Honestly, I lost track a long time ago."

"That's okay."

"It is? That doesn't scare you?"

Cora shakes her head. "I'm not afraid of you."

"You should be."

"You'd never hurt me," she whispers.

My heart skips a beat, and I grow grateful that even though she doesn't know much about me, she's at least aware of that one, very big truth.

"Never on purpose," I tell her and hope she realizes that I would do anything but bring her any discomfort. "Oh, and something else..."

"Yeah?"

"It's not my apartment."

Cora blinks at me a few times. "What?"

"This isn't my apartment. It's yours. That's why your things are in it."

She sits up and looks at me. "What?"

I laugh and lie back, folding my hands and resting them behind my head. "You heard me."

"That's insane," she says, glancing around. "This entire unit? It's mine?"

I nod and a strange warm sensation flows over me. Is this...happiness?

"It's yours, I promise. You never have to go to your parents' house ever again if you don't want to."

"I can't afford to live here. This place must be expensive to upkeep."

"When are you going to get it through your thick skull that you don't have to worry about stuff like that anymore? I'm loaded, babe. Whatever you want, it's yours." I'd give her the fucking moon if I could. But on second thought, maybe I know a guy who could make that happen.

"Miller, this is too much." She slumps her shoulders and holds her bear to her chest.

"For you, nothing is too much." I'd rip the beating heart out of my chest if it wouldn't kill me immediately. "Oh, and that reminds me, it's not decorated because I thought you'd want to do it yourself. However you choose to do it, it's on me. Just use the black Amex I gave you. No limit, so go crazy."

Cora breathes in deeply and takes another look around. "I don't know if I can accept this Miller, it doesn't seem right."

"There's a gym on one of the floors, and a spa, too. You have full access to both. I think they're even putting a coffee shop in the lobby or something."

She grins. "You do realize I'm supposed to be the one pitching *you* on the building, not the other way around. God, and it's yours, you own this entire thing."

"Our building, babe."

Cora side-eyes me and shakes her head. "Am I still dreaming?" She lays her head on my chest and curls up beside me.

I keep one arm behind my head and free the other to play with her hair as I study the delicate features of her beautiful face. Not too long ago I had only imagined being this close to her, and here I am, lying in bed with her, our happily ever after just within reach.

I don't know what it means that she has feelings for Silver and Alec, too, but right now, I don't care. The only thing that matters is that we're here, together, right now.

"Hey," I say softly. "Who's Jerry?"

Her blue gaze darts to meet mine like I said something completely forbidden. "What?"

"You mumbled his name in your sleep. I was curious is all."

Cora's eyes glisten, and I wish I could take back the question and shove it away to be uncovered on my own and not bother her with it.

"Um." Cora swallows harshly. "I've never really talked about it."

"You don't have to, not if you don't want to."

"God, I haven't even heard his name in years..." She shivers and her chest rises a bit faster than it was a second ago.

I tug the blanket over her body and pull her a little closer to me. "You're safe here."

"Can I ask you something?" Cora looks up at me through her lashes.

"Anything."

"Do you ever...this is probably going to sound crazy, or stupid, I don't know..."

I wait patiently for her to continue. Even if the suspense is killing me, I don't let it show.

"Have you ever had something bad happen and you store it in a little file in your brain and shove it aside? Maybe you plan to think about it another time or later or whatever but you never go back to it, you just sort of keep adding the bad things over time, until there's this big pit of bad shit stuffed into this corner of your mind that you do everything you can to ignore but the more it grows, the harder it is?" She says the words like she can't get them out quick enough, and then she sighs. It's almost like a weight lifts off her shoulders at the admission.

"I believe what you're referring to is something called a coping mechanism, Cor. You figured out if you could disassociate yourself from the situation, the bad parts, that it could help you through it."

"I think...I think I've put too many things away." A single tear rolls down her cheek. "I don't think I have room for anything else."

"You don't have to be strong anymore. I'm here." I wipe the tear away. "And as much as I hate to admit this, Silver and Alec are here, too. Let us carry that burden for you. Let us be your rock."

Cora slightly shakes her head. "It doesn't work like that."

"Why?"

"Because I have to be the strong one. If I'm not, everything else falls apart."

"That's how you got into this situation, isn't it? You felt like you had to save your parents, like you were the only one capable of figuring it out."

"It's true," she says. "And now my life is ruined."

I hold her a little closer, leaning up to press my lips to her forehead. "Your life is far from ruined; I promise you that. This shit with Ricardo, we'll get it figured out."

"How? There's no way out of it, he's made that clear."

"Don't underestimate what we're capable of doing. This isn't over until it's over, and I assure you, we will come out on top. I will *burn* the world down for you, Cora." I say the words to convince her, even though they're partially for me, too. I'm not lying—there isn't anything Silver, Alec, or I wouldn't do for her, but I would be lying if I said it was going to be easy.

For the first time in my life, I'm terrified of the unknown, especially when I have a feeling one of us won't make it out of this thing alive.

33
CORA

 y entire body aches, starting at my head and going all the way down to my toes. Even my mind is riddled with tormented memories of my past and what lies ahead of me in my future.

But lying here, my face resting against Miller's chest, it's a comfort no pain reliever could ever bring.

If only I could stay here forever.

"Have you heard from the hospital? About London?" I ask him, the question haunting me even in my dreams.

"No. I called a few hours ago, and there wasn't an update."

I pull my lip between my teeth and tug at it.

Miller reaches up and frees it from my hold. "She's going to be okay."

"You don't know that."

"I don't, but we have to hope, okay?"

It's strange how the tables have turned—I used to be the obnoxiously bubbly and optimistic one, and here is he, the murderous stalker who is telling me not to lose faith.

I should probably be concerned about the stalking and the murder, but nothing seems to surprise me anymore. It's as if my mind has grown numb to the terrors of the world and they've just become...normal.

Most guys don't put in an effort, at least Miller is thorough, even if that means breaking into my house, stealing my things, and stalking me.

Some would call it a crime; I call it romance.

Or maybe I really have gone and lost my mind.

"Do you want to unload some of the things you keep in there?" Miller presses his finger to my forehead. "I'll lock it up in here for safekeeping." He brings that same finger to his temple.

I draw in a breath through my nose and bring that memory to the surface, fragments of it jarring my thoughts like flash photography in a dark room. My hair tangled, sand on my knees, my bikini tattered and barely hanging on.

"It was uh, my dad's friend." My heart stutters at the admission of saying it out loud. "I was sixteen."

Miller plants his hand along my jaw, his touch calming me more than he'll ever know.

"He was twenty-four." The smell of the beach comes washing over me and suddenly, I feel dirty, like there aren't enough showers to rid me of the filth I felt on that day. "I'd known him my whole life. He'd come to visit here and there, play a game of poker with my dad and his friends. I'd bring them all beer or chips, you know, whatever little dumb errands they'd send me on." I force a smile and continue. "But that summer, he had made comments about me blossoming...and I was just a kid, a stupid girl. I didn't hate the attention, not at first."

Miller doesn't let go as I tell this story for the first time in my entire life. Not even the therapists my parents forced me to go to knew of what happened.

"We had all gone to the beach, and my parents left early so he offered to stay and watch me and drive me home. I didn't think anything of it. I should have known it was foolish to stay with him. Even my parents didn't blink an eye and told us to have fun. My mom gave me twenty bucks to spend on the boardwalk and told me not to eat too much ice cream. I was mortified. How dare my mother treat me like a child. But if there was some way to turn back time, I'd go back to that moment and beg her to take me home, not to leave me there with him."

"Cora..."

I keep on with the story because if I stop now, there's no way I'll ever start again. "He was drinking, and as the sun started to set, I knew he had too much. I had my driver's permit, so I said I could drive us home. I didn't want to get in the car with him behind the wheel." I shake my head. "But that wasn't the worst of what could have happened...because before we even left the beach, he pinned me to the ground underneath the lifeguard tower and stole my innocence."

Miller wipes the tears that fall down my cheek.

"I cried on the way home, and I remember wishing that we'd crash, or the police would pull him over. I pictured myself running to the cops and telling them what he had done, but nothing happened. No wreck. No cops. Nothing. And when we got home, he laughed at my parents and said that I fell down and scuffed my hands and knees, that's why I looked the way I did and why I was crying. Neither of them even questioned it, they fully went along with his every word and even scolded me for being so clumsy. I remember locking myself in my room but never really feeling safe. I don't think I left my bed for days. I told my parents I was sick, that maybe I got the flu or something from all the people at the beach that day."

Miller stays silent for a minute while he strokes my hair. When I don't say anything else, he finally speaks, "Thank you for telling me, for trusting me." His voice is gentle. "I am so sorry this happened to you. And I'm sorry that the people who were supposed to keep you safe weren't there to do so. No one should ever have to go through what you did."

I fidget with the tag on my bear. "I thought it was my fault, for the longest time. Heck, a part of me still does."

"Cora, no. You were a child. There was nothing you could have done that would ever make what he did to you your fault. You have to understand that."

"Maybe it was what I was wearing, or a look I gave him, I don't know. Maybe I didn't say *no* or fight back enough. Maybe I could have done something differently, and everything would be different."

Miller tilts my head up to look into my eyes. "Never, and I repeat ever, will I allow you to take the blame for that, Cora. That man was in the wrong, one hundred percent. Pretend this is someone else this happened to, would you blame her for his actions?"

"No." I sigh.

"Then you need to forgive sixteen-year-old you for something she didn't ask for."

We sit in silence for a moment, and Miller's phone rings, his attention lingering on me.

"Answer that," I tell him. "It might be the hospital."

He hesitates before wiggling out from under me and leaning over to get his cell from the nightstand. Miller slides his finger across the screen and presses it to his ear. "Hello?" He turns toward me. "Yes, okay, that's great. Thank you. Six p.m.? Okay. Thanks, again. Call me if anything changes."

"Who was it?" I blurt out the second the line disconnects.

"You were right, it was the hospital. London is out of surgery and in recovery. They have her heavily sedated but she's stable for now. Visiting hours are until six."

I throw the covers off me. "Then let's go."

Miller slowly leaves the bed, no urgency in his movements. "This is dangerous, Cora. He could be there."

"Don't you have eyes on him?" I ask while rushing to the closet to find something to wear other than the sweatpants I've been rotting in all day. I slip out of the loose T-shirt I'm wearing, throw a crop top on, and settle for a pair of ripped skinny jeans that fit me like a glove. "Hey, is there someplace I can burn..." But my sentence is halted when I step out of the closet and find Miller taking his shirt off with his back to me.

"I had no idea you had..." I step closer to him, my hand reaching out toward him. "Tattoos." His entire torso is covered in an elaborate black and white piece and as I approach him, I make out a medieval-looking castle in the center with other things around it. A grim reaper, various skulls, flowers..."It's so, beautiful."

Miller's chest rises and lowers, and he glances over his shoulder.

But when I press my fingers along his skin, tattoos aren't the only thing I find. Underneath the gorgeous artwork is skin that is raised, scarred.

I skim my knuckles along his flesh. "What happened?"

Miller finishes pulling another shirt over his head and turns toward me. "My dad."

"I'm so...sorry."

"It's not a big deal."

I stare up at him and wonder if this is how he feels every time I tell him things are fine when they really aren't? "May I?" I point to his back.

He pauses for a moment before turning around.

I grab onto the bottom of his shirt and lift it up, my gaze scanning the marks lining his entire back. How could someone do this to him? *Why* would someone do this? He mentioned he was practically homeless when he found his old boss, so he must have been a kid when this happened.

I bring myself closer to him and press my lips against his scarred skin, kissing him gently and moving over nearly every inch of his back I can reach. I continue leaving soft gentle pecks and lower his shirt down with a sigh.

Miller turns around, and his eyes glisten as he looks at me. "Other than my tattoo artist, I've never really shown that to anyone. Not in years, at least."

"Thank you," I tell him, resting my hand on his cheek. "For showing me."

His blue gaze flashes between mine. "You wear your scars in here." Miller kisses my forehead. "And I wear mine on my body."

"Maybe we aren't so different after all." I rise onto my tiptoes and kiss his lips, nothing hurried or frenzied about it, just pure, undiluted, soft intimacy.

Miller breaks away but remains close. "Get ready and I'll make you coffee." He leaves me there, reeling with his touch and the image of what his father did to him a long time ago.

I can't fathom the idea of sweet Miller having done anything to deserve or warrant a reaction that extreme. From the depth of the scars, he must have been beaten badly for them to heal that way. And over and over again...not a square inch of his back not marked by the remains of an abusive man.

My heart aches thinking about that version of him, the young and terrified Miller, the one who never knew a proper adolescence because it was stolen from him. In a way, we really are one and the same, our youth hoods stripped from us by men who gave us no choice in the matter.

If only there was a way I could make it up to him, to rewrite history and give him the childhood he deserved. The one we both deserved. But that isn't possible, because we're almost out of time, our story ending far too soon because of yet another man who set claim to what isn't his.

I run my fingers through my hair, the tangles catching each of them. Groaning, I grab the brush and attempt to get them out. I never should have gone to sleep with my hair wet without brushing it first. My side aches as I contort to free my ratted hair, and I clench my jaw through the pain.

Miller pops his head in the door. "Hey, do you want hot or cold coffee?"

I drop my hand, and my hairbrush remains stuck in the knotted mess.

"Do you need help?" Miller abandons his question and continues toward me until he's standing right behind me.

I let out an exasperated sigh. "Kind of."

Miller, as gently as fucking possible, removes the brush from my hair. "Where's the spray I got you?"

"I didn't see any," I tell him, despite not having looked very hard. I was trying to hurry so we could leave sooner rather than later. I figured I could snoop through all the goodies he got me later once I confirm London is okay.

Miller opens the double doors and peers inside, pulling out a bottle a second later. "Here." He holds the thing out in front of me. "Have you tried this stuff before? The lady at the store said it was the best they had."

"On my budget?" I chuckle and cross my arms over my chest, the embarrassment of not even being able to afford anything other than the detangler setting in.

"Well, let's give it a try." He spritzes some of it into my hair and sets the bottle on the counter, returning his attention to my tangled hair. Miller bunches it up in one hand and slowly starts from the bottom, untangling a little at a time until finally, he's reached the top of my head.

It doesn't take him long to get through it, and surprisingly he didn't pull or hurt me at all.

Miller carefully brushes my hair a few more times, making sure to tread ever so lightly and ensure every inch of my hair has been covered. "There, is that better?"

"Yeah." I smile at him in the mirror. "Thank you."

He takes both of my shoulders with his hands and leans toward me, kissing the side of my temple. "Anything for you."

"Hot, please," I tell him, finally answering the question he came here for.

Miller presses his lips against my face again. "Good deal. I'll leave you to it. Let me know if you need any more help."

I push my rampant thoughts away and do as instructed, getting ready in the lavish bathroom that Miller so gratefully secured for me with no shortage of supplies at my disposal. Even tucked into one of the drawers is a complete setup of makeup, everything I use on a daily basis, only new and not years old and gross like the stuff I have at home.

I apply a thin layer of mascara and tinted lip balm before pinching my cheeks and leaving the bathroom, grabbing a pair of sneakers from the closet on the way through. Pausing at the door, I rush back to my nightstand and grab my very busted phone and head to the kitchen, where I assume Miller is.

At the thought of coffee, my stomach growls, reminding me that I'm not sure when my last meal was.

Miller looks up from his spot at the island as he pours something into a bowl. "I made you some oatmeal." He slides it across the counter to where a steaming cup of coffee sits with a few various small bowls nearby.

I approach to find they're each filled with raisins, brown sugar, and walnuts.

"I can cut up an apple, too." Miller snatches a green one from the selection of fruit.

"No, this is perfect, thank you." I hold out my hand. "Really, unless you want it." I climb onto the seat and stare at the selection in front of me. How did he know this is how I liked my oatmeal...down to every last ingredient?

Miller hesitates but drops the apple gently in with the others, and pours himself a bowl of hot oatmeal. He claims the seat next to me and spoons some of the stuff into his afternoon breakfast.

I reach for my coffee, blowing on the top before taking a sip. "Mmm, this is good."

"Vanilla oat milk latte," Miller says and takes a bite of his food.

Is there anything he doesn't know?

"Do you even like oatmeal?" I ask as I side-eye him.

"Not until recently. At least, I wasn't aware of it." He drinks some of his coffee, his black instead of matching mine.

I don't mind mine without anything in it, but it makes it a more enjoyable experience with a little added flare.

"Oh," Miller says between bites. "Here." He shoves a white box toward me, the Apple logo on the outside.

"What's this?" I ask him and eat another spoonful of the oatmeal.

"A phone." Miller scrapes what's left of his oatmeal into his mouth and gets up from his seat to rinse his bowl in the sink. "You broke yours, so I got you a new one."

"You did what?" I lift the lid off the box and pull out the pale pink phone, turning it over in my hand. "What model is this?"

Miller shrugs and reaches for his coffee. "The new one, I suppose."

I flip the box over and read the small print on the back. "Um, this isn't even out for another couple of months."

He lifts his shoulder again and goes to work cleaning up the little bit of a mess he created.

So, he's thoughtful, murderous, a bit of a stalker, *and* cooks and cleans.

"I can't accept this," I say and lower the phone back into the box.

Miller shuts off the faucet and reaches for the top of it, sliding the hose out and pointing the nozzle at me. "Cora, sweetie, you're going to take the phone and you're going to like it."

"And if I don't?"

"If you don't like it, I'll buy you a different one. If you don't take it, I will soak you and not feel an ounce of remorse."

I eye the way his fingers twitch toward the handle and come to terms with the fact that he is probably not bluffing. He never is.

"Fine," I huff. "But I'll do it later so I can upload all my stuff."

Miller returns to the dishes and says, "No need, it's already on there."

I roll my eyes at him. "Of course, it is."

Once I'm finished with breakfast, I attempt to help him clean up, but he insists that he has it under control. I've never felt so...taken care of, in my entire life, and if I'm being honest, I have no idea what to do with it. My hands are fidgety and I mindlessly tidy up the kitchen that sort of belongs to me.

All of this is strange and I can't seem to wrap my head around any of it.

"You ready?" Miller dries his hands and hangs the towel on the dishwasher handle.

"Shit." I pause after a few steps.

"What did you forget?"

"My purse..."

Miller continues toward the door, ignoring my declaration, stopping just at the table near it and turns around, my Alexander McQueen clutch he had bought me in his grasp. "You looking for this?"

My mouth drops open and I close the distance between us. "How did you?"

A sly grin forms on his handsome face. "I keep telling you, there isn't anything I can't get for you." He plants a kiss on my forehead and grabs a key from the bowl next to where my purse must have been sitting. "Speaking of which, we're going to take your car."

"My what?"

He does that thing where he ignores me again and weaves his fingers through mine. "Come on."

I follow along because what other choice do I have, and gladly hold his hand as we walk out the door and wait for the private elevator to arrive. One of the perks of very few of the units in this building is their private elevators, perfect for A-list celebrities who need a little extra privacy from even their neighbors.

I'm a nobody though, and that perk is wasted on me, but it sure is nice to have the added bonus.

"What kind of key is it?" I ask him and try to peek into his other hand to see for myself.

Miller holds the key fob in his palm and I recognize the Porsche logo immediately.

I nearly gasp. "You bought me a Porsche?"

"Maybe." He pauses and says, "Maybe I just bought you this." Miller waves the key in the air and squeezes my hand gently. "Hey." His tone shifts. "You feeling okay? I know you're eager to see London but you really do need your rest."

"I'm good, really." And because I know he won't believe me, I decide to elaborate on the truth. "Don't get me wrong, I feel like I got run over by a bus, but it's not unbearable. I can handle it, seriously. I need to see her, and then I promise I'll go back to resting. Well, until I have to go to work tomorrow."

He pivots his body toward me. "You're going into the office tomorrow?"

"I need to."

"Can't you say you're working from The Wellerton for a couple more days? I can call and have it arranged, it's not a big deal."

"Miller." I place my hand on his shoulder. "While I appreciate everything you do for me, this is *my* career, *my* job. Please don't interfere with that."

His jaw tenses, and I worry that he's going to explode on me, the idea of him getting mad somehow making me regret putting my foot down.

But then he surprises me by saying, "I understand."

"You do?" I ask him, unsure if he's fucking with me.

"Yes." He tucks a strand of the hair he brushed for me behind my ear. "I'd be stupid to try to control you. Doesn't mean I won't try from time to time, but I know, ultimately, every decision you make is yours." Miller moves a bit when the elevator reaches the bottom floor. "I won't be another man in your life that takes that away from you."

The elevator dings before the door opens, both of us standing there, our eyes locked on each other.

"Are you real?" My voice is barely a whisper.

Miller smiles softly. "Yes, babe, I am very real."

"You're just so..." I try to think of the right words to say but all of them seem to fall flat. "Thoughtful? Nice? Considerate? Romantic?" I step out of the elevator and glance in both directions, unsure which way to go.

"Don't tell anyone." Miller follows me out. "I have a reputation to uphold." He winks at me and tilts his head. "This way."

"Oh, right, your *reputation*." I laugh. "How many people have you killed this week?"

He glances back at me. "Just two. It's been a slow week."

I wait for him to break his serious character, but he doesn't. "You're not joking."

"No. I'm not." He stops walking in front of a white Porsche, holding the key fob out and unlocking it.

I halt beside him. "This is *not* mine."

He nudges my arm gently with his elbow. "It is, but when we're together, I drive." Miller focuses on me. "No more Ubers and walking around town. You have a car now."

"What if I like walking?"

"Then I'll get you a treadmill."

"What if I like walking outside?"

"Then I'll take you to the park."

"What if you're busy working or something?"

"Then I'll have Silver or Alec take you. I'm sure they need zero convincing."

"What if they're not available?"

"Cora, I will hire you a bodyguard, someone better than Simon is for June, and they will escort you." He pauses for a second and adds, "Just promise me you won't fall in love with them, I don't think I can share you with anyone else."

I tilt my head toward him. "Wait what?"

"You know, how June and Simon fell in love after she and the guys already established their relationship."

"No, I get that. But hold on, back up a little bit. You're telling me you're okay with Silver and Alec?"

Miller runs his hand through his hair and crosses his arms. "I mean, no, not really, but what other option do I have? I'd ask you to choose but I'm too fucking afraid you won't pick me."

My heart breaks from seeing this vulnerable side of him despite being grateful he's showing it to me at all. There's no denying that Miller is a naturally reclusive man. He's made it known that he's not the best at expressing his feelings or emotions, yet here he is, doing that very thing. He's overcoming his fear of putting himself out there because if he didn't, this wouldn't work.

I could learn a thing or two about healing and growing from him.

And if time were on my side, I would get the chance to. Every step we take closer to being together I'm reminded that it's just out of reach. He might be willing to sacrifice everything to keep me safe, but there's no denying that come next week, my body belongs to Ricardo Gardella.

Even if Miller marched over there and put a bullet in his head, the fate of my parents would still be in limbo. Ricardo has my mother captive somewhere, and I wouldn't put it past him to have safeguards in place upon his untimely death, my dad no doubt being one of the people at the top of the list of who dies, my name not far behind.

If Ricardo dies, my parents die. And anyone I'm associated with. Miller. Alec. Silver. London. June...her men. Anyone who's crossed my path that Ricardo has been made aware of is not safe from his wrath if things don't go according to plan.

But right now, in this very moment, none of that matters, because for this terribly short time, Miller is standing in front of me saying what I've always wanted to hear: he chooses me.

And because I can't live without him, or Silver or Alec, I mutter, "I won't fall in love with anyone else, I promise." There is no one for me other than these three guys. I'd never put myself out there for it to even happen.

I never meant to fall in love with three different men in general, but I went into each relationship with the mindset that it wouldn't last, that it would be temporary and help me enjoy what little moments I had between then and when Ricardo took me. None of it was supposed to blossom into what it became, although it's what I've always wanted.

Connection. Devotion. Love.

Unconditionally and irrevocably.

I thought I'd never experience it with one man, let alone three.

I'm not even entirely sure if I'm in love with Silver, but the feelings I have for him definitely lean in that direction. I've known Miller and Alec longer, the connection between us solidified long before we ever made the first move.

Miller flits his gaze at the car we're in front of. "I was going to get you a pink one, but it was going to take too long to get it in. Then I figured I ought to ask you what color you wanted. I can still have this one painted pink."

"I don't need a pink car."

"No one *needs* a pink car, but do you *want* one? It can be arranged. I can order it custom, and you could drive this one in the meantime or..."

Standing tall, I interrupt his words with my lips, kissing him until he stops talking and weaves his arms around my waist, making sure to be extra gentle against my ribs.

I shouldn't be moving like this, my ribs and shoulder both pissed off, but how can I not throw myself at the man who would give me the world if it were possible?

"It's perfect," I tell him, my mouth a breath away from his. "Entirely too much, but perfect. Thank you."

He releases me and strolls over to the passenger door, opening it up for me. "I can have it be pink, just say the word."

I climb into the seat and meet his gaze. "Pretty sure I'd stick out like a sore thumb. Aren't you all about flying under the radar?"

"True." He closes me in and walks around, my sights locked on him the entire time.

Everything he does is sexy. The way he holds my hand, the little thing he does with his tongue when he kisses me, even how obsessed he is with me brings heat straight between my legs, even if it is borderline illegal.

The Miller I met so long ago was quiet and reserved, well-dressed, and overly mysterious. He's still all of that today, just surprisingly caring and sympathetic, too.

"So, about these people you killed..." I settle into my seat and look over at him, imagining him following through with ending someone's life.

"Yeah?" He raises a brow and leans across me to grab onto my seatbelt. "You really need to start buckling up."

"I'm used to being in the back of an Uber." Although I'm not exactly upset with having him this close to me and if not putting my seatbelt on is what makes it happen, I'm going to continue *forgetting* to put it on.

Miller hovers just inches away from my face. "Even in the back of an Uber, babe."

I swallow and say, "Kiss me."

He glides his nose over mine and lowers his lips, our mouths reuniting after what felt like forever apart. Miller tugs my bottom lip between his and sucks on it gently, and the thought crosses my mind that I'd like to see how far this seat will go back.

His strong hand grips my thigh, inching its way upward until he stops, along with his mouth. "I thought you wanted to see London."

I nod my head a bit too aggressively. "Yes, yeah, I do. You're right."

Miller grins, returns to his seat, and shifts into drive, the car lurching forward with a throaty groan.

"About those people," Miller says. "One got caught doing something he wasn't supposed to be doing, and the other was covering for him."

"What were they doing?"

He glances over at me briefly. "Things that are off-limits."

"Gotcha," I reply without really knowing what *things* referring to. "What about torturing? Do any of that this week?"

Miller side-eyes me with his brows furrowed. "Are you wearing a wire?"

I laugh and reposition in my seat. "Yes, Miller, I was able to put it on in between getting ready and eating breakfast."

He shrugs and pulls onto the main road. "Never know."

"To confirm, I am not wearing a wire. Where would I even get one? And who would be listening?"

"People, probably."

I smack his shoulder. "When did you become such a smart ass?"

He keeps one hand on the steering wheel and puts the other on my leg. "Just now, is that okay?"

"Yeah, I think I'm good with that." I weave my fingers over his. "I was asking though, because I'm curious about your life, your work, what you do when you disappear. You told me you were having issues; did you get it figured out?"

"Actually," Miller says and puts on his turn signal before switching lanes. "Turns out, I'm pretty sure Ricardo is responsible for the *issue*."

"Oh?"

He continues to drive with his knee and runs his hand through his hair, checking the rear-view mirror and fixing a piece that goes a little wild.

I ignore the veins in his forearm as he grips the steering wheel again and wait for him to continue.

"I don't know how much of our world you do know, but since you're going to be around it, there's no sense in keeping things from you. Look what good that did June..."

"What good did it do June?"

"That's a story for another day. Are you still not speaking to her?"

"No." I bite at the inside of my lip, the bridge that's collapsed between us too far gone to repair. She was my best friend, but she lied to me, kept things from me, and sabotaged my potential happiness. How can I ever forgive her for that? And how could she ever forgive me for the outburst the other night and the mean things that I said to her and Simon? I don't have much longer until my fate is sealed with Ricardo, and I'm not ready to consider whether we could salvage things. It's better if I leave what we had in the past and accept that it's one less loss I have to deal with in a week if I deal with our demise now.

"It'll take time," Miller says, confirming my exact train of thought.

Time that I don't have.

"Anyway," he starts again. "Dom and Johnny are aligned. West and East Coast. Following me so far?"

I nod. "Yeah."

"I work for Johnny. I handle things for him."

"Okay."

Miller speeds through a light as it turns yellow. "Essentially, that means I'm the one dealing with stuff on the West Coast, the alliance and its business together."

"Right."

"Some of that said business has been having trouble lately. Logistical trouble. Shipments going missing. Being confiscated by the police. Big ones, little ones, even the decoys."

"And you're convinced Ricardo has something to do with this?"

"Exactly." Miller slows down to stop at a red light, his hand still gripping my thigh. He looks over at me, sighs, and grabs my chin to pull me toward him as he kisses my lips. "Goddamn, you're breathtaking." He returns his attention to driving, my heart speeding up as quick as the accelerator of this car is.

Does he have no idea the effect he has on me when he does things like that?

"So far, I haven't been able to prove it, but there's no way it isn't him." Miller carries on with his story unbothered. "I got the name of a guy working for Dom who is supposed to be the double agent, the one working both sides."

"I'm familiar with what a double agent is, I watch TV."

"Right, yeah." Miller laughs dryly. "Supposed to be meeting him tomorrow with Silver."

"I want to come."

"Absolutely-fucking-not."

"Why?" I ask him even though I know he's going to mouth off some shit about keeping me safe.

"Do I need to explain, really?"

"I'd be with you and Silver, are you seriously worried something's going to happen to me when I'm with you two?"

Miller keeps his sights trained ahead like I may have brought up a valid point. He slows to turn onto the street the hospital is on.

"And, you wouldn't have to wonder if I'm okay while you're doing your thing, because I'd be with you."

Miller pulls into an open parking spot and puts the car into park. "Not happening."

I cross my arms over my chest, ignoring the pain that shoots through me. I hate how fragile my stupid body is.

"You can pout all day long."

I push out my bottom lip and bat my eyelashes for extra emphasis.

"You're killing me."

My lips curl up into a smile. "Is that a yes?"

Miller rolls his eyes. "It's a *let me think about it.*"

I reach for the door, and he glares at my hand.

"Don't you dare touch that."

I pause like it might set me on fire and wait for him to exit his side, come over to mine, and open the door for me. "Such a gentleman."

He even extends his hand for me to place mine in to help me out. "For you, always."

"But for everyone else?" I shove my clutch up under my biceps and slide my hand up under his.

"I don't care what anyone else thinks about me." Miller leads me across the walkway and into the front of the hospital, his gaze scanning the place for threats, no doubt.

I do what I can to keep an eye out, but I'd be lying if I said I knew what I was looking for. Other than disgusting Ricardo and the men he's had snatch me off the street, I wouldn't be able to tell anyone else apart from any of the other random people in this place.

"This way." Miller points ahead, and I follow him without question.

It's not hard to notice the way people step out of his way or don't look him directly in the eyes as he passes. There's this strange authoritative dominance to him that causes people to respect him, to fear him, but to me, he's just Miller—the super sexy stalker who vowed to hold onto my secret when it became too heavy for me to carry any longer.

Suddenly, Miller tugs me to his side and his entire body stiffens as he reaches under his shirt. It all happens so fast, his reflexive movement, the grip on his gun. The way he positions himself between me and the obscenely loud man who barrels down the hallway.

His face is bloodied, his shirt covered in crimson. The man calls out, "You have to help me, someone help me. Where is she?" His chest rises and falls rapidly as he darts his wild gaze at each passing person.

Finally, a hospital worker in blue scrubs approaches him, his hands reaching out trying to calm the frantic man. "Sir, are you injured? Follow me and I'll get you help."

"Don't touch me!" the man yells and swats at the worker.

Miller, with his back still toward me, one hand reaching to keep hold of me and the other on the gun still in his waistband, inches us along the wall and slips us past the guy. He doesn't remove his hand from around the gun, not even once we're no longer in the same hallway. Instead, Miller comes to my side, his free hand finding my lower back. "You okay?"

"I am," I reassure him and silently hope that the man finds whatever it is he was looking for.

Miller nods ahead. "Room two nineteen."

Once we reach the door, Miller pauses, "Wait here." He scans the hallway before slipping inside and returning less than twenty seconds later. "Come on."

I follow him in, my sights immediately settling on London, lying there on the bed with beeping monitors surrounding her. Rushing over to her, I slow down and gently take her hand in mine. "London, hey, it's Cora," I say quietly.

Her face is swollen, bruised, and cut. An uncomfortable brace is around her neck, and there's a cast on her right leg and left wrist. London's gorgeous red hair is matted to her head, and I sort of wish I would have brought her a hairbrush and some things to make her more herself despite her incredibly unfortunate condition.

The condition that is all my fault.

Maybe when I come to visit her tomorrow I can bring her some things to help her feel more at home and less trapped in a hospital room.

Her green eyes flicker open, both speckled red with busted blood vessels. "Hey," she barely croaks. "What's up?"

I sigh and sit along the edge of the bed, taking her hand between both of mine.

"Hey, pretty lady. How are you feeling?"

London's lashes flutter. "High as a kite."

"That's good." I fight the urge to cry and keep a straight face for her. "I'm so sorry."

She tries to shake her head but gets hardly any movement. "It's been worse; this is nothing." London's gaze shifts past me to Miller who stands guard at the door. "It's not safe for him here."

It's then that it dawns on me how completely stupid this was. Ricardo may have let me temporarily off the hook, but if he finds out Miller is here, he'll no doubt send his goonies to snatch him up so he can get his revenge. I wouldn't be surprised if Ricardo has posted people in the hospital to keep a lookout for who's coming and going from his daughter's room. The plan was to make him think nothing was going on with me and Miller, but if he's smart, he'd see right through our thinly veiled lie.

"It's fine," I tell her. "I needed to come see you. Make sure you're okay." I squeeze her hand gently. "You're so strong, London. So fucking strong."

London licks at her dry lips and smacks her mouth.

"Do you want a drink?" I reach for the cup of what I think is water sitting on the bedside tray.

"Could..." She pauses to her clear throat. "Could you get me a soda?"

I nod a bit too enthusiastically. "Of course, yes. What kind?"

"Sprite, if they have it."

"On it," Miller says from the door. "I'll be right back. Scream if something happens."

I focus my attention back on London. "What else do you need? What can I do for you?"

"I'm kind of cold." She wiggles her toes as they hang out from the bottom of the blanket.

"I can fix that." I rise from the bed and rummage through the drawers and closet until I find two extra blankets to layer over her. "Here you go."

"Thank you," London manages to get out with what she can of a smile.

Her face is fucked up and I wish it were possible to take her place, but I'm not sure if we switched if things would be any better for her in my shoes. Both of our lives are currently not going well, I'm not sure which is worse. Not that this is a competition by any means, I'd just like to put her in the position with the strongest chance of making it out of this alive.

"Do you need anything else?" I ask her.

"The company is nice." She blinks slowly and sighs. "I've never really had friends." London swallows and from where I'm sitting, it looks like it causes her a great deal of discomfort. "I mean, I have friends, but they're superficial, you know?"

I nod and sit on the edge next to her, taking her hand in mine again. "I know." Patting her hand I say, "I'm here for you, whatever you need. You're not alone in this."

"He's never going to let either of us live through this." London's bright green eyes meet mine. "I'm sorry you ever got involved."

I think about her words and consider my life without having met Ricardo. Sure, it would be different, but I'm not entirely sure it would be for the better. I never would have met Silver, and perhaps the circumstances never would have pushed Miller and me past the awkward unknowing phase we were stuck in. Maybe things with Alec would have progressed, but it's not certain. One thing is though, if I hadn't sealed that fateful deal with Ricardo, London and I never would have crossed paths, and she would be doing this all on her own. If I'm forced to find the silver lining in this incredibly unfortunate situation, it's that maybe this happened so I could help her.

But if we don't come up with some kind of plan soon, we're both doomed.

3 4
ALEC

"*J*ust what the doctor ordered," I say as I walk through the door holding two bags of take-out.

"The doctor, or you?" Cora slides off the stool at the counter to come over and take one of them from me. "This thing is heavy. What did you get?"

"Everything."

Cora places her bag on the counter and starts pulling boxes out and going through it. "Mmm, tuna sashimi, my favorite."

"I got those crab rangoon things you love, too." I glance around at the vast space. "Where are the guys?"

Cora rolls her eyes. "Off in another room having a *private* meeting."

"That's dumb."

"You're telling me." Cora finds the rangoons and bites one of the corners off before continuing to put things on the counter.

By the time we're done, the entire surface is covered with take-out containers. I smile triumphantly and discard the bags into the trash. "What do you want to drink?" I open the fridge and wait for Cora to answer me, my hand already inching toward the Sprite in the corner.

"Sprite," she confirms.

I take out two of them and place hers next to her water and coffee, and hop onto the chair next to her.

Cora hands me a pair of chopsticks and takes one for herself. "I was starving, thank you." She places a quick peck on my lips before latching onto a container of fried rice and eating straight from it.

"Do you want a plate?"

She shrugs. "No sense in dirtying dishes. We've all shared germs if you think about it."

I have thought about it, and part of me wonders if there's something wrong with me because I'm not as mad as I imagined I'd be at the girl I love spending her time with two other men. It's not ideal, but the fact that there are two additional guys equally obsessed and willing to make her happy and protect her isn't as terrible as it seems. It's kind of a relief, honestly.

I've known for a very long time that Cora had a crush on Miller, and it was reciprocated, so I'd always suspected I'd have to compete for her affection with him. I had held off for a while, not confessing my feelings, in order to give them time to work out their attraction for each other on their own. The second I found out Cora was going on a date with another man, though, I had to step up and do something. If Miller wasn't going to shoot his shot with her, I sure as shit was going to.

Only, he happened to decide on pursuing her at the same time I did, complicating matters of the heart.

For a long while, I accepted that Cora was not obtainable, that she would forever be out of reach. Mainly because she is way out of my league, but in great part because June and her men insinuated that it was forbidden for us to be together. I respected that, toeing the line every chance I got by flirting with her. It was innocent, nothing ever crossing the line, but the more it went on, the more I could no longer withstand the feelings that had been building for what felt like forever.

Every chance I could get, I would make it a point to say hi, ask how she was doing, spend any second I could get with her. June caught on easily, poking fun at my crush on occasion. She had joked about things evolving with Cora and me, but her men made it clear that it couldn't happen.

And because Cora's happiness has always been my priority, I kept that wall between us hoping that someone better would come along. Someone without complications or a dark past or things that haunt them in the night. Someone with a solid job and a steady life that didn't put them in harm's way.

I might be pursuing a career in architecture, but I still work for some of the biggest criminals in the city. I'd be a fool for involving Cora with that, even if it was supposed to be a means to an end. I wanted to secure that future and once I had, if the opportunity was still available, I'd take that leap and see if she was interested.

Sometimes life doesn't always go to plan, though, and when I found out I'd be driving her to a double date, my jealousy and selfishness got the best of me.

I was so fucking happy her date didn't show up, but seeing the look on her face, feeling the disappointment coursing through her, I had to do something. I nearly chewed off the inside of my lip as I battled with what to do: take her home or risk it all and offer to go with her.

Ultimately, my heart and brain got on the same page and my mouth opened, blurting out the feelings I've always held for her.

Goddamn, it felt amazing getting it off my chest, but the second it was out, I grew immediately worried that it was not reciprocated. Sure, she flirted with me, but that was Cora, she's a flirt with everyone. It's part of her bubbly personality. She's a bright shining light, and it's part of what pulled me to her, only it was the darkness that lingered within that kept me there. I could tell there was much more depth to her that she didn't share with just anyone that I was dying to uncover and learn about her.

The night Cora told me she didn't love me, it ripped me in two. Even though I was convinced the words she cut me with were lies, it still pained me all the same because it's what I've always worried—that Cora would never, could never, love me.

Confessing to her might have been the most terrifying thing I'd experienced up until that night at the baseball game, but now, being this close to having her and not knowing how to fix what she's going through, that's hell on an entirely different level.

I even got a little teary-eyed with Silver that night as I crashed in his living room, just to make sure that Cora was okay. I couldn't fathom the idea of leaving her, not after she had a breakdown like that, not after my suspicions only heightened with each new piece of information I uncovered.

Silver's not very chatty, but he reassured me that Cora was probably trying to hurt me to push me away, not because she meant any of the things she said. He told me to be patient with her, that anyone can be a friend when things are good, but it really counts if they show up when shit gets bad. Those are the people that matter the most, and if I could be that for her, she would, hopefully, eventually, recognize that.

At one point, he chuckled and said, "I don't know why I'm saying any of this to you. You're in love with my girl."

But without really discussing it, there's an understanding, that the goal is to keep her happy, to maintain her safety, and if sharing her is what it takes, that's what we'll do...at least, for now.

"Are you going to eat?" Cora breaks my concentration from my rampant thoughts.

"Yeah." I use the chopsticks to grab a piece of sushi. "How is it?" I ask her.

She nods with her mouth full, mumbling something I can't

quite make out, a smile on her face. Cora's shoulders move as she does a little happy dance while she's eating, and if I ever thought I'd witness her doing something more adorable, this definitely tops the cake.

Miller and Silver enter the room, their hushed conversation dying out as they approach. Each of them goes to one end of the island filled with food and exchanges a final glance.

"Nice of you to join us," Cora says with an undertone of annoyance. "Care to tell the class what you two were talking about?"

"Thanks for getting food," Silver says to me as he reaches for a pair of chopsticks. He tosses a set across to Miller.

"Yeah, thanks," Miller agrees, the two of them no doubt making Cora angrier at their avoidance of the question.

"When are you leaving?" Cora continues to question them.

"Where are you going?" I add in because I wouldn't mind being included in the conversation, too.

Silver and Miller look at each other like they're trying to decide who's going to say what and how they're going to evade both of us.

Silver clears his throat after he swallows his food. "We are going to torture someone we believe is acting as a double agent on Ricardo's behalf."

"Oh," I say.

"And we're leaving in the next half hour," Silver tells Cora.

"I'm going," she blurts out.

"No, you're not," Miller says without allowing a second to go by.

"Well, can I go?" I throw out to test the waters.

"No," Miller and Silver say at the exact same time.

I throw my hands up, my chopsticks still in my grasp. "Damn guys, tell me how you really feel."

Silver runs his hand through his beard. "This is a sensitive matter."

"I'm going and you can't stop me." Cora crosses her arms over her chest.

"Angel..." Silver reaches out to touch Cora but she jerks back, nearly falling off her stool.

I catch her just in time.

"Listen," Cora says. "There is no way out of this. Either you take me willingly, or I wait until you leave and Alec and I will follow you wherever you're going. Not only will that complicate matters, but it will put both of us at risk. Are you telling me you're okay with that?"

I don't utter a damn word even though this is her plan and not mine because Cora is hellbent on getting her way and there's nothing I can do to change her mind.

The sooner the guys realize this, the better.

"You're injured," Miller adds, no doubt tossing fuel on Cora's internal fire.

"You're benching me because of a couple bumps and bruises?"

"Your ribs are broken, Cora, that's no—"

Cora cuts Miller off. "You're failing to realize this isn't a negotiation. I'm going. End of discussion."

Miller glances at Silver in what I assume is a cry for help.

Silver averts his stare and reaches for a piece of sushi, popping it into his mouth and chewing to avoid having to make Cora angry any more than they already have.

"How about this?" Cora's tone shifts a bit softer as she focuses on Miller. "You agree to let us go, without resistance, and I won't go into the office the rest of the week."

I chew my food and watch Miller's jaw tense as he considers her offer. It's more than I thought she would give him, and honestly, he'd be an idiot for not accepting. He's been begging her to exclusively work at The Wellerton this week, why wouldn't he see this as a giant win. She continues to work from the safety of this massive home, and he keeps an eye on her during this interrogation thing.

"Fine," Miller huffs. "But the both of you will not get involved. Spectating only."

I shrug because I really have no idea what's going on, I'm just here for the ride. Sure, I'd love to check out what a day in the life of a criminal looks like, but I don't think I'm ready to get my hands dirty. I'm guessing the same goes for Cora, too, even though she's already had her hands covered in blood before.

Cora grins triumphantly and hops off her chair. "What should I wear?" She leaves a second later, not waiting for an answer and disappearing in the direction of her bedroom.

Miller glares at Silver. "What the fuck, dude?"

Silver shrugs and reaches for another piece of sushi. "You saw her, there was no winning that battle."

"The battle you didn't even fight?" Miller places his hands along the edge of the counter and exhales way too fucking dramatically. "She shouldn't be there. She shouldn't see that."

"What are you so afraid of?" I ask Miller. "You do remember her killing her boss, right?"

Miller shoots me a look that borderline sends a chill down my spine, but I remain firmly rooted in place because I won't allow him to try to intimidate me. "She's already lost so much of her innocence, do neither of you care about the rest of it?"

"She wants to go," Silver says. "We're not forcing her; we didn't suggest this. It's her own doing. You want her in your life, you need to accept that she's going to be a part of all of it. You can't pick and choose."

"He has a point," I throw out. "Look what happened to June when the guys tried to keep things from her."

"Whatever," Miller huffs and reaches for an open box of fried rice. "If this goes south, it's on you two."

"It won't go south," Silver reassures him.

"And you..." Miller turns to me. "Do you know what you're getting yourself into?"

"No, not really," I admit. "But it won't stop me from coming, either. Cora's a part of my life, and you're a part of hers. So, I guess that means we're stuck together unless she chooses one of us."

"That isn't going to happen," Silver is the first to say. "And I'm not going to be the one to force her hand."

"I'm not either," I tell them.

Silver and I both settle our sights on Miller, the last one in question.

"Don't look at me," Miller says and shoves a heaping pile of rice in his mouth.

It isn't exactly an answer, but it isn't a declaration that he's going to be the cause of trouble in our sort of complicated relationship we have going between us.

The conversation dies down and the three of us eat our food in silence. I glance up at them here and there and wonder if I should say something, make awkward small talk or try to learn about their lives. If we aren't going to fight to the death over Cora and agree with the dynamic we have going on, shouldn't we try to get to know each other a little bit better? Or maybe I'm massively overthinking this and should just keep my mouth shut.

Luckily, Cora returns, drawing every single set of eyes in this room.

"Fuck," I mutter as I take her in.

Skintight black pants hug her body in all the right places and her top exposes the greater part of her stomach, showing off a bit of her bruised ribs. The top is sheer, showing her lacey black bra through it, but not excessively, just subtly. She's wearing boots although I could totally imagine her wearing this same outfit with a pair of heels on one of those nights that she goes out with June.

My heart stutters as she approaches, and I ignore the way my cock twitches in my jeans.

"Does this look okay?" Cora motions to her body and continues toward us.

Miller coughs, and when I turn toward him, he's pounding on his chest like he's choking. His eyes water and he drinks his water before saying, "Okay is an understatement."

Cora grins and does a little spin.

"We should go before I get any ideas." Silver reaches for a napkin and wipes his face.

Were his ideas the same ones that crossed my mind?

---

*A*fter we clean up the kitchen together, Silver drives us across town to a warehouse I've been to in the past, a place I've driven June's men on occasion.

The vehicle creeps to a stop, and I sort of wish that Cora and I were waiting in here while they went and did their thing. Not because I wasn't prepared for whatever gore they had in mind, but because I'm dying for some alone time with her. We spent the ride with her hand on my thigh, my arm thrown over the seat behind her as she leaned into me, her warmth making my mind run wild with desire.

Not just sexually, either. I'd be thrilled with lying down on this back seat and holding her in my arms while we both drifted to sleep. Anything to be near her would be enough for me.

But, if life has taught me anything, it's that we don't always get what we want, and right now is no exception to the rule— I'm just grateful for what I can get.

The four of us climb out of each side of the vehicle and meet around the front, Miller and Silver are obviously in charge of what's going on, even if Cora is the boss of both of them.

444

"At any given time," Miller starts. "If the two of you need to leave, return to the car and lock yourselves in."

Silver hands me the keys. "It's perfectly normal to get uncomfortable with what we're about to do."

I slide the keys into my pocket and imagine the things he could be referring to. Obviously, they're here to torture someone, it's not like I'm expecting rainbows and butterflies. I've accepted that they're going to hurt this man, otherwise, I wouldn't have come.

It's Cora I worry about, not me. But even then, she volunteered, and literally forced the issue of her coming, so there's a sense of responsibility on her own behalf that she's going to have to come to terms with.

"Are we going to stand out here all day or what?" Cora says while tapping the toe of her boot to the ground.

"Come on, Angel." Silver slides his hand around hers and takes off toward the door to the building.

Miller walks a bit faster to get in front of them, and I follow up the rear because I don't really know my place in this. He opens the door for the rest of us and we step inside, the scent of dirty metal and plastic hitting me the second I'm inside.

It takes my eyes a second to adjust, finally settling on the man tied to a chair in the near distance, thick plastic coating the concrete floor around him. A single bulb dangles in the air above him, lighting up the space like he's the opening act at a show. Near him are various trays and if I'm not mistaken, they're lined with countless devices to torture him with. Although, from my spot near the door, I can't quite tell.

Another guy greets Silver, the two of them exchanging a few words before the man walks past us and slips out the door we just came in, leaving the rest of us behind.

Miller turns toward us, his attention focused on Cora. "You can leave at any time, okay? You don't have to be here if you don't want to be."

Cora stares up at him. "I want to be here." She doesn't appear nervous, not in the slightest. I can't tell if that's good acting or if she really is totally okay.

"Aren't you worried he's going to be able to identify us?" I ask Miller, my gaze trailing past him to the guy who's tied up.

He lowers his voice. "He's not going to make it out of here alive."

Cora doesn't even flinch, she simply blinks at him as if what he said was a completely normal thing for a person to say.

I knew shit would be brutal in here, but killing someone, was I really prepared for that?

There's no backing out now, especially since Cora is on board with whatever it is Miller and Silver have in store for this guy.

"Let's get this over with," Silver says. "You two keep your distance."

I nod in agreement because what other choice do I have.

Silver and Miller leave me and Cora where we stand, the two of them approaching the man they wish to harm.

"You good with this?" I lean over and ask Cora.

"If it gets us answers, yeah." Cora turns her head toward me. "Are you?"

"Yeah, for sure," I lie.

She points ahead to a pillar a bit closer but still far enough we shouldn't pose a distraction. "Let's go over there."

I place my hand on the small of her back and guide her over to the spot she suggested, pretending in my head that this is some kind of date we're on.

Cora leans against the sturdy surface, and I place myself behind her, still being able to see over her head with ease.

We don't speak as we watch Silver and Miller start what they came here for.

Miller snaps something underneath the nose of the man who was sitting there, unmoving.

He jolts to life abruptly, his head whipping around until he settles on Miller. "The fuck?" he blurts out.

"Harry, my guy, good morning." Miller crosses his arms and looks down at Harry.

Harry pulls at his confinement, his forearms attached to the metal of the chair arms, and his legs secured to the bottom. There's no escaping and I can only imagine he's just realized this. His sights land on Silver, who is busy determining which torture tool he plans on using first.

"What's this about?" Harry asks, turning his main focus onto Miller.

"I think you and I both know what it's about," Miller tells him. "Now, you can tell me what you know, and we can make this painless, or well, do I really need to explain the rest?"

"I'm not saying shit." Harry chooses the worst option possible.

"Very well." Miller tilts his head toward Silver.

Harry laughs. "What is this? Some bullshit good cop bad cop thing?"

Miller, his tone cool and collected, says, "Oh, no, you're mistaken. There is no good cop."

Silver comes over with a pair of pliers in both of his hands. He gives one of them to Miller and each of them holds one of Harry's wrists as they position the plier in place.

"Last chance?" Miller offers him.

"Get on with it," Harry tells them.

Silver and Miller comply, both latching onto a fingernail on each hand and ripping it off in one solid yank. Harry grunts and cusses but holds it together rather well.

I pinch my lips together as the phantom pain rips through me. Cora remains in front of me, seemingly unbothered from where I stand.

"Is that all you got?" Harry taunts his tormentors.

Is he fucking stupid, or has he completely lost his fucking mind?

Miller nods at Silver, and they waste no time ripping another fingernail off each hand. Miller follows it up by slamming the pair of pliers into Harry's hand, the excessive crunching sound no doubt confirming the broken bones.

Miller stands and gives Silver his pliers. "Get a hammer," he tells him.

Silver calmly returns to the table of torture tools, discards of their pliers and retrieves Miller's requested item, picking something up for himself, too, that I can't quite make out from here.

"I've already figured out that you're the mole," Miller tells Harry. "Which makes total sense. You were a great worker bee, until lately..."

"What I want to know," Silver says when he approaches. "What did you gain from it?"

"I'm not telling you shit." Harry spits on the ground near Miller.

Miller takes the hammer from Silver and shrugs. "Okay." He lowers himself and says, "Are you sure?"

"Fuck off."

Miller draws the hammer back and thrusts it right down onto Harry's foot, breaking it to go along with his smashed hand. He spares him no mercy and reels it back again, hitting him harder the second time around on the same foot. Even with him wearing a shoe, there's no saving him from that impact.

"Goddamn it!" Harry yells and winces.

Silver latches onto Harry's ear and holds what I think is a knife along the rear of it. "Talk to us, Harry. It doesn't have to be like this."

But Harry isn't ready, or willing, so Silver tugs on his ear and slices it clean off, discarding the dismembered flesh onto the crinkling plastic sheet beneath them.

"Step back," Silver tells Miller as he tosses his blade onto the tray and rolls up his sleeves. "Let me have a little fun with him."

Miller complies, standing to give Silver some space and watches as he lands blow after blow across Harry's face.

Cora reaches her arm between us and leans into me. She fumbles with my hand and brushes against my dick, the thing betraying me and going hard at the slightest touch.

She abandons her pursuit of my hand and cups my cock through my pants, stroking it gently.

My eyes close, and I breathe her heavenly scent in as I ignore what's really going on around us.

But it's impossible, because what I see when I close my eyes is blood, and although that should make my erection disappear, it doesn't, and that worries me more than anything.

Cora turns around to face me, her hand quickly unbuttoning my pants and sliding under the waistband of my boxers. She licks her lips and nudges me backward, just out of immediate range of Silver and Miller.

"Cora," I whisper, my breath catching.

She grins at me and drops to her knees, her hands going to work to free my traitorous cock.

"Fuck," I moan as she licks at the precum coating me. I weave my hand through her hair to get it off her beautiful face, my heart pounding at the sight of her on her fucking knees in a place like this.

Flitting my attention toward the guys, I realize they can totally see us even from here but come to terms with the fact that I really don't fucking care. No, the only thing that really matters is Cora's perfect little mouth taking me into her.

Cora grips the base of my shaft and squeezes it firmly, her mouth working me in a way that makes me question how long I can last. She looks up at me through her long lashes and takes me in deeper, my cock hitting the back of her throat. Pursing her lips, she sucks me harder, swirling her hand along the edge of her lips, increasing every bit of pleasure consuming me.

"Baby," I say. "You're such a dirty fucking girl."

She grins around my cock and the shift in pressure is enough to make me crumble right here and now, but I don't. Instead, I brace myself on the pillar we're sort of concealed behind and take my other hand to grip the base of her chin.

Cora pulls me out of her, still stroking me as she bats her pretty blue eyes up at me. "I want you to come in my mouth," she says, a bit out of breath, her lips touching the tip of my twitching cock.

And with a final glance at the men who are torturing someone else near us, I push myself back into Cora and buck my hips, my orgasm nearing.

"Fuck," I moan as my cock fills her warm and wet mouth.

Cora holds out her tongue and opens wide, jerking me to completion right into her fucking mouth. The sight something that will be etched into my memory for as long as I live. My cock twitches, sending what's left of my orgasm onto her cheek.

She sucks me dry, my body twitching with every movement, and swallows my load, surprising me when she wipes at her cheek and licks her finger, getting every last drop of me.

"That was so fucking hot," I tell her, my chest heaving as she stands from the ground.

I take her face into my hands and kiss her deeply, the salty remains of me still lingering.

Cora breaks away long enough for me to shove my dick back into my pants and button them up. She grabs my shirt and tugs me around the corner so we can continue watching Silver and Miller torture a man.

It dawns on me how fucking wrong all of this is, but what's worse is that I'm not convinced that I care. I recognize how fucked up this is, that much is true, and still, the only thing on my mind is how fucking happy I am.

What the hell is wrong with me?

Maybe I'm not as good of a guy as I think I am...and maybe that's okay with me.

Silver shakes his fist, blood from the man's face, flying off it and onto the plastic below him. "You still not ready to talk?"

Harry coughs and hangs his head sloppily.

Cora looks over her shoulder at me. "I'm going in." She takes off without even allowing me to process what she said, my chest tightening with each step she takes from me.

I'm right on her heels, but there's no stopping her, not when she's already made up her mind. I could throw her over my shoulder and carry her out of here, yet she'd still find a way to finish what she started.

Miller does a double take, his face hardening at her approach. "What are you doing?"

Cora stops a few feet from the beaten man, her boots crumpling the plastic under her. "He has a daughter, right?"

Harry's attention darts to Cora.

"He does," Miller confirms.

Silver returns from the selection of tools, a towel in his grasp as he wipes at his hands. He doesn't seem bothered at all that Cora made it a point to march over. If anything, it's like he expected it to happen.

"College student," Cora continues.

Miller nods.

Cora crosses her arms and looks between Harry and Miller. "I think I should pay her a visit."

"Wh-what? No," Harry blubbers, his words not coming out quick enough. "Leave her out of this."

Cora breathes in, her shoulders rising before she exhales. "I'm afraid we can't. I mean, if you aren't willing to talk, she's the one who's going to have to pay."

It's fucked up, especially considering she's literally paying for her father's mistakes.

"I'll talk, I'll say whatever you want me to say, just please, don't hurt my daughter." Tears well in Harry's eyes, tears that weren't there a moment ago even when Silver was beating the shit out of him. "I'll talk. Where do you want me to start? What did I gain? He promised me a spot on his council. Told me he was going to take over Dominic's organization one shipment at a time."

Holy shit, it actually worked, Cora got this guy to talk without even inflicting any harm. Somehow, even despite fucking her face a minute ago, my cock throbs with desire at seeing her take charge like this, and the idea of bending her over that table of torture devices crosses my mind.

Miller lets out a laugh. "There's no fucking way."

"It-it's what he said. He's working on restructuring things, bringing it back to the old days." Harry coughs and blood speckles his lips.

"Who's he working with?" Silver asks him and throws his towel onto the ground.

Harry blinks a few times like he's trying to access the file in his mind of the names. "Uh, John, Tony, Vito, you know, the old-school mobsters. Ricky's longtime friends."

"What about Carlo, Dean, and Sam?" Miller asks Harry.

"They wanted nothing to do with it. Said they wouldn't betray Dominic."

"So, all these guys are aware of Ricardo going behind Dom's back to overthrow him?" Miller continues to question him.

"Yeah, Vito's son, Joe, he's the one who bought Ricky's daughter. Ricky gave him a vested part of the deal, some exclusive cut. I don't know all the details, I'm just the middleman." Harry pauses, his head swaying. "Don't hurt my daughter, please."

Cora looks to Miller. "You satisfied?"

Harry shifts his tone. "Fucking bitch, don't think I don't know who you are. Ricky's going to ruin you when he puts his fucking seed in you. I just wish I was there to watch it happen."

Rage, unlike anything I've ever felt, builds up inside of me. I find my feet moving my body, my gaze scanning until it finds what it's looking for. My fingers wrap around the hard surface, and I scrape it against the ground on my way over to the man who just said such vulgar things to my sweet, twisted girl.

I look to Silver, and he nods a sort of agreement before I turn my sights to Miller.

"Yeah, I'm satisfied," Miller says, a clear sign that things are done here.

"The fuck you think you're going to do with that, boy," Harry speaks to me.

"Step back." I nudge Cora out of the way and ready the base-ball bat like I'm about to swing, but instead of aiming at a ball, I train the explosive blow on the side of his fucking face, caving it in with the first hit.

His skull collapses in easier than I thought it would, making me regret not hitting him less aggressively.

I wanted him to suffer, to understand that he would never get away with talking to her like that, but my swing had something else in mind.

Reeling back, I hit him again, and again, not satisfied with my torment until my ears ring and Cora's gentle hands are on my back.

"Alec," she says. "Alec. He's gone."

I stop, the sudden realization of what I've done causing the bat to fall out of my hands. It thuds once and then twice, landing near my shoes. Glancing down, my hands are covered in speckled blood, as are my forearms and most of the front of my body.

"Damn," Silver mutters. "You got him good."

"I..." I take a step back and nearly trip.

Miller reaches out to steady me. "You good, dude?"

"Yeah, I..." I turn around to face Miller and Cora, unsure of how they're going to react to my outburst.

I should have never done what I just did. I should have stayed away like Miller had asked of us. I shouldn't have taken things into my own hands, and I never should have thought I could beat a man to death with a baseball bat and get away with it.

35
CORA

*A*s soon as we got back to The Wellerton last night, Alec left.

He hasn't answered my calls or my texts, and I have no idea what that means—for him, or for us.

Silver and Miller both tell me to give him time, but how can I give him something I don't have?

I wake up alone, my body still sore from Ricardo's beating, even three days later. I'm assuming the worst of it is upon me, and its only improvement from here on out.

The apartment Miller so graciously gave me is eerie when I'm left alone, and it takes me one very slow hour before I decide I've had enough of the solitude.

I promised Miller that I wouldn't go into the office this week, but I didn't say anything about not leaving The Wellerton at all.

The shower has no shortage of hot water and feels great against my aching frame. Every inch of me is grateful for the excellent water pressure and expensive bathroom supplies that Miller has given me. I get ready in somewhat of a hurry, blow-drying my hair and styling it with a round brush. I settle on a pair of dark denim skinny jeans, a black crop top, and a pair of white Air Forces—all courtesy of Miller. Aside from the few things that he brought from my parent's house, everything else is picked out by him, and not only fits me, but is something I like, too.

Once I'm somewhat satisfied with my appearance, I make my way to the kitchen, poking a few buttons on the fancy espresso machine he bought me and making myself a drink. While it's brewing, I pop half a bagel in the toaster and pull out the other half of the avocado that Alec didn't finish yesterday morning.

My chest tightens as I think of him but I shove the thought away because it does me no good to worry about something I can no longer control.

Do I worry that things went too far last night, and Alec realized how very fucked up the rest of us are and that he wants nothing to do with us? Yes, absolutely, but I can't allow my mind to revolve around that, not when there are other pressing matters at hand. Like the fact that there are only four days until I have to go to Ricardo's house, and a week until he claims me as his. We may have uncovered some information during the interrogation but if we don't figure out what to do with it, all of this will have been for nothing.

I smear the rest of the avocado on my bagel and sprinkle some everything bagel seasoning on it. I'm not really that hungry, but I did promise Miller that I would eat when I woke up, and if I'm going to go behind his back and leave, I might as well follow through with one thing I said I'd do.

I eat half of the bagel before throwing the remains in the trash and placing the plate in the dishwasher, along with my empty mug. I may not have eaten all the bagel, but I refuse to let a drop of that damn good coffee go to waste.

Grabbing my clutch off the table near the door, I reach for

the key to the car that Miller got me. It feels strange to have a car at all, let alone a fucking Porsche.

Before I come to my senses and change my mind, I leave the apartment and use the private elevator to go into the parking garage. A car alarm beeps in the distance, and I watch over my shoulder as I make my way to my car, not letting out a breath until I'm in the driver's seat with the doors locked.

I punch in the address into my phone's GPS and wait for it to connect. The drive isn't that long, and I'm grateful because I didn't figure out how to navigate the stereo prior to leaving, and I didn't want to distract myself too much while driving. Wrecking the beautiful car Miller gave me the first time I take it out isn't exactly going to win me any bonus points with him.

I find a parking spot and put the car in park, giving myself one more chance to turn around and return home.

But this trip isn't just for me, it's for her, too.

The Porsche chirps when I press the lock button and each step away from it reminds me how vulnerable I am here, completely exposed to anyone who might walk by.

"You're just a girl, Cora. In a city of a fuck ton of people. No one will notice you," I whisper and make my way across the parking lot and through the double doors. I don't stop until I'm slipping into London's hospital room, my shoulders relaxing like I'm somehow safe in here, even though I know that's a lie. If anything, this is the most dangerous place for me to be.

"Hey," I say and approach her.

London raises her arm to shut the television in the corner off, a smile forming on her bruised and swollen face. "Hey, you're here."

"I am," I tell her. "How are you feeling?"

She brings her hand around her neck, where the brace is no longer. "They finally took this thing off, so I feel a hell of a lot better."

"I bet."

"Plus, I'm hopped up on drugs."

"That's always a plus." I scoot a chair over to the edge of the bed and lower myself onto it. "What were you watching?"

"Some baking show."

"You can turn it back on, if you want to."

"Nah, it was boring anyway. I'm going out of my mind in here. I'd much rather talk to you."

I sit on the edge of the seat. "Do you need anything?"

"No. I'm good. Unless you can convince them to let me go."

"Have they told you how much longer they're keeping you?"

"Few more days. They're pretty vague when I ask for specifics." She points toward the wall. "They gave me those crutches to get around with." London drags up the blanket to reveal her leg. "And they put this cast on me."

"You'll be back to new in no time." Although she and I both know that's impossible. The things that her father did to her will stick with her forever.

"Yeah, probably." London tries her best to reposition toward me. "How are you feeling?"

"Better." I raise my shirt to show her my bruised side. "Nothing like yours."

She draws in a breath. "I'm so sorry you ever got involved with him." Her gaze flicks to the door and back like she's afraid someone will overhear her.

"I am, too, but if I hadn't, we wouldn't have met." I fidget with a fray on my jeans. "Maybe fate crossed our paths so I could help you."

"Cora," London says sternly enough to draw my attention. "I'm a lost cause. You need to save yourself."

I shake my head. "No. I refuse to believe that."

She fumbles to find the remote for her bed, pushing the button to raise the back up a bit more. "He's tried to kill me numerous times, and one of these times, he won't change his mind. That day is coming sooner rather than later. I've accepted it."

London pauses and then adds, "If he doesn't do it, the guy he sold me to will. There's nothing left for me."

I stare at this beautifully broken girl and wonder what it is that I can say to make her realize I'm not giving up, not yet. Time might be ticking away but there must be something that can be done to save her—to save me.

"You've made it this far, why would you give up now?" I ask her.

"It's not that I've given up, I just don't have much fight left in me." London motions to her body. "Look at what he's done to me. This isn't the first time he's broken bones or left me in the hospital. Every single time I think there's hope to escape him, but he does what he always does and finds a way out of it. He's like a fucking cockroach."

"Then, together, we will fucking smash him. Once and for all." I lean forward, taking her hand in mine. "I'm not kidding, London, we're going to make it out of this." I don't know who needs to hear the words more, her or me, but regardless, I use them as motivation for both of us, because it's clear we need it.

Tears well in London's eyes. "Why do you want to help me? I'm no one to you."

"*No one* should have to go through what you have. What he's done to you, what he's *doing* to you, it's wrong. I'm not going to stand back when I can help."

"It's only going to put you in danger."

"I'm already in danger. At least this way, maybe I can help you, too."

Our conversation is abruptly interrupted by a man entering the room, my heart nearly lurching out of my chest at his intrusion.

"Well, what do we have here?" The middle-aged man storms into the small space like he owns it, walking around the side of

London's bed and stopping. He leans down, pressing a disgustingly sloppy kiss on London's mouth, completely disregarding what condition she's in.

I rise from my seat, noting how much bigger than me he is. "Excuse me?"

The man extends his hand toward me. "Joe Cassidy." He glances down at London briefly before returning his greasy stare at me. "London's husband-to-be."

I shake his hand, and he squeezes mine a bit too tightly, the bones crunching together uncomfortably. "Sarah," I lie. "A friend of London's."

"Any friend of London's is a friend of mine." He licks his lips and raises his brows, showing me exactly what kind of man he is.

For a split second, I consider hitting him in the head with the metal bedpan sitting off in the corner but decide against it. There's no telling if he has any of his pals with him, or if I'd bring London more harm than good. If I'm going to assault this guy, it's going to have to be final, not temporary.

"Heard you were laid up." Joe turns his attention to London. "Ricky told me you took a fumble down the stairs." He shakes his head. "Clumsy girl."

London smiles politely but I can see straight through that expression...she's no doubt having murderous thoughts, too. "Yeah," is all she manages to say.

His phone rings and he only takes a step away to get it out and press it to his ear. "Joe here," he practically yells into the receiver. "Oh, yeah, I can handle that. I'll be right there." He hangs up and claps his hands together. "Well, I've got to jet, baby doll. Rest up, we have a wedding to plan." He plants another kiss on London's lips, not caring at all that she isn't reciprocating and points to me. "Sarah, baby, I'll see you at the wedding."

"Wouldn't miss it," I tell him because if it comes to it, I'll be the one putting a bullet in his fucking skull as he waits for his bride to walk down the aisle. Anything to get her away from this sick man.

The second he leaves, I reach for the bottle of hand sanitizer and pump some into my palms, scrubbing aggressively and offering some to London. She gladly accepts, going as far as to rub some of it onto her face, too.

"He was..." I fall short of words to describe that man.

"Disgusting, repulsive, unacceptable."

"Yeah, that."

"Why wouldn't someone hot agree to marry me?"

"I heard," I lean in closer and lower my voice. "That it was part of a business arrangement between your dad and his dad, Vito."

London seems surprised at my knowledge. "What? How did you figure that out?"

"Well..." I scoot my chair toward her and speak quietly. "It's kind of a long story, but some guy working for your dad told us, last night."

"Last night?"

"It's probably better if we don't discuss details," I tell her.

She nods. "Yeah, you're probably right." London meets my gaze, hers growing more serious with each passing second. "You really weren't lying, were you?"

"About what?"

"About trying to find a way out of this?"

"I wasn't."

London stares at me for a long moment like she's assessing which path to take next. Finally, she says, "What can I do to help?"

And for the first time in a great while, I actually feel something bubbling inside of me that resembles what I can only imagine is hope.

36

SILVER

I drive to a place that doesn't belong to me because inside it is the woman who has stolen my heart.

Ideas of how to navigate this situation consume nearly every single one of my thoughts. Never in all my years have I been this fucking determined to solve a problem than I am now, and the fact that it's taking this much effort to figure it out is driving me fucking insane.

There are so many variables I'm not often faced with. Casualties I cannot disregard just for the sake of saving Cora from her doomed fate with Ricardo.

Her life is obviously at the top of my priority list, but then there's her parents to consider too. She doesn't have a great relationship with them yet they're the reason she's in this mess to begin with. I must determine how to keep them alive, along with Miller and Alec, too. If she loses any of them, I will have failed her.

Then there's the added variable of her new friend London, who happens to be the enemy's daughter. A complication I never accounted for that will pose a great risk to this entire fucking mission. It's clear he doesn't give a fuck about his daughter, and she's only alive as a means to procure him more money on his endless pursuit of whatever it is he's hoping to achieve.

It's laughable that he thinks he's going to overthrow Dominic. The likelihood of that happening is quite literally slim to none, but it still muddles business in a way that is not tolerable. Some disruption is expected, but what Ricardo is doing is downright pestilent.

And now that Cora's enemy is also Dom's it massively fucks with the whole keeping this a secret thing she's sworn me to.

I'm not supposed to know that Miller is dealing with this on Dom and Johnny's behalf, and Cora doesn't want us discussing things with anyone other than ourselves, so that leaves us all spinning our feet as we navigate the situation to the best of our abilities.

However, if Miller tells Dominic that he hired me to help him with the shipment situation, maybe that will allow me to discuss things with Dom, without telling him about Cora's involvement. If I can eliminate Dom's problem, using his resources, maybe that would, in turn, save Cora from her deal with Ricardo.

I'll have to talk to Cora and see if she's okay with me pursuing this option, because I'd love to get her permission first instead of begging for her forgiveness later. But, if she says no, that's exactly what I'll be doing, because this is the only way forward that I can settle on.

And while I'm waiting on a few leads to surface, discussing matters with her just came to the top of my to-do list.

I park in the garage, next to the car that Miller bought for Cora, and make quick work on getting upstairs, inputting all the codes that they gave me to access different parts of the building. I'm grateful for the level of security in place, but I'm not convinced we couldn't beef it up a bit more to keep her protected.

Once I'm through her front door, I toss my keys into the bowl and listen carefully to locate her.

When I don't hear anything, I accept that she might be sleeping, and this conversation I thought we'd be having may have to wait.

I kick my shoes off and head toward her bedroom, rolling my sleeves up to my elbows along the way. But the second I'm in, I don't notice her in the bedroom. My gaze shifts to the bathroom, the door ajar. Silently, I go over there and peer inside, my heart breathing a sigh of relief at finally laying my eyes on her.

I knock gently on the door.

"Come in," Cora says from her spot in the bathtub. She wipes at her cheeks and it's then that I see the tears lining them.

I rush over to her. "Hey, what's wrong? What's the matter?"

She shakes her head. "Nothing. I'm fine." Cora sniffles and it practically brings the grown man in me to my knees.

I don't waste another second—still, with my clothes on, I climb into the full bathtub with her, submerging myself completely, and pull her to my chest. "Angel." I smooth the hair from her face and press soft kisses on her forehead.

Cora resists at first but melts into my embrace, no doubt wondering if I've lost my mind having climbed in here totally clothed. Doesn't she realize that she matters more to me than anything else, and so what if I get a little water on me, I'd go to the ends of the Earth for her.

"Do you want to talk, or do you want to just sit here?" I ask her.

"I don't know."

Holding her close to me, I whisper, "That's okay. You don't have to know." I wrap my arms around her small, wet frame and wish that I could take away her pain.

Cora breaks away from my chest and looks up at me, her nose red from crying. "You're still in your clothes."

I shrug. "They needed to be washed anyway."

Cora rolls her eyes and repositions herself in my lap, straddling my waist. "What are you afraid of?" she questions while staring at me.

I do what I can to ignore the fact that she's completely naked and I'm completely clothed, my hands on her hips. "Nothing," I tell her.

It's a lie and we both know it.

"Nothing at all?" She sits back a bit, exposing her perfectly perky breasts.

I bring my left hand up to run my thumb along her cheek. "It's a secret."

"I'll keep it safe," she says encouragingly.

"I'm afraid...of you."

Cora narrows her glare. "You are not."

"I promise." I take that same hand and hold my pinky out to prove just how serious I am.

"Why?"

"Because you hold the power to break me, Angel." Every word out of me is the truth and I've known it from the very first second I laid my sights on her. For someone to come into your life so fucking abruptly and stirs up feelings like she has, she absolutely has the means to ruin me.

Cora lays her hands lazily around my shoulders, her gaze meeting mine. "I wouldn't. Not on purpose." She leans forward, pressing a kiss on my lips.

I kiss her back, grateful that she even likes me. I wanted to withstand the sudden feelings I had for Cora, and maybe a better man would have been able to, but every stolen kiss and flittering glance has only proven one thing totally certain—I am completely and utterly hers.

"Distract me?" Cora says, her mouth still hovering next to mine.

And all it takes is that one single request and I am submitting to her fully.

Cora climbs onto my lap further, her knees going on both sides of my hips. She deepens our kiss and tangles her hands in my hair.

I reach into the water, gliding my fingers over her clit and down until I penetrate her. She whimpers and tightens around me and my cock reacts by pushing against my soaked dress slacks.

Cora breaks away to allow herself space to unbutton my pants and grab onto my dick. She licks her lips and strokes my length, climbing back in place and aligning my tip with her entrance.

Without allowing me to protest, to ask her if she wants more time to warm up, to make her climax at least once, she sits down onto me, my cock spreading her open.

"Fuck," I moan as I fill Cora's tight pussy. Careful not to hurt her, I don't thrust my hips, I just give her the reigns to control the depth and tempo. "You feel so fucking good, Angel. You take me so well."

Cora grins and slides herself up and down my shaft, her pussy so fucking taut around me. She looks me directly in my eyes as she says, "Pull my hair."

I reach up, slowly grabbing a fistful of those beautiful blonde locks and tug them. "Is this hard enough?" I ask her while continuing to refrain from thrusting into her. It's taking everything I can do not to shove her down onto me and slam into her.

"Harder," Cora says through gritted teeth. "Don't hold back."

Her words go straight to my fucking cock, and I do exactly that, gripping her hair harder and tilting her neck toward me so I can kiss every inch of it. I skim my teeth along her collarbone and maintain my grip on the fistful of her hair, dragging her face toward me and crashing my lips onto hers.

Cora rides me more aggressively, her body reacting to the change in dynamic.

I keep my hand in her hair and wrap the other around her waist and hold onto her as I buck my hips into her, fucking her deeper than before. Water splashes all around us and neither one of us seems to care about the mess we're making.

"Silver," she moans into my mouth and pushes herself down, burying me balls deep inside of her.

How her body can even handle all of me is a question for Mother Nature herself.

"I'm so fucking close," she whimpers. "Don't stop."

I allow our joined bodies to slip a bit further in the water, my back almost horizontal with the bottom of the tub, my grip on her waist and hair not letting up.

Our mouths don't break apart as I push us under the water, both of our heads completely submerged.

I maintain my hold on her and slip my one hand over her ass and find her hole, penetrating it gently as I don't let up on her pussy. Instead, I hope like hell she's able to hold her breath.

Cora doesn't pull away, instead, she goes completely along with my insanity and allows me to fuck her under the water, her pussy clenching around me. She continues to slam up and down my shaft, the movement bringing my orgasm closer and closer until I explode harder than I ever have in my entire life, my cock filling her full. Her climax follows a second later, her mouth still on mine, both of us no doubt dying for air as we orgasm onto each other.

I keep my hips moving as I shove against the foot of the tub to bring us above the surface of the water.

Cora gasps and I'm not sure if it's from being underwater or the orgasm itself.

"That was fucking intense," she says, her forehead against mine, her body still shuddering in the aftermath of what we just did. "Have you ever done that before?"

I rock my hips gently and revel in the warmth of her sweet pussy pulsating around me. "Never."

Our mouths meet for another round of heated passion and as much as I want to stay here with her, live in this moment forever, I remember that I came in here for a reason. The goal was to talk to her about communicating with Dominic regarding what's going on and move toward finding a resolution, sooner, rather than later.

But then I remember that she was crying...and I'm not convinced I want to dredge up any negative thoughts or emotions right now, not when she's already in such a vulnerable state.

"Have you?" I ask her, suddenly curious about all the things she has and hasn't done with a partner. A strange sort of jealousy rises in me, but I shove it away. She's allowed to have a past, as long as I'm part of her future.

Cora laughs. "No. I most definitely have not." She releases her hold on me and scoots away in the rather large tub.

I stand, ringing what water I can from my soaked clothes before stepping out of the tub and drying off. "I'll get you another towel since I stole yours." I return a moment later with a fresh one to lay next to the tub. "You okay?"

She nods with a fake smile on her gorgeous face. "I'm better now. Thank you."

I graze her cheek with my hand and stare into her eyes. "I care about you, Angel. I hope you know that. I hope you know you can always talk to me, too. Whatever it is. I'm here for you."

"I know," she says, her voice soft and low, but not entirely convincing. It's almost like she wants to believe it, she's just a bit unsure.

I can't say I blame her though; trust has never been my strong suit either.

Our moment is interrupted when Miller barges into the room, his jaw tense and his body more rigid than usual. He's pissed, that much is obvious.

He stops beside me, the space between his brows creasing at

the state of my outfit, but he focuses on Cora. "You left The Wellerton today?"

Cora tilts her head toward him and leans back in the tub. "And?"

"That wasn't part of the agreement. You said you'd stay here."

"Actually, I said I'd work from home this week. I never said anything about not leaving the building." Cora props her elbow outside the tub and sets her head in her hand. "Technicality."

Miller's chest heaves and narrows his gaze. "I'm not happy about this."

"Join the club," Cora says, her sarcastic tone making me pinch my lips together to suppress a laugh.

That's my girl, I want to mutter but decide against infuriating Miller any more than he already is.

"Plus," she adds, "I got some dirt." Cora stands in the tub, not caring at all that she's completely nude in front of both of us, my cock having just been inside her moments prior.

With my help, she climbs out and dries off, wrapping the towel around her body.

"Meet me in the kitchen in five." She waves her hand to shoo us off and it works like a charm, both of us leaving the bathroom in an instant.

I step into her bedroom and make my way over to the bag of clothes that I've been keeping here, looking for something to change into.

"What was that all about?" Miller asks me.

I glance over my shoulder. "I have no idea. You know as much as me."

He lets out a sigh before leaving me there to undress without his eyes on me, not that I would have cared; we've had to strip out of bloody clothes in front of each other in the past. What's so different about mine being wet?

Once I'm dressed, I stroll to the kitchen and wait for Cora, making her a latte in case she happens to be craving one, and pour her a glass of water, too. I'm positioning the cups on the counter when she walks in, a sort of glow about her that lights up the space in my chest where my heart belongs. For years, I thought it was empty, but she reminds me that it may not have been lost after all.

"So, what's this dirt?" Miller says, barely giving her a chance to enter the room.

She continues forward and climbs onto the stool that has become hers in the few days she's been staying here and takes a sip of her water. Cora then grabs onto the mug and offers me a soft smile, a sort of non-verbal thank you. She's in no rush to answer Miller's question and I find it hilarious.

"Mmm, this is good." Cora licks at her lip to remove the froth left behind. Slowly, she lowers the mug onto the counter and turns toward Miller. "I met London's future husband today."

Miller tightens his hand into a fist. "What?"

"His name is Joe, and apparently he's Vito's son." She pauses and says, "I introduced myself with a fake name, and he seemed stupid enough to buy it."

He loosens his hand, his fingers twitching a bit. He should really consider going to anger management. Maybe read a self-help book. I'm no stranger to being filled with rage, but it tends to not manifest itself so obviously the way his does. Although, I do have quite a few years on him, giving me an edge on controlling the beasts that live within me. I wasn't exactly a great example of calm and collected when I was in my twenty-something's either.

"I've interacted with him a couple of times," I tell Miller and Cora. "Real arrogant kid, definitely not very bright. But he's entitled, and dangerous. Not a good guy." I recall the girl he had roughed up and paid off to keep her mouth shut. That was the last job I would ever work for him.

"London mentioned that her dad was close with this Vito guy, and there's this group of old dudes that meet with him pretty regularly. Sometimes at his house, sometimes at a place called...uh, what's it called?" Cora draws a blank and taps her finger on the counter.

"The Manor," I add.

She nods. "Yeah, that, what is it?"

"The Manor is a neutral ground for criminals to get together. Very strict rule of no violence of any means." It makes sense that he would have those meetings there if he was trying to convince them to come over on his side in his attempt to overthrow Dominic.

"That must be the place I saw Ricardo..." Cora tells us.

"You were at The Manor?" Miller asks Cora before I get a chance to.

"Not like, *there* there. I was with June; Alec was driving us to the game and we picked Simon up from there. Ricardo was talking to him and came over to forcefully introduce himself to me and June." Cora shivers at the memory. "Simon said he wanted to kill him, but that he couldn't because he's powerful."

At least I know Simon feels the same way about him as the rest of us, making me only more convinced that I should discuss things over with Dom to come up with some kind of power play to take him out.

If he's meeting with guys at The Manor, that complicates things, because he's truly untouchable there. It would be an act of treason and blatant defiance to hurt a single hair on anyone's head at that building. Not only would you be barred from doing any business with anyone who is anyone, if they catch you, they kill you. Simple as that.

As far as them meeting at his house, that's a different story, and if I could get creative enough, maybe I could make a silly little accident happen to wipe them out. Miller has already proven how well he can sneak around without being caught, so maybe this very loose plan is more possible than not.

"London also told me that her dad was involved in some

medical trials." Cora glances between me and Miller. "He often talked to a guy named Bill. Does that ring a bell?"

I had already started looking into the trials that Ricardo has his dirty hands in to uncover anything I could about the condition of Cora's mom. This entire situation is because of her mother, and she's been a variable none of us have any knowledge of. "I'll ask around," I say, making a mental note of the new name.

"Don't ask the wrong people though, I don't want it to get back to Ricardo that we're trying to undermine him." Cora nervously fidgets with her latte.

"I've been doing this a long time, Angel. I know how to be discreet," I reassure her even though her concerns are totally valid. Ricardo is a snake and has spies everywhere. "I have an idea." I reach for my phone and take a step back from the counter, putting a bit of distance between us. Punching in the number I have memorized; I wait for it to connect.

It rings three times before it does.

"What?" the grumpy person on the other end says.

"Archer, it's Silver, I need a favor."

"No."

"You owe me," I mutter those three magic words that work like a charm for anyone in our industry. No one, and I repeat no one, enjoys being indebted to someone else, especially in the form of favors. We sure love to collect them, but we go out of our way to avoid owing them.

"How did you get this number?"

"Does that really matter?"

"I'm retired," Archer tells me even though I'm already well aware of the distance he's put between himself and the criminal world.

It's unfair of me to pull him back in when he's already made it clear he's done, the loss he experienced causing him to burn a bunch of bridges before he secluded himself completely. I've kept tabs on him, partly because I'm nosey but mainly because he's a great asset.

Miller trains his gaze on me like he's trying to figure out what I'm doing before I've done it. His impatience is something he could stand to work on, too.

"You don't dabble, not even a little bit?"

"What do you want, Silver?"

"I need eyes and ears."

"On what?" Archer sighs and I grow confident he's at the very least entertaining the idea of helping me.

"The Manor."

Archer lets out one abrupt laugh. "Yeah, right."

"And Ricardo Gardella's house."

"I'm hanging up now," Archer says.

"I'll consider us even."

He breathes in deeply and sighs. "Even?"

"Even," I confirm.

"And I never have to hear from you ever again?"

"Never."

"They could kill me for this," he tells me what I already know.

"I wouldn't ask if it weren't absolutely necessary."

"You must be desperate if you're calling me."

"Can you do it?"

"Child's play, Silver. Of course I can do it. It's whether I'm willing."

"Please." I hate how the word sounds slipping out of my mouth but come to terms with the fact that I would say anything to get him to agree.

"Fine. Send me details. I can get you in for a few days, but that's it, do you hear me? I won't risk my life any more than I have to for you." Archer hangs up, not giving me a chance to thank him.

"Who was that?" Cora asks me.

473

"Only the best hacker I've ever come across."

"He can really get a feed in The Manor? How's that even possible?" Miller leans against the counter and looks right at me.

"There isn't anything this kid can't hack, I'm telling you, he's damn good." With my phone still in my hand, I know there's another phone call I need to make, one that I don't want to do in front of them. "I have another lead I need to follow up on. You two okay or are you going to fist fight?"

I could cut the tension between Miller and Cora with a fucking butter knife. The two of them need to fuck it out of their systems and get over it. I don't know who's more stubborn, and it isn't helping our situation.

"I'm fine," Cora says, her default statement I'd love to erase from her vocabulary.

Miller shrugs. "I don't know what you're talking about."

I roll my eyes and step toward Cora, kissing her cheek briskly. "I'll see you later, Angel." Grabbing onto Miller's shoulder on the way to the door, I tell him, "Don't fuck this up."

He doesn't bother responding and I don't care either way. I leave them behind to deal with whatever is going on between them and dial Dominic the second I'm in the parking garage downstairs.

"Yeah?" he answers.

"Dom, it's Silver. Can we talk? It's urgent."

"When?"

"Now."

"Meet me at The Manor." He hangs up, and I head directly there, not wasting another moment or allowing myself to feel guilty about not discussing this with Cora first.

Her trust is important to me, but it means nothing if I lose her to Ricardo...and I refuse to let that happen.

The drive is short, made even shorter by the broken speed limits and red lights I've run. I don't care about anything other than the steps that need to be taken to free Cora from Ricardo, and the sooner I do that, the sooner we can begin our happily ever after—whatever that might be.

I pull up in the line of cars, park behind a construction truck, and hop out of mine, hitting the lock button on the key fob and marching straight into The Manor. People attempt to make eye contact with me, and I have to navigate around construction workers, but I don't pay a single one of them attention, the only person I'm here for is that big and brutish old man.

Catching his eye, I continue walking, not turning around or acknowledging him. I head straight into one of the secluded rooms off the lobby and wait for him to follow me in.

"What's this about?" he says once he's inside.

I take in his perfectly polished exterior—the tailored suit and shiny cufflinks. Dominic is a man of class and sophistication, something Ricardo knows nothing of. He's brutal and known for his ruthless nature, and I wouldn't be surprised if he could crush me with one word to any of his henchmen.

"I know about your *problem*," I start. "I found your mole. He's dead. But not before he told me who he was working for."

"Let me guess." Dominic runs his hand over his greying beard. "Ricardo."

I nod stiffly. "He's making a move to overthrow you. So far, he has John, Tony, and Vito on board."

"The old council." He pauses and asks, "What about the rest of them?"

"They claimed they didn't want to betray you."

"And yet none of them told me what was going on."

That's a fair point that I hadn't considered. In all my concern for Cora, I never actually stopped to think about how this might be impacting Dominic, only how I could benefit from the cross-over in their shared enemy.

"Who was the mole?" Dominic asks me.

"Harry."

He grips the backrest of a chair, his fingers digging into the plush leather. "That explains why he's been unreachable."

"Apologies, sir. I should have told you sooner. I've been trying to neutralize the situation."

"Who hired you?" His dark eyes bore into me.

"Miller," I lie, although it's not entirely false; Miller really did hire me, just not for what I'm referring to.

"He really should have told me, too." Dominic rubs his hands together and turns his body toward mine.

I can no longer sense his reaction, although I'm certain it can go in either one of two directions. Going along with my involvement in things, or him ending my life.

Here's to hoping he chooses the former, not the latter.

"There's only one thing we can do." Dominic stares at me intensely.

I wait for him to continue.

"We have to kill them all."

"Sir?" I attempt to wrap my head around what he just said. "You mean John, Vito, Tony, and Ricardo?"

But Dominic simply shakes his head. "No. I mean all of them."

"How?" I ask the question that has been weighing heavily on my mind.

"I don't know, not yet. But we'll figure it out. Give me a couple of weeks to discuss this with Magnus and Coen. We'll relay the plan once we're sure."

I want to tell him that we can't wait two weeks. That the time is ticking on this entire situation, but if I did, I would be betraying Cora more than I already am.

But if I don't...what if we can't pull this off ourselves?

37
CORA

I convince Miller to let me visit London one more time that week without throwing a fit. I would have done it anyway, but I wanted him to know instead of being blind-sided again. We negotiated that he would accept it if I allowed Silver to escort me, which allowed Silver to grill London on some of her dad's dealings.

It was a win-win for all of us, even though London is still going through hell in the hospital.

Doctors say she will eventually heal fully but may have aches and pains that will live with her for the rest of her life. Not to mention, the impact on her mental health.

She says she's fine, that she just wants out of that cooped-up room, but I know better than to accept she isn't deeply bothered by what's happening.

Thursday and Friday went by in a blur. Other than visiting London, I was able to focus on some portfolios I needed to put together for work. I assembled them mindlessly and waited for the guys' returns, hating every minute that they weren't near me.

I only heard from Ricardo once, and I don't know whether I should be alarmed or relieved.

June sent me a few texts and called me twice, but I never got back to her. I don't want to. Not when I still have no idea if our plan is going to work.

The plan that we spent the entire evening Friday going over, and the better half of this morning.

"Should we go through it again?" Miller asks us.

I shake my head, glancing at Silver and Alec to see if they need another recap.

"No," Silver says. "I think we're good."

"And you're good with this?" Miller focuses on me.

I nod. "I am."

Alec speaks up, "What's next?"

I take another glance between them and raise my hand. It shouldn't be the first thing on my mind, but if things don't work out, this very well could be my last chance to spend with all of them.

Collectively, they look to me to continue.

"Sex," I say bluntly. "Would anyone like to have sex?"

Silence, complete and utter silence befalls the room.

"Okay then," I slap my thighs and stand up from the couch. "Glad I made that awkward. I'm going to leave now." I turn to walk away and Silver latches onto my wrist, holding me from going any farther.

"Where do you want it?" Silver tugs me closer until I fall into his lap. His hands roam under my shirt and up my back.

"Like, together?" Alec circles his finger in the air in front of him. "All of us?"

I shrug. "I mean, you guys seem pretty okay with whatever we're doing here—the whole *sharing* me thing. Why not at the same time? Could be fun?"

"I'm game." Alec stands from his spot in the chair next to the couch. "Although, I've never had a foursome before, so I don't know what I'm doing. Heck, I've never had a threesome, either."

"This is probably new territory for all of us," I say and reach out to him.

"Or is this an orgy?" Alec comes over and sits next to me and Silver.

"I think an orgy is when we're all fucking," Miller finally speaks. "And I'm not having sex with anyone but her."

Just when I'm convinced he's not going to go along with my idea, he surprises me and comes closer. "Whatever makes you happy, our Queen."

A smile breaks across my face, and for the first time in my whole life, I'm convinced I really have died and gone to heaven. I've only ever dreamed of something like this, and it was only with two of them, not all three of them.

My core tightens at the thought of their hands on me, their mouths kissing my flesh, their cocks filling me up. I'm overwhelmed by the possibilities, and if I'm being honest, can't believe they've all agreed.

Silver swipes the hair off my shoulder and presses his lips against the sensitive skin of my neck. "Is there anything off-limits, Angel?"

I swallow down the anxious nerves that rise at his question and tell him, "You know what I like."

"I think we should take this to the bedroom." Silver wraps his arm around my waist and stands with me in his grasp, carrying me away like a rag doll and setting me gently onto my mattress.

The guys follow us and stand at each side of the bed as Silver remains at the foot of it.

Their eyes on me are enough to make my skin pebble with goosebumps and heat to rush straight between my legs.

Silver unbuttons his shirt and looks at the guys. "You plan on staying clothed or?"

LUNA PIERCE

Alec strips his shirt off without hesitation, and I'm reminded of Miller's back.

"You don't have to," I tell him.

Miller's jaw tenses before he decides to face his fear and expose himself in a way that I never thought he would with them. Pride swells within me. He climbs onto the mattress next to me and sighs.

"The things I'd do for you..." Miller's mouth finds mine, and he kisses me softly at first, his intensity picking up almost immediately.

The mattress moves, and I break away slightly to find Alec at my other side, our lips meeting and melting together.

Miller draws his attention to my chest, tugging my already pretty revealing top down to expose my chest, his breath cascading over my nipple before he pinches it between his teeth.

I moan into Alec as hands grip the waistband of my bottoms and drag them over my ass.

Heat lingers on my sex for a second prior to a warm tongue sliding ever so gently over my clit. Silver continues on his journey, kissing my thighs and digging his hands into them as he licks at my center.

He shoves a finger inside of me, and then another, spreading me open and taking his other hand to assault my aching clit. Silver places one more inside my pussy, filling me and arching them upward on my G-spot.

The sudden urge to pee hits me but I succumb to the pleasure of his torment and climax hard and fast.

"Fuck," I all but yell in Alec's mouth, my breath catching.

Silver grins up at me and pulls his hand out to lick his soaked fingers. "You're so fucking wet for us, Angel."

I sit up, yank my shirt over my head, and throw it on the floor with theirs. "Cocks out, now," I demand now that I'm fully fucking naked and hungry for them.

480

Silver is the first to unbuckle his belt, and I'm not surprised in the slightest. They might say they're willing to give me whatever I want, but he's the least afraid of actually following through with what that entails.

He grips his cock in his hand and looks right at me. "Where do you want it?"

I reach out to Miller and Alec, my hands skimming their cocks before falling to the comforter. "I want you all inside of me. At the same time." I don't even know how it's possible, but I want it.

Silver walks around the side of the bed, going past Miller and climbing onto the mattress. He settles in and pulls me onto his chest, my back to him. "Let's see what we can do about making that happen, Angel."

With Silver's help, I slide down onto his cock, my pussy already stretched and wet from him fucking me with his fingers.

I whimper and spread my legs apart on both sides of his, allowing him to fill me more.

"Think you can fit another?" Silver asks while keeping his hands on me, his hips gently thrusting upward, his cock hardening inside of me.

"Mmhm." I glance at Alec and extend my hand toward him, turning my attention to Miller. Licking my lips, I take his cock into my hand as he inches closer, stroking and spreading his precum onto his shaft. He might not be totally into this, but his cock sure is.

Alec climbs between my legs and lowers himself to lick my clit, making my entire body tense up. He rises on his knees, his thick cock in his grasp. "Are you sure?"

I nod while stroking Miller and move my legs farther apart.

His tip is warm as it slides against my entrance, looking for its own way in. Alec pushes along Silver's dick until he finds a spot to shove in.

I cry out at the fullness and do everything I can to relax and adjust to the way they fill me. How did I think it would be possible for all three of them to be inside of my pussy? And why am I still eager to figure out if we can make it happen?

"Is this okay?" Alec slowly continues, his dick sliding in with Silver's, both stretching me wider than I ever imagined I could be.

Miller's cock twitches in my hand, and I focus on him, pulling him toward me and grazing his tip over my lips. I open my mouth and take him in, my throat dying to be fucked until it's raw and my eyes water.

I clench around the two cocks buried inside of me and rock my hips as I suck on Miller.

Silver increases his movement and cups both of my breasts in his hands. "You're taking us so fucking well, Angel. You were made for us."

Alec leans back, his thumb pressing on my clit. He deepens his thrusts and moans. "Goddamn, baby. You really do feel so fucking good." He slams into me, and I moan around Miller's cock.

Miller grabs a fistful of my hair and takes control of the movements, his other hand wrapping around my throat as he fucks my face.

I gag but don't dare pull away, no, this is too fucking good, and I never want it to end.

"Tell us if it's too much, Angel," Silver says.

I reach out to Alec, my fingers trailing the hard lines of his abs until my hand lands on top of his to apply more pressure to my clit. Together, we move my orgasm even closer, my pussy clenching around them as they harden inside of me.

Moaning against Miller's cock, tears trickle down my cheeks, and I glance up at him, my head bobbing to the tempo he sets. He slows his stride but deepens his thrusts, hitting my throat until he's spilling his orgasm down the back of my mouth. I swallow every drop of him, and with Silver's fingers pinching my nipples hard and Alec's thumb rubbing my clit, I climax onto them, my pussy squeezing them so hard they orgasm, too, both of them grunting and filling me full.

I lie there on Silver's chest, my body nearly convulsing with pleasure, my breaths jagged as I try to catch them "Fuck. Next time we'll have to try all three of you at once..."

Alec, very carefully, pulls his throbbing cock out of me and holds onto my hips to release Silver's, too. "You're dripping with us, baby." Alec leaves a sweet kiss just above my pubic bone and collapses to the side on the bed.

Silver holds me to his strong, broad chest. "If anyone is putting a baby in you, it's us."

Miller, with his cock still in his hand, tells Alec, "Watch out." He climbs past him, taking the spot where Alec just was, and strokes his shaft along my entrance, getting himself hard again.

"What are you doing?" I ask him.

"Making it impossible to figure out who's putting a baby in you." Miller surprises me by shoving his cock inside of me, my pussy oozing with the remains of two other men. He leans down, finds my mouth with his, and kisses me with an intensity I've never experienced with him. He keeps one hand pressed to the mattress to keep himself upright and takes the other to weave along my jaw, tilting my face toward him as he kisses me with a renewed passion.

I moan into him, my core heightening with desire I thought was satiated until he made his declaration.

Silver holds me in place, his dick twitching against my ass, but otherwise remaining in place. He's allowing Miller to claim me, and I don't know what's hotter, Silver and Alec watching or Miller taking charge like this.

Miller lowers his hand around my throat again, pressing the sides of it gently, restricting my airflow. He swirls his tongue in my mouth and pulls away to look me in the eyes.

He deepens his thrusts, his cock slamming into me as he buries himself balls deep. "You. Belong. To. Us." Every word is another buck of his hips. "Do. You. Understand?"

I nod and rake my bottom lip between my teeth, tugging it so hard it breaks the skin. Blood trickles and Miller spots it, leaning down to smash his mouth onto mine again.

Whimpering, I tighten around him, his cock sparing me no mercy and throwing me over the edge of bliss once again, his own climax coming at the same fucking time as mine, both of us constricting with each other.

"That's. It. Baby. Girl." He fucks me the rest of the way through my climax, making sure to fill me with every drop he has to give. Miller, finally satisfied, rests his forehead on mine. "I fucking love you, Cora."

Silver nuzzles against my ear. "I love you, too, Angel."

"Yeah, me too," Alec says from his spot on his side, his elbow propped up with his head on it like he's watching his favorite TV show and not his girl getting railed by another guy.

I smile, my heart just as full as my pussy, and sigh. "I love you guys, too."

But just as soon as I'm overwhelmed by joy, I'm reminded that if things don't go to plan tomorrow, nothing will ever be the same. Not me, not them, not us.

3 8
CORA

I take an Uber to Ricardo's house because I don't feel like ruining the plan immediately by explaining to him where I got a very expensive Porsche.

Things are already complicated enough without risking it any more than they are.

Walking up the front pathway, I brace myself for what's to come, and plaster on my best fake smile to get me through. If I can make it past today, maybe, just maybe, our plan will actually work.

I knock on the door and wait impatiently to be greeted.

It only takes a moment until the large door opens and one of Ricardo's minions motions for me to step inside before slipping out the way I came in and shutting the door.

It's sort of strange that Ricardo doesn't have more people surrounding him at all times, but maybe I'm just seeing what he wants me to see.

I've been made an idiot underestimating what a man could do in the past, I refuse to let that happen again.

"I'm back here," Ricardo says from down the hall in his creepy jerk-off room.

I approach, my footsteps pattering against the floor and doing a poor job of blocking out the sound of my racing heart.

Entering the room, Ricardo holds out his finger to me and continues with the phone call he's on.

"Uh huh, I understand." He pauses. "Yes, call me back when you have more information." He hangs up and faces me with a sigh. "There's my pet." Ricardo coughs and pounds on his chest with his fist. "I'm glad we'll have no distractions today."

He's referring to London, who's still in the hospital, but I don't dare say that to him and rile him up before we've even begun.

"Shall we get started?" I walk in further, trip over the corner of the rug, and fall into a heap on the floor, my clutch spilling open the contents.

"Clumsy bitch," he slurs and doesn't bother moving from his spot to help me up.

But that's what I was counting on.

"I'm so sorry," I say as I reach for the items, making sure to leave the false tube of lip-gloss tucked under the couch it rolled beneath. I brace myself on the corner table, sticking another one of the bugs underneath the bottom of the surface. "I'm such a klutz."

"Whatever." Ricardo lowers himself onto the couch and wafts his hand in the air. "Stop wasting time. Clothes are in the bathroom down the hall."

I nod in compliance, slip out of the room, and breathe a sigh of relief at the first phase of the plan working. Now, here's to hoping I can pull the rest of it off.

My stomach coils at the pile of measly fabric waiting for me, but I come to terms with the fact that this must be done. It's the only way forward. I maneuver myself into a bright red piece, the sheer lace barely covering my most private areas, and slide into a pair of heels sitting on the floor. In the mirror, I adjust my tits and mentally give my reflection a little pep talk.

With every ounce of confidence I can muster, I strut down the hall and into the room, catching his attention the second I'm through the door.

"Damn, pet, you're really wearing that one." He licks his lips and reaches for the waistband of his dress slacks. "I'm already hard just looking at you." Ricardo points. "Come, stand here while I take a closer look."

I walk over to the spot and muster the courage to remain in place while he violates me with his stare. "I wanted to ask you...about my mother."

Ricardo's brows pinch together. "After, pet, not right now." He pulls out his drooping cock and squeezes it in his hand, stroking the length to get himself harder.

"I just thought I'd be more compliant if, you know, I knew she was okay."

Ricardo clenches his jaw and his hairy nostrils flare. He smacks at the couch to locate his discarded phone, his eyes still trained on my body as he jerks himself. He only glances away briefly to push a couple of buttons on his screen, the speaker crackling to life.

He doesn't take his hand off his cock as a voice comes through the speaker.

"State your name," a man says.

"Suzannah Price."

My mouth nearly drops open at hearing my mother's voice.

"And state your current condition, on a scale of one to five," the man asks of her.

She clears her throat. "A four, maybe. I'm feeling quite better, honestly. Very pleased with the results and ready to go home."

I chew at the inside of my cheek to stop myself from crying. I had worried so fucking hard this entire time that I never pushed to find out how she was because I couldn't come to terms with the idea that maybe this had all been for nothing, that my mother was already dead.

But upon hearing her voice, I'm filled with hope that this really might be over soon. That my mother might make it out of this alive, despite the cancer that I only recently found out she had.

Ricardo clicks off his phone and tosses it aside. "Happy?"

I nod and step closer to him. "Yes. Thank you."

"Turn around, pet, let me see that ass of yours."

I go along with his demands, even if they make me sick, because every moment I distract him is another that the guys have to get done with their part in all of this.

"So fucking perky, pet. I can't wait to have you. I'm going to have so much fun wrecking that little cunt of yours."

I stand there and do what I can to block out his disgusting remarks. Honestly, it helps that he had me turn around because then I don't have to watch what he's doing to that sad excuse of a cock of his.

"Go put the pink one on, and hurry back."

Without a single ounce of hesitation, I leave the room and return to the bathroom. I swallow down the bout of nausea that rises and yank the red strappy thing off me and throw it on the floor. A sigh leaves me as I try to make sense of the pink article he ordered me to wear. I step into it, nearly falling down, and steady myself against the wall as I shove both of my feet through what I assume are the right openings and pull them up to cover my body.

Cover being a massive overstatement. My nipples show through the sheer fabric, and there's no concealing my pussy lips with the minimal fabric.

"A means to an end," I remind myself. "Pretty soon, this will be over."

Or, pretty soon we'll all be dead, or worse, Ricardo will get his wish of taking my body as his property.

"Yeah, pet, I knew you'd wear that one well," he spits out once I return to the room he's in. Ricardo strokes his cock harder, so hard I wonder if it must hurt but quickly realize that I don't care about him or his dick. "Come here and stand so I can see you."

I approach, settling in the spot I was just a few minutes ago.

"Closer," he tells me, his face contorted as he jacks off faster. "Let me smell your cunt."

But before I can be subjected to his demeaning nature, he ejaculates onto his dress pants with a grunt.

"You made a mess of me, pet," he says while looking at his lap. His phone rings, distracting us both from his embarrassing condition. Ricardo reaches for it, swiping to connect and putting it between his face and shoulder. "Talk to me," he tells the person on the other end while reaching for a tissue to clean himself up.

I stand there because I don't know what else I'm supposed to do.

Ricardo frowns and straightens himself, holding the phone with his hand. "What do you mean, he's *dead*?" He wipes at the ropey semen coating his pants and pinches it between his tissue-covered fingers to pick it off him.

I avert my gaze in an attempt to distract myself from vomiting on him.

He flicks the tissue aside without any consideration for where it lands. Ricardo stands, shoves his tiny cock into his pants, and buttons himself up. "How is that possible? How did he die? A fucking car accident, you're kidding me? What do you mean that's not all?"

I continue to remain in place, grateful that his attention is on something other than me.

Ricardo shoves past me and goes straight over to his bar, pouring himself a drink and downing it in one swig. "Carlo and Sam are *both* dead. Has anyone checked on Dean? He's the only one who didn't..." He pauses his statement and turns his back to me like that will somehow block me from being able to hear his top-secret conversation. "He's the only one left who didn't agree. Are John or Vito in on this? Have you called Tony? Let me go, I'll call him now."

He hangs up the phone and pushes a few buttons before pressing it to his ear again.

"Tony, yeah, it's Ricky. Have you heard the news? You have? Are you in on this? You need to tell me if you are. I didn't authorize this." He stumbles over his words and it brings me great joy that he has no idea that I'm knowledgeable of what happened.

It was all very clever, really. Carlo is a careless drunk driver, making his death so very easy to pull off. Sam on the other hand, his health wasn't that great to start with, giving him a heart attack was like taking candy from a baby. Dean, though...poor guy was highly allergic to fish. Such a shame his new maid was careless with the soup she prepared him for lunch. It took the guys no time to stage each of their deaths, but now? Now things depend on what Ricardo does next. That part of the plan is already in motion, too, but if he doesn't react the way we think he will, fate will have to take the wheel on what happens to all of us.

"I'm calling an emergency meeting, you know where. Yes. *Now,* you fucking imbecile." Ricardo hangs up and swallows another unhealthy swig of booze, his nerves seemingly getting the best of him. He slams the glass on the tray and exhales oh so fucking dramatically. Slowly, he turns toward me. "I'm afraid I have to leave. There's something rather pressing and urgent I have to attend to."

I press my hand to my chest. "I hope everything is okay. Can I do anything?"

Ricardo walks over, pausing right in front of me. He takes my chin into his hand and yanks my face toward him. "You're being entirely too obedient today, pet."

He narrows his gaze and I grow worried that I may have just spoiled this entire fucking plan by being a fucking brat.

"What you can do," he says, his hot, nasty breath nipping at my nose. "Is get that little pussy of yours ready, because come Wednesday, I'm going to put my fucking seed in you. I need an heir now more than ever."

I nod as much as I can while he still holds me in his grasp. "Yes, of course."

"Yes, what?"

"Yes, sir."

He releases me abruptly, shoving my face away, my neck cracking at the force of his hand. Pain shoots down my side as I brace myself from falling, and I ignore it all because this is almost over. Everything is going according to plan. Three of the six men that he calls his allies are dead, and my mother is alive and doing well. A few weeks ago, I thought I'd never make it through this, and here I am, the ending so close I can fucking taste it.

"Be here at six p.m. on Wednesday. I'll be waiting for you. Get changed and get the fuck out of my house. Don't touch anything or I'll make sure to make you pay for it when that cunt finally becomes mine in just a few days." He leaves the room, my heart pounding in disbelief that everything has worked so far.

Are we really going to pull this off?

I hesitate before leaving the room, not wanting to follow too closely on his tail. Gathering my things, I slip into the bathroom and change out of the ridiculous outfit and into my regular clothes. Leaving the rest of the garments there in a heap and shoving my clutch up under my arm, I march down the hall with my chin held high and leave this place for what I can only hope is the very last time.

The outside air hits me unlike ever before, smelling fresher and cleaner than I recall. A smile creeps across my face but I try to hide it until I'm down the walkway and turn onto the side-walk. I decide to stroll a little further, putting a couple houses between me and Ricardo's place prior to ordering an Uber.

I pull out my phone, stop near an intersection, and click on the app, tires squealing drawing my attention from my screen to the car zooming in the near distance. Stepping back, I watch as it approaches and slams on the brakes in front of me. I lose a breath as Silver gets out of the driver's side, his face solemn, not matching the look on mine. I blink, unsure what could possibly be wrong when everything else is so right.

My lips part, and I go to say something but it comes out jumbled.

"I came as soon as I found out," Silver says, something seriously haunting in his tone.

"Found out what?" My heart tightens at the endless possibilities running through my mind. I glance around him, not seeing Miller or Alec with him. "The guys? Are they?"

Silver shakes his head. "They're fine, Cora, it's about your mom."

"Oh," I say, so sure of myself. "She's fine, I just heard a recording like ten minutes ago." I throw a thumb in the direction I came but my words don't seem to pacify his distraught nature.

"Cora, Angel, I just came from the morgue. Your mom, she's dead."

This time, it's me shaking my head. "That's impossible. She, she's fine."

"I need you to listen to me, Cora. Your mom is dead. She's been dead a while now. She's been on ice."

"I don't believe you. There must be some mix-up." I refuse to accept what he's saying because it can't be true. "Take me to her."

For the next few minutes, it's like I'm frozen in time, my mind racing and my heart pounding but nothing making any sense. How could he possibly know who my mom is or that she's dead? Especially when I just heard her voice.

I step onto the ground behind what I'm assuming is the morgue and walk toward the back entrance of the building.

Silver opens the door for me and points ahead once we're inside. "This way," he says, but it sounds like he's in a tunnel, or really far away.

I glance at him to confirm he's right next to me and continue walking, one foot after another, closer to the woman who cannot possibly be my mother. There must be a mistake, that's the only explanation for any of this.

Silver nods an acknowledgment at the man standing in a cold room, the guy latching onto a handle and pulling out a long tray with what I can only assume is a covered body on it.

I approach, convinced this is a mix-up, and reach for the cover to reveal the body.

Silent tears stream down my cheeks, and I stare at the woman who looks just fucking like my mom, only she's pale and grey, her face somehow sunken in despite her appearing bloated.

"No," is all I can say.

Every shred of hope I had gained rips out from under me in one solid motion as my legs grow weak and I collapse into Silver's arms.

He holds onto me, and my world falls apart, everything I sacrificed up until this point has been for nothing.

39
MILLER

We accounted for so many variables, just not the one where Cora's mom was already dead.

This whole entire situation was fucked up, but there was still hope, a chance that we could right all the wrongs and make her suffering mean something.

But that reality is a thing of the past with the recent news that her mom is gone and has been for quite some time.

I only got limited information from Silver, but from what I did gather, Ricardo put her mother on ice at the morgue when she died, probably to buy him more time with this sick fucking deal he made.

What kind of sadistic, fucked up person would force someone to go through with their end of the bargain when they no longer had the leverage to uphold theirs?

The one singular saving grace is if we can follow through with the rest of the plan and eliminate Ricardo, giving Cora some semblance of knowing he is dead.

And hopefully, in the next hour, we can deliver that.

I glance down at the broken girl in my arms and back at the screen in the distance with various cameras showing different viewpoints of The Manor, courtesy of Silver's hacker content. The mere fact that he was able to get us these feeds is a true testament to how skilled he is. That place is supposed to be impenetrable, totally safe from this sort of attack.

Cora wipes at her face and sits up, surprising both Silver and I who were holding onto her. She points her finger in the general direction of the screen. "Where is he? Why isn't he there yet?"

Silver and I scoot to the edge of our seats and scan the feeds.

"I don't know," I say, my impatience getting the best of me as I rise to my feet. "I'm going there."

Silver stands, too. "No. I will."

Cora continues to keep her gaze trained on the screen. "No one is going anywhere."

"He'll spot you from a million miles away," Silver tells me. "He's not looking for me. I won't draw his attention." He shifts his attention to the girl between us. "You need to stay here with her."

Silver's right—after my stunt with shooting Ricardo, even in his paranoid state, he'll notice me the second I walk through the front door. Silver, on the other hand, he'd never blink twice at him wandering around The Manor. He'd be just another face in the crowd of criminals, no one to cause his suspicions to grow.

He lowers himself back onto the couch and puts his hand on Cora's knee, careful not to startle her. "Hey, Angel." He keeps his voice low. "Do you need anything before I leave?"

"I need you to stop treating me like I'm a bomb that's ready to explode. I'm fine." She wipes at her cheeks again. "And I'll be better once he's dead. I had my pity party, now it's over."

I walk closer to the screen and point at a small, but rather large figure. "There's Vito."

"Are you sure?" Silver comes over, taking a better look. "Yeah, that is him. Won't be much longer until the rest of them are there." He looks to Cora. "I'll be back once it's done. Okay?"

She nods and reaches for the glass of bourbon he poured her earlier. Cora swallows it in one gulp. "Where's Alec?"

"He's with Dom on the other side of town, like we talked about," I remind her.

"Okay. Just making sure." Cora sets the glass down. "This will all be over soon."

Silver meets my gaze, a sort of silent agreement falling over us. I tip my head briefly and he does the same.

"Call me if there's any trouble," I tell him as he's walking to the door.

Once he's gone, I return to Cora's side, watching this real-life thriller movie play out before us. Everything was going so fucking well, until it wasn't, and now, if anything else goes wrong, I'm not sure how Cora is going to cope. If Ricardo dies, there will be a silver lining, but if he manages to cock-roach his way out of the situation...I'm scared for the state of her mental health.

Minutes pass and we watch the screen together, silence falling between us.

Cora anxiously rocks, and I put my hand on her back, unsure how to make her worries disappear. Part of me wishes that I would have stood up to Silver and insisted I went to The Manor, just to put a bullet in Ricardo's skull. But if I had, I would have been killed on the spot, making Cora grieve for more than just the loss of her mother.

I hate sitting here, not knowing what the outcome is going to be or being able to do anything about it, and not being able to reassure her that everything will be fine, when it very well might not be.

"There's John and Tony," I say while pointing at the left side of the screen.

More time passes, and I check my watch, Silver no doubt having arrived at The Manor by now.

Cora chews at her nail. "What if something happened to Silver?"

"Silver's tough," I tell her and tug her closer to me. "He's been through worse, and plus, The Manor is the safest place for him."

However, how can I say that when I know what we're planning for Ricardo? Hopefully, that thought doesn't cross her mind, too.

Cora's phone buzzes on the table in front of us and I grab it, reading the notification that comes across. "Alec says he'll be here as soon as he can."

"Okay," she says, not taking her eyes off the television. "Is that Silver?" Cora hops up from the couch and walks over to the screen. "Right there?"

"That's him," I confirm, scanning the rest for the man we're still waiting on.

Silver glances up at the camera near him and raises his fingers slightly to acknowledge us.

"See, he's good, everything is going to be fine." Although, I don't know whether I'm trying to pacify myself or Cora.

My eyes trail over every inch of the feeds, wondering and waiting for that stupid fuck to appear.

"Where is he? What's taking so long?" Cora crosses her arms over her chest and paces in front of the TV, her gaze never leaving it.

I could ask the same question but I don't want her to think I'm as worried as I really am. Maybe Ricardo saw through our plan and decided going to The Manor wasn't actually the best thing he could do. Maybe he got suspicious of the men he's working with and figured they might be plotting against him. What if any number of things happened, preventing him from stepping foot in that place?

But just as the endless what-ifs completely consume me, Ricardo Gardella walks into one of the frames.

"There." I point, a bit too aggressively. "Right there."

Ricardo makes his way over to his so-called friends and traitors of Dominic's, the four of them huddled together, no doubt whispering amongst themselves. It's hard to tell exactly through the small section of the screen he's in. Ricardo talks with his hands, while the other three's body language seems more closed off, skeptical even. Ricardo throws his arms wide, as if gesturing to the building they're in, and waves at someone in the distance.

A hotel worker immediately takes action, stalking toward the group of men. A moment later, he's leading them further into the building, past the construction closing off the first-floor conference area, and toward the elevators.

A construction worker finishes doing something to one of the out-of-service elevators, giving the guys a thumbs up and moving the sign out of the way.

Ricardo slaps the man's shoulder and stops him to talk, the guy accommodating his request.

Cora remains stiff next to me, her hands clutched to her chest, her breaths short and jagged, mirroring my own.

Silver moves from one feed to the next, trying to get a better vantage point on the action.

A couple walks past Ricardo to use the newly opened elevator but Ricardo cuts them off, shoving himself in front of them to get on first, his comrades following him in with the annoyed couple coming up the rear.

Fuck, that wasn't part of the plan.

I dig my fingers into my arm as I watch the door to the elevator close, the feed only showing part of it on the screen. I start to relax when I'm certain we've succeeded, only to be let down by a hand shoving through the open space and making the door open again. Ricardo steps outside of the elevator, turns to tell the rest of the people something, his finger held up in the air toward them and his cell phone in his hand.

Fuck, fuck, fuck.

I drag my own phone out, dialing Silver's number immediately.

Staring at the screen, I see the moment it connects on his end, him reaching and sliding it out of his pocket, him putting it to his ear.

"Yes?"

"Abort mission," I tell him. "Abort fucking mission."

He does no such thing, instead, he takes off in the direction of the elevators.

"What's happening?" Cora asks me. "What's he doing? Why isn't he leaving?"

"Silver, get out of there. *That's an order,*" I all but yell into the phone.

But he doesn't listen, or at least he doesn't obey. He lowers his arm to his side and practically slams into Ricardo when he rounds the corner.

Everything else happens in a flash—the camera feeds shaking, the dust cloud, the loud explosion that drowns out the mild chatter that was once filling the feeds. The feeds crackle, not a single one of them left running once the final part of our plan was set in place.

Cora presses her fingers to the screen where Silver just was and a tear rolls down her cheek. "He..." She turns toward me. "He wasn't supposed to be there."

My heart constricts and the unknowns of the situation hit me like a ton of bricks.

Ricardo was not on that elevator. The one that we orchestrated to collapse with Ricardo and the last three men who were causing issues. We never thought anyone else would be on it with them, let alone what would happen if Ricardo got off at the last minute. None of us were supposed to be in the building, we thought it would be better that way, drawing less attention to the fact that it was us who carried this inconceivable mission out. This was fabricated to appear like an accident...and now one of us is down and our target was not taken out.

I dial Silver, and it goes straight to voicemail. I hit the call button again and get the same response.

"He's fine," I say. "Silver's fine, don't worry. He's smart, he would have never..." But I don't finish that statement, because I never thought Silver would have gotten that close to the elevators to begin with. He knew it was going to crash, why would he be so foolish to be near it when it happened.

My phone rings, Cora and I both jolting our attention to it.

"It's Alec," I tell her and hit the button to connect. "Hey, Alec, you're on speaker."

"Did it work?"

I share a glance with Cora and hate the overwhelming feeling that I failed her sweeping over me. I promised her that I would make this problem go away, and not only did I not succeed in that, but I may have just gotten someone she loves killed.

"No," I answer. "Everyone but target."

Cora steps closer. "Silver was there. We can't get ahold of him. I don't know if..."

"We'll be right there," someone on the other end of the line says, their voice gruff and familiar.

The call disconnects and Cora stares at me. "Who was that?"

"Dominic."

"Why is he involved?"

I tilt my head, unsure of how anything I have to say is going to impact her. She swore us to secrecy, yet Silver went and involved Dominic anyway. I thought that she had suspected it, but the look on her face right now tells me that she didn't, that she trusted us when we promised to keep it between us.

She sighs and shakes her head. "It doesn't matter. The only thing I care about now is if Silver is okay." Cora positions her body toward the screen that is filled with static, and I'm left wondering if I've made the biggest mistake of my life by letting him walk out of here.

40

ALEC

oot pressed to the floorboard; I drive as fast as I can across town to The Manor with Dominic in the passenger seat.

He doesn't say anything, and I don't either. There's nothing to be said, other than the fact that we fucked up.

Our plan was tight, carefully laid out, and working like a charm until we found out Cora's mom was dead, and since then, everything has fallen the fuck apart.

I hate it. For her, for us.

The streets surrounding The Manor are chaos, with cars driving the wrong way, and people running as a fire engine blares through.

"Follow it," Dominic points ahead at the emergency vehicle clearing a path.

I get right up on its ass and do exactly that, not stopping until we're in front of the building.

We both get out in haste, a police officer yelling at us that we can't park there.

Dominic glares at him and the officer throws his hands up.

"Sorry, Mr. Adler. I didn't realize it was you."

We rush past the people standing in front of the building, clutching their trembling bodies, and muttering to each other about what happened.

The entire lobby is filled with thick, dusty air that makes it impossible to see well. I squint and scan, looking and hoping and wishing I could find that dumb old man who insisted on coming here.

Paramedics rush by with someone on their stretcher and my heart drops the second I recognize them.

It's not Silver, no, it's the man we meant to kill, Ricardo fucking Gardella.

He doesn't appear too injured, a bit covered in soot, but aside from the oxygen bag they have covering his face, he seems okay.

Dom and I exchange a glance and push further into the building, stepping over rubble and overthrown furniture.

"We've got another one!" a medic yells to his colleagues, waving his arm over his head.

I run over, my hands gripping the debris covering him and toss it aside, not caring that it's slicing my flesh.

"Fuck," I say and keep doing what I can to free him. "Help me," I tell Dominic as he approaches. The two of us, with the help of the medic, yank stuff off Silver.

"You shouldn't be back here," the medic tells us even though it seems more like a formality than anything.

Dominic grunts and nearly falls backward as he heaves a massive hunk of concrete off Silver.

Silver gasps for air, his face almost unrecognizable with all the soot covering him.

The other medics approach with a stretcher and reach for Silver to hoist him on top of it, but Silver has other plans. Instead of climbing on, he smacks their hands away and pushes himself up from the ground.

I weave a hand under his arm to help him despite him clearly having it covered on his own.

He dusts his torso off, doing next to nothing to actually clean himself and mutters, "I'm fine, help someone who needs it." Silver glares at the medics who, at first, don't take no for an answer, until they finally do.

Dominic clears his throat. "I'll get him to the hospital. You look for more casualties."

Silver doesn't bother waiting for Dom or me to help him, he simply steps over some of the shit we pulled off him and continues forward like the fucking Terminator.

"Shit," he blurts out, glancing over his shoulder. "My phone."

"I think the phone is the least of your worries," Dominic tells him and pushes on his back to keep him moving. "We need to get out of here, *now*."

Once we're outside, I cough and blink, my eyes watering at the lack of shit floating in the air. I hadn't realized how terrible it was inside until I was free of it all. Glancing down, I see that I'm covered in dust particles from the accident.

"Here." I hand Silver my cell. "Call Cora."

Silver snatches it out of my grasp, dialing her number and pressing the phone to his ear.

We continue moving toward the SUV, all of us loading in without a second thought.

"Yeah, I'm fine," Silver tells what I can only assume is Cora. He clears his throat, hacking a bit, his gaze trailing to his blood-covered palm. "That's not good."

Dominic sighs. "Take us to the hospital."

"I said I'm fine," Silver barks from the back seat.

I shove the vehicle into reverse, bumping into the car behind me to free up space to get out. Perhaps I shouldn't have parked as close as I did to the fire truck when we arrived. Either way, I don't give a fuck, this isn't my car and there are tons of distractions to mask my petty crime.

Silver shoves my cell toward me. "Here."

But when I take it, the screen is off. "So, how did it go?" I glance at him before taking my phone and tossing it into the cup holder.

"She's pissed." Silver wipes at his forehead. "Can't say I blame her."

Dominic turns in his seat to get a better look at Silver. "Do you two want to tell me how Cora is involved in all of this?"

I meet Silver's gaze in the rearview mirror, hoping like hell he will take the lead on explaining this one.

And thankfully, he does.

Silver fills Dominic in as best as he can, leaving out key details here and there, like the fact that Ricardo is planning on using Cora as his personal baby-making machine. Cora is indebted to Ricardo, Silver just redacts explicitly how. He explains the somewhat complicated nature of our relationship, Dom nodding along, his own relationship making that part of the story easy to digest.

"So, the deal is off then, if her mother is dead?" Dominic says.

"In theory, yes, although there's still the matter of her father, and the debt that is owed."

"How much is it?" Dominic asks the question we all once wondered, too.

"It doesn't matter. Ricardo already accepted her as payment." Silver scoots to the middle of the back seat, that confession no doubt solidifying Cora's debt to Ricardo in Dominic's mind. "And," he adds. "I'm not certain if Ricardo is aware that Cora knows her mom is dead."

Dom, with his hand on the middle console, turns toward Silver. "She's supposed to go there Wednesday?"

Silver nods and I hate the direction that this conversation is going.

The two of them don't say anything else, a sort of silent understanding falling between them, the same one settling over me.

I grip the steering wheel and keep driving because there's no way I can convince them of what they're already certain of.

41

CORA

"𝒥 got you something," Miller says in the doorway of my bedroom. Slowly, he steps inside, a box in his grasp.

I watch him in the mirror until he's right behind me.

"What is it?" I ask and consider the possibilities. At this point, doesn't he realize that I hate surprises?

"Well." He spreads his hand over the top and pulls off the lid, revealing something shiny and exquisite. "I told you that I'd get you a crown." Miller carefully takes the thing out of the box and says, "May I?"

"You're not serious," I tell him as he sets the delicately jeweled crown on my head. My fingers graze over the hard and cold surface of the crystals and I suddenly grow very curious about how much this damn thing cost. Not because the value matters, but because I'm not convinced he didn't spend an arm and a leg just because he could.

"I want you to wear it, today, to remind yourself that you are our queen, that I have every faith in you." Miller fixes my hair and settles it over my shoulders. "I am so proud of you, how far you've come, how far I know you will go." He presses his lips to my cheek and meets my gaze in the mirror. "I love you, Cora. I believe in you."

Taking a deep breath, I exhale and study the extravagant thing on my head. It's stunning and belongs to someone much more worthy. And yet, I still feel empowered by wearing it, and can't bring myself to take it off. I press the edges down, noting how sturdy it is, how it fits me perfectly, as if it was custom-made for the specific measurements of my skull. Although, I wouldn't put it past Miller to have done exactly that. He had once told me he would get me one and that it wouldn't be *too flashy*, but when has he ever not gone above and beyond?

"I love it," I tell him and turn to face him. "I love you."

He lowers himself and gently kisses my lips, my heart swelling with admiration.

"Do you have everything you need?" He asks me, his hands landing on my shoulders as he looks me over.

"I do," I say, the remainder of our plan having to be revised and me stepping into the role of the only one who could ensure things get finished.

Sure, one of them could have marched up to Ricardo's place and fought their way in, risking their own life to *maybe* end his, but my way, it's the guaranteed win—even if I have to go in there alone and put myself in danger.

The plan isn't without risks, we're aware of that, but it's the reward that outweighs them and ironically, with Dominic now included in our loop, he was the vote that pushed the decision in my favor.

I was the one who started this, and I will be the one to end it.

Even if I lose my life in the process. Ricardo may have tortured me, hurt me, scared me, but no one will ruin my life other than me, and today, I'm going to make damn sure of it.

And so, I give one farewell kiss to each of my men and leave them behind in the lavish apartment that Miller bought for me.

Ordering an Uber, I wait impatiently at the front of The Wellerton—my temporary home.

I should feel afraid, but instead, all I feel is the deep-seated desire to have this done and over with, no matter the outcome. I cannot live in fear anymore, and the sooner this is finished, the sooner I can find peace, whatever that may mean.

"Damn, girl, nice tiara," the young Uber driver says when I climb into the back seat.

"It's a crown, actually," I correct him.

"Oh, shit, my bad. What's the difference?" He pushes a button on his phone and pulls out onto the street.

"A crown is a complete circle, worn to represent power and authority. A tiara is something worn by beauty pageant winners and the occasional bride." Among other things, but I won't bore him with the details, especially when they aren't important.

"I see, I see. That's sick." The guy looks over his shoulder at me. "So, you're like royalty or some shit?"

I force a smile. "Or some shit."

"Cool." He gives his attention to the road, and I'm grateful that he doesn't bother asking any more questions. It's not that I don't mind answering them, but my mind is laser-focused on the task at hand—not fucking this up.

I imagine all the ways I could end Ricardo's life, my thoughts turning into something darker than I ever imagined. What have I become in the last month? The person I am today is nothing like the girl I was then. And I worry that she might be someone I can never return to, a past version of me that died along the way because of the traumas she'd experienced.

Would I even want to be her if I could? That girl was scared and alone, insecure and afraid of letting anyone in. Sure, she was not as cynical and murderous, but that girl was weak, and I never want to be weak ever again.

"Here we are," the Uber driver says as he pulls up in front of

Ricardo's mansion. "Damn, you really are royalty, aren't you?" He cranes his head to take a better look at Ricardo's house.

I slip out, not saying another word, and slide my phone out, tipping and rating him before I forget. It would be a shame if this mission failed like the last one and I died; this poor Uber driver thinking he isn't worthy of his gratuity.

Exhaling, I square my shoulders and bring my chin up, summoning every single ounce of bad bitch energy I have within me. "You've got this, Cora, don't back out now."

One step in front of the other, I close the distance between me and my so-called fate. The knocker on the door is hard in my grasp as I slam it against the surface and wait for what's on the other side.

"You're late," Ricardo says the second he opens the door, his usual annoyed expression written all over his disgusting face.

I glance at my wrist even though I'm not wearing a watch. "By a couple of minutes, maybe." I shouldn't be mouthing off to him this soon, but it's hard when I know what I have in store for him.

He grabs my arm and yanks me inside, that shoulder injury of mine flaring up and shooting a hot lance of pain through me. "Get inside before someone sees you." Ricardo pokes his head out, looking one way then the other, and slams the door.

"Is everything okay?" I ask him like I have no idea what could possibly be causing his paranoia to flare up.

"Yes," he spits out. "Everything is *fine*." Ricardo's cold gaze trails over my body. "And it will be better soon enough." He narrows his focus on my head. "What on earth are you wearing?" He licks his lips. "Never mind that. Finally, you're all mine. I can't wait to have my way with you."

I do my best to not let his remarks bother me. "Where should we get started?" I probably never should have worn this gaudy thing that Miller got me to Ricardo's house, but it surprisingly does make me feel a hell of a lot more powerful, and knowing Miller, he probably planted a camera on it to get a front-row seat to the action. Miller is generous, that's for sure, but he's calculated, too. Him putting that tracker in each of the purses he bought me proof of that.

Ricardo latches onto my hand and takes off down the hall. "How about the room we've shared so many memories in?"

I go along with him, my feet stumbling underneath me as he pulls me aggressively, the plan in place jumbling around in my head and growing fuzzy. What if I get this wrong? What if I can't pull it off? What if Ricardo is the one who comes out on top and succeeds in taking my body against my will?

Suddenly, all that confidence I once felt is left on the front doorstep of Ricardo's mansion.

He releases me with a push, tossing me into the room he jerked off to me, not only once, but twice. The same one where he beat his daughter to her near death, and the place Miller shot him. I recall each of those instances and channel the rage I felt at being so fucking helpless.

Never again, I remind myself.

I plaster on a seductive grin and turn toward Ricardo, growing bold and planting my hand on his shoulder. "Why don't you have a seat and allow me?"

He eyes me carefully and after I'm convinced he's not going to agree, he does, settling into the oversized chair he pleasured himself in.

I set my clutch on the table, walking toward him, one foot in front of the other. Once I reach him, I turn around, lowering my body onto his lap and grind my ass into his crotch. I nearly vomit but continue, the only way out of this mess being through.

Bending at the hip, I succumb to his grimy hands on my waist as he groans.

"Oh, yeah, pet, this is what I'm talking about. I knew you'd give in to me and give me what I want."

My fingers graze my stiletto heels and I weave them under the straps to unbuckle them. "Let me get more comfortable," I tell Ricardo as I slip out of my shoes. I stand from his lap and drop down onto my knees in front of him, his eyes lighting up like a kid on Christmas morning. After I stroke the length of his thighs, I break away to unbutton my top, reaching into my bra to pull out the blade that's meant to slit his fucking throat.

But Ricardo senses the threat before I've secured the weapon, his hand latching onto my wrist with great force. "You fucking bitch. Think you can outsmart me."

My heart pounds hard, my vision going light and dark all at the same time. I should have waited, I should have been more careful, I should have done anything other than rush this because rushing it is exactly what gave me away. Why did I think I could pull this off? Because I killed my boss? I murder one fucking person and suddenly I'm a master at it?

Frantically, I reach with my other hand, desperately searching for anything to help me.

Ricardo grips me tighter, the circulation to my hand being cut off with each squeeze.

I take hold of the only thing I can think of, my fucking heel, and glance down at it, wondering what the fuck I'm going to do with it. Only, those murderous tendencies running through my veins gives me what might be the best and worst idea of my life. Seizing the place my foot was a moment prior, I yank my arm backward and heave it forward, slamming the pointed edge of the heel directly into Ricardo's cheek.

He drops me immediately, reaching for his face.

I hit him again, this time with more force, the heel penetrating his flesh.

"You fucking bitch," he yells at me while holding onto himself.

"You. Said. That. Already," I tell him, each word another blow to the face with my stilettos, courtesy of Miller. Climbing back onto Ricardo's lap in a way that he never expected, I don't let up. Not when he tries to shove me, not when he cries out for help. I keep smashing the sharp edge of my heel into his face until he's unrecognizable, his body twitching with what life is left in him.

It isn't until moments later, when hands grip my shoulders, that I realize I won.

And how fucking anticlimactic of a victory it is.

I'm pulled off what remains of Ricardo and the murder weapon is taken from me.

"Cora, Angel." Silver meets my gaze, his voice soft and gentle. "You did it." His face is speckled in blood, and I'm not sure why or how, but he seems okay, and that's all that matters.

He's okay. I'm okay. This is over.

"We have to get you out of here," he tells me but all I want is to turn my attention back to Ricardo and make sure he never hurts another person ever again.

"But I..." I try to get free of Silver's hold on me. "I have to make sure."

"He's dead, Angel. I promise."

But his promise falls flat, because he's made and broken them before.

As if he senses my exact thought, he releases me and pulls out a gun from his waistband. "Here." Silver shoves the gun into my hand, flicking off the safety and taking his own hand to guide mine to point it at Ricardo.

I pull the trigger, shooting Ricardo's motionless body, once, twice, however many times until the trigger no longer produces a bullet, the thing clicking as I tug it back. "It's not enough," I whisper, the satisfaction I expected nowhere in sight.

Seeing him dead is great, but it will no doubt repay him for the torment he inflicted on others every second he was alive. I should have been more prepared, I should have figured out a way to prolong his death, make it more painful, make him fear ever stepping foot into my life.

But I can't change what's done, the only thing I can do is breathe easier now that he's gone.

Miller rushes into the room, his steps halting when he focuses on me. "We have to get you out of here."

My ending Ricardo's life wasn't the last part of our plan, and if we stand any chance of pulling this off, I have to get my head out of my ass and focus on completing what we started, once and for all.

42
SILVER

"Did you guys seriously blow up his house?" Alec asks us even though he already knows the answer to the question.

"Yes," I say. "Should have been there."

"That's so cool." Alec opens the fridge to look inside, only to shut it a moment later, his hands empty.

"Are you searching for something?" I take my focus off the computer in front of me and settle my sights on him.

"No."

"Very well."

"But like, have you seen those fruit cups?"

"Right side, bottom drawer," I tell him and try not to sound too fucking annoyed. He's like a child but I see what Cora sees in him. He's a nice guy. Very polite. A bit oblivious to the dangers of the world but treats her with more kindness than I could ask him to.

Cora waddles into the room, her cardigan hugged around her chest, her eyes puffy and tired. She rubs them and yawns. "What are you guys doing?"

Alec returns from the fridge with his treasure in hand, a

smile across his face. "You hungry?"

She stops behind me and leans her head on my shoulder. "No, not really." Cora nods to the screen. "What are you doing?"

"Well, I can't really go into details, but I heard you when you said you were worried about what would happen to London last night. I'm working on helping her disappear." I close the screen so she doesn't see details that could jeopardize making that happen. "This sort of thing is rather delicate, so for now, the less you know, the better."

I worry Cora is going to get mad, demand to have every bit of information I have, but instead, she wraps her arms around me and says, "Thank you."

I've spent most of my life alone up until this point, only answering to myself and the jobs that I'm tasked to handle. I'm not used to caring for another person, let alone fulfilling their needs when they're not explicitly stated. But ever since Cora met London, I've sensed a connection between the two, and if I'm not mistaken, Cora feels bad for the role she's played in making things potentially worse for London.

With Ricardo out of the picture, London is free from him, but in a way, she'll never fully escape him, considering he sold her off before his death to some scumbag. I'd like to think I could eliminate the threat for her, but with the uproar all these deaths have caused, Vito's son has more protection than he ever has, making him harder to kill than Ricardo ever was.

And honestly, I don't really want to risk my life for her, not when the threat to Cora's life is finally over and we have a chance to be happy, together, all four of us.

So, I'll do what I can, what I do best, and solve the problem how I see fit.

Helping London disappear.

Here's to hoping she takes the opportunity and doesn't fuck it up, because I've put my life on the line far too many times and

I'd like to stick around a bit longer and try this whole happily ever after thing.

"Can I say goodbye to her?" Cora asks me, still leaning on my shoulder.

I press a kiss to her forehead hoping it'll soothe the hurt I'm about to cause her. "I'm sorry, Angel, it's too risky. It's better this way."

Cora stands straight, her nose twitching like she's holding back tears as she nods. "Okay." She turns around, leaving me behind with the weight of helping her and hurting her all at the same time.

43
CORA

I don't have a funeral for my mother.

I don't tell my father that she's dead.

Instead, with the guys' help, we make arrangements to have her body buried in a cemetery where some of her family rests.

Holding my arms around myself, I stand a few feet from her casket as it's prepared to be lowered into the ground. I never got to say goodbye to her, not really. I never got to tell her how the job I had gotten would change my life forever. How I met three men who would do anything for me, and how I was starting to come to terms with the fact that maybe I deserved all the love they showered me with. I never told her about my fight with June, and how her betrayal cut deep. She would have given me advice, and maybe it would have been terrible, but it's what she would have done, and I would have been grateful for it, even if I didn't accept it.

I lost the woman who brought me into this life, the one who I thought might be there one day if I got married, to teach me my grandma's recipes, to help me move into my apartment. I lost all these versions of the mother who was supposed to grow old and guide me through life.

517

I hate my father for that. I blame him. Not for her cancer, but for the path he took with it. Every choice he made led to this outcome, the one where I never got to tell her how sorry I was for not seeing the signs sooner and doing whatever I could to save her.

"What's he doing here?" I say, the words like venom out of my mouth as I watch my father walk toward us.

"Don't be mad." Silver places his hand on my lower back.

I shrug him off and march around my mother's casket to meet my dad halfway. "I don't want you here."

Tears well in his eyes but they do nothing to simmer the rage within me.

"You don't mean that, Cor," the man before me says. The man that I no longer recognize or want in my life.

"You were supposed to protect me." I shake my head. "You're nothing but a coward." I stare him directly in the eyes as I mutter, "I never want to see you ever again." I don't bother waiting for him to respond, yet I take one parting look and say goodbye to the man who helped bring me into this world.

I leave him behind and don't stay for my mother to be returned to earth. I lost her weeks ago, today is just some formality I'd rather not be a part of.

Miller catches up to me as I'm nearing the vehicle Alec drove us here in. "You okay?"

"I want to leave," I tell him and reach for the door handle, my entire body and mind going numb to everything that's happening—that's already happened.

Miller mumbles something to Silver and Alec, the three of them climbing into the SUV with me and sitting in silence the entire drive to The Wellerton as I watch out the window, everything passing by in a blur.

The silence stretches out into the elevator ride up to my unit, and only stops when we near my front door.

Their attention turns on me, collectively, and I wonder what could possibly happen next for them to be acting like this.

"Before you go in there," Alec says. "Just know that we love you, and we're here for you. No matter what."

Silver and Miller nod in agreement, and I go inside because I cannot handle their mysterious nature anymore.

But once I'm in my apartment, I wish I could grow invisible and vanish into thin air.

June is the first to approach, a plate in her grasp, her expression nothing like the normal resting bitch default she's usually in. "Cora." She reaches out to me, wraps her arms around me, not caring that I don't hug her back. "I'm so sorry." She sighs and squeezes me tighter, and I try to recall her ever hugging me before. If she had, I don't remember it, at least not immediately.

She releases me, keeping her hand on my shoulders. "I made you cookies."

Magnus comes over, nudging June out of the way and hugging me next, hard and so aggressively it lifts me off the floor. "Cora bora." He drops me gently and wiggles me back and forth before finally letting me go. "Whatever you need, we're here."

I swallow the anticipation of who's going to approach me now that June and Magnus have had their turns, a great part of me hoping that this is the end of my pathetic welcome party.

Simon strolls toward me and envelopes me in his arms and kisses the top of my head. "I'm sorry for your loss." He joins Magnus and June at my side.

I wait for Coen, knowing damn well June put him up to offering me his condolences, too, even if we never really have been very close. June tells me he's a nice guy, and I believe her, but he has this off-putting, murderous vibe about him that usually keeps me at a distance. He kind of reminds me of a dog that is very protective of their owner, always lingering and ready to bite someone's head off if they fuck with her.

"Come on," I tell him. "Get it over with." I wave Coen over and he offers me a sympathetic smile before throwing an arm over my shoulder and giving me a one-armed hug. It's more than enough, especially from him.

Dominic stiffly nods at me, the two of us no stranger to this conversation since he's been around the last few days anyway.

June wraps her hand around my forearm. "Can I talk to you, alone?"

I glance at my men, sending them daggers with each glare as they avoid saving me from this kidnapping. I sigh, knowing damn well there's no getting out of this. "Fine." I lead June out of the front area and deeper into the apartment until we reach my bedroom. I slip from her grasp and go over to the closet, desperate to get out of these depressing clothes. "Talk," I tell her as I search for something else to wear.

June waits for me to change as she noses about my room, no doubt examining the wealth of things Miller has spoiled me with, within our short time together. She settles onto the edge of my bed, her feet dangling just above the floor. The plate of cookies at her side.

I sit a couple of feet away from her and cross my arms over my chest. "What is it?"

June swallows and repositions her legs to face me. "First of all, I want to tell you how sorry I am, about your mom."

I hold my hand out. "June, please, if I hear one more apology about my mom, I'm going to lose my mind."

She nods. "That's fair. I get it." June clears her throat. "What I really want to apologize for has nothing to do with your mom and everything to do with our friendship. I miss you. I fucked up. I did the very thing that had been done to me so many times over, and I was an idiot for thinking my reasons justified it. I see the error of my ways now, and I hate that I didn't sooner. I wanted to protect you. I never wanted you to get hurt, especially if I could prevent it from happening. I didn't realize how much of a wall that put between us. I'm so sorry you had to deal with all of this on your own. I should have been there for you."

"But that's the thing," I tell her. "I didn't go through it alone. I had Silver. Alec. Miller. You know, the guys that you tried to sabotage me from being with."

My words slice through June like a blade, and I hate how I immediately regret the cadence of my voice. At the end of the day, I never want to hurt her, either, even if what she did hurt me.

"You're right," she admits. "I did do that. I thought that if I drove you away from them, that maybe it would keep you out of harm's way." June chuckles. "We're so much more alike than you think. I would have done the same thing if I were you."

"I've been so mad at you," I say, relief flooding over me. "But I missed you, too." I hug my arms around my torso, suddenly feeling so cold now that the guys are in the other room. "And since when do you bake cookies?"

"Since I had to figure out how to apologize. It was Magnus's idea, so if they suck, blame him. What else can I do?" June asks me, her gaze serious like she truly wants to make this right.

"For starters..." I huff. "Don't lie to me ever again. I still don't know everything that's happened, or what it is you do for a living, but it's time that I find out. This life, I'm in it now, whether you want me to be or not. Silver and Miller are a part of it. Alec is too, in his own way."

June does a terrible job hiding a smile. "Can we talk about the fact that you're dating three men?"

"Apple doesn't fall far, does it?" I roll my eyes and shove her playfully. "But seriously. No more lies. No more walls between us. There's a difference between being private and hiding things from me. I know you're a reserved person, you've always been that way. But you have to talk to me. You have to tell me things. I want to be there for you, June."

"I know. I should have been honest. I just didn't know how.

I'm working on it, the being open thing. It doesn't come easy. I'm sorry it came between us. I recognize now that we can't be there for each other if we don't communicate." June tucks her jet-black hair behind her ear. "I won't lie to you anymore. Not about things that matter."

"Don't add a disclaimer like that." I point at her. "No lies, ever. Deal?"

She holds out her hand, her pinky toward me. "Promise. But same goes for you."

I look at her outstretched hand and then her.

"I don't want anything to come between us ever again," she says, a hint of something I've never seen her exude...it's almost like she's being vulnerable for the first time ever, at least, with me.

I slide my pinky around hers. "Deal."

When I woke up this morning, settling things with her was not something I thought would happen, even if it was something that I deeply wanted, even if I wasn't willing to admit that to myself fully.

June has been, in her own unique way, a great friend, even if her methods aren't ideal. The thought of moving forward past what I've been through without her wasn't something I yearned for. Sure, we have more to discuss and the trust between us to rebuild, but the great thing about life is, we have time.

Something I thought I had lost, the stiletto piercing Ricardo's skull giving me back what I thought he had stolen.

But even though I regained that freedom from him, I still lost my mother and my father, despite him living to tell the tale. I hate that he gets to continue breathing when my mom is the one who deserves to be alive.

"June..." I meet her gaze.

"Yeah?"

I ask her a question I've been holding onto for far too long. "Have you ever killed anyone?"

She chuckles and rolls her top lip between her teeth as if she's pondering the answer to the question. "Lately?"

My eyes widen and I clasp my hand over my mouth. "What the fuck, dude, really? How many?"

I scoot onto my bed and June does, too, both of us kicking our feet up and confessing things that would absolutely land us either in prison or a mental institution. Nothing about what we've done is right, but I'm reminded of the thing Miller told me when I struggled with the guilt of not feeling guilty after killing my boss: just because something is illegal, doesn't make it wrong.

And after she's told me some of the things she's gone through to get to where she is today, I come to terms with the fact that he was right.

June and I aren't bad, we've simply figured out a way to overcome what's been forced on us. It was our lives or theirs, and we chose to live.

A knock draws my attention to the door, Alec standing there in the doorway, his arm reaching to the top of the frame. "Did we interrupt?"

"We?" I look past him, the rest of the guys, June's and mine, filling the hallway.

Magnus shoves past him, two bags in his grasp. "I ordered take-out." He comes right over, plopping onto the bed next to me and June, making himself right at home.

And in a way, my heart recognizes that's what this is: home. Not a place, but here, with these people surrounding me, uplifting me, loving me, despite going my whole life thinking I'd never find what I have with them. I thought I knew what I was missing until I was overwhelmed with their presence around me.

We might be killers. We might be the villains of this story.

And they might not be blood, but they are my found family.

EPILOGUE – CORA

$\mathcal{T}$he expensive bourbon is hot in my mouth as I swallow it down. Setting the glass on the table in her living room, I look over to June.

There's something about her that's new and unfamiliar, almost like she's shed this protective layer concealing the true parts of her that she had kept hidden.

Sure, there's plenty I've yet to uncover, but since our fight, she's been much more open about the things in her life. Even if they're often laced with violence and crime.

For a long time, I thought that June was the main character, that she was the only one capable of a happily ever after, but I was wrong. We're all the centerpieces in our own story, and it's up to us how that story will end.

Life can either happen to you, or for you. And I choose my own fucking destiny.

"Are you listening or daydreaming again?" June interrupts my thoughts.

"Totally listening," I lie.

"Uh-huh, and what did I say?"

"Something about how much you love me." I shrug and settle

into the extremely comfortable couch, dragging one leg up over the other and facing her.

Magnus strolls over, stopping right behind June. He rubs her shoulders. "Are you gossiping? Can I join?"

It's so glaringly obvious how much he adores her but now that I have my own version of that, his affection no longer repulses me the way it once did.

"Actually, I was just asking June what was going to happen now that all those old dudes are dead. Should we be concerned or something?"

"Don't worry. I took credit for it." Dominic walks into my line of sight, adjusting the collar on his suit jacket.

"Is that allowed?" I take in his rough exterior as he moves toward June.

Dominic reaches for her hand and presses a soft kiss to her knuckles before focusing on me. "I call the shots. This way I claim it as a power move and your men get to live another day. It's a win-win."

I reposition myself, putting my arm over the back of the couch. "But like, isn't that dangerous for you?"

"Listen, Cora, I know you're new to this world, but danger isn't. Every choice comes with a price. Killing off numerous prominent members of our industry wasn't a decision I took lightly, but ultimately, it was my decision. Did your men act on it? Yes, yes, they did, but unless you want them to die, too, this is the way it has to be. Anyone involved needs to know this was my doing, and that I was involved every step of the way." Dominic pauses and then adds, "And it's been made clear that any future undermining is considered treason." His intense stare bores into me.

I swallow harshly and nod. "Yeah. Of course."

June swats at him. "Don't talk to her in that tone."

"What tone?" Dominic feigns shock.

"The murderous one. That's my best friend, dude."

Dominic rolls his killer eyes and scoffs. "I was doing no such thing."

"I don't know, man," Magnus chimes in. "Had me shaking in my boots and you weren't even talking to me."

"You're not even wearing boots." Dominic folds his arms over his chest and shakes his head. "Why do I even bother? You're always ganging up on me." He stalks away without another word and reminds me how even though he appears like he could kill me with just a stare, he still has feelings.

"You big softie," Magnus calls out after him.

June presses her finger toward me. "Hang on, I'll be right back." She stands from the couch, elbows Magnus, and takes off to comfort Dominic. She returns a moment later, the door to their garage closing a moment prior.

"Everything okay?" I ask her.

She sighs and settles back into the couch. "He's not used to having another woman around. Give him some time, he'll eventually warm up to you. Oh, by the way, Magnus told me to tell you bye."

"I didn't think he did anything wrong," I tell her honestly. "If anything, I should thank him for his transparency. That's what I want. To know the good *and* the bad."

"Speaking of good," June quickly changes the subject. "What's it like living with three guys?" She reaches for her bourbon, sipping it while waiting for my response.

I draw in a long breath and exhale. "You know, I thought it was going to be hard, or weird, but it's been good. I mean, it's only been what, two weeks?"

"Honeymoon phase is definitely still there."

"I keep waiting for the shoe to drop, for them to realize they made a mistake or that they can't do this."

June reaches forward and grips my hand. "Hey now, have a little faith. They chose this. They chose you."

But doesn't she realize that just as easily as they did, they could choose to change their mind, too. And now that the constant threat of having to give Ricardo an heir isn't looming in my every thought, I'm struck with the reality that I'm riddled with insecurities and a plethora of my own issues. Even prior to what happened, my mind was a dark and scary place. What if they decide they don't want to deal with that? With me? What if what I have to offer isn't worth the price they have to pay?

"Do you want to tell me what this is really about?" June squeezes my hand before letting it go. "I'm here for you, Cor. I'm sorry I haven't always been, but I am now."

It warms my heart to see her be open with me, vulnerable even. It's what I've wanted from the start, but it took almost losing our friendship until she came to terms with the fact that she couldn't push me away and expect me to stay there.

"I think..." I consider my words carefully, unsure how to properly string them together to make sense of what it is I'm feeling. "I think I just need time. Time for them to stay. Time for them to keep choosing me. Time for me to realize I'm not the problem."

"Well," June says. "Until then, I'm here for you. I choose you." She shifts her tone. "And if any of them step out of line, I'm here to kick their asses, too." June smirks and suddenly, I'm consumed by guilt at not having been there for her when she was no doubt going through the same thing. She's the one who kept me at arm's length, but still, she suffered through the unknowns alone.

At least now, we have each other.

"Thank you," I tell her, really hoping she understands how much I mean it. "But for real, I do have a very important question for you..."

"Uh oh." She points to her cup. "Do I need more bourbon for this?"

I snatch my glass. "Probably."

June downs the rest of hers and wipes her mouth. "Okay, hit me."

"Umm." I fidget with the rim of the glass.

"Come on, spit it out."

I avoid her eye contact as I find the courage to mutter the words. "What's your sex life like?"

June laughs. "You mean because I have four boyfriends?" She gets more comfortable on the couch and continues. "I mean, it's interesting, to say the least. And never-ending, it seems."

"What do you mean?" I glance up at her, my cheeks blushing.

"Come on, Cora. You and I both know I was always a bit promiscuous. Now, instead of sleeping around with random guys, I'm sleeping around with the same four. It's..." She pauses for a moment. "Fun and exhilarating and somehow, consistently fresh. Just when I think we've surpassed any level of crazy, the guys surprise me with a new position, a new toy, a new goal."

"What do you mean, *goal*?" I question even though I probably shouldn't.

"Well, sometimes they have these little competitions over how many times they can make me orgasm. Willingly, or forced. Sometimes it's total, or individual goals. It varies, but still, it's like a twisted side quest they come up with."

My face flushes even more than it already was at the idea of them repeatedly making my best friend climax.

"Cora, you're turning bright red." June leans forward and pushes on my shoulder. "It's just sex, don't get all embarrassed."

I lick my lips and blink away my awkwardness. "No, I'm not. I'm fine, I'm totally fine."

June rolls her eyes. "What's the problem? Is the sex boring? Are they bad at it? You know you can practice, right? They can get better. You'd be surprised how well men can listen if something as carnal as sex is on the table."

"No," I cut her off. "They're good at it. Trust me." I tuck my hair behind my ear and choose my next words carefully. "They're like *really* good at it."

"Then what's wrong?"

"I just...I just didn't know if there's a line, or a limit."

June throws her arm over the back of the couch. "That's on you to decide. You call the shots. Whatever you want, I'm sure they'd give it to you." She taps her fingers and stares right at me. "What's the craziest thing you guys have done?"

"Oh my God, I can't say that." My cheeks light up again and betray me. Who knew I'd get this fucking weird about talking sex with my best friend.

"How about this..." June pokes my knee. "If you tell me and it's not something I've already done, I'll give you whatever you want. Name it."

I narrow my gaze at her. "You're trying to trick me."

She shakes her head, her dark hair swaying on her shoulders.

"Okay..." I chew at my lip. "So, this one time, we uh...we, well, I asked them to...to do two at the same time."

June blinks as if she's processing what I just confessed. "You mean, like you and two guys or two dicks in the same hole?"

"June!" I blurt out.

"What? I'm only trying to understand the scenario."

Drawing in a breath, I wonder why I ever brought this up to begin with. "Two *dicks*, at the same time. In the same hole." I add that last bit quietly.

"That's like, a normal day for us. Double vaginal penetration is a good way to warm up."

My eyes widen. "Warm up to what?"

June grins, her smile resembling something of the Cheshire cat. "Triple."

"Triple dicks? In the same hole. Is that actually possible?" I cover my mouth and glance around as if I'll somehow get in trouble for blurting it out.

June laughs and bobs her head up and down. "I can assure you; it is possible."

I consider her confirmation and recall that instance where I had said I wanted all my guys at the same time. Then, it was an impossible thought that had crossed my mind in a frenzied haze of lust and desire and the idea that it might be our last time, but now, with her sitting right in front of me, living proof, it might be a reality I'm willing to explore.

"Did it hurt?" I ask her, my mind running wild at the new questions that have formed. "And like, how? That's a lot of legs."

"I mean, it wasn't without effort, especially the first time."

"First time? You mean you've done it multiple times?"

June shrugs. "I mean, practice makes perfect." She winks at me and continues. "The first time was a challenge figuring out who went where, and it kind of depends on if the guys are comfortable with each other or not. Simon and Coen have their differences, so that complicated things, but they knew it was what I wanted, so they made it work."

I imagine the logistics it would take to pull something like that off but draw a blank on how it would work. A woman's body is truly a magical lifeforce—the idea that three dicks could fit inside isn't what's hard to wrap my head around...but the way the guys would have to enter...and the position I'd have to be in to make it happen.

Regardless, if my best friend says it's possible, it leaves me with one thing incredibly certain: I want to try triple vaginal penetration, even if the thought of it borderline terrifies me.

---

*A*lec takes my hand and guides me into the private elevator outside of my apartment that Miller gave me at The Wellerton.

Miller joked and said he would rename the building after

me, but I insisted that a multi-million-dollar unit was far more than enough.

"Nothing is ever too much, for you, my Queen," Miller had said. His love and generosity truly knowing no bounds.

"Where are we going?" I ask Alec as he cups my hand in between his in the confined space.

"It's a surprise." He breaks away to push a button I've never pressed before. Alec kisses my knuckles, one at a time, the elevator chiming once he's caressed his lips over the last one.

I glance from him to the open air outside of us. "I didn't know this went to the roof."

Alec guides me out, his hand lingering on the exposed part of the small of my back. "Did I tell you how gorgeous you are tonight?"

We round the corner and step into the lit-up terrace, the whole thing illuminated by fairy lights that are strung about. My heart stutters as I take it all in, the memory of what he wanted our first date to be coming to me from all those weeks ago. I had a feeling he wouldn't let it go; I just wasn't positive he'd actually follow through with it now that our relationship has already been established.

"Alec...the date." Tears glisten in my eyes. "You didn't have to do this," I say the words even though I'm so fucking grateful for the incredibly thoughtful gesture.

"Cora." Alec turns toward me, cupping my cheeks in his hands. "I want you to know how much I love you. How much you've changed my life. There isn't anything I wouldn't do for you. Truly. I will promise you many things but let me promise you this...I will never *ever* stop taking you on dates." Alec leans in close, his cedar cologne lingering between us. He rubs his nose against mine. "Even when we're grey and old, babe."

I kiss Alec's lips before I full-on cry and melt into his embrace.

He fumbles with something in his pocket, a second later, a

soft piano melody playing from some random speaker system. Alec breaks away and holds out his hand. "May I have this dance?"

I grin at him and slip my hand in his. "Always."

We dance close, my head resting on his chest, his heartbeat singing a sweet lullaby. He holds me, and for a fleeting moment, I forget about everything other than us. But that's all it is, a temporary reminder that there's still one thing hanging in the balance I've been too afraid to bring up.

Alec kisses my forehead and guides us over to a small table with two covered trays on top. "I was going to hire a private chef...but then I thought...that's not very Cora."

He pulls out the chair and pushes it in when I sit down, going so far as to grab the cloth napkin and set it in my lap.

"I present to you..." Alec grabs onto the handle of the domed cover and reveals two slices of pizza with pepperoni and pineapple.

A laugh slips out of me, and I clutch my hands to my chest. "This is perfect." I sniffle and smile up at him. "You're perfect."

"And because I know you..." Alec reaches into a silver canister and pulls out a jug of Sprite. He pours some in one of my cups and fills another with water. "I also brought you this."

"Is that what I think it is?" I take in the familiar cup as he turns around the logo.

There's something special about the twinkle in his eye that makes me want to hold onto this memory for the rest of my life.

"Your favorite." He pushes the iced vanilla latte toward me. It's hands down the best coffee in town, if you don't count the at-home versions. Those are made with love, so obviously they top all the others.

"Just don't tell June I betrayed her by going somewhere other than Bram's for coffee," I say even though I'm certain the secret is safe with him.

"She's going to find out sooner or later." Alec pulls out another bottle. "And bourbon, just in case."

"You know..." I drink some of the heavenly coffee. "I once thought three drinks was plenty, but I think you're right. Fourth really is the charm."

Alec grins and pours me two fingers of the bourbon before settling into his seat and doing the same for himself. When he's done, he puts his hands in his lap and sort of stares at me with an expectant look on his handsome face.

"Everything is perfect, Alec. These decorations, the thought-fulness, this night...you." I reach across the table and take his hand in mine. "Thank you. Seriously. I mean it."

Alec squeezes my hand back and for another fleeting moment, everything is right in the world.

"Can I ask you something?" The words slip out of my mouth before I've had time to reel them in. I guess they had to come out sooner rather than later, but here's to hoping they didn't completely ruin our perfect evening.

"Yeah, of course. What's up?" Alec's expression shifts and I hate that I'm the cause of it.

Why couldn't I have waited until the night was over or kept my mouth shut for all of eternity?

"Well," I start. "I was wondering about...New York."

Alec blinks a few times and I wonder if this is where he comes up with some sort of lie or cover-up to hide the truth. "What?"

"Your job offer, in New York?"

"What are you talking about?"

"You don't have to lie about it, Alec. Simon told me."

At first, his face is tight, but the moment I mention Simon, he breaks into a smile and leans back. "Oh my God, Cora." He holds his hand to his chest. "You seriously had me worried there."

He chuckles but I don't find it at all funny.

"I'm confused," I tell him, my fingers desperate to fidget with anything sitting on the table, the corner of the tablecloth my most current victim.

Alec leans forward, grabbing onto my anxious hand. "Cora. *That* was a lie. I told Simon about a made-up job offer because I don't want him to get used to me always being around. I want him to realize my place in his business is temporary, a means to an end."

I let out a breath and stare at his beautiful face. "Really?"

Alec nods. "Christ. You thought I was going to leave you? Are you crazy?" He shakes his head. "You can't get rid of me, not that easily."

Suddenly, the world really does seem right. The weight is lifted from my shoulders, and I come to realize that maybe these good things I thought were potentially only short-lived might actually be capable of lasting.

Maybe in this book called my life, I really do get the guy...or better yet, *guys*.

iller checks the blindfold wrapped around my eyes. "Okay. I think we're ready."

My stomach grows wild at the possibilities that rack my brain. Where could he possibly be taking me? And why does it require a blindfold?

"I'll come around and get you," he says before slipping out of the driver's side of his Porsche and opening my door. "My Queen." Miller takes my hand and guides me out of the car, gravel crunching under my shoes.

"Where are we?" I ask him even though he's not going to tell me, at least, not yet.

"I'll give you a hint."

I pause and wait for him to continue. "I'll take a hint."

"You've been here before." Even without looking, I can sense that he's grinning, perhaps a smug look caked on his face. He gets that way when he's certain he's got a clever idea. And most of the time, he usually does.

That's how Miller is. He's fanatical about being thorough, about knowing everything, especially when it involves me. Obsessive is another great word to describe him. Whatever it is, it's so very him, and it's one of the things I love most about him. He's like that because he prefers to control every potential variable he can. He doesn't like to be wrong, and if it were up to him, he would call the shots about everything. It settles his nerves and keeps his anger at bay. I wouldn't call him controlling, because he isn't pushy about those things, but Miller prefers to do the thinking, and if I'm being completely honest, it's nice to not have to think for a change. I do enough of that on a daily basis. And considering Miller is more in tune with my wants and desires than I am, I'm not exactly missing out on anything by not having a say.

Although, when I do, he's willing to adapt and accommodate what I want. And that's why I'm okay with things being the way they are, because at the end of the day, his true desire lies with keeping me happy, and that keeps him happy.

So, I go along with the blindfold and breathe in deeply to assess my surroundings in an attempt to figure out where the hell we are.

"Wait." I hold out my hands and rub my shoe into the gravel, a sense of familiarity coming to me. Tilting my head, I listen to how eerily quiet it is and recognize the place immediately.

"You figured it out, didn't you?" he asks me.

I turn toward his voice. "Did you bring me here to kill me?" I plant my hands on my hips. "Because if you did, I would have worn something nicer to die in."

Miller chuckles and takes one of my hands while placing the

other one of his on my lower back. "Ah, come on. You look stunning. I promise."

"That's not very promising," I tell him even though I know he wouldn't hurt me. If anything, I'm the safest with Miller. Or with any of my guys. June's included, unless she's there, then obviously they would probably throw me in front of a moving bullet to save her.

Miller leads me across the pavement and to a door I remember from our first and only time here.

The thing creaks open, making the same sound it did that day, too.

Only, today, I'm not sure what could have brought us here.

The scent hits me immediately—metal mixed with dirt and dust.

With a click, the door shuts, sealing us inside this desolate warehouse on the outskirts of town, the sound reverberating through the building and settling into my bones.

"This way," Miller says, his voice soft and even.

We step onto plastic, the thickness of it crinkling underneath our shoes. A tell that someone has, or will, die here.

Why else use the good stuff?

Miller stops and moves to my backside to remove my blindfold, the untying taking entirely too long.

But once my vision is freed from its confines, I consider putting it back on.

I suck in a short breath and take in the man tied to the chair, the one who looks like someone I used to know, only older, ragged, worn down—aging having done nothing to preserve the features I once thought were attractive. The features that lured me in with a false promise of safety and stole my innocence.

His head is slumped, his arms tied behind him, his legs secured to the chair.

"Is he?" I whisper unsure if this man's fate has already been sealed.

Miller steps to my side and crosses his arms. "No, of course not. I wouldn't deprive you of that satisfaction."

I swallow and hug my chest, suddenly cold and entirely too insecure about the shirt I'm wearing. Is it too revealing? Am I asking for something to happen? But I know the answer to that, so I shake my head and rid myself of those intrusive thoughts.

"Wake him up," I tell Miller and move a little closer.

Miller complies with a smile on his face, quickly going to action and putting smelling salts under my assaulter's nose.

He snaps to life, frantic at first, his sights scanning the place, his chest heaving, until he settles on me.

"Hello, Jerry," I mutter, stalking toward him but not too close.

Jerry blinks a few times and I consider slicing his eyelids off to prevent him from shielding himself from what's going to happen next.

"Co-Cora?" he blurts out. "Wh-what's happening?"

Miller stays near me, his presence like a warm blanket keeping me safe.

I don't answer him, instead, I stalk over to the tray full of torture devices and contemplate my options. I could cut him, stab him, rip his fingernails off, beat him, electrocute him...the possibilities are endless, and yet none of them seem good enough for what he did to me, what he took from me. And would doing any of those things actually make me feel any better, or will they reduce me to being no better than him—my rapist?

Miller places his hand on the small of my back and leans in close. "You can take your time, Cora. Whatever you want. However long it takes."

I chew at my lip and reach for the gun sitting on the tray, the grip cold and hard.

"Come on, Cora. Talk to me, tell me what's going on." Jerry rocks his body and tries to free himself. "There must be some misunderstanding. There's no need for this. What would your dad think?"

Taking the gun in my grasp, I turn and march toward him. "My dad? You mean the man who is no better than you? The one who failed to keep me safe?" I rock my head slowly. "Not from you, not from this world."

Jerry laughs. "Is that what this is all about? All those years ago? C'mon, Cora. Don't act like you didn't want that, too."

"You realize I'm holding the weapon, right?" I point the barrel at him but keep my finger off the trigger.

Jerry jerks but remains rooted in place, the ties holding him there not budging. "Cora, baby, relax. I was drunk, you were a tease, that's the end of it. I don't know what you think happened..."

"What I *think* happened?" I dart in front of him, shove the tip of the gun into his temple and hold his shoulder with my other hand to steady him. "You don't remember holding me down, pinning me to the ground under the lifeguard tower? You don't remember me telling you no, begging you to stop and fighting you? You don't remember my cries for help or the blood that coated your dick after you fucking violated me?" I drag the gun down and pop the barrel into his mouth, chipping at least one of his teeth with the force. "I should fucking blow your brains out right now."

He mumbles against the gun and his eyes remain so wide that this image of him will forever stay in my head. Instead of him on top of me, *this* is what I'll remember—him, helpless, pissing his pants in fear of the girl he assaulted.

I shove the gun forward with force and remove it, watching as he coughs and fights to catch his breath. "You're a pathetic waste of oxygen."

"You-you don't understand," he blubbers. "I have a wife, a child, you can't do this."

538

"*I* was a child," I yell at him. "And I trusted you. My parents trusted you."

"I'm not that man anymore, Cora. I'm s-sorry." Tears fill his eyes and roll down his cheeks. "I hate what I did to you, okay? Is that what you want to hear? That I'm a sick fuck, that I regret doing what I did to you?"

"Say it," I tell him through gritted teeth.

He furrows his brows. "Say what?"

"What you did to me." I glare at him, the gun tightly pressed in my hand at my side. "Say the word."

"I...I raped you."

And with his admission, I've gotten everything I could have asked for—validation of the truth.

For all these years, I carried the burden of that day with me like a ball and chain, unable to free myself. He had tried to gaslight me, and even convinced my parents that I simply had an accident at the beach. Every single day I wondered what I had done wrong to ask for that, why it happened, but the truth of it is: this is his fault, not mine. And the second the word *rape* left his lips, that solidified what it really was, what really happened.

It does nothing to erase the torment I've held on to, the nightmares that will probably never end, but it offers me something I never thought I would have, something most victims will never receive, and because nothing will change what he did, this will have to be enough.

I turn toward Miller, his expression tense and rigid. "Here." I shove the gun toward him. "I got what I wanted. You can finish him off."

He nods stiffly and without him truly understanding the situation, and the feelings that have haunted me since then, I know he's doing his best to understand why I'm asking this of him. "Do you want it quick or painful?"

"Painful," I say with a sigh.

"Very well." Miller raises his arm without hesitation and pulls the trigger, the first bullet landing in Jerry's stomach. Miller shifts his focus to me momentarily, ignoring the shrieks that Jerry lets out. "Pull up a chair, this might take a while."

Jerry coughs and screams, and it's strange how numb I am to the sound. Perhaps if he hadn't ignored my muffled cries on that fateful summer day, I would come to his aid. But no, he's proven that he doesn't deserve what he isn't willing to reciprocate.

So, I do as Miller suggested, and settle into the cold metal chair near the table of torture devices and watch in awe while one of the men I love brutally assaults the man who hurt me.

Each gunshot rings assurance through me that the end is near, not just for him, but for the torment he's caused me. I will no longer live in fear of Jerry and what he did to me.

Today, I am reborn in the blood of my rapist, stronger than ever and determined to never allow that to happen ever again.

"Where are you taking me?" I ask Silver the same question I had asked Miller not too long ago. Haven't they figured out that I hate surprises? How can two people claim they know so much about me and yet fail to recognize this one very certain fact?

"It's a surprise," he confirms.

I groan and cross my arms but perk up the second we pull onto a long gravel driveway.

We had been in the car for nearly an hour, driving farther and farther away from town and slipping into a rural area I don't think I even knew existed. Each minute that passed put us deeper into no-man's land and made me wonder if maybe Silver was taking me out to murder me, too, the same way I thought Miller was when he brought me to that warehouse to kill my rapist.

But he didn't, and that surprise turned out great, so why would I assume this one wouldn't either?

"Is this a farm?" I turn toward Silver and take in the expansive pastures all around.

We crest a hill, revealing a gigantic building in the near distance with a massive horse statue in front of it. Silver pulls us up near the entrance of the structure and shifts the car into park.

"I don't understand," I tell him because I really have no clue what's going on here.

"Trust the process, Angel." He climbs out of the driver's side and strolls over to open my door, extending his hand to help me out of the car. "Do you remember that first night we spent together?"

I wrap my hand up under his biceps and walk at his side as we make our way closer to the building. "Yeah?"

"Well, you jokingly said you were tempted to ask me for a horse just to see if I could get you one."

"Okay..."

"I followed it up by asking you if you actually wanted one. Do you remember what you said?"

I recall that evening and the events that led to it, shaking the memory of my boss's murder off, and focusing on the parts that include Silver. "What did I say?"

"You said, and forgive me, I'm paraphrasing here, something along the lines of yes, but that you didn't have anywhere to put it."

A soft-spoken older woman greets us the second we're through the doors. "Hello, welcome in Mr. and Mrs. Franco."

I don't dare correct her that my last name is not Franco, because regardless of it being wrong, it has a nice ring to it.

She smiles politely at each of us before saying, "Ready to pick out your new horse?"

The woman turns on her heel without allowing me to respond, my mouth falling open as I gawk at Silver.

"You're buying me a freaking horse?" I whisper-shout at him and shove his strong, broad chest.

Silver grins and I'm not sure which is more surprising, the sheer happiness radiating off this ruthless man or the fact that he refused to let go of that very not-serious comment I made about getting a horse. Either way, I settle with the fact that I'm the luckiest girl in the world.

"Maybe," he says with a smirk. "Only if you find one you like."

"Where are we going to keep it?"

"Here," he tells me. "Until we get it a proper home closer to us. You can come visit whenever you'd like, and you can even take lessons here."

"You thought of everything, didn't you?" I shake my head. "You're unbelievable."

Silver leans down and presses a gentle kiss on my lips. "Thanks, Angel. You're not so bad yourself." He winks at me and tilts his head in the direction the lady went. "Better not keep her waiting, *Mrs. Franco.*"

"I'm still not entirely sure that's possible," Alec says from his spot at the kitchen counter. He holds his hands out in front of him, carefully examining his fingers. "Where do the legs go?"

I laugh and say, "That was my concern, too. But listen, I did some research, and it's totally possible."

Alec's eyebrows perk up. "Research?"

Miller shifts his focus from his phone to me, too. "What research?"

"Visual research." I grab my cell and turn the screen on. "Come here."

Alec wastes no time, rushing to stand behind me. Miller, clearly intrigued, joins us, leaving Silver to glare at us overtop his newspaper.

"Fine," Silver huffs. "I'm coming."

"That's what she said," I mutter and click a few buttons on my phone.

"Wait, did you seriously search *triple vaginal penetration?*" Alec asks me.

"Yeah, because if you just search TVP, it brings up textured vegetable protein. And that's in Google...you have to go to a private browser and search the hub if you want to find something good." I lower my phone and continue, "But like, here's the part where it gets complicated. Most searches bring up triple penetration, not triple vaginal penetration. Big difference."

"What's the difference?" Alec asks me like he's sitting in the front row at a college lecture.

Miller chimes in. "Triple penetration would be any hole: mouth, ass, vagina. Triple vaginal would be, well, all in the vagina."

Alec nods his head in understanding.

"Also, did you know that has a name?" I glance over my shoulder at Miller.

"What?" Miller questions

"The filling of the ass, mouth, and vagina all at the same time," I explain.

"Airtight," Silver says out of nowhere.

I wink at him. "Yeah. It's called airtight." I can't believe I was being bashful with June about sex and here I am, discussing sex terms with my three boyfriends.

"So, the research..." Silver clears his throat. "Show us."

"Right, yeah." I bring my phone back up. "Anyway, like I was saying, a lot of these are triple but not vaginal, and most of the vaginal ones are with toys, not actual humans. But here—" I click on one of the thumbnails and the video loads. I turn my phone to the side to bring it to full screen and ignore the silence that falls in the wait for it to start playing.

A short trailer of the video begins, with the girl by herself, teasing her pussy and moaning. I skip ahead, fast-forwarding over the *regular* sex stuff, skipping the anal, and find the spot I want to show them.

"Here," I say while pointing at the screen. "Triple vaginal, three guys."

"Huh." Alec hovers his finger toward the phone. "So, one dude is on his back, the girl is back to chest with him, that guy is standing in front of them, and the other dude is squatting over her. His quads must be on fire."

I chuckle and nod along. "Yeah. Basically. That's how they make it work."

"So," Miller speaks. "This is what you want to try?" He moves from behind me and stands at the side with his hands planted on the counter.

"Yes. But only if you guys are up for it."

Miller scratches his chin and glances at the other guys. "I mean, I'm game if you guys are."

Silver rubs my back. "Whatever you want, Angel. I just don't want to hurt you."

"Did you see that thing stretch?" Alec motions to the screen. "Vaginas are magic. You can't convince me otherwise."

"What made you want to do this, Angel?" Silver moves my hair from my shoulder and presses his lips on the exposed skin, sending goosebumps all over me.

"I mean, the idea itself was conceived on its own but...June said she did it, so I kind of have to try it, you know?"

Silver's beard grazes my skin as he continues to leave a trail with his lips. "And you didn't think you wanted to one-up her?"

I crane my head around at him. "We don't exactly have four dicks we're working with."

Silver grins. "I have something in mind for when the time comes. Speaking of which, when did you want to try this?"

I consider my options but quickly decide there's no better time than now. "Like, this very moment, if possible."

I'm already feeling the courage and want building from having this conversation itself, so why not continue that into actually following through instead of thinking about it too much and talking myself out of it? The idea and imagery make it seem fun as fuck, but I'd be lying if I said I wasn't a little nervous about having three, rather large, cocks inside of my vagina at one time. I won't tell them that, though.

"Okay then." Silver clears his throat. "Hold that thought. I'll be right back."

"You sure you want to do this?" Miller asks me the second Silver has left us.

"The idea of feeling you all...inside of me...at the same time." I get lost in the daydream of it for a moment, my core tightening with heated desire. "It's hot as fuck."

"You're telling me," Alec chimes in, his hand going to his groin. "I've got a chub just thinking about it."

I reach for his cock, feeling it through his pants. "Damn, you do." I stroke the length and look up at him, licking my lips. "May I?"

Alec's eyes light up and he nods a bit too aggressively as I hop from my stool and stand in front of him to unbutton his jeans.

"Only if I can get a taste." Miller comes up behind me, reaches for my waistband, and yanks my leggings over my ass. "Is that okay, my Queen?"

I kick at my feet to free myself from my bottoms and spread my legs for him as an answer.

"Fuck," Alec mutters the moment before I bend at the waist and take his cock into my mouth.

Miller wastes no time, his mouth finding my sex, too, his tongue licking my already wet entrance. He grips my thighs and buries his face in my ass, coating himself, no doubt, in my desire.

I moan against Alec's cock and revel as he hardens.

Alec holds onto my hair, pulling it out of the way and bucking his hips. "God..."

Miller shoves at least two fingers into my hungry hole and jerks them aggressively in and out, slamming his knuckles into me. He licks at my ass and finger fucks me harder, my body backing into him, my pussy tightening around his torment as I climax hard and fast, just how he wanted me to.

I pant and shiver, stroking Alec's cock against my lips.

Silver comes into the room. "I see you started without me." But that doesn't seem to faze him, because instead of leaving, he approaches me from behind, not caring at all that Miller is knuckles deep and Alec's cock is in my mouth.

"Relax, Angel." His strong hand grips my hip. "Miller, put this in your mouth." A second later, something cold pushes along my asshole. "Relax," he tells me again. "I promise you'll like this."

I comply, giving in to whatever he has in store for me, and allow him to penetrate my asshole slowly.

He doesn't let up until I feel a slight pop, and the fullness consumes me. "Good girl," he whispers and smacks my ass gently but with enough force that it will probably leave a mark.

Miller keeps rocking his fingers and I find myself inching my legs farther apart, so fucking ravenous for more.

"Let's take this to the living room," Silver suggests, his callused hand resting on my lower back.

I release Alec and stand upright, adjusting to the sensation of the butt plug. My pussy quivers and I grow excited for what's to come next.

"But first..." Silver grabs onto the hem of my shirt. "We should remove this." He pulls my top over my head and his gaze trails over my naked body, so exposed, especially considering they're all fully clothed. "You're so fucking gorgeous, Angel." Silver runs his thumb over my cheek.

I stand on my tiptoes and press a quick kiss to his lips before turning on my heels and leaving them behind to watch me go. Glancing over my shoulder with a grin, I ask, "Are you guys coming or what?"

Alec is the first to react, his shirt landing on the floor next to mine a second later. He goes to work slipping out of his pants as he trails me to the living room.

Miller and Silver follow us over in no major rush, making the wait that much more antagonizing. Don't they realize that now that I've gotten this idea in my head, I need to see it through? They've sparked something inside of me that will be insatiable until I'm completely full of them.

I stop next to the oversized couch and watch them approach, eyeing the three sexy men who are somehow mine.

Silver unbuttons his shirt, one button at a time, each one revealing his broad, strong chest. He removes it fully, folding it in half and laying it on the nearby table. His fingers move to his pants, unbuckling his belt and sliding it out. His eyebrow raises like an idea strikes him. With his pants hanging open, he approaches with the belt in his grasp. "Kneel on the couch, Angel."

I swallow and comply, my body acting on its own as it climbs onto the plush surface, my back toward the guys.

Silver comes up behind me and plants his hand on my shoulder. "We need a safe word, Angel. What will it be?"

"Pineapple," I say without really thinking about it, my mind focused on whatever it is he's about to do.

"Very well. Pineapple it is." He slithers the belt across my back and over my ass as he leans down to whisper into my ear. "Don't be afraid to use it, Angel."

I nod and hold onto the back of the couch expectantly.

Miller comes toward us and says, "Bend over and spread your legs."

Leaning down, I arch my ass at them, exposing myself and the butt plug.

Silver teases me with the belt again, grazing it against the soft flesh of my ass before hitting me with it.

The pain is hot and fast, and fades quicker than it came.

I look over my shoulder and say the words I know I'll come to regret. "Is that all you got?"

Silver grins and smacks me again, this time with a bit more heat. He wastes no time, going again and again until my pussy is throbbing with desire, the masochist in me having entirely too much satisfaction from this.

I reach between my legs and moan as I rub my fingers over my soaked entrance, dipping them inside to appease my hunger.

Silver grabs a handful of my ass with his free hand and smacks me a second later. "Now, now, Angel. You have three men here; do you really feel the need to pleasure yourself?"

But I don't dare remove my hand, instead, I arch my back more to give them a view of me slipping my fingers in and out, letting out a soft moan to top it off.

I glance back at Silver as he shakes his head and draws his arm back to crack the belt across my ass, this time the leather hits the delicate skin of my labia.

Biting down a whimper, I drag my fingers out to spread myself open for them to see how badly I want them. "Someone needs to claim this or I'm going to."

Silver exhales and drops the belt on the floor, grabbing his cock a second later. He lines it up with my pussy, stroking the length and teasing my entrance. "Is this what you want?" Each stroke makes me ravenous with desire.

I shove myself backward, slamming onto him as he gives in, driving his hips forward and filling me full of him.

He grabs my hips and fucks me hard and fast, sparing me no remorse as he buries himself balls deep.

My tits bounce, and I dig my fingers into the back of the couch as I buck against him, my knuckles turning white, my orgasm building and building until I'm almost...

But Silver stops abruptly and pulls himself out of me, slapping my ass with his cock. "You think I was going to give in that easily?"

Panting, I try to catch my breath and wonder how mad he'll get if I finish myself off.

Silver plops down onto the couch next to me and drags me over. "Climb on, Angel. We're only getting started."

I do as he says, quickly filling my throbbing pussy with him and finding my rhythm. Each time I try to pick up the pace, he holds my hips and prevents me.

Miller approaches me from behind, his gentle touch on my ass alerting me to his presence.

Silver and I both slow down, allowing Miller to rub his cock over my soaked entrance and find his way in.

"Fuck," I moan as he slides in beside Silver, my pussy stretching to accommodate their girth.

Silver reaches up to move the hair from my sweat-glistening cheek. "You're doing so great, Angel."

I tighten around them, his words of affirmation somehow turning me on even more.

"You like it when I tell you what a good job you're doing?" His dark gaze melts into mine.

I whimper and nod as I tug my lip between my teeth.

Miller picks up his pace, sliding his cock deeper and deeper along Silver's, the sensation intense, especially with the butt plug in place. "You're taking us so well, my Queen. I'm so fucking proud of you." He pushes on the plug and takes his other hand to wrap around my waist to find my clit.

Silver positions himself lower, giving his mouth access to my nipple. He applies the soft pressure and then bites down hard.

I cry out, my orgasm rattling through me as I moan louder than I ever have in my entire life. My entire body shakes and my pussy clenches tightly around the two cocks buried inside of me.

"I think you're ready." Silver presses soft kisses on my chest and pops my nipple into his mouth before releasing it.

I exhale, my breath shuddering as I rise off the back of the couch and look down at him. "Think so?"

Miller pulls himself out of me and Silver guides me off of him, turns me around, and lowers me onto his lap, the change in position hitting so many new nerve endings.

I bounce on his cock and take in Miller and Alec, who haven't gotten much of my attention since we entered the room. Miller strokes his wet cock beside me, and Alec holds his in his hand a few feet away.

"Come here," I tell Alec and motion for him to approach.

Silver leans back on the couch, scooting further and dragging me with him. He pulls me onto his chest and spreads my legs. "I'm just jealous I'm missing out on that view," he says.

Miller smirks. "It's a damn good view." He strokes his length and looks me up and down, his gaze lingering on my pussy which is currently inhabited by another man's cock.

Alec comes to my side, and I take him in my hand immediately, spreading the precum over his tip and jerking him. His eyes flutter and his cock throbs.

Silver reaches his hand across my waist and slides it between my legs, his fingers grazing over my clit and swirling around my entrance. "You're so fucking wet, Angel."

"Make me wetter," I tell him as I tighten my pussy around his cock. "I want you guys to fuck me until I'm begging for mercy." The words that leave my mouth surprise me but speak nothing compared to how badly I want them, how I'd let them do anything they wanted to me. If only they knew how devoted my body was to theirs.

"Your wish is our command." Silver's cock hardens inside of me, and he rocks his hips slowly. "Who's got the stronger quads?"

Miller and Alec exchange a glance and Alec tilts his head to Miller, giving him the go-ahead.

"You should go first," Alec tells Miller. "I need to focus on my thighs otherwise I'm going to come in like twelve seconds."

Miller shrugs. "Suit yourself." He approaches again, this time I get to witness him as he lines his shaft up with my hole and slides it around to find his opening.

I brace myself for the stretch and grin when he slowly moves into me. "Fuck," I moan, my head falling back onto Silver's chest.

"Good girl," Silver whispers and holds onto me. "Such a good fucking girl." He continues to glide his fingers over my clit, rubbing against both his and Miller's cocks as they penetrate me.

Miller flits his gaze from his cock to me. "This okay, baby girl?"

"You guys actually think I can take all three of you at the same time?" I clench around them, my pussy so fucking full yet so fucking happy.

"You sure you want to find out?" Alec asks me with his cock growing harder in my hand.

I tug on him and nod. "Yes. Are you ready?"

"Ready as I'll ever be to stick my ass in some dude's face." Alec plants one foot on the couch and heaves himself up, taking the other and straddling over me while my legs remain outside of his.

I take the opportunity to grab back onto his shaft and stroke the length, teasing the tip of him with my mouth.

"You keep playing with that thing and I'm going to bust before we can find out," Alec says jokingly.

"Dude, watch your ass," Miller tells him and repositions to give Alec some room despite there not being much to give while staying inside of me.

I suppress a giggle, but it finds its way out anyway. "This is more entertaining than I thought it was going to be."

Silver shakes his head, or at least, I think that's what I feel happening behind me.

Alec continues to try to find a comfortable spot, kneeling on his left side while keeping his other leg bent to give himself a proper angle to approach my already crowded entrance. He glides his dick around my clit and circles it in place.

"Spread wider for him, Angel," Silver tells me. "And make sure to relax. You're not holding your breath, are you?"

"No," I lie and inch my legs out farther to give him more room.

A minute goes by, and Alec still hasn't found entry, my pussy growing impatient with the wait.

"Give it to me," Silver tells him, reaching forward and grabbing onto Alec's cock.

Alec doesn't protest, yet releases his hand and watches Silver move his dick right into place.

"Push," Silver guides him. "There we go."

Alec goes along with Silver's direction but takes his eyes off his cock and stares into mine as he applies pressure and slides into me.

I gasp and shudder, my pussy spreading and filling and stretching...

"Talk to me, baby. Are you okay? Is this too much?" Alec asks me.

"No." Tears well in my eyes even though I'm fully fucking enjoying this newfound fullness. "It's perfect."

Alec grabs onto the back of the couch to brace himself and shoves in more, his cock gliding against two others. "You feel fucking incredible, Cora." His chest heaves and his cock throbs as he buries himself as far as he can go.

My eyes flutter closed, and I moan, my pussy aching. I wrap my arms around Alec's muscular torso and drag my fingers over his back. "Don't hold back," I whimper and dig my nails into him. "None of you hold back. Please."

Silver groans against my ear and bucks his hips, him no doubt having the hardest position to move in, yet he still manages to thrust into me. "Goddamn, Angel. You're taking us so well. I knew you could do it. I knew you'd take us like the good girl you are. How does it feel to have three cocks inside of you?"

"So. Fucking. Full." I move my hips and rock against them, desperate to have every inch of them inside of me. "So. Fucking. Good."

Miller picks up his pace, slamming into me and shoving Alec in, too.

Silver slides one hand up and wraps it around my neck and the other to shove two fingers into my mouth.

I suck on him, and he applies pressure to the sides of my throat.

He removes himself from my mouth and slides down my front to find my clit, circling it with his spit-covered fingers. Silver grips my throat harder and heightens my arousal, his fingers trailing my clit and around the three cocks inside of me.

I moan and feel them individually throb inside of me; my mind unsure of which cock is which now that they're all in there. Instead, they become this one, giant unit, buried balls deep and fucking me harder, deeper, in unison.

Miller mutters, "I'm so fucking close."

"Thank God," Alec pants. "I've been holding off since we started."

"We can feel you clenching, Angel," Silver says. "Are you ready to finally come?" But he knows exactly what it is that he's doing, so he tightens his hand around my throat and rubs my clit slower, harder, more intentionally, sending me spiraling over the edge and climaxing intensely on them, my pussy squeezing them so fucking hard they follow me over the cliff and fill me even fuller of them.

Miller bucks hard with a groan and Alec shudders as he allows himself to finish. Silver groans and holds onto me, his cock spilling over into me.

I convulse around them, my body trembling harder than ever at an orgasm. I practically become a pile of nothing on top of Silver, completely unable to move any part of myself aside from the involuntary shivers. My chest heaves and I smile, my eyes closed as I revel in the bliss, not just at having all three of them inside of me at once but coming to such a heightened state at the same fucking time with them.

Alec sighs heavily and presses off the couch to kiss my lips. "My quads really are on fire," he admits.

I chuckle and open my eyes to stare up at him. "Good thing you work out."

He grins. "I'm going to have to do leg day more often if this is going to be a reoccurring thing."

Miller slowly pulls out of me, my pussy adjusting to the newfound room at his exit. "That was intense." He plops down onto the nearby chair, his dick in his hand, his other hand resting on his forehead.

Alec climbs backward, careful to slide out of me with ease, his gaze lingering on my exposed body. "You're truly stunning, Cora, and I'm not just saying that because my dick was just inside of you."

With only Silver's cock remaining, I wonder how the fuck I'm going to move and free him of the weight of my body.

But Silver simply wraps his arms around my chest and holds me tight, burying his face in my neck. "Are you okay, Angel? Did we hurt you?"

My pussy quivers and I place my arms over his and bask in this heavenly embrace. "For the first time in my life, I assure you, I am perfectly fine." I sigh and look at Alec as he collapses onto the couch next to us. "And if I have any say in it, you should definitely work on those quads." I wink and smile. "But next time, I think we should get a toy and go for four. Just to say we could."

"You're out of your mind, Angel." Silver kisses my cheek. "And I absolutely love it."

I lie there, against him, surrounded by my lovers, feeling truly content, truly safe, truly loved.

I don't know what the future has in store for me, for us, but with them by my side, and sometimes lingering in the shadows, I am fully prepared for whatever comes our way. Whether we are sinners or angels, we have each other, and that's all that matters in this dark and dangerous world.

Six months later
From the passenger seat of Silver's car, I swipe my phone screen open and click on Instagram. I type *London Gardella* into the search bar and get the same results I have had for quite some time.

Nothing.

I sigh and click on Facebook, doing the same thing but coming up with another dead end.

London is gone, and I cannot find her. She leaves behind no

trace and gives me no clue as to where she went, but I guess that's the point...she was supposed to disappear.

"What's wrong?" Silver asks me as he tightens his grip on my thigh.

I shut off my phone and slide it between my legs. "You can't even tell me where she is? If she's okay? Why can't I, I don't know, talk to her?"

He glances over at me. "We've talked about this, Angel. It's better. For her and for you, this way. I know it sucks, but you have to trust me."

I focus my attention out the window and wonder what she might be doing, and if she really is safe and sound. I hate that I can't confirm it for myself, but I guess I'm going to have to take Silver's word for it.

"You promise me, like pinky freaking promise me, that she's okay?"

Silver's pinky twitches up off my thigh and lingers in the air. "I promise. London is safe. At least, she is for now."

Don't miss your chance to find out what happens to London Gardella...

Or dive into the rest of the Sinners and Angels Universe!
Johnny & Claire's book: Broken Like You (MF romantic suspense)
June & her men's duet: Untamed Vixen and Villain Era (mafia why choose)
Banks & her men's novella: Wings of a Devil (MFM dark romance)

DEAR READER:

This year was a challenge, both emotionally, and physically. I never deny the fact that I struggle with my own mental health issues, and this year was no exception. I often write myself into my characters, whether in small or big ways, and Cora had pieces of me woven in from the start. I went on a journey with her, as I do with all of my book's characters, and I thoroughly enjoyed witnessing Cora's story unfold and watching her come into her own. Life does not always give us happily ever afters, and for Cora, hers was a bit messy, but it's the one her character deserved. I hope that, if you related to any of the things that Cora has experienced, you felt some comfort in watching her overcome the things that were thrown her way. As a sexual assault and domestic abuse survivor myself, I know how difficult it is to live with the things that have been done to us, so I wanted to give Cora a chance to get something that we never got. It might not be much, but in a way, it healed a little piece of me that I thought might never recover. It doesn't change what happened, but it makes me feel a little less alone. I can only hope the same for you.

I wrote this book during a challenging point in my life,

where I struggled with health problems and the unknowns of my mystery ailments. I'm still going through it, and I'm not sure what the outcome is going to be, but I want you to know how special this book was to me, and how it truly kept my mind at peace while writing it. It might have been the very thing to get me through, honestly, and I just really want to say thank you for wanting Cora's story, and for loving these characters hard enough to want to read their HEA.

If you're struggling, know that you are not alone. I see you. I feel for you. I care about you. I want nothing but the best for you. It's not your fault. And from the bottom of my heart, I am so sorry that life has been unkind to you. But I want to remind you, you've made it through all the hard days so far, and I believe in you to keep going. And don't forget, you're allowed to ask for help, to reach out your hand. You don't have to go through this alone.

Sending you all my love x

xo Luna

ACKNOWLEDGMENTS

I have to say a gigantic THANK YOU to the readers, because without your love for this dark and dangerous universe, Cora's book never would have happened.

You screamed your support for Simon, and you never stopped asking for Cora to have her own group of obsessive guys!

I am forever grateful that you love these characters and I'm so sorry if you relate to their struggles. But just know, you're not alone, and I'm sending you a gigantic hug right now.

Tiffany Hernandez, I would be lost without you. Thank you for always believing in me and sticking through every single rough patch.

Michelle—so grateful for everything you do. You're an incredible human.

Kate—my manifestation partner and forever cheerleader.

My Patrons over on Patreon—Robin, Mel, Natasha, Payton, Kiana, Heather, Ellie, Clayton, Tyler—your generous support means the world to me. THANK YOU.

Cassie at Opulent Swag & Designs. The covers for this series would not shine without you. Tori at Cruel Ink Editing & Design, I appreciate you putting up with my chaoticness.

Cassia—for convincing me that I had to kill someone off and always being the best at bouncing ideas back and forth!

Taylor Swift—for always delivering on a bangin' playlist to get me in my feels.

Tember—for all those daily hype voice memos.

Carol—I'm sorry this book made me neglect you.

Mini me—thank you for helping me pick out the chapter headers, I love them so much, not not as much as I love you!

Everyone over on #Booktok—thank you for joining me on this wild ride, I can't wait to see where the next one takes us! <3

Now, let's go find out what happened to London Gardella...

ALSO BY LUNA PIERCE

Sinners and Angels Universe

Broken Like You (Standalone)

Untamed Vixen (Part One)

Villain Era (Part Two)

Wings of a Devil (Standalone novella)

Ruin My Life (Standalone)

London & Archer's Story (Standalone)

The Harper Shadow Academy Series

(PARANORMAL ACADEMY REVERSE HAREM)

Hidden Magic

Cursed Magic

Wicked Magic

Ancient Magic

Sacred Magic

Harper Shadow Academy: Complete Box Set

Falling for the Enemy Series

(PARANORMAL REVERSE HAREM)

Stolen by Monsters

Fighting for Monsters

Fated to Monsters

ABOUT THE AUTHOR

Luna Pierce is the author of gritty romance, both dark contemporary and paranormal. She adores writing broken characters you won't help but fall for on their journey to find themselves and fight for what they love. Her stories are for the hopelessly romantic who enjoy grit, angst, and passion.

When she's not writing, you'll find her consuming way too much coffee, making endless to-do lists, and spending time with her daughter and cats in small-town Ohio.

Join the exclusive reader group: Luna Pierce's Gritty Romance Squad

Join Luna's newsletter to receive updates at: www.lunapierce.com/subscribe

If you enjoyed reading Cora's book, please consider leaving an honest review on Amazon, Goodreads, Tiktok, and/or BookBub.

Made in the USA
Monee, IL
20 January 2024

52112355R10333